Lucy Dakota
Adventures of a Modern Explorer

Book 1
Rocky Mountain Beginnings

C.S. Shride

My Piece of the Puzzle, LLC
Lakewood, Colorado

CONTENTS

AUTHOR'S NOTE

Reflecting on my life, I realized I have had an amazing journey that I wanted to share with others, particularly teenage girls. My daughter will soon be a teenager and I wanted to share with her not only my adventures but also the some of the lessons I have learned along the way. So *Lucy Dakota: Adventures of a Modern Explorer* was born.

Lucy is my alter ego, a combination of who I was at her age and who I could have been if I had had a better sense of self. All of the adventures she endures I experienced throughout my more than 25-year career of high-altitude mountaineering and adventure guiding around the world that began with my first climb of Colorado's Mt. Bierstadt at age 15. Of course, the timeline in which Lucy experiences everything is more condensed than my own—otherwise there would be plenty of quiet, down time, just like in real life!

Book 1 chronicles how Lucy got started on her adventurous life in Colorado. It shows the angst and discomfort she had experienced as a middle-schooler and the challenges she faced as she started to discover who she was. Just like any teen, Lucy makes a few poor decisions based on her desires to be loved and accepted. Eventually, through her connection to nature and her outdoor adventures—particularly a month-long mountaineering course—she starts to know her own strengths and grow into the leader she was born to be. Future books follow Lucy on her adventures around the world.

To research this first book, I not only drew upon my memories but also resurrected my old outdoor education training manuals, journals and the topographic maps we used. I studied recent accounts of Colorado River expeditions from Glenwood Springs to Grand Junction to recall some of the details from my first rafting trip and pored over maps of the Black Ridge Canyons Wilderness area. Even though the wilderness area didn't actually exist as a designated protected area like it does now, the courses of the canyons and many of the names haven't changed during the past 20 years.

I want to acknowledge Donald York for illuminating many dark places I hadn't seen before, and my daughter, Reyna, for inspiring me to always be more than I think I can be. My writing coach, Harry Pickens, reintroduced me to the value of self-reflection, taught me the use of EFT (Emotional Freedom Technique) to counter mental and emotional blocks as they arose, and supported me during a year of coaching calls. I want to thank Satyen Raja from the Get A Life Company whose vision of the "Gift of My Heroic Journey" program inspired me to start this project and who connected me with Harry. As with any worthwhile endeavor in life, especially one that requires growth and expansion, I had to face a number of my own demons while writing this first book, particularly my own sense of self worth. I had to look closely at the creative ways I had developed to sabotage my progress and success, and I had to teach myself new habits and disciplines.

My editor, Kelly Smith, was invaluable in taking my rambling, verbose writing and transforming it into something readable. Thanks to my friend and former adventure travel client Linda Pohle for giving me Jenna Browning's name. Jenna ultimately put me in touch with my creative team: Kelly, the editor; my fabulous designer, Kimberlee Lynch; and Lindsay VanDeWeghe, the illustrator who did an amazing job bringing Lucy to life. I also have to thank Jenna for her editing and proofreading skills, as well as my friend Karen Thompson, who used her great talent at finding mistakes to help proofread this book.

Finally, I want to thank you, the reader, for choosing this book. I hope you see a bit of yourself in Lucy and that her story inspires you to follow your dreams and be more than you think you can be.

To my daughter, Reyna, and my teenage mentee, Vanessa,
with thanks to both of them for being an inspiration
and with hope that Lucy can be the same for them.

PROLOGUE

Hi. My name is Lucy Dakota and this is my story—or, at least, the beginning of my story. Actually, that's not right, either. The very beginning involved growing up and all the usual kid stuff, so I skipped over it and started my tale in middle school. That's when things started to change.

I was just like a lot of girls that age: lonely, insecure, even bullied. I made some stupid mistakes while trying to fit in and make people like me. I would really rather not revisit that part of my life because it was hard and I messed up some, but right in the middle of these difficult times I began to discover the keys to unlock my future. Without the challenges, I would never have escaped through the door into the adventures that not only saved me from my loneliness, but also launched me into the most incredible life I could ever have dreamed of.

And so I invite you, my newest friend, to come along and join me on my journey, through all the ups and downs of adolescence and beyond. Trust me, it's gonna be a great ride!

Lucy

Part I

A Rocky Start

Chapter One

I never knew I would be an explorer. Nothing in my childhood or early school days would lead me or anyone else to think I was adventurous or daring. It took me a few years to figure it out, but I did, thanks to narrowly escaping being knocked off a mountain by a falling boulder and sucked into a giant whirlpool, a chance encounter with a mountain lion, and nearly going crazy by myself in the woods.

Things had begun to change for me during middle school. Every morning during the summer after seventh grade, I would wolf down breakfast, tell my mom goodbye and bike to the pool to meet my friends, including my best friend, Keri. There, we would slather on tanning oil and bake in the sun, never worrying about future wrinkles or possible skin cancer. We listened to hit songs as our bodies browned and our hair bleached. It wasn't about the swimming; we would lie on our towels and talk, and then hop in the pool when it got hot, chasing and splashing around before going back to lie out. That was it. All summer long.

Something had happened to my body over those summer months between seventh and eighth grades. The changes that occurred in me might have had something to do with riding my decrepit, yard sale, hunter orange, ten-speed bike five miles each way to the pool where I hung out with my friends. I was exercising every day, and I didn't even realize it; I rode at least 50 miles a week for the entire glorious summer. Maybe the changes occurred because of my new attitude. I was happy. No, I was joyous! I was out in the fresh air every day and I had friends. My troubles with Keri, Lisa and her gang seemed to be behind me (more on that later). I felt the freedom of having my own wheels, even if they didn't work all that well and I had to pedal to get where I was going. I could go! My mom trusted me to come and go throughout the day, the weather was ideal, and the words in the songs we listened to moved me. Life was glorious, sublime, and perfect that summer.

No matter the cause, I had morphed into someone I didn't know. My body thinned out and nature took its course. Suddenly, I had slender legs, perky breasts, and a waist. My reddish hair was long and straight, with natural, golden streaks from the sun. My brown skin highlighted my deep green eyes and my teeth were straight and white. The daily climb on my bike up Florida Street to the pool had strengthened my legs and lungs, and when I returned to PE class in the fall, I could actually run the 100-yard dash at a reasonable pace. I wasn't the fastest but I ranked among the top 10 runners in our class! And I was still smart.

What a change from the year before! I had hated seventh grade. Back then I was chubby and awkward, just getting over the baby-fat years of elementary school. OK, I admit, mine was more than baby fat. I had a chubby tummy, big wide butt, and chunky arms and thighs. Stress eating and puberty had combined to create my charming seventh-grade figure.

Physical education was my least favorite class. It was required, so I was tortured every single day. Those lumpy arms of mine would give out after only three embarrassingly short seconds, each and every time we had to hold ourselves up in a chin-up on the horizontal bar. It didn't matter that I practiced at home, in the rain or snow, on my old swingset in the back yard. I never could hold it for more than three seconds.

My short, thick thighs felt like they were pumping quickly during the 50-yard dash. I could, just briefly, see myself running fast in my mind's eye. My time of 15 or 18 seconds told a different story. Only Kevin Taylor, the fattest kid in class since kindergarten, with his thick, black-rimmed glasses and asthmatic wheeze, was slower than I was.

I never participated in sports or outdoor activities at that time. My family's preferred form of entertainment was sitting around the television on brilliant Colorado Sunday afternoons, watching Dad drink beer with his eyes glued to a football game or car race. We couldn't do or say anything because it would interrupt his concentration. If we did, he would yell at us to shut up.

Even on a sunny Saturday afternoon, our family would gather to play gin rummy in our smoke-filled living room. I never saw Dad walk anywhere except from his car to his office or a restaurant, or back into the house at the end of the day. When we did anything outdoors, it was to take our classic 1968 Ford Bronco four-wheeling.

Mom tried to expose me to the outdoors and exercise. This was an amazing feat since she was about as far from sporty as one could get. She had been raised a small-town southern belle, the only child of a doting physician father and a social-climbing, stay-at-home doctor's wife. It was too hot and humid in the Oklahoma summers and too bitter cold in the winter to be outside. In my grandmother's mind, outdoor activities were unladylike, so Mom never spent time in the great outdoors despite her parents owning a cattle ranch.

Mom was my Girl Scout troop leader, though, and she took us camping twice when I was in elementary school. Camping wasn't really the word for what we did; we rolled our sleeping bags out on foam mattress bunks in a wooden cabin that had a full kitchen and either dormitory-style bathrooms or smelly outhouses. No fires required, no freezing temperatures to be endured and no elements to contend with. We were, however, in the mountains, and we did go on short walks. We walked slowly, with Mom always dragging on a cigarette, and the Girl Scouts talking and laughing along the way.

I despised the way I looked in seventh grade. I had frizzy, red, shoulder-length hair, thanks to Clairol's home permanent kit and my mom. It was a beautiful auburn color, but I hated it because no one else in school had red hair. All the popular girls were blonde or brunette. Pimples covered my forehead, nose and chin and I had large, shiny, silver braces on my teeth, courtesy of Dr. Fuqua, the orthodontist.

Braces weren't the norm when I was a kid. Very few teens had them because not many families could afford the high cost of straightening their teeth. Plus, there weren't the cool colors that make braces the fashion statement they are today. My braces came with headgear. This scarlet, nylon contraption had two flat straps, each about an inch wide, that went over the top of my head, down past my ears and along my jaws to fasten to the front of my teeth. The headgear was designed to pull my extra-large pearly whites into place more quickly, and it worked; my mouth constantly throbbed with a dull, aching pain. Once a month, this became sheer agony when Dr. Fuqua tightened the wires that looped in figure-eights around my teeth. This debilitating pain would last about a week, during which time I wore the headgear night and day, rather than the typical nighttime-only wear.

Sporting the headgear during the day was mental torture as well as physical. Not only was it painful; it made me look like I was wearing a big, red cage on my head and face, making me a target for everyone's stares and comments. Of course, the red straps flattened sections of my frizz against my skull while allowing the rest of my hair to poof out like Ronald McDonald's clown curls. Lovely. As much as I wanted to shrink into a corner and hide, people couldn't help noticing me. I felt like a freak, like I was wearing a glowing dunce-cap and every eye was on me.

I heard girls call me "metal mouth," "freakazoid" and other cruel comments behind my back. They would whisper just loud enough so I could hear, yet quietly enough that no teacher heard or knew what was going on. No one ever got into trouble and the name-calling didn't stop, so I assumed the teachers didn't know.

Halfway through seventh grade, I started my period. Mom hadn't talked to me about what to expect, so it was very uncomfortable and disconcerting for me. For whatever reason, Mom always found conversations about the body, its functions and sexuality to be unnerving, and she avoided speaking to me about those topics. So each month, I endured gut-wrenching cramps, not really understanding what was happening to me. The whole experience was new and awkward enough, but on top of that, she insisted I use sanitary pads rather than tampons.

There I sat sweating in class, embarrassed, sure everyone could smell the acrid scent of blood that assaulted my own nose. To make it even worse, I was afraid to use the bathroom. The idea of encountering the bullies who hung out there between classes, terrorizing girls who weren't part of their clique, paralyzed me with fear. I was such a coward I stayed away from the bathroom all day. By the time I got home, I nearly wet my pants! Between my period and my braces, two full weeks of every month sucked.

I did have one thing going for me: I was smart. I liked to read and I liked learning, but it was exhausting to stay awake during some of the most boring classes to ever exist. Some of my teachers would have made better prison guards; it was clear they were doing time until retirement and punishing us for their own misery. They didn't seem to enjoy their subject, their students, their job and quite possibly their lives, and they seemed determined to share their suffering. So not only did I not like the way I looked; I also didn't like the way I felt in seventh grade and I had no refuge. I was miserable.

My best friend was Keri. She had long, wavy, strawberry blonde hair and freckles. She was cute in a wholesome, Irish-country way that I couldn't even dream of being. People liked her, so by being friends with Keri, I could kind of have friends, too.

I met Keri in fourth grade. She hadn't been crazy in elementary school and we did everything together, so I don't know if it was puberty or her home life, but starting in seventh grade, she started acting really weird. Keri would be my best chum for a month or two, and then all of a sudden, she would hate me. She might hate me for a day or two or her mood could last a couple of weeks. It was an insane on-again, off-again friendship.

When she liked me, everything was great. We were inseparable. We went to football games and basketball games in the evenings to see our friends and watch the boys. On weekends we hung out at the mall or her house all day and watched hours of movies. We spent all the time when we weren't together on the phone.

When Keri was mad at me, all of that changed. She wouldn't talk to me or return my calls. She would harass me herself or even send someone who would threaten to beat me up. So I descended into my own personal nightmare during those days or weeks when Keri was angry. On those days, my stomach ached more than usual. My head throbbed more than normal. I would do anything to stay at home and avoid going to school because she would be there, calling me names and ganging up against me with the bullies who hung out with Lisa Johansson.

I don't know what Lisa's problem was. She was beautiful on the outside, with long, straight blonde hair and smooth, tanned skin. She had neither a blemish on her face nor an ounce of fat on her body. She could have been a poster girl for the California surf, sand and summer The Beach Boys sang about. That was the outside. Something must have gone terribly wrong with her on the inside. She was one of the meanest people I knew, always looking to pick a fight with someone and always ready with the perfect cut-down.

Somehow Keri had become friends with Lisa and the bully girls, who for some reason were already looking to beat me up. Maybe it was because I was a coward, and Lisa and her gang just sensed my fear like wolves positioning themselves for the kill. I don't know. I just know that it sucked to go to school, especially during those days when Keri was angry and annoyed with me.

I was so afraid of Keri and the gang she hung out with during her angry moods that I befriended my ancient English teacher, Mrs. Knopps, and began going to her classroom at lunch. Mrs. Knopps must have been at least 60 years old; she had permed, short gray hair and a nasty demeanor. Along with that, she had extremely high expectations of her students and didn't let anyone off the hook. It's possible she was as unpopular as I was.

Maybe that was why she took pity on me and became my seventh-grade savior. I don't know how she knew I needed a place to hide or even that I was being picked on (the other teachers didn't seem to notice), but one day she asked me if I would like to help her grade and file papers. I pounced on the opportunity and from that day on, I sat in her tiny, paper-strewn office filing term papers and book reports for her while eating my lunch. It was a 35-minute respite from the torment of the rest of my day. Of course, it only added to the fire when the bullies found out. "Teacher's pet" replaced "metal mouth" as my nickname. To make matters even worse socially, I got straight A's on my report cards without much effort—always had. I had loved elementary school, and would have enjoyed middle school, except for everyone else who had to attend along with me.

Books had always been my sanctuary at home. To escape my dad's moody behavior, I could go to my room, shut my door and travel anywhere I wanted with a good book. Books also distracted me from the tortures of middle school. I had kind and loyal friends in my books. I was the beautiful, athletic heroine in the stories I read. I learned about love and romance through tales like *Gone with the Wind*. I went on grand adventures all over the world and I began to think of deep, spiritual ideas through Hermann Hesse's *Siddhartha* and J.R.R. Tolkien's Lord of the Rings trilogy. Somehow, with the aid of my beloved books and the kindness of a cranky middle-school English teacher, I survived seventh grade.

Chapter Two

About halfway through eighth grade, I started becoming accustomed to my newly svelte body. I even tried out for the track team, running hurdles because I still wasn't very fast, but I discovered I was fearless. Other girls, the fastest team members, would run up to a hurdle and stop or hesitate before crossing it. I, on the other hand, could just run right over them like the coach told me. It was exhilarating.

Boys started noticing me for the first time in my life. I had my first crush on one very muscular, deep-voiced jock, Kenan Dewitt. He used to give me notes he had created using words and slogans from magazine ads. One read, "You're not getting older, you're getting better." Another one said, "When you've got it, flaunt it," and my favorite read, "M'm! M'm! Good!" Sure, it was dorky, but at the same time, it was totally fun having a guy send me homemade notes.

I wasn't accustomed to attention from the masculine members of the planet. I would have been thrilled having any guy send me notes, but Kenan was cute and he was popular. It was intoxicating. I loved the attention but I was shy so I didn't know what to do next. People thought Kenan and I might become an item, and I secretly hoped deep in my heart we would.

I watched him play basketball all winter, and had gone to some of his baseball games over the summer. He was as much an athlete as I was a bookworm. I went to his games to watch him play, but also to enjoy my new friends, newfound popularity and the sheer joy of hanging out with other people besides Keri. We were still best friends and she was not nearly as weird or crazy as in seventh grade, but it was gratifying to have more than one friend for the first time in my life.

I loved the sensations at a game: the sweat of the players, ripe in the air; the sugary sweet smell of kettle corn and cotton candy wafting from the concession stand; the deafening sounds of voices shouting cheers, along with the drums and horn section of the band, all accompanied by hundreds of feet stomping on bleacher seats. The tension of not knowing who was going to score the last basket or hit the final home run, and the thrill, oh, the rush of finally having friends.

This was really what brought me to the games; they were addictive, these new feelings of being sought-after, of being liked. It was a high that would eventually lead me to make one of my worst decisions ever.

It was a crystal-clear, sunny spring day following a big, wet, Colorado March storm. The warm air still held a coolness but the snow was melting fast. I had gone to Kenan's basketball game at the high school. Although he was on a junior-high team, they were playing for the championship, so the quarterfinals and finals were held at the new high school. Our team had won and I was giddy. The excitement in the air and coursing through my body came from more than just the thrill of winning—it came because I was walking home with A BOY!

Besides sending me occasional sweet notes, Kenan had never asked me to do anything with him but watch him play his sports. He always said hi to me at his games, but we really had never talked much. I think he was as shy as I was. But this glorious day, he had asked me if he could walk me home!

"Hey," Kenan said, wiping sweat from his brow.

"Great game," I stammered, turning bright red as I often did when Kenan and I actually spoke to each other.

"Yeah, it was," he said. "Can I walk you home?"

I mumbled a stuttered yes and waited while he changed in the locker room. Soon we were walking out of the building, heading east toward my house. I was surprised to look down and see my feet touching the ground.

We didn't talk much and we didn't hold hands. We talked a little about the game and how cool it was going to be to go to high school next fall in the new building. Other than that, we acted pretty awkward with each other. I guess when he didn't have magazine phrases to use, Kenan was as much at a loss for words as I was. It wasn't exactly how I had envisioned the start of my first "date."

That day, like nearly every other day of eighth grade, I was wearing a skirt—a short, baby blue, corduroy skirt with panty hose and a white blouse. I was so enamored with the idea of being "cute" for the first time in my life, I discovered early in the fall that I could roll up the waistband of the skirts my grandmother had sewn, to the point that they barely covered my rear end in back. I could leave the house with my hem falling just above my knees as my mother liked, and when I got to school, I could morph into the little sexpot I imagined myself to be. With my nice legs and a shapely butt after all those fat years, I thought I was the sexiest thing alive. I probably looked ridiculous.

I was not dressed properly for the walk ahead of us. There was a steep hill behind the high school, covered with wild grasses and knotty, thigh-high sagebrush. For years, people had used the hill as a dumping ground for junk, rather than driving another couple of miles out to the landfill. Bulldozers used during the school's construction had uncovered some of the car parts, bumpers, doorframes, windshields, glass bottles, refrigerator doors, and other bits of trash that lay scattered across the ground, but a lot of the junk was still buried. The snow, which had fallen the day before, covered the ground, making for a lumpy, sharp mess.

I don't know why we decided to use this hill, which didn't have a trail, as a shortcut to my home. We could have taken the longer route following the sidewalks and streets. I guess it felt exciting to head cross-country. Also, somewhere deep inside, I wanted to show off to Kenan, to prove I could handle it.

After slogging across the top of the hill and sinking into the snow halfway up my calves, I looked over at Kenan. My legs were freezing and my feet, in their cute, strappy, platform shoes, were numb. He must have realized I was miserable because he said, "Hey, Lucy, do you want to try sliding to see if we could get down the hill quicker?"

I wasn't sure. I didn't see anything to slide upon and I realized that I wasn't dressed for the occasion but I didn't want to seem cowardly. So, with more courage than I felt, I said, "What the heck? Let's give it a try!"

He led the way, dropping to his jean-covered knees and starting to slide.

"Woohoo!" he shouted.

"Hey! It's working!" I shouted back as he careened down the slope.

Kenan was already halfway down, going fast, and I didn't want him to leave me behind. So I lowered my nylon-sheathed knees to the snow and started to slide. The snow was slick and fast, and I barely noticed my pantyhose getting soaked through. My feet and legs no longer felt cold as adrenaline took over. I was two-thirds of the way down and had almost caught up with Kenan, who was standing on the sidewalk that circled the church parking lot at the base of the hill, when everything went wrong.

My left knee collided with the metal trim of a rusty car bumper. Wham! Crunch!

The quarter-inch-thick steel sliced through the skin of my knee and the meat underneath, almost down to the bone. Adrenaline could no longer hide the discomfort in my legs, and tears sprang from my eyes as searing pain registered in my mind.

My nylon hose hung in shreds from my legs as the snow at my feet turned red with blood. Soaking wet, I shivered from cold as well as shock. I stood up, looked down the hill and, through blurry eyes, saw that Kenan had disappeared!

He's probably gone to get help, I thought to myself, hopeful he had not abandoned me.

I turned my head this way and that, but my "friend" Kenan was nowhere to be found. Hot tears ran down my face, not only because of my throbbing, bleeding knee but also because I realized he had not gone for help. He had left, unable to deal with the disaster of my cut knee.

My heart ached as much as my knee. My first potential boyfriend proved himself a bigger coward than I was. I couldn't believe it. I couldn't believe he had left, right when I most needed help.

I felt humiliated, stupid and basically wretched. I wanted to shout and scream at the world, but I was bleeding profusely. I stumbled down the remaining hundred yards of the hill, blood gushing from my torn knee. I limped across the church parking lot. The empty lot told me the church was closed. I was still a half-mile from my house, and there was no way I could walk home.

I hobbled across the street to an apartment complex, probably looking like an assault victim—torn clothes, messed-up hair, tear-stained face and bloody stockings.

I knocked on the first door I came to and a woman in her late 20s opened the door. She took one look at my knee, my torn clothing and my tears, and immediately invited me in. She brought me a wet, green, paisley-patterned washcloth and wrapped it around my leg. I called my mom and she rushed over; the color drained from her face when she saw me lying on the sofa with a blood-soaked washcloth on my leg, tattered hose around my ankles, and mud and dirt soiling my blouse and face.

"What in the world happened to you?" she asked me, hysteria barely concealed beneath her calm voice.

"I don't want to talk about it!" I wailed. "Just take me home, now!"

I was overwrought from the accident and both my knee and my heart screamed in agony. I also had a huge fear of needles, and so far in life, had avoided getting stitches. The thought of being sewn up at the ER put me over the edge. Mom thanked the kind woman for taking me in, and we drove the half-mile home. The entire way, I frantically begged her not to take me to the hospital. Instead, she took me into the bathroom, washed the cut and taped my knee up as best she could. I was lucky I didn't get an infection as it was such a deep cut.

Now I have a thick, ragged scar from that little incident, reminding me not to do stupid things like sled down a hill without the right gear just because someone else is pressuring me to do so. I also still have the green-patterned washcloth. I kept it as a token of that woman's kindness and my gratitude that she found it in her heart to help a stranger in need.

I guess the whole event freaked Kenan out. He never spoke to me again. I, of course, took his absence personally and thought there was something wrong with me.

Later that spring, on a beautiful day in May, my desire to be popular and not go back to being nerdy, bookworm Lucy led me into another disturbing situation.

I had met a seventh-grade boy earlier in the year, and I thought he was hot. The total opposite of Kenan, Matt had chocolate-brown eyes, black hair and olive skin. He was nicely built but was not an athlete, and he was a "bad boy" if I had ever seen one. We had been in ski class together all winter. We sat together on the hour-long bus ride up to the ski area every other Wednesday, and at some point during that time, as we chatted, I felt my attraction to him build. Eventually, we sat close together on the bus, talking less and snuggling more. Tingling feelings

I had never felt before overcame me, and I did not want them to end. It was always a disappointment when the bus journey ended and we each went our own way.

Our ski lessons ended in late February, and Matt and I barely saw each other after that. Our schedules were way too different and we had different friends. Still, I never forgot those days on the bus and the sensations that made me quiver and set my heart racing.

One hot afternoon in May, as I cooled off after track practice, I looked up and there he was. Matt and a buddy of his, Kevin, whom I had never liked, were leaning nonchalantly against the storage shed that housed the hurdles and other field equipment.

He looked over at me with those beautiful brown eyes and my heart started thudding as if we had never been apart. I was flush with nerves and excitement.

What was he doing here? What did he want?

"Hey," I said, as casually as possible. "What's up?"

"Oh, not much," Matt shrugged. "We just came to watch you practice."

"Oh. Well, we're finished now so there isn't a lot to see," I said.

"Have you ever been down in the gully?" Kevin asked abruptly. The guy gave me the creeps. Behind the track field was a series of open spaces where we could sometimes see deer and rabbits among the brush. "No. I've never been there," I admitted as my heart soared over just talking to Matt again!

"Do you wanna go check it out with us?" Matt asked.

Matt was asking me to explore with him!

"Of course I want to go!" I practically shouted. I thought he was the cutest thing alive, and here he was paying attention to me again! Life couldn't get any better. I gathered up my sweatshirt, slipped on a pair of jeans and put the last of the hurdles in the shed.

We walked around the track and started down a bone-dry dirt path that wound through the scrubby rabbitbrush, sagebrush and yucca. The sun beat down on our heads while little puffs of dust floated up from under our feet. Billowy white clouds dotted the cobalt sky. It was a perfect spring afternoon.

I didn't know where we were going or what we were going to do, and I didn't care. All I knew was the feeling I had felt when Matt and I sat together on the ski bus had roared back. I was ecstatic!

We hadn't gone far into the gully when Matt and Kevin stopped. I stopped, too, wondering what was going on.

"What's up? Did you guys see a deer or something?" I asked quietly, not wanting to disturb the wildlife I assumed we were looking for.

"No," said Kevin, and Matt took my hand. "Have a seat," Kevin said, gesturing to a patch of sparsely covered dirt. I don't know why, but I did as I was told.

Matt sat beside me, still holding my hand. I tingled all over and my heart raced.

Maybe he's gonna kiss me, I thought to myself, hoping he would, yet afraid that he might. I had never kissed a boy before. Matt was the first boy I had even held hands with and he was the only one I had snuggled up against. I could barely breathe.

Matt lay back on the ground and I followed along. The dry grass poked my back and the sun blinded my eyes but none of that mattered; I was lying next to Matt. In my mind's eye, I could see us snuggling together here in our own private gully. In my excitement, I totally forgot about Kevin. All my attention focused on the feel of Matt's hand in mine, dry and scratchy, and the fluttering, flipping sensation in my stomach. I even managed to push aside the little niggling suspicion that something wasn't right as my common sense kept trying to get my attention.

I was a nervous wreck, knowing I would soon be kissing him and wondering how I was going to do it.

Where do I put my tongue? Alarms went off in my head.

How's my breath? Thank God I got my braces off!

I panicked as the questions ran through my mind.

I knew kissing a boy involved more than just touching lips like I did when I was a kid with Mom or my grandparents. I had read about kissing in my romance novels and had seen it done in a bunch of movies. I knew it could last a long time and it often had something to do with the tongue.

While these worries were passing through my head, I felt a tugging at my pants. I must have closed my eyes in anticipation of that first kiss, and the next thing I knew, Matt and Kevin were unzipping my jeans.

I opened my eyes and began to sit up, but at the same time, Kevin's hand shot down my panties.

"Whoa!" I shouted in fear and disgust. "Take your hand out of my pants!" I screamed and his hand withdrew. This was not what I was expecting at all. No boy had ever touched me down there before, and I always thought when someone did, it would be someone I liked. Someone I was in love with. Someone like Matt. Not some grubby, yucky guy like Kevin.

"Get away from me!" I yelled, scrambling to my feet. I was shaking all over. The boys backed off, then ran toward the school, laughing. I zipped my pants and trudged up the hill to the track.

I don't even remember the journey back to my house. I was dazed with confusion. Part of my experience had felt good, stirring up my emotions and my already raging hormones. I had dreamed of sharing a kiss with Matt. I had longed for physical closeness, hoping it would be with a cute boy I loved. Other parts of the day's event seemed dirty and weird. I felt used and betrayed by Matt. The whole encounter didn't last long, just a few minutes, but it put an end to my crush on Matt, the cute boy.

He ignored me the next day, and that was fine with me. I was hurt—my heart was broken again and I couldn't figure out what I had done wrong. I blamed myself for not being good enough or pretty enough, when really it was my desire to fit in, to have friends, that had clouded my judgment in both of my eighth-grade encounters with boys.

The jagged scar on my left knee reminds me of my misadventure on the snow-covered hill with Kenan, and I never will forget how distant Matt's laughter sounded as he ran up the gully with his friend. Both boys had left me hurt, confused and alone. I didn't know it at the time, but I was much stronger standing on my own than alongside any boy who didn't have my best interests in mind.

Chapter Three

Ninth grade was a much better year than seventh and eighth grades had been.

I finally had a group of girlfriends—all players from the basketball and volleyball teams. Although I still wasn't a natural-born athlete, my desire for friends led me to try out for, and eventually make, the junior varsity teams in both sports. My involvement in these teams radically changed my lifestyle and started changing my perception of myself.

For the first time, I had to exercise and take care of my body. We practiced every day after school and I learned how to work out and eat nutritiously. Soon I felt stronger and healthier than I ever had. I felt energized and excited, with a sense of power and control that I had never known before. I was in the best condition of my life. It was a whole new sensation for me! It was better than being popular. I imagined it was even better than having a boyfriend. I was on top of the world!

Suddenly, boys were noticing me all over the place. Who knew that getting into shape and feeling good about myself would make me more attractive to boys? I had my first real boyfriend in ninth grade, Stephen Aaronson. We went to football games together. I didn't have to go watch him play; I sat beside him in the stands. Stephen was not a jock, even though he played baseball in the summer and had played Little League football. He played the guitar and I loved hanging out with him. Plus, all my girlfriends from the volleyball team went to the games, so there was one big group to hang out with. I imagined it was more fun than I had ever had in my life.

Unfortunately, I was still making stupid decisions based on my desire to be popular. The morning of the homecoming game, my two best friends, Keri and Angel, and I had headed over to the mall just to hang out. We would often get a snack and spend hours walking around looking at the stuff in the stores. It was a normal routine for us but I guess we got bored that day because for some reason we decided to start taking stuff.

I don't remember if it was Keri's idea or Angel's, but somehow it had become a dare between us so we started doing it. At first, we took little things like nail polish, lip gloss, cheap necklaces and candy bars. Before long it became a game for us.

We started seeing if we could take something from every store in the mall. We might have gotten away with it had we not gotten cocky and decided to return to one store to get more things. We had already taken some makeup from there that morning. Apparently the security guys had seen us before and they were on the lookout for us to return. And return we did.

All of our focus was on what we were going to take. We weren't looking around or even really paying attention to anyone but ourselves. We never even knew what hit us, but just as Keri put a pair of earrings into her purse, a huge man with a balding head and a grip like a pair of Doberman's jaws grabbed us from behind.

"Thought you'd get away with it, didn't you, you little punks?" he snarled in our ears. "We've been watching you all day." He shoved us through the racks of clothing and across the store into a little room. It was small and bare with dirty white walls and three straight-backed, metal chairs. I expected to see a bare light bulb hanging above our heads like in the movies.

"We have to call your parents," the man growled, handing us a tablet of paper and a pen. "Write their phone numbers here."

We did what he told us to despite our shaking hands. He snatched the paper as soon as Angel finished writing and left the room, closing the door behind him. There were no windows, no posters on the walls, nothing to look at while we waited for security to call our parents. It felt like it took forever; none of us had a watch, and there was no clock in the room and we were too shaken to notice the time on our phones.

My friends started to freak out. Angel cried about how her father was going to beat her when he found out. "I'm dead," she kept crying over and over.

Keri agreed. She was sure she'd not only get beaten but grounded. "My brother, Mike, got in trouble for stealing last year and my stepdad was all over his case. Mike is six years older than I am so there wasn't a lot Butch could do to him, but he told him if he got in trouble again, he would have to move out of the house. Do you think he'll make me leave the house?" she sobbed.

I shrugged my shoulders. They were driving me crazy and for some reason I felt very blasé about the whole thing. It had really been their fault. The whole thing had been their idea and they had taken a lot more stuff than I had. I just didn't really think my parents would care all that much.

We sat there stewing for about an hour, Angel and Keri were busy texting friends while I just sat there, shocked. And then our parents came. Keri's stepdad was furious, with a furrowed brow and red face.

She's going to get killed, I thought to myself as he grabbed her and pulled her out of the room.

Angel's dad was hysterical. He kept shouting at her in Spanish and shaking his fist. He would look up at the ceiling and growl and then stare at her and shout again. She left looking terrified.

I was the last to leave. When my parents finally arrived, Dad seemed unruffled. Mom was tense, her lips mashed tightly together in a little straight line. No smiles there. Dad thanked the security guy and put his hand on the back of my neck to steer me out of the room. When we got into the car, he calmly told me to hand over my phone and then announced I was grounded until the end of Christmas vacation.

In the privacy of our own vehicle, Mom started crying and before long she was hysterical, sobbing about how we could never tell my grandparents about this. "Your grounding starts today, young lady, right this minute," she shouted at me as we pulled out of the parking lot. Dad nodded his head in agreement. *Oh, great,* I thought to myself.

"You'll call your friends, including Stephen, when you get home and tell them that you will not be going to the homecoming game tonight," Dad said.

"What? That's not fair!" I shouted furiously.

"You should have thought of that before you started stealing stuff from stores, Lucy," he replied quietly.

"I hate you!" I screamed. "I hate both of you! You've ruined my life!"

I hated my dad. In my mind I called him every name I could think of, although I was not brave enough to say any of it to his face. Or maybe I didn't say anything because I was smart. I didn't need more time added to my sentence.

"Please, please, just let me go to the homecoming game," I begged. "Stephen and I have planned this since the beginning of the school year. We're going to get pizza before the game and hang out with all of our friends."

"I am sorry, Lucy," he said. "You really should have thought about the consequences of your actions before you started stealing things. You know that was wrong. There is no way you can go to the homecoming game tonight."

"I hate you!" I shouted again, knowing full well that Stephen would drop me as a girlfriend when he found out I couldn't go to the game. I stormed into the house, slamming doors behind me. I stomped into the kitchen, where the family phone was, and called Keri first.

"Hey," I said sullenly. "Did you get beaten?"

"No," she answered cheerfully. "I'm grounded, but it doesn't start until next week! I can still go to homecoming tonight. What about you?"

"I am grounded now," I growled. "I just had to call and tell you I can't come to the game, and that you're not allowed to call me until January."

"Oh, man, that's harsh," she replied.

"Yeah, I know. Tell me about it. The first thing Dad did was take my phone. Guess I'll see you at school Monday."

"Yeah. OK," she said and hung up.

Next was Angel.

"Can I speak with Angel?" I asked timidly when her father answered the phone.

"No vay!" he shouted with his thick accent. "Shees in her room, and shees not allowed to speak with you, Lucy Dakota." And he hung up on me.

Great, like this is all my fault! OK, last on the list: Stephen. I braced myself as I dialed his number.

"Hey, Lucy," he answered the phone. "Keri said that you guys got into trouble today."

Fantastic, I thought. *What was she doing calling my boyfriend?*

"Yeah, that's an understatement," I said. "We got caught shoplifting.

I'm grounded until January. I can't come to the game tonight and I can't talk on the phone. I'm sorry," I said.

"Yeah, that was pretty stupid of you," Stephen replied. "Why did you do it?"

"I don't know," I said. "I think I was just bored, then Keri and Angel dared me. I knew it was wrong but after a while, it seemed fun and we made it into like a game, not to get caught, you know. But obviously we did. Have fun at the game. I wish I were going," I concluded, choking up as I spoke. I hung up the phone as tears burned my eyes.

Dad sent me to my room once I had made my tearful phone calls. As part of the conditions of my being grounded, I was not allowed to talk on the phone (any phone, not just my own phone) or have contact with anyone outside of school. I couldn't watch TV, get on the computer unless necessary for school, or listen to music. All I could do was my homework, help out around the house and read in my room. Thank God I still liked to read, but it was going to be a brutally long three months.

I survived the grounding and Stephen didn't break up with me as I'd feared, but gradually, he became as strange as Keri had been in junior high.

When I came to school on Monday after the shoplifting incident, he acted as if nothing had happened. We ate lunch together like normal, and talked when we saw each other in the halls. Then, about two weeks later, out of the blue, he started acting angry with me.

As far as I could tell, nothing had caused it. One day, he just wouldn't talk to me. The first time, it only lasted for a few days. Then, everything was fine again. We were on good terms for a couple of weeks, and then suddenly, he did not like me again. This time it lasted for a couple of weeks. Then, just as quickly as it had come on, he was over whatever it was and started liking me again. It went on like this for the next two months, with him acting friendly for a bit, then angry, sullen and refusing to talk to me. He'd call me "Crazy Lucy" or "Lucy the Thief" and tell people at school that he was convinced I was seeing other guys behind his back.

Sometimes, on the days he and Keri were both mad at me, I'd get a stomachache so bad, I would stay home from school. I was still a coward and I hated confrontations.

Christmas break came and went and finally, it was January. My parents set me free from being grounded. Stephen and I had gotten accustomed to not spending much time together, but when we did go out again after break, he got mad at me. This time was the worst. He was rude and abusive at school, yelling at me in the hallway and telling people that Keri and I were much more than just friends. He finally broke up with me in February, after I had endured another month of stomachaches and name-calling.

Stephen told everyone the reason for our breakup was that Keri and I were lesbians. That lie formed the second rift in my friendship with Keri, the first being her crazy behavior. Although her mood swings were the worst in seventh grade, they lasted throughout our relationship. I suspected she had an anger problem because of all the stuff she had to deal with at home: a drunken and abusive stepdad, a violent older brother and an absentee mom who resented having to always work to support the family. All I knew was that I often felt sorry for Keri.

Fortunately, the rest of the school year and summer went by without major incident and before I knew it I was in tenth grade.

Though I'd begun to enjoy the benefits of being part of an athletic team, such as the friendships and staying physically fit, I still didn't consider myself athletic or particularly outdoorsy. All of that changed, as did my life, my last three years of high school.

The Adventures Begin

Chapter Four

During my sophomore year, Keri and I joined a group of kids from our high school in adventure scouting. I had never heard of it before, but later learned that an adventure scout post was basically a Boy Scout or Girl Scout troop with a theme. I had one friend who was in a post focusing on being a veterinarian, and another whose troop was learning about firefighting. When one of our friends, Mack, invited Keri and me to a meeting, we went.

The posts were co-ed so both boys and girls were able to participate, and we didn't have to do things to earn merit badges or help the elderly cross streets, which was fine by me.

The theme of our adventure scout post was just that—adventure. Living in Colorado, it seemed perfectly natural to have adventure as a theme, with all the beautiful tall mountains, wilderness areas and national forests. Our post leader was Mack's father, Carl Lewis. The active Lewis family skied every weekend during the winter and hiked and climbed all summer long.

So there we were, eight or 10 sophomores, juniors and seniors trying to be "adventurous." One of the cool aspects of adventure scouting was that the kids were in charge. Carl Lewis took this concept seriously. He was there to make suggestions and give guidance, but we planned what we were going to do, where we were headed, what we needed to bring and how it was all going to work out.

Our first adventure was a spring climb up one of Colorado's fourteeners, Mt. Bierstadt. A fourteener is a mountain with a summit at least 14,000 feet above sea level. Colorado has 54 of these, and Bierstadt was a good choice for our first trip. Located about an hour west of Denver, it is considered a non-technical, walkup peak meaning that, in theory, any reasonably fit person should be able to climb it. No special skills were needed.

Since the mountain was so close the city, we decided to make it a weekend trip, skiing on Saturday at a nearby ski resort, camping overnight in the highlands at the base of the mountain and climbing the peak on Sunday. It sounded like a grand adventure and I was both excited and apprehensive. The only activity of our planned weekend I had ever done previously was ski. I had taken skiing lessons in seventh and eighth grades as part of our PE program, when I rode on the bus snuggled up with Matt. I had never been tent camping before and I certainly had never tried to climb a mountain.

Keri was coming, too, along with Carl and Mack Lewis and a few other guys from school: Alan Meyers, Tate Gritdal and Andy Ferigano. Mike Ferigano, Andy's dad, was joining us as an adult assistant. Come 6 a.m. on Saturday, four of us plus Carl piled into Carl's old Subaru with our gear. The other two drove up with Mr. Ferigano in a tiny Honda.

We arrived early at Geneva Basin, a small, family-owned ski area. It was perfect—not many people skied at "GB," as Mack and his ski-team buddies called the area, and the Lewises were friends of the owners, so we pretty much had the run of the hill.

Keri and I goofed off as much as we skied. We spent a lot of our day in the bathroom of the base lodge, warming our hands, and in the main lodge, flirting with the guys. We did about half a dozen runs down the "green" (easy) trails, which didn't take long at Geneva, as there were only four lifts and about 15 runs on the whole mountain.

Mack and Tate skied by us a couple of times, spraying us with snow when they slid to dramatic hockey stops right in front of us. It was an awesome day—perfect spring skiing conditions, sunny and cool with crystal-clear Colorado blue skies. We had a blast.

When the lifts closed at 4:30, we loaded ourselves back into the cars and drove the three miles up to Duck Lake, a little glacier-created pond right at tree line, at about 11,000 feet in elevation. We parked and set up our small camp.

That night was to be my first time ever camping out in a tent. Keri and I had borrowed a tent from Carl, and a neighbor had lent me a down sleeping bag. We didn't have sleeping pads or mattresses to put under our bags, but the tent was waterproof and cut the wind. We had no idea what to bring for clothing or how to dress to spend the night at tree line.

Our camp sat in a glade of fir trees overlooking the lake. All around us, stunning, snow-clad mountains turned lavender, mauve, gold and amethyst as the sun set.

We ate canned beans and tortillas while sitting around a blazing fire. The sky was magnificent, with stars appearing so close I felt that I could reach out and touch them. I had never seen such a sky. The only other time I had ever even slept outdoors was on the flatbed of a truck in Oklahoma one Fourth of July when I was about eight, and then the stars had been obscured by the hazy, humid southern sky.

As we sat around the campfire telling jokes and teasing each other, a big bull elk walked within 10 feet of our little campsite. One moment I was watching the fire and taking a bite of beans. The next, I looked up and there was an enormous deerlike animal standing just behind the boys. From where I was sitting, it looked like an entire mountain had moved in front of us to block out the hills in the background.

The elk looked me right in the eyes, steam rising from his nostrils as he breathed in our scent. His massive head was just starting to show the stubs of the four-foot-wide antlers that would grow later in the season, and dark fur covered his neck. We stared at each other for what felt like forever, but was probably more like 10 seconds. Then, just as I started to tell the others to turn around and witness this magnificent beast, he vanished, as quickly and quietly as he had come. Later, I wondered if I had imagined the whole thing. I also wondered if maybe he was there to tell me something. The more I thought about it, I realized he was probably there to remind me to savor every moment and stay alert as I never knew what might pop by. Whatever the reason, the elk sighting got my first camping night off to a very cool start.

Keri liked Mike as a boyfriend, but they weren't going out yet—although that would soon change following this trip. I watched them snuggled together by the fire while Mack and Tate teased them relentlessly. They seemed happy and I wanted that for myself. I felt jealous of them. Even though I felt happy hanging out with my friends, I realized I still wanted someone who would hold me and hang out with me, someone with whom I could share my thoughts and feelings and be accepted for who I was.

Although it was bitterly cold at 11,000 feet, no one realized it while sitting by the warmth of the fire. I was wearing jeans, sneakers and a thick wool sweater under my ski jacket. I didn't wear a hat for fear of messing up my hair, so I was getting cold. I was envious of Keri being able to cozy up to Mike and stay warm. I was wishing I had a boyfriend, too, but after last year's experience with Stephen, I wasn't in too much of a hurry to take on another romantic entanglement.

Carl stood up and stretched. Then he checked his watch and announced it was time for us to turn in. He said we would be rising early so we could reach the summit before any bad weather came in.

"Here in the Rockies," he explained, "especially in spring and summer, thunderstorms can build in the afternoons. It's dangerous to be exposed on a granite peak when lightning rolls in, so we have to get going early tomorrow."

"Goodnight, Mr. Lewis," Keri called out, raising her head off Mike's shoulder.

"Yeah, goodnight, Dad," Mack said.

"Goodnight, kids," Carl said as he strode toward the A-frame tent he was sharing with Mr. F.

The stories the boys had told earlier about being up high when the air became electric just before a lightning strike were enough to convince me we needed to get an early start. I didn't want to experience every hair on my body standing on end, hear the distinctive crackling sound or see the blue glow of St. Elmo's fire, which would indicate a strike was imminent. So, Keri and I headed over to our little tent. I quickly tore off my clothes, toasty warm from the fire, and pulled on my pajamas.

"Oh, my God," I cried out. "It's freezing in here!"

"You got that right," came Keri's muffled voice as she dragged her sweater over her head.

"What do you think the temperature is?" I asked, teeth chattering.

"I have no idea," she replied. "But I bet it is at least 32 degrees. I could see everyone's breath as we left the fire."

"Yeah, me, too," I said, listening to the wind rattle our tent. "I can feel the wind blowing right through this tent."

"I know," Keri said, crawling into her sleeping bag. "It's going to be a long night."

"Yeah, it sure is," I agreed as I slipped into my own nylon-covered down bag. "Brrr! It's flippin' cold in this bag! How's yours?"

"Frigid," she said.

I could feel the hard, cold ground under my back. My head, ears and nose were icy to the touch. We both lay there for what seemed hours. I could tell by the rustling noises and the sound of her breathing that Keri was still awake. We could hear deep breathing from the boys' tent and snoring from Carl's own shelter. It seemed everyone else was sound asleep.

"Keri?" I called out softly. No answer.

"Keri?" I called a bit louder. "Are you still awake?" She didn't reply, probably hoping I would be quiet and go to sleep. I couldn't. I was too cold.

"Psst," I whispered. "I know you are awake. I can tell by your breathing. Are you cold still? I'm nearly frozen over here."

"Shhh, Lucy," she replied. "You're going to wake everyone up and we'll get in trouble."

"I won't," I said defensively. "Are you warm enough?"

"No, I am still freezing," she said.

"Do you want to share a bag to get warm?" I asked.

"OK," Keri replied. "Whose bag?"

"Let's use yours, since it looks bigger," I suggested.

"OK," she agreed.

I crawled out of my borrowed mummy bag into her square bag, and pulled the zipper up. It was a tight fit, but almost instantly we were snug and warm, and soon we both fell asleep. Sometime in the night, we must have moved wrong because her zipper popped open. Cold air came streaming into the bag and we both snapped wide-awake.

"What the heck?" Keri cried out. "What happened?"

"I don't know," I said.

"Oh, man!" she exclaimed, struggling with the zipper in the freezing dark. "The bag is busted! I can't get it to zip closed again! What are we going to do?"

"I don't know," I admitted. I was freezing again! This time, however, after having been so warm and snug, I was afraid to get cold again. I quickly crawled out of her bag and into my own. Now that I was warm, my bag didn't feel so bad and it started to warm right up.

"Hey!" Keri whispered vehemently. "What about me? Move over so I can get into your bag with you! You broke my bag."

"We can't do that, Keri," I replied sleepily, already dozing off in the warmth. "My bag is a mummy bag, and it's really skinny. You know we won't fit in it together. That's why we got into yours to begin with."

"Well, that just sucks," she growled at me, but I was too cozy to care. I fell asleep, snug and warm in my bag, while my best friend lay next to me, freezing in the tattered remains of her sleeping bag.

At first light, Carl came by our tent, telling us it was time to get up and have some breakfast. As soon as we opened the flap on our tent, we realized how much warmer it was inside than outside. The wind was still blowing as we stumbled out into the crisp morning air. A layer of frost covered all the tents and a thick mist rose from the lake. Carl had water boiling for coffee and tea, and we gulped it quickly, washing down our granola bars at the same time. Keri was obviously still miffed about her bag being ruined and having to sleep in the cold all night. I didn't really blame her as I had let my fears get the best of me. She glared at me through narrowed eyes as we drank our tea.

"How'd you sleep, Lucy?" she asked sarcastically.

"OK, I guess," I replied. "How 'bout you?"

"Oh, just peachy," she responded, her words dripping acid. "I had my back against the cold floor of the tent and a nice cool breeze blowing under either side of my broken sleeping bag. Plus, my brother is going to kill me when I get home."

"I know," I said, sheepishly looking at her as she tried to kill me with her gaze. I felt like such a coward and cad, I couldn't keep eye contact with her. So I stared at the ground instead and mumbled, "I am sorry, Keri. I hate to be cold. All I could think about was finding a way to be warm. I was definitely not a very good friend."

"You got that right," she spat.

"I know. I was only thinking of myself. I am sorry," I added lamely.

"Yeah, me too," she said icily as she turned her back on me to talk with Mike.

After eating, we packed our hiking gear into the back of the wagon, squeezed in together and drove the couple of miles to the trailhead. We parked the car in a rutted dirt lot and put on jackets, hats and gloves in preparation for our climb. Carl made sure everyone had a full bottle of water, some granola bars for snacks and a lunch. We shoved all of this plus any extra clothing anyone wanted to take into our small daypacks and were ready to go.

Chapter Five

When I looked across the tundra, the mountain appeared miles and miles away rather than just three miles distant. At the same time, in the clear air it seemed to tower above us. Large blotches of snow covered the ground like a patchwork quilt, growing more uniformly white in the valley between the trailhead and the base of the peak. The tops of smaller evergreen trees just barely peeked through. I wore the same pair of jeans as the day before with a T-shirt and sweater and threw an old down jacket on top. A wool hat, a pair of gloves and a pair of sneakers completed my outfit for the hike. On a summer day, sneakers would probably have been fine; however, walking through snow meant my feet got wet and cold immediately and stayed that way all day.

Because of the snowpack, there was no trail. Again, in the summer, a clear, dirt path led to the mountain's base and then up through the rock scree to the summit. As it was, we made our way cross-country, keeping the peak before us and trying to pick the best possible route. Mack, Tate and Mike led the way with Carl and Mr. F. bringing up the rear. Keri and I walked in the middle of the group although not together at this point. She was clearly still angry with me. She kept glancing my direction with hatred in her eyes and would purposefully move away from me if I came anywhere near her.

Man, this is going to be a long day, I thought, watching her huff away, calling out to Mike.

Scott Gomer Creek flowed through the small valley that lay between the trailhead and the mountain's base. During the summer months, it was a large stream. Fortunately, it was still mostly frozen this early in the spring. After wandering for several minutes among the red-tinged, "wait a minute" willows lining the stream banks we found a snow bridge to cross over safely. We called them "wait a minute" because they blocked the direct path, causing hikers to double back two and three times find a clear route. Their branches were springy, like all willows, and they tended to make deep scratches in exposed skin that could take weeks to heal. Fortunately, all of us were either wearing jackets or long-sleeved shirts, so we didn't get any cuts.

After crossing the river, we ascended steadily for about 45 minutes. We hiked through the edges of a pine forest where stands of evergreens were interspersed with open, marshy meadows. A lot of snow still hid among the trees. Coming out of the forest, the trail got steeper and we passed above a granite rock face. I was very glad we didn't have to climb that, as rock climbing was unknown and scary territory for me. At 11,800 feet, the trail began to climb up a shoulder of the mountain. We continued above tree line and into the open tundra. The wind picked up as the trail switchbacked up the hill, gaining another 500 feet in elevation as we reached the north end of the shoulder.

At this point, the route became clear although many parts of what would be a trail in the summer were still snow-covered. We headed left and then curved around to the right to reach the base of the steeper slope near 13,000 feet. From here, we followed a clear trail as it climbed south and then southeast.

Now, we started climbing in earnest. The steeply pitched, rocky trail made it clear why our Rocky Mountains had their name. On the lower segments of this summit push, the rocks were huge. Rocks the size of Volkswagen Beetles dotted the slopes; they were easy to go around. Soon, however, those turned into refrigerator-sized boulders stacked one on top of the other so that after three hours of hiking, we were climbing hand-over-hand. We hauled ourselves up a rock using our knees, our butts, anything to gain a hold and ascend in elevation. Just as soon as we surmounted one rock, we came to another. Even though the sun was shining, it was freezing. The wind whipped around us, stirring the snow up into miniature tornados. Our gloves were soaked. Our jeans were dripping, and of course, my sneakers were sopping wet. Even though I was drenched in sweat, I was shivering all over from the dampness of my clothing.

We just kept climbing, one foot in front of the other. Stop. Breathe deeply and slowly, and then repeat. Gradually the rocks gave way to talus, smaller boulders and stones, some that were six feet wide, some only a foot or two. The smaller the rocks became, the harder it was to walk on them. They were tippy or slippery so you had to be always on the look-out for your footing.

We moved at a snail's pace. Keri and I hiked side by side now, not talking as we were focused on walking and breathing, but at least no longer mad at each other. The boys and Mr. F. walked ahead of us and Carl trailed just behind.

As I looked for a place to put my foot, someone shouted "Rock!" from above my head. I looked up to see that Tate had dislodged a boulder the size of a toaster oven. It was bouncing and leaping downhill, careening off other rocks and gaining speed as it fell. Keri and I had time for one quick, frightened look into each other's eyes before we each hugged into the rock face. We heard a sharp ping as it struck just to our right and then whizzed away down the slope.

"Whew! That was close," I exclaimed, looking over my shoulder and shaking gravel from my hair. I noticed a two-inch piece of granite had chipped off the boulder as it bounded by me, so I reached down, picked it up and stuck it in my pocket.

"Yeah," Keri breathed a sigh of relief as she watched the boulder bounding down the mountain, and then we continued our ascent. I guess a near-death experience was enough to help her forget her anger at me.

Finally, after four hours of nonstop hiking, we came to the last ridge leading to the summit. We still had another 250 feet of elevation to gain, but after already climbing 2,000 feet, it didn't seem like it was very much. I could tell everyone was re-energized knowing we had only a short distance to go as the pace picked up again and I heard the boys whooping up ahead.

Thirty minutes later, Keri and I topped the ridge, and the summit came into view.

"Woohoo!" I smiled at Keri. "We're going to make it!"

"Yeah!" she smiled back. "I can't believe we're going to stand on top of a fourteener!"

"I know, right? Who'd've thought Lucy Dakota could ever do this?" I was giddy.

A flat stroll took us to the actual summit, which was marked by a brass medallion placed by the United States Geological Survey, a summit register and a few rock cairns. The cairns are piles of stones that can help point out a path, or in this case, just a cool way to mark the summit. The summit register is a scroll of paper stuffed inside a waterproof tube; the National Forest Service supplies them, and climbers sign the register to prove that they made it to the top. Buffeted by the wind but warmed by the sun, we hid behind some rocks and ate a quick sandwich. The boys took photographs, since neither Keri nor I had thought about bringing a camera or our phones. We signed the register and then headed back down.

The going was slow on the descent because we had to watch our footing. Carl and Mack were the only ones who had ever climbed a mountain before, and they helped us learn about climbing downhill, which was almost as hard as going up. If we stepped too close to the uphill side of a rock, it would slide a foot or two down the mountain, threatening to make us lose our footing and tumble down the mountain. It was nerve-racking.

I was frozen and couldn't feel my feet inside my soaked sneakers. My hands were cramped and my fingertips were numb. My legs hurt, I had a headache, and I had started to cough. I knew I didn't have a cold, but it felt like I had gotten water in my lungs somehow. Every time I took a breath, I could feel a gurgling sensation, particularly when I had to breathe deeply. I assumed that I had gotten water in my lungs when I drank on the way to the top even though I couldn't remember choking or swallowing wrong. So I quit drinking water on the way down. Basically, once the elation of reaching the top subsided, I was tired, cranky and ready to go home.

We slowly climbed down the refrigerator-sized rocks, lowering ourselves on our bottoms. Sometimes, the guys would have to stand below us and give Keri and me a hand down. Leaving the rocks, we made better time as we half-slid and half-ran down the snow slopes. My cough was getting worse and it was getting colder. Clouds started to build to the west and a feeling of snow filled the air.

The sun settled behind the surrounding mountains just as we finally arrived back at the parking lot. Exhausted, we threw our backpacks into Carl's wagon and piled in to return to camp and Mr. F's car. Soon, we were warm and drowsy, driving back to Denver; I quickly fell into an exhausted sleep. I slept the entire ride back home, coughing along the way.

The next day my cough was about the same and I could still feel the gurgling of fluid in my chest when I breathed. It had not gotten any worse, but it didn't seem to be getting any better. I was certain the water had come from drinking on the climb. Somehow, I concluded, I must have gotten water into my lungs while hiking. My mom consulted with my granddad, the Oklahoma doctor, and he agreed that while unlikely, it could be possible. He told my mom to keep me warm and fill me up with hot tea. I felt miserable and was determined never to drink water again on a climb.

Exhausted and miserable, I spent the next three days in bed, coughing. My mom finally relented and took me to a local doctor, and it turned out I had contracted high-altitude pulmonary edema, a potentially life-threatening disease caused by the altitude. My flatlander country doctor grandfather, for all his skill, wasn't familiar with the condition. On the mountain, I hadn't mentioned it to any of the adults, so they had no way of knowing how much trouble I was in. Fortunately, the best treatment for pulmonary edema is to return to a lower elevation, which I did when I came home to Denver. I slowly recovered but would never forget that gurgling sensation in my chest.

It took two more days of bed rest for me to recuperate enough to return to school. As I lay in my room thinking about the climb, my eyes fell upon the piece of granite I had put in my pocket, now lying on the nightstand. *Mom must have taken it out of my pants,* I thought as I picked it up and slowly turned it over in my hands, admiring the sparkling bits of mica flecked in among the gray and black of the stone. Immediately, it took me back to that moment when the boulder came bounding past Keri and me. It had been scary, yet at the same time exhilarating, just like the climb. Inexplicably, I felt drawn to the mountains, despite how badly I felt, and I vowed I would return someday.

Suddenly I realized just how lucky I was: not only narrowly escaping the falling rock on Bierstadt but stumbling upon the proper treatment for altitude sickness, and a few years earlier, knocking on just the right door in the apartment complex where a kind stranger cared for me. I summoned the strength to walk to my dresser and opened up my sock drawer, where I dug out the green washcloth that kind woman had used to tend to my hurt knee. I gently placed it on top of my dresser and set the granite shard right on top. I then flopped back into bed, awash in a sense of awe and gratitude before dozing off.

Chapter Six

My next adventure took place the following month. My cough finally cleared up about three weeks after our climbing trip and over that time we planned our next adventure. Mack and his dad had done a float trip on the Colorado River the year before, so Mack suggested that we try the same route together as a troop. We all agreed it sounded like fun.

We purchased four bright-yellow, four-person, inflatable rafts from a local sporting goods store and started designing a trip down the Colorado River. We would run the river 20 miles or so each day and sleep at night in camps we set up on islands. We couldn't camp on the riverbanks because the land on either side of the river was privately owned, whereas the islands that formed in the middle of the stream, whose size and location varied from year to year depending on the amount of water flowing through the canyons, were public domain.

We decided to go over Memorial Day weekend so we would have three full days for our journey. We would leave Denver on Friday after school and drive to Glenwood Springs. We would put in Saturday morning and follow the river for about 60 miles, all the way through the 15-mile-long DeBeque Canyon, just outside Grand Junction. If everything went as planned, we would take out Monday afternoon with enough time to drive back to Denver that night and get some sleep before school on Tuesday morning.

I was both nervous and excited about this trip. I really was not a strong swimmer, even though I had taken swimming lessons as a child. I looked forward to the trip because it sounded like a grand adventure and I would be with my friends. Keri and I were to share a raft—our friendship had survived the camping trip and climb a month earlier. Dudley the Dog, Carl's family's pet, came along so altogether there were a total of 12 of us heading out, 11 humans and one canine. We would be in five rafts, four each with two people in them and one with three people in it. Dudley would travel with Mack and Carl in the raft they used the year before.

It can snow in Colorado in May, especially in the high country, at the Colorado River headwaters. I couldn't even imagine snow, since the temperature was already in the 80s in Denver, but Carl told us to plan on cool weather.

OK, I thought, *I have no rafting experience whatsoever, and Carl says it is going to be cold. Geez, I have no idea how to pack.*

Personally, I was hoping it would be warm and sunny just like it was in Denver and I could get a tan during our little adventure, so in the end, I packed jeans, shorts, T-shirts, a warm sweater, and my swimsuit into my dad's old Navy duffel bag. I had the same down sleeping bag I had borrowed for our first camping trip and we bought an Ensolite, a thin foam pad for under my bag. Mom was smart and made me wrap everything up in big trash bags to help keep my stuff dry.

Friday, May 27, dawned clear and beautiful in Denver—another hot day for late May. My hopes soared high and my patience wore thin as I sat through half a dozen classes waiting for the end of the school day. Everything was packed and ready to go, waiting for me at home. Finally, after an hour of torture in chemistry, 2:30 came and I could leave. I half-ran, half-walked the whole way. Keri headed home to get her gear and then came up to my house.

Carl picked us up at my house around 4 p.m. Mr. Ferigano came along as chaperone again, driving his old Chevy Suburban this time, rather than the tiny car he took on the camping trip last month. He had the rafts and most of the gear in the Suburban. Tate, Mike, Heather Maloney, Tom Matthews and Paul Cuevera had already piled into Mr. F.'s car; it was stuffed to the gills. Keri, Mack, Alan and I rode with Dudley and Carl.

Everyone was in high spirits as we started out west.

"Ready for your second camping trip, Lucy?" Mack asked from the front seat.

"Yeah, I think so," I replied.

"You and Keri gonna share a sleeping bag again?" Alan inquired to my left in a teasing voice—I was squished in the middle of the back seat between him and Keri.

"Ugh! How'd you know about that?" I asked.

"Everyone knows about it," he said with a smirk. "Everyone knows what 'close' friends you two are," he added jeeringly.

"Shut it, Alan," Keri snarled from my other side.

"Just giving you a hard time," he said.

"Anyhow," Mack interrupted, "it's a fantastic trip. Beautiful scenery and fun rapids—not too hard. Dad and I had a blast last year, huh, Dad?"

"Yes, we sure did, Mack," Carl replied.

We continued chatting about last month's adventure for another half-hour or so as we drove up into the mountains. I got the distinct sense while we talked that Alan felt quite jealous and left out because he had not gone on that trip.

Maybe that was why he was so sarcastic with his earlier comments.

It was a five-hour drive to Glenwood, and even with the spectacular countryside and dazzling sunset, I was tired and slept most of the way. Every now and then I could hear Keri and Alan having quiet conversation while Carl and Mack talked in the front seat. Dudley had his head perched on the seat behind me. Thank God he didn't drool.

I woke up as we pulled into a campground just outside of Glenwood. It was a beautiful evening, with the last remains of light silhouetting the mesas to the west. There was not a cloud in the sky and we could hear the river rushing somewhere in the dark off to our left. A thrill ran through me as I imagined us hurtling down the rapids. Everyone knew the Colorado River was big water, dangerous and scary! I couldn't wait for tomorrow's adventure to begin.

We pulled out our sleeping bags and quickly set up a couple of tents. We munched on beef jerky and candy bars and jumped into our bags. Soon everyone was sound asleep, including me, despite my earlier four-hour snooze.

Saturday morning dawned bright and clear. Birds chirped in the trees and shrubs around the campground. Carl and Mr. F. had coffee brewing and were putting together a breakfast of bacon and pancakes. It smelled wonderful. As we ate, Carl went over some safety instructions.

"Alright, guys, listen up. If you fall out of the raft, the first thing you have to do is not panic," he said, walking back and forth before us like a college professor lecturing on the rise and fall of some ancient civilization.

"According to the guidebook," which he waved in the air, "as well as Mack's and my experience last year, we shouldn't hit any whitewater bigger than Class 3, so most of our trip will be just an easy float." He smiled reassuringly as he walked. Suddenly, I felt the urge to laugh out loud. I don't know if it was nerves or just the sight of Carl at five-foot-six with his full beard looking like a yard gnome lecturing us. I snickered behind my hand and both Alan and Keri shot me dirty looks.

"When we do hit whitewater, if you fall out of the boat, just float on your back, keeping your head out of the water. Point your feet downstream so that you can push yourself off any rocks you might encounter with something other than your head." A few of the guys laughed at his joke.

"Seriously," Carl continued, "huge submerged boulders are what create the rapids, so it's important that you navigate around them if you are floating through them outside your raft. One of us, either I or Mr. F., will come to help you as soon as you are out of the rapids. Any questions?" he asked, looking around to make sure we were all following him.

"Are we going to be using life vests?" I asked hesitantly, not wanting to appear afraid or stupid but I didn't remember us purchasing any life vests.

"This is just a float trip," Carl replied. "But it's always better to be safe than sorry. We've got vests for everyone, and we'll start fitting them as soon as the safety talk is done. Any other questions?"

"What if we can't swim?" I persisted.

"Is there anyone in the group who can't swim?" Carl asked, surprise registering in his voice.

"I don't swim really well," I said.

"Then you better not fall out," Tate mumbled in the background.

"No duh, Tonto," I snapped, flashing him a nasty smile.

"You'll be fine, Lucy," Carl assured me.

"I hope so," I said, feeling intimidated.

"OK, if there aren't any further questions, I'll explain how things are going to work," Carl continued, pacing back and forth. "Either Mr. Ferigano's boat or mine will go first. ALWAYS. Next will be your three boats and then one of our boats will bring up the rear. That way, there will always be an adult available for rescue, and an adult reading the river." He looked around to make sure everyone was listening. We were, avidly.

He resumed his lecture. "You'll each have a paddle, which you will use to propel your boats through the slower sections of the river. You hold the paddle with your thumb hooked under the handle and your hand resting on top, like this," he added as he showed us how to hold the paddle.

"Then, you reach forward and pull the water back alongside the boat. That will move you forward," Carl proceeded, demonstrating as he talked. "Got it, everyone?"

We all nodded and I raised my hand again.

Carl looked my direction. "Yes, Lucy?"

"What if we need to go backward?" I asked.

"Then you paddle backwards, dummy," I heard Tate mutter and I shot him a furious look. *What's up with him today?* I wondered.

"You will push the water forward along the boat by levering the paddle using your top hand as the anchor," Carl explained patiently and showed me how it was done.

"Thanks," I mumbled, feeling embarrassed and stupid, courtesy of Tate's rude remarks. I didn't know why he was in such a foul mood. I'd have to ask Keri when we got into our boats.

We inflated our rafts and put them on the water. Carl had brought along a power pump that plugged into the car lighter, and it went quickly. Less than 30 minutes later, all five boats were full of air and ready to go. We loaded our duffel bags and camping gear onto the rafts and carried them to the river's edge.

"Alright, gang," Carl called out. "Mack and I will go first. Lucy, you and Keri should follow our boat. Then, Tate and Alan followed by Tom and Paul. Mr. F., Mike and Heather will follow in the sweep boat, making sure everyone is OK."

Carl and Mack put their boat in the water while Keri and I watched intently, since we had never done this before. We noticed that they put the front end in the water and Mack got into the raft. Then, while Mack stabilized the boat, Dudley jumped in and Carl pushed it into the water, jumping onto the rear just as it left the bank.

Wow, I'm not sure we'll be able to do that, I thought, watching the others.

"Ready?" I asked Keri.

"Ready as I'll ever be," she replied with a grimace.

"Do you want to be in front of the boat or the rear?" I asked her as we carried our boat the last few feet to the water.

"I'll go in the front if that's OK with you," she said.

"Sure," I replied, holding the raft steady as she climbed in. She crawled across our gear to the front and grabbed her paddle.

"Here I come!" I shouted as I shoved the raft forward and tried to jump in. I missed and fell face-first into the water, still holding onto the raft. The water was freezing! I jumped up, embarrassed and cold, and crawled into the boat before it floated off into the current.

"Bummer!" I cried out as I reached for my paddle and looked back to see everyone else getting into their boats. I could see Tate smirking at my mishap.

Soon, we were all aboard our crafts, heading down the river. What we didn't know as we started out that day was that the runoff, or snow melting from the high country, was close to its peak that weekend. That meant normally quiet sections of the river now had rapids, and the Class 3 rapids were now running high enough and strong enough to be classified as Class 4 water. That meant bigger waves, deeper holes, and faster, colder water than usual.

The river pulled us downstream immediately. The current moved a lot faster than I had realized watching from the shore. We rounded a curve in the river and immediately hit a big rapid, Class 4 whitewater. Keri and I had no idea what to do. Luckily we didn't lose our paddles as we plunged into a deep hole and shot out the other side. We were thrown into the center of the boat, and had no control at all. We just hung on, hoping we didn't hit a rock and flip over. Water splashed over the sides and drenched us both.

After the first big hole, we bumped across half a dozen waves and then, looming before us, was another gaping opening in the water. We could hear the river roaring into it. At this point, we were doing nothing to control our boat. We were at the mercy of the river, holding on for dear life. Fortunately, the river tends to take things along the path of least resistance. Unfortunately, that meant going into the hole. We hit it straight on, which was our only chance of getting through without flipping the boat. The jolt of dropping into the opening in the water and then the impact of hitting the standing wave on the far side was so severe that Keri nearly fell out.

Without thinking, I reached forward and grabbed the waist of her jeans and threw myself into the bottom of the raft. Our combined weight moving around must have somehow dislodged us from the hole, too, because as soon I fell into the boat, we shot out the far side of the hole like a speeding bullet. Somehow both of us managed to stay in the boat, and we held onto our paddles. We were, however, soaked to the skin as we joined Carl's boat in a large eddy, a quiet spot where the river actually runs back upstream, to wait for the others to come through the rapids.

"Wow! What did you think of that?" Mack exclaimed. "Wasn't it totally awesome?"

"Nnnnooo," I stuttered both from shock and cold. The sun had gone behind the clouds and I shivered, hoping it would get warmer soon. I wondered where had all that water had come from.

"It was scary," Keri said, also shaking from the chill.

"Yes, the water is significantly higher than I expected," Carl said. "However, that should be the biggest rapid we hit the entire trip," he added encouragingly.

Soon everyone made it through the rapids. Keri and I seemed to have gotten the worst of it because the rest of our party appeared pretty dry. Even Dudley the Dog was drier than I was. I didn't say anything because I didn't want to seem weak around my more experienced friends, especially with Tate being such a bully. I just held my arms tightly around my chest and silently shivered.

Before long, we reluctantly left the gentle eddy, continuing our downstream run.

"Hey," I called out to Keri. "What's up with Tate today? He is usually pretty nice."

"Yeah, I know," she answered. "I don't know. Maybe he broke up with his girlfriend."

"Really?" I asked, intrigued. "I didn't even know he was seeing anyone."

"Yeah, he has been going out with Bailey," Keri replied.

"Bailey? You mean Bailey Greenberg?" I asked in amazement.

"I know," Keri said earnestly. "They don't seem like a good match."

"No, not at all," I said. "No wonder he's crabby. 'Course, if he's broken up with Bailey then he should be happy."

"I know! You'd think," Keri said.

"I don't know," I said. "I'm not sure that's it."

"Hmm," Keri said, grabbing onto the side of the raft as we hit another section of whitewater.

Unfortunately, my sunny day never materialized. Instead, it got colder by the minute. We kept bumping through the whitewater that wasn't supposed to be there and the waves that crashed over the sides of our little boat continually soaked me.

I warmed up some at lunch, but the wind started to pick up once we got back on the river in the afternoon. Clouds covered the sun and grew thicker as the day wore on.

our tents and gear, the sun beamed high in the sky—a glorious day.

After a full day on the water, we learned how to read the river. We now knew to navigate over to the side of the river with the higher bank because the deeper channel was there. We learned to watch for the smooth pillow of water that meant a huge, submerged rock might hide a deep, sucking hole behind it. We discovered the importance of paddling like crazy through the rapids to keep our boat straight and give it momentum, which helped keep us dry. And we mastered the art of relaxing on the swift, quiet sections, taking in the spectacular scenery all around us.

Although we ran two or three sections of Class 3 rapids, most of the morning saw us passing through gentle riffles with just enough waves to bounce us around a bit and keep us moving swiftly.

Just before noon, we came to the remains of an old highway bridge. The enormous concrete support pillars still stood in place on the left side of the river. They looked gnarly, covered with vines and with huge chunks missing. Rebar poked sinisterly out through the gaping holes. Looking forward toward the monoliths, at first, we did not see the danger ahead. We didn't realize it, but the far left pillar was creating a gigantic whirlpool, and we were headed straight into it.

The sound drew our attention first. We heard a low, roaring noise, and one by one, each of us turned to look in the direction from which it came. We saw the center of a whirlpool, a six-inch-wide hole completely free of water! We listened to the gurgling sound as water, branches and debris were drawn closer to the center and then down into the core.

"How in the world are we going to get past that monstrosity without being sucked down?" I wondered in panic.

Steep, cactus-covered cliffs formed the banks opposite the whirlpool's center, allowing no way to portage around. There was a marshy bog on the other side, where the main whirlpool formed, fenced in by barbed wire. It was clearly private property, and there was no chance to use it to carry our rafts around the challenge.

Carl motioned us all over to an eddy on the far bank.

"OK, gang," he said, trying not to appear worried. "This was not here two weeks ago when we scouted the river. I know it looks scary, but we will be able to get past it. It will just take some hard paddling."

Then, I saw Carl and Mr. F. exchange glances. Keri and I looked at each other. I could see the fear in her face and knew it reflected my own terror.

Following Carl's lead, we headed out. Keeping as far from the sucking current as we could, we paddled furiously, digging into the water and pulling on our oars with all our might. We could see Carl making headway. His raft moved past the midpoint and the boys in the raft ahead of us had already made it halfway across the danger zone.

Keri and I, however, were at a standstill. No matter how hard we paddled, we couldn't move forward. We weren't being sucked toward the middle, not yet, but we weren't moving ahead either.

The two rafts that had started out behind us came abreast of us and started to move past us. Looking around, we realized everyone was passing us and making it through!

"Keep paddling, Lucy!" Mr. F. shouted as his raft passed us. "Don't give up, Keri!"

"We can't stop to help you or else we'll get sucked in," called Alan.

What were we going to do? I felt helpless and hopeless and could see by the set of her shoulders that Keri felt the same way.

By now our arms were tiring and we wanted to quit. Our muscles burned intensely and sweat poured off our foreheads. If we stopped, we were doomed to be sucked into the center, where the current pulled even stronger than it did on the outer edges, where we were. Visions of movie scenes where adventurers were drawn to their horrible deaths in the center of a whirling storm of water passed through my mind.

This is it. My life is over, I thought to myself. I was certain that Keri and I were going to drown.

But we kept paddling. Amazingly, some way, we kept our arms moving, pulling water past our small, yellow-orange raft. Every inch of my arms screamed in agony, the burn more intense than anything I had ever experienced.

By this time, everyone else had avoided the danger; they had beached their rafts on a small rocky shore just downstream. They cheered us on and encouraged us to keep at it. Even though we couldn't hear them, we knew they were on our side.

I realized that we were moving. I hadn't noticed before because I had been so caught up in visions of a watery death, but Keri and I had imperceptibly inched forward. We now hovered near the halfway mark on the 60-yard-wide circle made by the whirlpool. Just a bit more and we would emerge on the other side where the current would actually help propel us out of harm's way.

"Come ON!" I shouted at Keri. "We're almost there!"

"I can't," she screamed back. "My arms are dying! I'm not going to be able to paddle any further!"

"Sure you can!" I yelled back above the roar of the water. "If you don't, we're going to die here on our first real adventure, and I'll probably hate you forever!"

That made her laugh and together we pulled a bit harder. Inch by inch, we pulled our raft against the outward flowing current and made it to the halfway mark just as our arms gave out. Fortunately, it was enough. One more good push and the current grabbed our raft and threw us out to the bank and downstream. We had made it!

"Woohoo!" I shouted, punching the air with the last of my energy.

"Yeah!" Keri yelled. We high-fived our paddles.

We could hear the rest of our group whooping and hollering as well. As we pulled over to the rocky shore where everyone waited, shouting and yelling, Mack and his dad waded out to haul our raft in. My arms shook with fatigue and I started to cry with relief. I hadn't realized how frightened I had been until our friends came over and gave us a hand to get out of our raft.

Carl apologized, "I'm sorry, girls. Like I said, there was no whirlpool last year when Mack and I rafted this section, and I didn't see any whirlpool two weeks ago when I scouted the river. As the spring runoff grew, the higher water levels must have created that whirlpool. If I had known how large it was, or that it even existed, I would have made sure each raft had at least one boy in it to help with the paddling."

"That's alright, Mr. Lewis," I heard myself saying, sniffling a bit and wiping my nose. "It was pretty scary. I'm just glad we didn't get sucked into the middle. What would have happened to us if we had?"

"I'm not sure," he replied, shrugging his shoulders and grimacing at the water. "I'm guessing that your raft would have been too large to get sucked under, however, you could have been swirled around for a very long time before you got out."

"Wow!" I said, shrugging off the fear I had felt. "Thank God we're a couple of strong chicks!" and I weakly flexed my arm muscles.

But I wondered what waited for us around next bend.

We ate a simple lunch of summer sausage and cheese there on the riverbanks below the whirlpool, taking it easy after the rush of adrenaline and emotions the whirlpool had stirred up.

Fortunately, the rest of the day proved quiet. The river widened out as it meandered through the rangeland of Colorado's western slope. Stately buttes, mesas, desert plateaus and mountains paraded by us as we drifted downstream. Although we encountered no whitewater sections, the river flowed swiftly, with occasional riffles to keep us from falling asleep. The sun shone brightly, afternoon light glinting off the water. I felt warm and contented as we floated along, with memories of my bout with hypothermia the first day nowhere in my consciousness.

That evening we camped on an island obviously inhabited by cows. Cow pies littered the ground, though the beasts themselves were not present, and I wondered how the animals got there. I still don't know if they swam the river to pasture on the lush grass growing there, or if, later in the season, water levels dropped low enough that they could just walk across to the island. The lack of cows did not stop Tate and Alan from threatening us with a cow pie fight.

"Don't even think about it," I growled as I caught a glimpse of Alan sneaking up behind Keri and me with a dry frisbee of manure in his hands. She spun around just as he tossed it and dodged out of the way.

"You're gonna pay for that," she grinned, picking up her own weapon.

"Oh, you think so?"

"I know so," and the fight was on, with dried cow dung flying everywhere. It was like a summer snowball fight. Fortunately there were no fresh patties to be found.

Carl came by at the peak of the battle. "Alright, guys! Alright! Enough fun, already," he tried to sound gruff even though he was grinning from ear to ear. "It's time to start getting ready for dinner."

"OK, Carl," we all agreed and shook dirty hands in a truce.

Giggling and shaking grass and manure out of our hair, Keri and I gathered armfuls of driftwood to build our evening fire while the boys cooked. As we sat in the fire's toasty glow eating tortellini in marinara sauce, everyone felt relaxed, companionable and comfortable after a full, fabulous day on the river. We all slept great that night.

Our final peaceful day of rafting rewarded us with robin's-egg blue skies scattered with milky white clouds. Cinnamon-colored soil contrasted with the Christmas green of piñon pines and the dusty silver gray of sagebrush on the towering mesas above us. Cattle grazed on the ranchlands bordering the river. The cottonwoods had just leafed out so their leaves were brilliant spring green. A couple of bald eagles soared over the river but we could have been the only people in the world for all we knew. Deer occasionally skirted the banks, darting off into the trees if we spied them or made too much noise. When Dudley the Dog spotted them, he barked like crazy and once even jumped into the river, trying to swim to shore and give chase. The current was too strong and the dog gave up quickly, needing then to be hauled back into Carl and Mack's raft.

The river braided into channels, with small and medium-sized islands created in between. For a while we played hide-and-seek on the water, choosing a channel apart from the other rafts, then seeing who would appear first, and from which channel they would come. Often the boat that had left a side channel first would lie in wait for the others, armed and ready to start a water fight as soon as an unwary raft appeared.

As the day heated up, we finally got to enjoy the water the way I had originally envisioned. We tied all our rafts together. With Carl and Mr. F. in charge of the boats, we jumped in and floated the river on our backs. There weren't any more rapids, so it was quite safe and refreshing. Back in the rafts, we lay in the sun enjoying the warmth of a beautiful May day. *This is why we live in Colorado,* I thought to myself.

Later, when we got too hot, we had a gigantic water fight, using paddles and bail buckets to splash each other until everyone, even Dudley the Dog, was soaked. What a fun and glorious end to a great adventure, one I always wanted to remember.

When we pulled ashore to eat lunch, a smooth, dark gray river rock caught my eye, so I bent down and picked it up. A white swirl in it reminded me of the whirlpool. Again, I was struck by how lucky I was to have survived that scary moment, and I realized that part of my "luck" came from being smart (ducking from the falling boulder on Bierstadt) and from being persistent (not giving up when I felt too tired to paddle past the sucking whirlpool). *Hmm,* I thought with wonder. I had never really considered good instincts and persistence as some of my strengths, but here they were! A sense of pride swelled up in my chest as I started to like and appreciate myself more.

After lunch, we floated another mile or so to the takeout, where Mack's grandfather awaited us. He had driven Carl's car and Mr. F.'s truck over from Glenwood with the assistance of a couple of cousins. After thanking them for their help, we deflated our rafts, loaded up the gear and headed back to Denver, ready to plan our next adventure. Back home, I laid the small, rounded river rock next to the jagged piece of granite on top of the green washcloth.

Chapter Eight

The summer between my sophomore and junior years was pretty quiet compared to the spring. We didn't go on any trips with the scout post, since it was hard to get together during the summer holiday, with families traveling and doing things.

I spent the summer hanging out with friends at the swimming pool and working for my dad at his engineering firm. Once in a blue moon my dad's business partner, "Uncle" Bill, would take us all out to the lake on his speedboat and we'd take turns water-skiing. It was a ton of fun and gave me a great chance to work on my tan.

I had played on the volleyball and basketball teams in tenth grade but never got past the junior varsity teams, so I dropped out at the beginning of my junior year. I wasn't on any teams, but I had learned how important it is to stay in shape. I was getting better at exercising once in a while. I joined a gym and took a pilates class twice a week starting the fall of my junior year. That, our monthly adventure scout post meetings, working for my dad, homework and my involvement with a group called BMCA, Business Marketing Club of America, were pretty much all I could handle that fall.

BMCA was an interesting class designed to help students develop skills for successful business careers, build self-esteem, experience leadership and practice community service. At our school it was a blend of super-easy business classes plus credit for working off-campus. I received two full credits each my junior and senior years: one for attending the class during the day and the second for my job at Dad's. How cool was that? I wouldn't complain about two super easy A's.

I loved my job. I was in charge of the printed circuit boards for an entire series of control panels. That meant stuffing, or poking, diodes and resisters into their appropriate holes, and then soldering them into place according to a schematic or plan. There were about 25 boards per panel, each with about 40 little ceramic pieces (the diodes and resisters that directed the flow of electricity along the circuits) that needed placing and soldering, and dozens of panels were on order for jobs around the world. So my job was pretty secure. Or so I assumed.

Dad started me out at piece rate, meaning I was paid a fixed amount, $8, for each completed board. Any mistakes my supervisor or Dad found had to be fixed on my own time, without pay. That inspired me to do well because I wanted time off to visit with the handsome 25-year-old guys who worked at the construction company next door to my dad's warehouse. Plus, I had my own sense of pride in doing my job well. In a short time, I got to be pretty quick at completing my work accurately, and before long, I was averaging $15 an hour with loads of time to hang out in the back. It suited me perfectly.

It didn't take long before some of the other shop employees began to complain about my freedom. They got 15-minute breaks in the afternoon, while I hung out, gabbing, for 30 or 40 minutes at a time. One day, I was taken into the manager's office and given a "promotion."

"Hey, Lucy!" Wally called out. I had known Wally and his older brother, Russell, since they were teens and I was eight. His dad and mine had worked together installing some of the ski lifts in Steamboat Springs.

"Yeah, Wally?" I called out, looking up from the board I was soldering.

"Uh, could you come into the office for a moment?" he asked hesitantly. Wally was a nice guy but he really wasn't a great manager. He was still young and anything that felt like a confrontation made him very uncomfortable. I could relate.

"Sure. Just let me finish this board. I'll be right there."

When I walked into his shabby little office, he held out a chair for me. I sat down, wondering what was happening.

"Lucy," he began and then cleared his throat. "Uh, well." His face turned beet red. "Some of the guys have been talking."

"Yeah?"

"Well, not really talking," he stumbled on his sentences. "I mean, I can just tell. You know. What I mean to say, is, well, you are really, really good at what you do but it makes some of the men jealous that you have so much freedom. They feel that it is because your dad owns the company."

"Oh. OK?" I said, shaking my head and wondering where in the heck this conversation was headed.

"So," he said slowly. "Your dad suggested that we give you a raise," he smiled wanly at me.

"That sounds great," I said. "So what's the problem?"

"There really is no problem, Lucy. It's just that when you are on a salary, there are more restrictions to your time and more rules you have to follow."

"Oh, I see," I frowned. "What sort of rules, Wally?"

"Well, you will have a set schedule that includes specific break times."

"OK?"

"Well, you will arrive right after school at three o'clock and you'll have one 15-minute break and your shift will end at 6:30."

"Oh. That doesn't sound all that great."

"It will take some getting used to, for sure," he said. "But I have faith in you. So does your dad."

Great. Just great, I thought to myself as I walked back to my bench. This meant I would be taken off piece rate and although my salary looked fantastic for any 17-year-old, it was still less than I had been making before and it meant I had a whole lot less freedom. Suddenly my job was not all that stimulating. That little experience taught me not to flaunt the good stuff or take my circumstances, especially the really great ones, for granted.

The one bright spot still was our adventure scout post. All fall we planned a winter trip to Steamboat Springs and I looked forward to those monthly meetings when I got to be with all my best friends. Most of them were skiers, like me, but a few would snowboard for a change of pace.

We planned to go over the long President's Day weekend in February and had a ton to do before the trip. We had to organize lodging, food, transportation and ski and snowboard equipment for those who did not have their own, plus we had to decide if there were any extra activities we might want to do besides skiing.

After a lot of research, we finally found an affordable place to stay. The local college was not full so it had some extra dorm rooms. We could stay there very inexpensively. Carl and Mr. F. both said they would be happy to drive us as long as we took care of their gasoline, and Mack had a Volkswagen Beetle he said he would take, so that covered our transportation needs. One of the local ski shops gave us a discount on rental equipment. We decided to eat at the school cafeteria for breakfast and dinner as it was pretty inexpensive, and we would use the ski area's snack bars for lunch. So, by the end of December, our plans were all set.

Before I knew it, February arrived and we were ready for our ski trip. We left right after school on Friday, stopping along the way for burgers. After the four-hour drive, we rolled into the dorm around 9 p.m. Everyone was tired, so we went to bed immediately.

The dorm rooms were pretty basic, with a pair of twin beds, brick walls the color of oatmeal and tired, worn-out carpet. They were nothing special, but this was my first trip with friends away from home that didn't involve camping, so I thought the accommodations were fantastic.

Keri had come with us, even though she was no longer active with our explorer post. She was on the varsity basketball, volleyball and track teams, and so she hung out with all the athletic girls rather than us. Although we were no longer best friends, it was fun to have someone along who I could ski with and it was great to have a roommate. We were the only two girls who had come along on the trip.

Carl came knocking at our door early Saturday morning.

"Lucy? Keri?" he called out.

"Wha, what?" I groaned. I felt like a train wreck. Even though we had gone to sleep early, I had tossed and turned most of the night. The mattresses were flat and lumpy and I had had a headache. And, I was not used to sleeping with someone else in my room. Keri talked in her sleep and I kept trying to listen in even though it was too soft to hear.

"Time to get up, girls," Carl replied cheerily.

"What time is it?" Keri asked.

"It's six o'clock."

"Oh, my God," Keri growled and covered her head. I remembered from some of our childhood sleepovers that she was not much of a morning person.

"We're up," I called out as I swung my feet over the side of the bed. Fortunately, my headache had gone away during the night.

"That's what you think," Keri groused from under her pillow.

"Don't worry," I said. "I'll go shower and grab you some fruit or something. You sleep a bit longer. I'll wake you up in half an hour."

"'K," Keri grunted and turned over in bed.

The showers were nearly as drab as the rooms. Beige tiles and concrete floors. I felt a bit exposed in the gang shower with its dozen heads even though I was the only female present. I got the feeling I wasn't going to be too excited about going to college in a year and a half and living in the dormitories. "Thank God I have another year to mentally prepare before that happens," I mumbled to myself as I rinsed my hair. Fortunately, there was plenty of hot water.

The cafeteria was better. At least it had huge windows with views of the surrounding mountains and bright, cheery plastic chairs. The food, however, was as bland as our room. I got a bowl of gloppy, gray oatmeal and a couple of bananas. I grabbed a bagel and an apple for Keri and slipped into a hard orange chair next to Mack.

"Hey, Luce," he grinned. "How'd you sleep?"

"Lousy," I replied. "How 'bout you?"

"Same," he said. "But I'm ready to hit the slopes. Just look at all that powder!"

"Yeah, it looks great," I said, not sure I was ready to learn to ski the powder. I was much more of a groomed-run girl.

"Aww. Come on! You'll love it," he said, sensing my reluctance as he dug into his breakfast.

I finished my oatmeal quickly and excused myself to take the food back to Keri. She was up when I got back to the room and was grateful for the breakfast.

We were among the first to hit the slopes that morning, and we had a blast. My middle-school ski lessons really came in handy; without them, I would never have been able to keep up. Werner Mountain was HUGE. It had miles of snowy trails and Mack and his best buddy, Tate, were fantastic skiers and ski racers. They flew all over the mountain—hitting jumps, darting in and out of the trees and running the moguls on the most difficult, "black-diamond" runs. Keri and I followed along at a slower pace, avoiding bumps and looking for the smoothest, flattest route but keeping up, more or less.

Mostly, we skied groomed, intermediate-rated "blue" slopes and tried sometimes to keep up with the boys on the easier black runs. Usually though we just met them at the bottom of the hill and rode up the lift with them. It was a fabulous day!

That night we returned to the college dorms, ate a quick dinner in the cafeteria and then walked into town. About midway through town, across the river, was a small ski area with a jumping hill called Howelsen Hill. Tate told us it was the oldest ski area with continuous use in Colorado and it had one of the largest natural ski jumping complexes in North America. He was into facts like that. As we walked past the darkened area, he and Mack suddenly got a crazy idea.

"Lucy, you and Keri wait here," they said, jogging off into the dark. "We'll be right back." And they left. We had no idea where they had gone, or even a good sense of where we were. It was dark and freezing cold, with snow piled on the ground around us, and we jogged in place while we waited for them to return. When they did, less than 10 minutes later, we could see that they had something stashed behind their backs.

"What were you doing? What do you guys have?" I asked, leaning to look behind them.

"Oh, we borrowed some food trays from the college cafeteria," Mack replied.

"What are you planning on doing with food trays?" Keri asked, with a puzzled look on her face.

"Just come with us and see," Tate said with a mischievous grin.

We followed the boys as they walked to the base of the ski area. Then we hiked about a fourth of the way up the hill and I started to get the idea of what Mack and Tate had planned.

"You girls just watch this first time," Mack said as he sat on a tray and went careening down the mountain.

"Yahoo!" we could hear him whooping as he slid. Tate jumped on his tray and quickly followed.

"Oh, great," I groaned as I remembered the last time I slid down a hill without a sled, prompted by a boy.

"What do you think?" I asked Keri.

"I dunno. It looks pretty fun," she answered.

"Yeah, but did you see how fast they were going?" I said apprehensively.

"Yeah, I know. Those trays look pretty small," she said as the boys hiked past, waving for us to join them, and then started down their second run.

"Yeah, they do. It's probably crazy and dangerous," I said, feeling worried and scared as they shot by like cannonballs fired at close range.

"I know," she said as she looked longingly at the boys. I could tell she really wanted to give it a try. They seemed to be having so much fun.

"OK. I'm going to give it a try," I decided. I didn't want to appear cowardly or keep my friend from having fun. "But I am going to start further down the hill," I explained, thinking this was a concession to safety.

"That sounds like a good idea," Keri said, and we both hiked a few hundred feet back down the hill. We met the boys as they were walking back up for their third run.

"Wow! That was awesome!" Tate gasped. He was covered in snow and out of breath in the high altitude, but he managed to squeak out some instructions as we got ready to ride. "Stay toward the center of the run— there are some nasty moguls on the left side. If you hit one of them, you're gonna crash, and it won't be pretty."

Mack was panting as he came up to us. His face was bright red and he had snow all over his hat and jacket.

"You definitely want to avoid the far side of the run," he wheezed. "If you get off the packed snow, the powder is about four feet deep."

"Thanks for the warning," I said. "That's partly why we're starting further down the hill."

"OK. See you at the bottom in a couple of minutes," Mack said as he and Tate headed up the run.

Keri and I stopped about 300 yards from the bottom of the run, sat on our trays and lifted our feet up. Before we knew it we were hurtling down the hill. Trees whizzed past us and tiny ice particles cut from the snow's surface knifed at our faces. The whole trip probably only lasted 30 or 40 seconds, but it was exhilarating. I felt my heart thudding in my chest and my breath was coming in gasps. I let out a whoop: "That was fantastic!"

"It was great!" Keri agreed, and we started back up again.

Part of the appeal was that it was also scary. We slid so fast, and it was pitch black around us. There were no lights, except the town lights

across the road from where we were sledding. We couldn't see the
spots, bumps or humps in the snow before we were upon them, sudd
airborne, and if there were any stumps or rocks showing through t
snow, we wouldn't have seen those either. Fortunately, we never encour
tered any on our dozen or so trips down the hill.

It was about midnight when we got back to the dorm, faces bright
red from the cold and stinging ice. Carl was waiting for us in the foyer.

"Where have you guys been?" he asked gruffly, eyeing our snowy
clothes and frozen faces.

"We were in town," Mack responded smoothly.

"You're all wet and you look like you're freezing," his father replied,
looking Keri and me over with skeptical eyes.

"Yeah, we went sledding over at Howelsen Hill," Mack said.

"Oh, I see." Carl sighed like he was accustomed to Mack heading out
to do crazy, adventurous things. "Nobody brought their cell phones on
this trip. What would you have done if one of you had gotten injured?"

"I don't know," Mack replied, scuffing his feet and looking appro-
priately abashed.

"Next time let one of us know where you're going, what you're going
to do and when you plan to be back."

"Yes, sir. I will."

"Sorry, Mr. Lewis," Keri and I said in unison as he frowned at us.
Then we all trooped up the stairs to bed.

I winced getting out of bed the next morning. Between the skiing
and the sledding, my body had taken a beating and I was stiff and sore
all over. Keri and I spent most of the day following the easiest runs and
hanging out at the Thunderhead food court, as our legs were aching and
we were both tired. The boys still roamed all over the mountain, checking in with us a couple of times during the day. That night, everyone was
exhausted, so we turned in early after a couple of rounds of poker in the
common area.

Monday offered up another excellent day of skiing: fresh powder and
clear skies. Keri and I returned to the blue runs that day, more or less
keeping up with the guys, and wishing we didn't have to go back to
school the next day. But we did, so we enjoyed every moment of the day
and being with our friends.

soon as the lifts closed, we jumped in the cars and headed back
enver. We got home late Monday evening, just in time for bed. As I
warm under the covers, just about to doze off, I thought back over
ie weekend. There had been a lot of fun and camaraderie, and the skiing had been fantastic, but for me the most significant moment had been
deciding whether or not to join the boys and Keri sledding. It had
taken several minutes to overcome my fear and give it a try. I was
proud of the fact that I had done so and happy that I had also taken into
consideration my feelings and justifiable hesitancy by choosing to do a
shorter, safer run. It really had been a great weekend. I sighed, "I love
my life," and drifted off to sleep.

Chapter Nine

My best friends outside the adventure post that year were part of the BMCA group. I didn't fit in with the jocks, and although I was smart, I really didn't want to be classified as one of the nerds. I wasn't a musician, a freak or a druggie, and the adventure post met just once a month, so I was limited as to people I could hang out with.

My boyfriend in eleventh grade, Dean, was also in BMCA. That's where we met.

Dean was handsome and exotic. He had moved to Denver from Boston; I loved his thick, back-bay accent. He was charming, and in some ways, he was one of the most popular boys in school. He was the stereotypical bad boy and I was the good girl. He smoked, did drugs and drank, none of which I had ever done or had ever considered doing. My parents both smoked and the smell of cigarettes disgusted me. I knew nothing about drugs, and my only experience with alcohol was when I had gotten up the nerve to try some of my dad's Scotch when I was home alone one afternoon. The earth-peat flavor of it was nasty, and the taste way too strong.

However, when Dean took an interest in me after a BMCA business competition, once again I let my desire to "fit in" dictate my behavior and override all my good sense.

Our chapter had driven to Longmont for the district competition. Mr. Manning, our BMCA teacher/supervisor, signed me up for the Professional Selling Event, but didn't tell me anything about it. I was happy to get away from school for the day even though I had no idea what to expect. I just went along for the ride. Or so I thought. Other students, particularly the seniors who had done this before, were nervously practicing speeches or working on projects during the hour-long bus ride.

It turned out that the sales contest consisted of two major parts: a cluster exam assessing math, analytical and communication skills, which I was very good at, and a 20-minute simulated sales scenario or oral presentation, which was weighted at twice the value of the exam score. For the sales pitch, we had to role-play selling a product. In my case, it was an iron, the kind you use to press clothing. I had 10 minutes to study the scenario, learn the features of the iron and prepare my presentation. I had never sold anything before in my life, but it seemed fairly straightforward to me. I told the buyer, who was the judge, all the various features of the steam iron I held in my hands. He came up with a couple of questions and a couple of objections, which I answered using the materials at hand, and that was it. It wasn't all that difficult, so I just shrugged it off as another experience.

At the awards ceremony later that day, the emcee announced my name as the first-place winner in the professional selling event! Surprised and dazed, I walked to the stage to receive my trophy. I had never won anything in my life, and immediately, people in the club paid attention to me.

No one had really noticed me until that moment. BMCA was considered super easy, and it attracted students who didn't excel in their other classes; most of them seemed to be kids who had taken a dislike to me over the years, for whatever reasons. Now, suddenly, Sheila Evans, Lisa Johansson and Terri Shultz (all former bully girls) and Dean Bryans wanted to talk to me.

Me! I was stunned.

The rest of the awards ceremony passed in a blur and we piled onto the bus to head home.

"We just knew you would win the sales event, Lucy," Sheila gushed. That should have had me worried; Sheila never gushed.

"You know, I'm really proud of you, Luce," Dean twanged in his throaty Bostonian accent, leaning over the bus seat to peer at me. I practically melted in place.

Wow, Dean Bryans was talking to me! I couldn't believe it. I couldn't respond. All of a sudden my head spun, my mind went blank and my voice box shut down. I nodded dumbly.

"Yeah, you're so smart," Terri said. "I don't know how you did those math tests. I took BMCA so I wouldn't have to take any more math, and there we were having to do equations with a time limit. OMG!"

I smiled and lay back against the seat, soaking up the praise and reveling in all the attention.

After that event, everything changed for me. Now the gang from BMCA was my group of friends. Sheila and Terri would ask me to come eat lunch with them and so I would crowd into place at the table along with all the girls who had wanted to beat me up in middle school! It was weird and I really never felt comfortable when Lisa Johansson or Stacy Treele ate at the same table. I didn't trust either one of them, but at least I didn't have to hide at lunch or eat alone anymore, and Lisa even smiled at me sometimes in class.

One girl seemed different from the others. Maybe it because she and I didn't have any past history and so I didn't prejudge her as a bully. Maybe it was because she didn't quite fit in with the other bully girls. Maybe it was because she was Hispanic and no one else was. I don't know. Her name was Florangel Martinez but everyone called her Fluffy.

She started a conversation with me one day at lunch: "Hey, Lucy! How's it going? What did you think of the marketing project in BMCA today?"

"I dunno," I shrugged, looking up from my bologna sandwich. "I am not excited to go out and ask people questions for my market survey. I didn't have a hard time coming up with the questions, but I just don't feel comfortable talking to random strangers."

"Yeah, I know what you mean," she said. "I think that won't be as hard for me as writing out the business plan will be once the survey is done. My mom will help me ask people questions. She's been involved in local politics for years and knows lots of folks. She doesn't have any problem talking to anyone and I guess I'm a bit like her," Fluffy said.

"You're lucky that way," I smiled at her.

"Yes, I am," she said. Just then the bell rang and it was time to head to class.

Fluffy and I started sitting together every day at lunch and she moved her seat in class to be closer to mine. Even though she was a year older and a senior, she soon became my new best friend.

Meanwhile, Dean was making it obvious he thought we should go out. He found excuses to seek me out in the hallway or after school. Usually he'd just say "hey" and we'd chat about trivial things, which was typically all I could think of to say when he was around anyway.

I don't know why my brain turned to mush so easily and quickly around him but it did. I felt tongue-tied and stupid, and at the same time gloatingly proud. Girls would glance our way with envy in their eyes every time we walked together down the hallway.

Because I had won at the local level in the BMCA competition, I went on to compete at the state level, along with other winning BMCA kids, including Dean, who was competing for the "Boy of the Year" award. State was a weekend-long event held in Colorado Springs at the ritzy Broadmoor Hotel. We drove down Friday after school, checked into the hotel and had dinner with Mr. Manning. The contests all started at 8:30 the next morning, so everyone went to bed early that night.

We spent all day Saturday participating in the events for our particular specialty. Once again, I had math computation tests, communication tests and a sales reenactment. I didn't really know what Dean and the others had to do and I didn't really care. This time, I knew what was at stake, so I practiced and studied and worried just like the seniors on the bus ride to Longmont. I had never competed at anything before our early spring event and suddenly I wanted to win, to be good at something. The problem was, I had very little experience, just the one event at the district level, and I didn't allow myself enough time to practice and study. Plus, I was now extremely nervous and I knew nothing about the mental game of success. All my worry ended up being wasted energy and a lot of time spent focusing on the wrong thing: not losing as opposed to winning.

None of us won at the state level. However, Mr. Manning had big dreams for the club for the following year, when many of us would be seniors. So, a few weeks later, he escorted five of us—Dean, Terri, Sheila, Fluffy and me—to Washington, D.C., to observe the national competition. He hoped some of us or maybe even the club itself would make it to the national level the next year.

Washington was a blast. We went to the opening ceremonies and the awards ceremony and got to speak with some of the competitors from around the country, but since none of us were actually competing we weren't allowed to observe the specific events, something about not wanting upcoming competitors to have an unfair advantage next year. Despite being barred from the competitive events, we had a fabulous time. We did some of the standard tourist things like visit the Washington Monument and Lincoln Memorial, walk through Arlington National Cemetery and tour some of the museums of the Smithsonian Institution. We also explored some of the funkier eateries downtown and enjoyed an evening out in Georgetown. But, what made it especially fun for me was that I had popular friends to hang out with for the first time in my life.

In the evenings, we all gathered in either Sheila's or Dean's room and that was when my judgment took a nosedive. I was so afraid to do something that would jeopardize our new friendships that I was willing to do just about anything.

Our first evening together, Dean brought out a pipe. I wasn't sure but I thought it was probably filled with marijuana. I panicked. I didn't know what to do. I had been taught about the dangers of drugs and had never tried anything except one nasty swig of alcohol, so I was really at a loss. I wanted to leave the room but didn't want to risk alienating my new friends.

Dean went out on the balcony to light the pipe. I was lounging on the bed. Sheila and Terri sat in the chairs and Fluffy was sitting on the bed leaning against the headboard. When Dean came back in, he passed the pipe around. First Sheila took a puff. Then Terri and Fluffy.

Fluffy handed it my way and I shook my head. "No, thanks," I said.

"Aww, come on Luce." Dean always called me Luce; it made me feel special. "Don't be a spoil sport. Take one puff for me." He smiled and came to sit down beside me. I couldn't say no. Actually, my tongue was tied again and I couldn't say anything but there was no way I was going to say no to Dean. In my mind, he was my passport to popularity.

Taking my lack of comment as a yes, Dean handed me the pipe. I took a deep drag like I had seen my father and mother do countless times with their cigarettes and immediately began coughing and spitting. It was horrible.

Dean laughed, "Take it easy! You don't have to inhale the whole pipeful on the first hit."

My eyes were watering and my head was dizzy as I blindly shook my head. It was hard to tell if I was agreeing with him or trying to tell him I didn't want any more. He assumed I was going along with him.

"Try another small puff," Dean said encouragingly, so I did. This time I didn't draw the smoke deep down into my lungs and I didn't cough.

"Much, much bettah," Dean smiled and handed the pipe to Sheila again.

By the time the pipe had gone round the circle three times, I was sleepy and completely unable to think clearly or even speak. I just sort of lay there sprawled on the bed in a stupor. It wasn't even remotely fun. I vaguely noticed that everyone had left the room except Dean, who was lying on the bed beside me. It was his room, of course. I couldn't put two thoughts together to form a sentence and I felt my shyness and discomfort around Dean amplified a thousand times. Somehow, too, I felt ashamed of myself for doing something I had been taught was wrong, so I just lay there.

After some time had passed, I perceived, as if through a fog, Dean running his hands down my sides and moving them forward toward my breasts. I froze. I didn't know what to do. My mind and body felt lethargic and slow but I somehow had the presence of mind to mumble "no" as I awkwardly pushed myself up to a sitting position on the bed.

My pot-fogged brain did not help at this time, but somewhere deep inside me I knew I was not ready to have a sexual encounter with Dean. Of course I had fantasized about him holding me, touching me and loving me. But the fantasy was a far cry from the reality of this moment.

Ours was a strange, uncomfortable relationship. Clearly we had very little in common outside of BMCA and it showed anytime we had the opportunity to talk to each other. We had nothing to say to each other. I was still tongue-tied because he was so lovely and I felt so undeserving of someone as handsome as he was even liking me. I have no idea why he was unable to converse with me; maybe he didn't have much to say, or maybe the fact that I was intelligent, even though it didn't show when I was with him, unnerved him. I never knew. I just knew we really couldn't think of anything to say to each other when we were together and so we often just sat in awkward silence.

That discomfort did not help me now. I had to say something to him. He was waiting, watching me with confusion in his winter sky blue eyes. "I...uh, I mean...," *Oh, God, would my brain please start working?* I tried again. "I really, really like you, Dean."

"Well, that's good to heah," he smiled his dazzling smile and reached for me again.

"Stop!" I said more strongly this time, pushing his hands away. "What I mean to say is, even though I like you a lot, I don't want my first time with a boy to be like this." I felt exhausted, embarrassed and exasperated. "I mean, sometimes I think about doing it with you, but not here in an ugly old hotel room, not now with my friends right next door! Not with me totally out of my mind!" Suddenly I was crying.

"Aww, Luce," Dean said as he cradled me in his arms. "I didn't know you felt that way. I have to say, I had gotten a different idear from you befoah."

"I'm sorry if I led you on," I said, sniffling as my crying stopped. "I didn't intend to. I guess sometimes I just don't know what's going on between my brain and my body."

"I understand," he whispered as he held me. He didn't try to touch me again that night and after a while, I stumbled back to my room.

The awkwardness between us only increased after that night. We were still "going out" but we spent less and less time together and never went out without friends. I felt badly about not going all the way with Dean, so with a guilty conscience, I fell into the habit of smoking pot with him and our mutual friends. It was never something I really enjoyed but I felt somehow I owed him something for having stood up for myself.

Dean did ask me to accompany him to our junior prom and I accepted, but as always being alone together was uneasy for both of us. He wore a navy blue tux that popped the color in his eyes and I found an amazing vintage burgundy dress: a straight-cut, jersey, floor-length gown with spaghetti straps and billowy, open sleeves falling to either side. I wore baby's breath in my long, wavy hair and felt like a goddess. Too bad I didn't know how to act like one; I was goofy and silent. We were a lovely couple (at least that is what everyone told us), however, we didn't dance and we had barely eaten before Dean suggested we leave. He was driving a beat up, old minivan he had borrowed from his mom.

We left the dance at about 10, drove through the city and started up the mountain canyon road. I had no idea where we were headed. Dean pulled out a couple of beers from a cooler and offered me one. I never really liked beer, but I took it because it gave me something to do so

I didn't feel as uncomfortable with the long silences.

I recognized the canyon we were heading up; it wasn't far from my home. I had driven up there the previous summer with Mack, Tate and some other friends to explore an old abandoned mansion. Everyone claimed it was haunted, but we never found any evidence of ghosts. We did see proof that someone was living there illegally, though. Some of the rooms had evidence of fires and one corner of the living room had been used as a toilet. I hoped Dean and I weren't headed there. It wasn't a very romantic spot and I had always envisioned prom as a romantic evening. I was already pretty disappointed with how things had gone so far.

We were about 12 miles out of town when Dean pulled off to the left. We drove a short distance on a dirt road and then Dean stopped the van. He gave me another beer, even though I hadn't finished my first one, and pulled a joint out of his pocket, offering me a hit as soon as he had lit it.

Of course, I thought sarcastically to myself. *He has no idea what to talk to me about nor any idea of something fun for us to do together, so he's going to use beer and marijuana to cover up his own discomfort.*

I was as guilty as he was because I always accepted what he offered me and didn't stand up for myself, but I was quickly losing any respect and awe I had originally felt for Dean. He seemed to be all fluff and no substance. Problem was, I was uncertain how to break it off with him, and I wasn't completely sure I wanted to end it. That meant I would lose my short-lived popularity if I ditched one of the most handsome, popular guys in school.

Against my better judgment, we smoked the joint. After that, Dean immediately wanted to make out. Even as insecure as I felt, I knew this was the last straw. I realized I was at a turning point, and this was the time for me to say no, once and for all, to Mr. Dean Bryans.

"Dean," I started.

"I know, I know," he said, annoyance coating his words. "You aren't ready. Right, Luce?"

"Yeah, that's right, Dean," I said, feeling sad. "You just don't seem to get it. I don't know what girl wants to have her first time be all muddled up with drink and marijuana, but it isn't me. Plus, here in this grubby old minivan is not my ideal spot for romance."

"I know. I know. It's just like in the grubby old hotel room in D.C."

"Yeah, I guess it is. This is really not working out for either of us."

"You can say that again," Dean muttered. Then he mumbled something about getting me home and I nodded in agreement. I hadn't told my parents I would be out this late. I hoped they weren't worried about me, but secretly I wanted them to forbid me from ever seeing Dean again. They weren't, and they didn't, but prom night marked the beginning of the end of our "good girl falls for bad boy" relationship. We went out a couple more times, but each date grew more tense and uneasy than the time before. After school ended in May we drifted apart over the course of the summer, and I turned my focus to work and other friends.

Chapter Ten

Our explorer post took a long, 55-mile bike ride in July. It was the farthest I had ever ridden my crusty old yard-sale bike and it almost killed me. We left our houses at 7 that morning planning to ride downhill to the reservoir. At least I thought it was going to be downhill. It turned out there were several steep, rolling hills between my house and the lake. From the lake we headed uphill, into the mountains, following a winding two-lane road. It felt like the churning, pumping of my legs that was slowly propelling me upward would never end. *I can walk faster than this,* I thought frequently to myself and then found out differently when I got off to walk for short stretches. The hill was endless.

It took an hour to ride to the lake, then three more to make it up the hill to the highway, where we turned and screamed back down the hill. It was an exhilarating 35-minute descent, followed by another hour or so of rolling hills, which, at that point, felt like the Himalayas to my exhausted legs. I was so sore I could barely move for the next four days. That's the problem with doing strenuous exercise when you're not accustomed to doing much, and it's probably what keeps a lot of us from continuing to exercise.

I didn't want to repeat the torture of those four days when my legs ached every time I just thought about moving, so at the beginning of my senior year, I began getting up at 4:30 every morning to go for a jog, eventually working up to a five-mile run. The challenge I felt during the bike ride motivated me to start running. I soon discovered it to be a lifesaver. It was a transformative experience, running in the dark, cold silence of the predawn morning. It was my first encounter with any sort of meditative practice and when times were tough during the year, my daily run helped me keep my head on straight.

The streets felt lonely at that time of day, with no cars on the road and no other people out walking or running. The solitude and peace allowed me to quietly think my own thoughts in the beauty of the out-doors. Over the course of the year I grew very fond of running and of having daily quiet time to myself. I thought about life in general, and where mine would be headed at the end of nine short months when I graduated from high school.

My family expected me to go to college. Mom and Dad both had college degrees from Colorado University in Boulder. I had good enough grades to get into CU or any school I wanted and I had done well on the SAT and ACT exams I took last spring.

I thought over boyfriend or girlfriend issues on those morning runs as both went through changes over the summer and early fall.

That fall, I began dating Mack, the son of our adventure scout sponsor. I don't know how it happened; at the time it seemed like fate. We had been friends for years and hung out together at our post meetings each month. We had gone through a funky period in ninth grade when Mack helped spread rumors that Keri and I were lesbians. Thinking back on those times, I believe it was probably jealousy that spurred those comments from Mack. Maybe he liked me even back then, and regretted the time I spent with my best girlfriend, or maybe he wanted his relationship with Tate, his favorite bud, to be equally close. I don't know. It was a strange, difficult period in all our lives.

I do know that being with the older, more mature Mack was fun. It felt like a homecoming for my soul. He was my best friend. We could talk about anything together and we discovered we had a lot of qualities and interests in common—such a relief after my few months with Dean. Mack was a musician (he played the piano like I had when I was younger and had switched to guitar) and a reader just like me. He was a bit idealistic, wanting social justice for everyone, and very romantic, yearning for the simpler times of the days of the cowboy. He loved nature and the outdoors and I discovered I shared some of the same values and passions.

He was also many things I was not. An accomplished artist, he had many pieces of work displayed on the walls at school. Mack was also athletic—a ski racer and a member of the varsity swim team. In our junior year, he started exploring his cowboy urges, taking up the sport of bull riding. Plus, he had an active and fun-loving family, a marked contrast to my own boring, workaholic parents.

So as best buds, we skied together, got to travel together when our post took trips and we planned our scouting adventures side by side with the other members of our post. So it just seemed natural that we would start going out. At least everyone told me that when they found out we were dating.

The first order of business for the scouting year beginning with our September meeting was organizing another weekend of skiing and boarding in Steamboat Springs. Preparations for that trip were easy since we had made a similar outing last year, and by the time our October meeting rolled around, everything was set for another President's Day weekend!

We also wanted to schedule a big three-day, two-night backpacking journey to commemorate the end of our senior year. The groundwork for such a big undertaking would require months, since we only met for two hours each month, so we began planning in October. There were so many details to handle to prepare for the backpacking trip. We had to decide where we wanted to go, based on what area would have decent weather for hiking and camping in mid-May, just before our graduation. We had to decide if we would stay in Colorado or go out of state. We had to think of what type of hiking would be good for our group. Several of us, myself included, had never backpacked in our lives. So, the route couldn't be too strenuous but it still had to be interesting enough for the more experienced adventurers in our post. We had to figure out how we would get to the trailhead and back to the city, and we had to plan food and equipment for the journey. It was quite an undertaking.

After several meetings spent studying various Bureau of Land Management and topographic maps, we decided to head to the canyon country in western Colorado. The desertlike terrain was similar to that of eastern Utah but we wouldn't have to cross the state line.

Temperatures in that area at the end of May averaged in the mid-80s, with nighttime lows in the 50s, so it wouldn't be too hot and we definitely wouldn't have to worry about any snow. If we had chosen to go to the high country, there would still probably have been deep snowpack from the winter, which would mean lots of slogging through wet, thigh-deep snow. That didn't sound like fun to anyone, and we thought it might prove too challenging for beginner backpackers in the group.

So we reviewed the maps and decided on the canyons outside the Colorado National Monument, in an area called the Black Ridge Canyons Wilderness. Located on the northwest flank of the Uncompahgre Plateau along the Black Ridge, it was basically an enormous elevated mesa, crossed by seven major red rock canyon systems, each draining into the Colorado River. The area's canyons varied in length from a few miles to more than 12 miles and every one of them contained interesting side canyons for exploring. We would see fascinating geological features including spires, balancing rocks, giant alcoves and spectacular red rock cliffs. Plus, the area contained the second largest concentration of natural arches in the country. It sounded just right. And Carl had hiked the area many years before so he had an idea where we were headed.

We ordered maps for everyone and began planning the equipment and supplies we needed to take. I did not have a backpack, so after calling several people my mom knew, we found a backpacking friend of the family who was willing to lend me his pack.

The usual high-school activities kept me busy my final year of school—football games, dances, friendships, Mack, BMCA, work at my dad's shop and our now twice-monthly adventure scout post meetings. We started meeting every other week so we could get all the strategizing done for the backpacking trip.

As I focused my time on all these activities, I found myself less and less interested in school so I started skipping a few classes. I also continued dabbling with marijuana, smoking some every day with Fluffy or with Mack, and my use of pot had an influence on my skipping school. I hadn't known Mack smoked pot until we started going out. Then he asked me if I did, and although I had only smoked those few times with Dean, I could finally say yes and be honest.

Even though I never really enjoyed it (I never got past feeling stupid and tongue-tied when I was high and it always left me lethargic and unmotivated), I found myself doing it more and more often. I was still insecure in my friendships and romances, so I kept saying yes, against my better judgment, so no one would dislike me. The more I ignored my own best interests, the more guilt and shame I felt, so my emotions spiraled downward. I began to feel ambivalent about myself and my future. That led to greater insecurity, so I continued missing a class here or there to go home with friends and have a few puffs on the pipe. I didn't know how to stop even though I knew it wasn't serving me or my future. I knew I needed to go to class to maintain a high grade point average so I could get off to a better start at college next fall, and I wanted to feel better about myself.

My daily runs helped. A little.

Meanwhile, Carl Lewis was actively involved in a secret project I would not find out about until February. He was completing applications for me and several others from our post to receive scholarships to attend a Colorado Outdoor Mountain School mountaineering course next summer right after graduation.

The holidays passed quickly and the snow was good, and soon it was time for our weekend in the mountains. We stayed in the college dorms again, skiing or boarding every day from when the lifts first opened all the way through the last run of the day. Thank goodness for my running; I had much more stamina than the previous year and I was able to keep up with the boys. Keri was no longer part of our post but that was OK since I was dating Mack. He skied with me every day, showing me how to improve my technique and where to find the best powder without leaving the groomed runs. It was a great weekend.

Chapter Eleven

During the troop meeting following our Steamboat ski trip, Carl announced that he had applied for scholarships for several of us to attend an Outdoor Mountain School program that summer, and that five of us had been accepted. Wow! I didn't even know what Outdoor Mountain School was but everyone else was excited as he called our names. None of us had known he was doing this, or expected it, and no one knew why he had singled me and the others out from among the dozen members of our post.

"Ellen Ferguson."

"Way to go, Ellen," voices called out to her. Ellen, a sophomore, was a very sweet girl. Though a new member, she proved a great addition to our troop—always upbeat and positive, never saying anything negative about anyone and always ready to lend a hand.

"Andy Ferigano," Carl called out next.

"Woohoo!" exclaimed Andy, looking around at the group.

"Yeah, Andy!" we shouted.

"Tate Gritdal."

"Alright, Tate."

"Way to go, dude!" Mack shouted.

"Cinday Summerland."

Wow, I wondered. *How did Cinday get accepted?*

Cinday was the least outdoorsy of any of us—even less so than I was, which I hadn't thought possible until I met her. Of course, I was getting better, with running and skiing, and I had gone rafting last year and climbed Mt. Bierstadt. Cinday hadn't done any of those trips; she mostly seemed to be concerned with her looks and what other people thought of her. The boys in the troop liked her because she was beautiful and pretended to be dumb and helpless. The girls in the troop regarded her with a measure of hostility, which was probably unfair because she really was a nice girl. I guess we were all just jealous of her.

Then Carl called out my name: "Lucy Dakota."

"Oh, my God!" I exclaimed as everyone turned to look at me. I could not believe it. I felt myself turning red at all the attention.

"Congrats, Lucy!" Tate shouted, and I smiled nervously at him.

"Way to go, girlfriend," Mack said, clapping me on the back good-buddy style, although I could tell he was disappointed; I would find out later that his dad had not included him in the scholarship applications because he wanted to give those of us who had fewer opportunities to be outdoors the chance. Mack and his family were always going hiking, backpacking, rafting or exploring. Even though it made sense, it didn't stop Mack from feeling left out and a bit jealous.

"Th…th…thanks, Carl," I stammered, feeling afraid and suddenly worried about what was coming up.

Yikes! I hope I can handle this! I panicked thinking about the fact that I had only been camping twice so far in my life. *What the heck am I going to do on a 25-day wilderness backpacking trip?*

Meanwhile, we had plans to make for our May trip so we quickly turned our thoughts toward that expedition. We had to finalize food and packing lists and figure out where we were going to camp, how we were going to get there and how long it would take. Troop members had to make sure they could join us, particularly us seniors as it was so close to graduation. There was plenty to do to keep us occupied throughout the late winter and early spring.

Soon enough, it was Memorial Day weekend and time for our adventure. As a troop, we had already discussed what was needed in terms of food and group supplies and each of us had gone out shopping earlier in the week. We were responsible for all of our own personal gear and food. Even though it was a group experience, individually we would handle our own cooking and meals.

My grandmother surprised me with an early graduation present: a new, royal blue down sleeping bag! Mom and I went to the store and bought canned beans, tuna, Parmesan cheese, tortillas and other hardy food supplies (I really had no idea what to bring). Then, I packed my jeans and T-shirts, underwear, rain jacket, water bottles and food into the ancient, aluminum-frame pack I borrowed. I tied the sleeping bag and a pad to the bottom of the frame and tried it on. It was heavy and uncomfortable but I guessed it would do. It was all I had.

We left Friday afternoon right after school for the seven-hour drive to Colorado National Monument, where we would spend our first night. We drove a couple of hours in Carl's big Ford pickup truck before stopping at a burger joint for a bite to eat.

Eight of the 14 troop members were going, including Carl. Cinday, Ellen and Tate sat up front with him in the cab while Mack, Andy, Jason Trowbright and I rode in the bed of the truck, along with all the backpacks and gear, under a big, waterproof tarp. The tarp made a loud flapping sound as we headed down the highway but it was cozy and warm with all of us huddled together in the middle, leaning against the gear on the outside edges.

We were dozing in the back when we pulled into the campsite. It was pitch-dark and late, so instead of putting up tents, we just crashed in the back of the truck, under the tarp, throwing our gear off into a pile and covering it with a second tarp Carl brought along.

Coyotes howled in the distance, their creepy yapping vocals making me think of a crazy woman roaming around out in the wilderness. It gave me shivers and I was glad I was huddled together with my friends and that there was an adult in the cab. I slept fitfully, trying to find a comfortable spot where the ridges on the truck bed's floor weren't digging into my hip or my shoulder. I finally dozed off, awakening with the early light.

We woke up about 6 the next morning. It promised to be a beautiful sunny day by the looks of it. There was not a cloud to be seen, and the sky glowed the brilliant baby blue so unique to Colorado. We quickly heated up coffee and eggs on the big camp stove Carl had pulled out of the pile. We wouldn't be using something so large and cumbersome on the backpacking portion of our trip but it sure was nice and convenient that first morning. A chill permeated the air, even though it was almost June in the desert. We stood at about 6,000 feet above sea level, and we could still see patches of snow up on the Grand Mesa and on the summits of the Bookcliffs in the distance.

Tate and Andy went for a morning jog. They asked me if I wanted to come along, but I declined. Even though I had been running daily for about nine months, I felt uncomfortable running with other people.

I really didn't think I could keep up with anyone. I was also accustomed to keeping my own company, and besides, I had no idea what to expect today in terms of physical exertion, so I wanted to stay as strong as possible. A little worry knot formed in my stomach as I thought about not being able to keep up with the others on the hike. I hated the idea of being last or holding everyone up.

When the boys got back from their run and everyone had eaten and cleaned up, we headed out to the trailhead. It took us another couple of hours driving because Carl had not been to this area in more than 20 years. We had maps but the roads in this remote region weren't well established and miles of developed backpacking trails didn't exist at the time.

We knew we had to find the Glade Park Store, a small market and gas station that Carl remembered being at a major crossroads of two well-traveled dirt roads. From there, he planned on asking directions; we just knew we would travel on a four-wheel-drive road for about six more miles before we would reach the area we planned to hike. Carl and his wife had hiked the canyon we were looking for when they were in their 20s, and he was hoping to explore it again.

The country was spectacular. Deep gorges cut into layers of red and white sandstone; dense stands of piñon and juniper trees peppered the higher terrain. There were occasional sagebrush parks or open, meadow-like areas but without the lush vegetation typically found in a meadow. The soil was sandy with rocks and boulders strewn about, like a giant's child had been playing with them, grown tired of the game and knocked them over.

Grasses filled the bottoms of the canyons, and the streams flowing through them were lined with cottonwoods, willow and box elder trees. The wind and water had cut arches in some of the canyons, and formed fantastic shapes out of others. Immense boulders balanced on slender spires, looking like they might topple over at any moment. In some of the canyons, Cadillac-sized rocks were thrown about like a Paleolithic junkyard. It was an impressive sight, like nothing I had ever seen.

At the Glade Park Store, Carl asked the elderly clerk for directions, we each got a soda and we filled up our gallon-sized water containers.

"It's dry going," Carl said. "We may not have any water until we reach the Colorado River, and even then, the water may be too silty to drink," he said. "So we had better carry in what we think we will need."

The boys would carry two gallons each while the girls carried a gallon. Along with that, everyone had their own personal drinking bottles filled with water. Altogether, we had nearly 14 gallons of water between us!

We loaded the jugs into the back of the truck and bumped along the dirt track for another 45 minutes before we parked.

"Well, this is it," Carl announced, spreading his hands wide as if introducing us to a dear friend. "We're going to try to find a trail down into that canyon over there."

He pointed toward the west and we could see a 700-foot-deep gorge yawning before us. There was no trail heading into the shaded depths as far as we could see. A hundred feet of loose dirt and rocks lined the upper sections of the canyon and topped a sheer, 100- to 200-foot-high, sandstone cliff followed by more loose dirt and rocks sloping down to the canyon floor. Everywhere we looked it was the same. The only challenge we could see was how in the world we would get down the cliff section and into the canyon.

"I know there is a place here somewhere," said Carl as we walked along the rim of the gorge, "where the stream has worn a path down the cliff face. We might have to do a bit of scrambling but we're not going to do any rappelling. Too many of you are greenhorns," he concluded with a grin.

Only Carl, Mack, Tate and Andy had ever rappelled before, and we had not brought along enough rope to span that great of a drop. Rappelling is a technique that rock climbers use to descend a sheer face. It involves running the rope through a special descending device, or else across your shoulder and through your legs if you didn't have climbing gear, and then walking backward down the face of the cliff. Since several of us were novice backpackers and had never climbed or rappelled before, Carl felt that it was best not to try this. So we kept looking for an easier descent, hiking along the edge of the gorge.

Finally, after about an hour in the sun, we found a way down. The time approached noon, so our daytime star was high in the sky and it was starting to feel really HOT. Sweat dripped down my arms at the elbows and little rivulets of it ran across my cheeks. Occasionally some would get into my eyes and sting. I hated that!

My borrowed backpack jabbed me in the ribs and burrowed into my hips, and it felt like it weighed a ton. It actually weighed about 60 pounds—a lot for a five-foot-four high-school girl weighing 130 pounds, on her first-time backpack trip—but I determined I would make it work. Most of the excess weight in my pack came from the water, which I had not thought about at home when I was packing my gear and determining how much weight I would carry. Plus, we were all carrying canned food, so our backpacking fare was not exactly lightweight.

The route down into the canyon proved steep but manageable. There weren't any sheer drop-offs, so even when our feet slid on the rocks and loose soil, we weren't at risk of falling to our deaths. We stumbled and slipped as we gradually made our way into the chasm before us, grabbing occasional juniper trunks to help us keep our balance. The pungent, bitter scent filled our nostrils as the bark broke open under our grasp. Sagebrush perfumed the air with its sticky, sweet scent and we spied a couple of deer resting in the shade of an overhang. They watched calmly as we trudged past.

It took us nearly an hour of hand-over-hand scrambling followed by dusty plodding to finally reach the bottom of the canyon. Here a small, crystalline stream meandered through waist-high grass and the canyon walls towered above us. The gorge was narrow where we had climbed down near the head of the ravine, probably 200 feet across, so just a strip of cobalt blue sky appeared overhead.

Chapter Twelve

Still no clouds on this hot, dry day. Sweat raced down my arms, creating little white streaks where it washed away the dirt and dust already accumulating on my skin.

My purple bandana, which I had tied around my head to keep the sweat out of my eyes, was soaked, as were the back of my T-shirt and the upper parts of my jeans. I soon realized that jeans, no matter how lightweight, did not make for the best attire while hiking in the desert. Both Tate and Cinday had worn shorts and their legs were already beet red and we still had a half day of hiking to go. So even though I was hot and sweaty, I was glad I hadn't worn shorts.

We kept going for another hour. Our route followed the stream and I relished the sweet coolness of the water each time we slogged through to cross to the other side. Fortunately, at the narrow end of the gorge, we had to cross over every time we came to a twist or meander in the canyon.

Around 1 in the afternoon, we stopped in the shade of a couple of towering box elder trees and ate a quick, dry lunch. We were glad we brought extra water with us, because even though there was a stream to follow, Carl said the presence of the deer and their droppings by the water's edge made it unsafe to drink unless we boiled it. It was too hot and we had way too far to travel to take the time to build a fire in the middle of the day, so we gladly drank the water in our canteens and refilled them from the gallon containers. Psychologically it was rewarding to feel the semi-cool liquid run down our throats and we loved feeling like we were lessening the weight on our backs!

As the afternoon trek continued, the canyon opened up to probably half a mile across, getting wider with every bend in the little creek we followed. To cut down on the number of miles we hiked we tried to stay as close to the middle of the canyon as possible, but sometimes we had to work around thick vegetation or piles of rock that had tumbled down from the canyon walls centuries before.

We were all getting very tired. The heat had drained our energy. We had covered about six miles already and Carl said we still had several miles to go before we would reach our camping spot. Collectively I could feel our spirits sinking. The walk had become a trudge. Somehow, some way, we kept putting one foot in front of the other. No one talked. No one laughed or looked around in amazement at the beauty around us.

By late afternoon, the sun had dropped behind the higher mesas, leaving large swaths of the canyon's bottom in shadow. It was a tremendous relief to slog through the grass and water in the cooling darkness, away from the sun's glare. Our pace picked up and I looked around at my companions. Everyone was sunburned. In his bluster to get going, Carl, a seat-of-the-pants sort of leader who sometimes got carried away in his enthusiasm, had forgotten to remind us to put on sunscreen, so noses were fiery red and arms, where exposed, glowed a bright crimson. Mack's neck was blistered (the Lewises were short, red-headed Irishmen so they burned easily), and poor Tate and Cinday's legs looked like boiled lobsters. I was extremely grateful not only for my long pants but also for the olive complexion my mom had given me. Thank goodness for genetics.

Looking up at the sky, we spotted a huge bird soaring overhead. It circled above the canyon, rising higher and higher.

"Look!" Andy exclaimed, pointing upward. "It's a vulture waiting for us to die so it can eat us." Leave it to him to come up with a morose comment that reflected how we all felt.

"You're not going to die," Mack said. "You just feel like it. Your mind and body can handle much more than you think they can. Everyone's can."

"So, if is it a vulture," I cut in, suddenly feeling better than I thought possible, "it will be disappointed."

"No meal for you!" Cinday called up to the bird, shaking her fist.

Stopping to look closer and longer, we realized it was not a vulture but an eagle.

"It's probably a golden eagle," said Carl. "Although it could be a juvenile bald eagle. They nest in this region, especially close to the river. When the birds are young, they don't have the white feathers on their heads so sometimes it's difficult to distinguish them from the golden eagles."

We watched in wonder as the bird lazily rode the rising air currents, not once flapping its wings. We had seen plenty of other birds along the trail that day including sparrows, magpies, desert scrub jays and ravens, but the sight of this majestic bird impressed us the most.

As we stood there transfixed, the trilling calls of the canyon wren echoed off the cliff walls, bouncing back and forth in their melodic, descending *treeeee, treeee, treeee, treeeeeee*. We could also hear the wind echoing off the rock walls around us. It created a haunting, soul-stirring sound that made me feel like the ancient ones who had first lived in this area still wandered around. A shiver ran up my spine.

Coming back to the present moment, we started walking again. Some of us were literally dragging ourselves along. Everyone was hungry now and we were tired beyond belief. I felt the same fatigue and I was ravenous, but something had changed in me as we stood watching the eagle fly.

I had a new rush of energy and enthusiasm. My legs didn't feel quite as exhausted as they had just a few minutes before. I could walk a little faster. I didn't know if it was the cooling air, now that the sun moved behind the cliffs, or the fresh smell transported on the breeze, but something signaled to the primitive part of my brain that the big river was not far away. I didn't know why but I suddenly felt better.

"You're just getting your second wind," Mack told me when I mentioned it to him. "It's something that your body does when you're under a lot of physical stress. You create chemicals, called endorphins, that help you feel better and keep going. Marathon runners experience it all the time."

"Maybe," I said while thinking to myself it was something more, something unique and special, like an ancient memory calling to my soul, telling me I once belonged here, I once lived a life like this in complete harmony, connection and contact with nature. I scuffed my foot in the sand and something black and shiny caught my eye. Bending down, I shifted through the loose soil and found an arrowhead about the size of the first joint of my thumb. It was perfectly shaped with small notches below the widest part. I shoved it into my pocket and hurried to catch up to the others as they had already started walking on without me.

"Just a couple more bends in the canyon," Carl called out cheerily, trying to raise our spirits and interrupting my thoughts.

Our little stream had grown throughout the day, after starting out as a narrow little trickle. It was not a raging river, but it was definitely too wide to jump across, and in places it looked to be waist-deep. We now had to search back and forth to find a safe place to cross.

"Watch out for quicksand," Tate called out.

"Right!" I shouted back. "I thought that was only in the movies!" I yelled jokingly.

"Oh, no, it is real enough," he said. "It doesn't suck you down like in the movies, but you could lose your boots and be stuck for a while."

"Great," I mumbled, thinking about how miserable it would be to hike with no shoes for the next two days. "What does it look like?" I called out more loudly. "How would I know where it is?"

"That's the problem. It's hard to tell the difference between the quicksand and the rest of the sand," Tate called back.

"Lovely."

"It has to be the right combination of water and sand," he continued. "In the case of quicksand, the water doesn't move to the surface, but remains mixed in with the sand. So the sand on top appears solid, even dry, and it can support leaves and other small debris. It won't, however, support your weight."

"Oh, great!" I said sarcastically. "We won't know it's there until we're stuck! I can't wait."

Tate was kind of a nerdy guy. He was into science and math in addition to the outdoors and skiing, and he loved sharing with his friends the myriad facts he had stored in his brain. Earlier in the day he had told us about the cryptobiotic soils in the upland area or mesas around the canyons.

"Biological soil crusts, as opposed to chemical crusts like those created by salt, are formed by living organisms and their by-products, or excrement, if you will, creating a surface crust of soil particles bound together by organic materials," he said enthusiastically as we walked along, his face breaking into a huge grin.

"Above-ground crust thickness can reach up to four inches in depth, although the crust is usually shallower than that. These crusts are predominantly composed of various algae, mosses and lichens," he continued, building up momentum. We all listened intently at that point, not out of real interest in the subject, but we couldn't help but get caught up in his passion.

"The mature crusts of the Great Basin and Colorado Plateau, which is where we are right now," he said, "are usually darker than the surrounding soil. Crusts generally cover all soil spaces not occupied by plants such as grasses, flowers, shrubs or trees."

We had all kept walking, thinking about the information Tate had just shared. He had gotten quiet while we trekked along, probably thinking about what to teach us next.

During our lunch break he continued his lecture. "Soil crusts are important members of desert ecosystems and contribute to the well-being of other plants by stabilizing sand and dirt, promoting moisture retention and fixing atmospheric nitrogen. Because of their thin, fibrous nature, cryptobiotic soils are extremely fragile systems. A single footprint or tire track is sufficient to disrupt the soil crust and damage the organisms. While some species within the soil crust system may regrow within a few years of a disturbance, the damage to the slower-growing species may require more than a century before the delicate soil returns to its former productivity," Tate concluded proudly. I almost expected him to take a bow.

Tate's sensitivity to the environment meant we were always trying to follow animal tracks, human trails or natural stone walkways rather than heading directly cross-country. This also meant that we did a lot of extra walking!

Fortunately, no one encountered any quicksand that day and we finally spotted the Colorado River at about 6:30 in the evening. Although the temperature was still hot, probably 80 degrees, there was a fresh, cool breeze coming off the river.

We finally dragged ourselves into a wide, shady site overlooking the water and set our packs down beneath half a dozen ancient cottonwood trees. We could tell they were 50 years old or older because their trunks were at least three or four feet in diameter and each one stood nearly 75 feet tall! The freshness from the water plus the slight breeze and shade under the trees felt delicious after a full day in the blazing sun.

I changed out of my jeans and into a pair of shorts. It was great to get out of the heavy, sweat-soaked clothing.

We quickly pitched our tarps. No one but Carl had a backpacking tent, so the rest of us created lean-tos and shelters out of big, blue waterproof tarps. We strung them up between the trees, tying off the ends as tightly as we could in case a wind came up that evening. None of us really knew any special knots but Carl had warned us of sudden winds in these canyons, so we tried to make them as secure as we could.

Looking them over, we decided we had done our best and started putting together our cooking fire.

I headed off to gather wood and find a private spot to relieve myself. Squatting under the trees, I noticed a bloody spot on my shorts near my right hip.

"What the heck?" I asked myself as I stood up. Looking down, I saw a big, raw spot right on my hip bone.

Seems the decrepit old backpack didn't fit me all that well, so with the extra weight from the water and canned food I was carrying, the waist belt and bottom of the frame had dug a hole in my upper leg.

Oh, great! I felt bummed out, frightened and intimidated. *Two more days of hiking with this is going to hurt.*

I headed back to camp with an armload of wood for our fire.

We ate under an amazing sky, inky black, darker than anything I had ever seen, with tens of thousands of sparkly points of light. They looked like so many hole pricks in a black blanket with a lamp shining behind it. With the atmosphere so clear, it really did feel like we could reach out and bring the stars down to us. We munched our beans and tortillas and talked about life, our upcoming graduation and our plans for the future. We watched the headlight from a train move eerily along the canyon wall well before we heard and then saw the locomotive. In the quiet of our isolated camp, the whoosh, clack and whine of the train was irritatingly loud. I covered my ears as it passed.

Soon everyone grew drowsy and slipped off to their sleeping bags. The night passed uneventfully, especially compared to my sophomore year's first-ever camping trip up near Guanella Pass beneath Mt. Bierstadt when Keri and I tried to share a sleeping bag and ended up splitting it apart! Fortunately, the high desert cooled off significantly at night so it wasn't too hot for sleeping, yet the air temperature never fell below 50 degrees so it wasn't too cold, either. I delighted in not freezing while I slept.

Oh, gag me, I thought. *She's just trying to get on his good side. She would love him to be her boyfriend rather than Keri's.*

Keri, of course, was my former best friend and even though we no longer hung out together, I still felt loyal to her. Keri and Tate had started going out this year after she and Mike had broken up. Plus, I was jealous of Cinday's good looks and the easygoing way she had with boys. I wished I had that much confidence.

The remainder of the day's short hike was uneventful. Soon after we set up camp near the entrance to another canyon, clouds started to form, billowing and swirling into dark, threatening masses. A sharp wind began to blow, shaking dead branches out of the cottonwoods. Unfortunately, we had set our tarp-tents in the shade directly under the trees, using the trunks and low-hanging branches to tie off the ends. We were lucky that none of the falling branches landed on one of our shelters or hurt anyone because, for much of the afternoon, they pelted down like hail.

We couldn't have a fire that night thanks to the wind; however, it was cooler so sleeping was comfortable and no insects bugged us. Without a fire or any camping stoves we ate a cold dinner: cheese, tortillas, tuna and sardines. Not the best meal on the planet, but it sufficiently fueled our bodies for the next day. Nobody sat around talking that evening. The wind and lack of campfire drove everyone into their shelters right after dinner.

I remember sleeping soundly for the first part of the night and then waking sometime around 2 a.m. I couldn't quite place what had disturbed my sleep. Was it a bad dream? I recalled ancient Puebloans in my dream. There had been some sort of a ritual taking place, with dancing, drumming and a big bonfire. Nothing scary. Nothing that would wake me up from a deep sleep.

Hmm, what was it?

I listened carefully. The wind had died down to just a gentle breeze so it wasn't necessarily a falling branch that had brought me to wakefulness. I listened more intently, straining to hear beyond my own breathing, which now seemed extraordinarily loud in my ears.

There. That slight sound. Almost like a whisper. Can you hear it?

I wanted to ask someone, but I was alone in my shelter. There was no tent mate to awaken and ask if she heard what I heard; no thin nylon shell to protect me from whatever was out there. Just a plastic sheet with grommets in the corners and nylon ropes snugging it to nearby branches and tree trunks. There was even a four-inch gap between the bottom of my tarp and the ground. Anything could crawl inside!

Suddenly I stiffened. I heard breathing outside my shelter!

It must be my imagination getting the best of me, I told myself.

I wished there was another warm body sharing my space with me. My skin broke out in goose bumps. I wondered to myself: *Do coyotes eat people?* We had heard a pack howling and yipping to each other earlier in the evening. Their noisy symphony had made my scalp crawl then; now I was practically jumping out of my skin.

"No, I don't think so unless they are rabid," I reassured myself, speaking softly out loud, in hopes I would frighten away whatever lurked in the dark.

I wondered if I had brought food into the shelter with me. No, everything was in my pack, leaning against the tree five feet away and secure under a big, black yard bag in case it rained. Plus, everything I had in the way of food was in cans or tightly wrapped in its original packaging.

"Are there bears in the area?" I mused. I didn't recall reading anything about bears but who knows, they could be anywhere.

I kept listening and could still hear the breathing, soft and even. It wasn't Carl. His snore was loud enough to wake any spirits that might haunt these canyons. But at the moment, all was quiet from his little pup tent. The nearest shelter to mine was probably 15 feet away so I didn't think the breathing was coming from there, either.

All of a sudden, I heard snuffling, like a dog was sniffing around my pack.

Oh, my God! This is it! I thought to myself. How loud would I need to shout to rouse one of my companions, and how quickly would they react? Could they get here and scare the beast off before it ate me?

I was paralyzed with fear, certain now that it was an animal prowling around outside my shelter. It definitely sounded larger than a packrat, which at 10 inches in length are about the size of a chinchilla, even though they weigh about a pound and a half. A coyote or a bear were the only two critters I thought it could possibly be as I prepared myself to be eaten.

Finally, after what felt like hours of straining to hear more sounds in the night, I determined that whatever had been stalking me had decided to move on without making me its midnight snack. My muscles ached from the strain of holding them tense for so long, and my ears rang from the effort of trying to listen so intently.

I tried to relax and realized I was drenched in sweat. I felt chilled and hot at the same time. Adrenaline coursed through my body and my mind was still racing so I tossed and turned, trying to find a comfortable space and fall asleep. Finally, after I don't know how long, I was able to doze off. All too soon, it was time to get up. Before I knew it, the sun brightened the sky and made the inside of my tarp glow bluish.

I heard people stirring. Carl banged the pot as he made coffee. I struggled out of my sleeping bag and stumbled toward the kitchen area, disheveled and sleepy-eyed. I rubbed my eyes and ran my hand through my hair, which stuck out wildly.

"Wow, Lucy! You look like you had a rough night," Andy commented as I approached the fire. Now that the wind had quieted down, it was safe to build a fire and everyone was looking forward to a hot breakfast before our big push back out of the canyons.

"Yeah, I did." The conversation continued as we sat around eating tortillas with scrambled eggs and coffee. "Did you guys hear anything unusual last night?" I asked the group.

"Wike mhaat?" Tate asked around a gigantic mouthful of food, barely understandable.

That boy can pack it away and still remain thin as a rail, I thought to myself, feeling slightly jealous.

"Did you hear any sounds? You know, like breathing, walking and snuffling," I replied.

"The only sounds I heard were Andy farting," Tate joked, elbowing his tent mate in the ribs.

"No, I'm serious. I woke up in the night and heard something smelling around my tarp and my backpack. I was sure it was a coyote or a bear or some other predator determined to eat me, so I couldn't get back to sleep. I finally started drifting off just before you guys got up to make coffee."

"Well, it looks like it didn't find you appealing," Cinday said, trying to be funny and make light of the situation.

"Hey, come look at these tracks," Mack called out. He had gotten up as I talked and walked over to where my pack was stashed against the tree.

We all filed over to see where he was pointing. There, in the soft, sandy soil between my tarp and the one Tate and Andy shared were two, palm-sized prints. It was a big pad with four round toe marks. There were no toenails showing off the toes, which meant only one thing.

"A mountain lion?" I managed to choke out. "Oh, my God! How on earth did I ever manage not to get attacked?"

I was nearing hysterics now that the evidence was clear that something had indeed been skulking around our camp in the middle of the night. "Oh my God oh my God," I kept repeating out loud, wrapping my arms around my chest.

"What's up, kids?" Carl called out. Mack motioned for him to come over and have a look.

"Well, well," he said, a grin splitting his full, mountain-man beard. "It looks like we had a visitor last night."

"Yeah, some visitor," I grumbled. "How come I'm not dead?"

"Probably for a couple of reasons, Lucy," Carl explained. "Cats are solitary, shy animals, seldom seen by humans. While they do occasionally attack people—usually children or lone adults—statistics show that, on average, there are less than 10 attacks and only one human fatality each year in all of the U.S. and Canada," he smiled reassuringly at me and I tried to smile back.

"Our feline friend last night was probably curious and not hungry. Maybe it was just passing through to a new territory, as lions need about 30 square miles to roam. I don't know, your guess is as good as mine. I'm just glad you stayed inside your tarp and didn't panic," he concluded, laying an arm across my shoulder.

"Me, too," I replied weakly.

Chapter Thirteen

We finished our breakfast, packed our gear and headed out on the trail early. Carl figured we had about 15 miles to hike and he wanted to get as much of it done as early as possible. We still had a five-hour drive back to Denver after the hike.

The canyon's mouth looked a lot like the one we trekked down the first day; it was wide and open with tall grasses and cottonwoods running through the center, following a dry creek bed. Unlike the first day, there was no water at all in the sandy channel leading to the Colorado River.

As the sun rose, we were glad we were carrying extra water. It was going to be a scorcher! I guessed it was already 80 degrees by 9 a.m. The first mile or two of our journey was basically flat but as the canyon began to narrow, the trail started becoming steeper. Thick stands of juniper and piñon greeted us as we started climbing.

After an hour of uphill walking, following a well-marked dirt path, we came to the end of the canyon. It was a box canyon, ending abruptly at a large, natural amphitheater with a hundred-foot cliff above it. In several places runoff stained the rock surface. A small trickle of water dripped down the center of the cliff; it probably formed a spectacular, and dangerous, waterfall during the sudden downpours common to this desert region.

Other sections of the rock were covered with a dark, shiny coating known in the southwest as desert varnish. Ancient tribes used to carve petroglyphs through the varnish, exposing the lighter rock underneath and preserving their drawings forever.

The end of the canyon reminded me of some of the gorges in Mesa Verde where the Anasazi built their cliff houses. We quickly looked around the base of the cliff but found no sign of previous human habitation. I was disappointed. It would have been fun to discover an ancient stone building out in the middle of nowhere.

Our concern now centered on how to get out of the canyon. No obvious trails existed on either side and the cliff was impossible to scale even with ropes and climbing gear, let alone with bulky, heavy backpacks. And no one wanted to walk back down the canyon to search the next gully upriver and see if there was a way out.

Carl told us to wait on a small rise in the center of the canyon while he, Mack, Tate and Andy took off their packs and headed toward the south side of the gorge to see if they could find a trail. The rest of us opened our granola bars and had a snack and a long drink of water. It tasted like heaven. I hadn't realized how parched my throat was.

Black cumulonimbus clouds were forming to the northwest and it looked like we were in for an intense rainstorm, the kind that often resulted in flash floods here in the desert. As we observed the dark, swirling mass of clouds, we saw a flash of lightning in the distance and heard the crack of thunder. The wind picked up and started blowing the trees around. For a brief moment, the coolness felt wonderful after the extreme heat of the morning.

The boys came back soon, shouting that they had found a trail and we needed to get moving because of the fast-approaching storm. Carl wanted us out of the canyon before the rain hit. Apparently, these dry riverbeds were notorious routes for the walls of water that came with a flash flood.

Everyone shrugged on their packs and started off at a brisk pace, heading toward the south wall of the canyon. It didn't look to me like there was any trail but as we got right up to the face of the cliff, I could see a section of rocks making what appeared to be a staircase. *OK, this is a staircase fit for a giant, not for me,* I thought. Thank God we had eaten most of the food I was carrying and had drunk probably half the water; otherwise I might not have made it.

The first couple of "steps" rose at least two feet high, so I had to put one leg up and kind of pull myself the rest of the way using my knees and hands.

Man. If it is all like this, it will take us hours to reach the top.

The good news was there were only half-a-dozen steps that high, then the trail became more manageable with the rocks varying in height from eight to 15 inches. Soon I had a rhythm going. Step, push, breathe, step. Step, push, breathe, step.

Time passed quickly as the rhythm put me into a meditative state and my fear of the approaching storm drove my legs onward and upward. Wind whipped sand and grit into my face. Lightning jetted across the dark sky with the thunder crashes sounding closer and closer to the flash each time. The tempest was nearly upon us.

After nearly an hour of the endless stair climber, we had reached the upper plateau surrounding the canyon.

Looking back, we said our mental goodbyes to the tough, uphill climb and the beautiful little box canyon out of which we had just ascended. Facing forward, we saw the storm was there, right on top of us! Lightning crashed nearby and the deafening roar of thunder reverberated almost simultaneously. Great drops of water splashed down, bursting like miniature water balloons.

"Come on!" Carl shouted, and we began running as best we could with bulky packs on our backs. He pointed straight ahead and we saw a small overhang where the wind had carved horizontally through the sandstone. We hustled into the tight spot just as the clouds above us let loose with a torrent of water.

It wasn't raining. It was pouring like someone had taken enormous buckets of water and dumped them straight down on the earth, like God's fire hose had been turned on to cool off the desert land. It didn't matter what it reminded me of—I had never in my life seen water coming down in sheets like it did that day!

"Thank goodness we are no longer in that box canyon!" Andy shouted above the roar of the water, pointing in the direction from which we had just come. Everyone looked where he pointed. We couldn't believe our eyes. Not only was there suddenly a major river pouring down the cliff face, creating the spectacular waterfall we all had envisioned while hiking; our little staircase trail had also become a stream overflowing with water.

"Yeah," I yelled back, not wanting to think what it would have been like if we had delayed half an hour longer and had been caught partway up that tricky slope with water rushing down around our feet and legs. I could see someone getting washed over the edge of that narrow trail and plummeting down to the canyon bottom—not a pretty vision. I shuddered and breathed a sigh of relief, feeling snug in our little cave.

The good thing about desert storms is that however intense, they are short-lived. After about 40 minutes, the rain slacked off to a drizzle and Carl said we needed to keep going.

We took off again, this time heading cross-country toward the southwest and hopefully our truck. It would have been nice to travel in a straight line across the desert and arrive as the crow flies to where our truck was parked, or even to find a dirt four-wheeling road that would make a beeline to where we wanted to go. Unfortunately, desert travel is not like that. There are small ravines, cliffs, hillocks and arches everywhere, and so the meandering path we took probably stretched to twice as long as it would have been in any other part of the country.

Grumbling under my breath about not being able to travel in a straight line, I looked up from watching my feet. The storm had raged on in the distance but right before me, twin rainbows graced the sky above a 30-foot-high natural arch—the most glorious sight I had ever seen. With the dark background of the storm, it seemed like the sky was on fire. *Man, I wish I had brought my camera.* There wouldn't have been time to take photographs, though, because Carl was a man on a mission. He wanted to have us back home by midnight because we all had school Tuesday morning, even though we wouldn't be doing much during our last week before graduation.

Finally, with sweat creating large circles of salt on my back and under my arms, we arrived, exhausted and sore, at the big, beautiful Ford.

"Whew! We made it!" I groaned as we unloaded our gear into the bed. Before climbing in after it, I stopped and took a last look at the desert. The air was perfumed with the scent of ozone and pine sap, and the land looked washed clean. Everything was crisp, outlined by the late-afternoon sun streaking through the remaining clouds. In three short days, I had grown to love this beautiful countryside, and I felt a hint of sorrow as I pulled myself into the back of the truck.

Tate volunteered to ride up front with Carl and help keep him awake during the long drive home. He promised not to put him to sleep with any more boring scientific explanations. The rest of us wanted nothing more than to lie down and fall asleep. Laying out our sleeping bags and huddling together, that is exactly what we did. One minute we were in the desert and I heard the truck's engine roar to life and the next, we were pulling into my driveway at home and Carl was telling my folks what a great trip we had while the boys handed me my pack. I left the pack in the garage, laid my precious arrowhead on the green washcloth with my other adventure treasures and crawled into bed, dreaming of flash floods, mountain lions and ancient tribes.

Chapter Fourteen

The two weeks following my first backpacking adventure were a whirlwind, between graduating from high school and getting ready for the 25-day wilderness backpacking course compliments of Carl Lewis and the Outdoor Mountain School. My parents weren't sure what to make of my desire to be outdoors and live without the comforts of home for nearly a month but they supported my decision to go.

Graduation day was beautiful and sunny, without a hint of the previous weekend's freak May snowstorm on the eastern side of the state. There were 700 of us graduating, so the ceremony took a couple of hours. Although I was sad for it to end, high school had not been my whole life as it had been for some of the kids I knew. I had friends whom I would miss but the highlights of my high school experience had come the last two years as I started getting involved in outdoor activities with my explorer post, and I was looking forward, with anxiety mingled in with anticipation, to my next adventure in the San Juan Mountains of southwestern Colorado. If I had stopped to think about the future beyond my summer backpacking trip, I would have felt nervous and worried about the end of a 12-year adventure as a student but I was going on to college that fall, so I assumed things would not change too much.

After the experience of having my hip torn open by the ill-fitting backpack I had borrowed for our canyon trip, I was delighted to receive a real, mountaineer's sack for graduation. My boyfriend, Mack, had taken a special Lowe Expedition pack on our trip and I coveted it. It was one giant bag with an internal frame, padded shoulder straps and a waist belt so it was a challenge in terms of organizing gear but it fit like a second skin. Anyway, my new pack was exactly the same as his, only it was a cosmetic second—somewhere there was a stitch out of place or the color didn't match exactly. I don't know. I never could find the problem and to me it was perfect! It was a beautiful royal blue that matched my new down sleeping bag and there were strips of nylon webbing underneath, which I would eventually use for tying my sleeping pad and sleeping bag to the outside.

Mom had helped me sew a down vest from a kit and we had gone to the Army-Navy surplus store to purchase wool pants, shirts and socks. She even converted an old pair of Navy sailor's pants, the kind with the double row of white buttons on either side, into a very cool pair of knickers. Checking the equipment list, we bought a pair of gaiters, which were sort of waterproof over-socks that kept snow, ice and stones out of your hiking boots.

"Boots! Oh, my God, I don't have any boots!" I cried to Mom while we were out shopping.

"Don't worry, dear," she replied. "Your grandparents are getting you a pair for graduation. All we have to do is go to the sporting goods store and find a pair that fit you."

"Oh, whew! OK. Thanks," I said.

So we headed over to the big sporting goods store. There, in the shoe department, I soon discovered that my foot was not designed for most hiking boots. My lovely feet are short and wide, size 5 women's, D width, with an extremely high arch—perfect for dancing, I was once told.

The overly helpful clerk suggested that I get a heavy-duty boot since I would be backpacking for 25 days and might encounter snow. Finally, I found a pair that fit decently, and walked around in the store. They felt as stiff as if I had two little coffins attached to my feet. Nothing bent or had any give to it.

We paid for the boots and as we were leaving, the young man said, "Be sure to give yourself plenty of time to break those boots in. They are pretty stiff and could cause you some significant pain if they aren't broken in properly."

"What do you mean by plenty of time?" my mother inquired.

"You should wear them for a couple of weeks at least," he responded.

"Oh, great," I grumbled. "I am leaving in six days. There's no way I'll get these boots broken in by then."

"You'll be fine," Mom reassured me, despite having no real concept of what lay before me. "I am certain the first few days of your trip will be easy, so they can count toward the breaking in of your boots."

"Sure. Sure they will," I muttered sullenly, acting very spoiled even though I was getting some amazing, expensive hiking boots. "And I'll be just fine," I added under my breath, starting to feel my nerves now that the bustle of graduation had wound down.

A week later, after having worn my new boots everywhere I went, I stuffed my backpack full with the required supplies—underwear, socks, bras, T-shirts, long johns, wool shirts, wool pants, gaiters, sleeping bag, foam sleeping pad, baseball cap, wool cap, gloves, down vest, rain jacket and pants. I also had two liter-size water bottles, a pair of sneakers and my brand-new Swiss Army knife with a can opener. It all fit very nicely into my cool new pack. I had no idea how I would fit food, tent, camp stove and the other group camping gear we were told to be prepared to carry, but I did grab my green washcloth and tucked the three artifacts from my most important previous outdoor adventures inside. As I set out on this new adventure, I figured they would serve to remind me of the outdoorswoman I was hopefully becoming, as well as what I had learned so far in the backcountry: listen to your inner guidance, don't give up, be prepared and remember where you came from.

On Friday morning, Mom drove me to the bus station where I caught a Greyhound bus for the nine-hour journey to Grand Junction, the small city right outside the national monument where we had hiked only two weeks before. She was tearful and probably worried about what her only child was getting into as she said goodbye and wished me good luck. Clearly she had no personal experience with the outdoors upon which to draw and she likely had a very vivid imagination as to what might happen. I had not shared with her anything about the mountain lion skulking around my tent just a couple weeks earlier. I know she had researched Outdoor Mountain School thoroughly before signing the papers allowing me to join the expedition. I guess that had appeased her because there she stood with wet eyes, waving wildly at me as the bus pulled out of the station.

"Bye, Mom," I said, adding "I love you" under my breath and wondering as well what I was getting myself into.

My Ultimate Challenge

Chapter Fifteen

Staring out the window, watching the rain fall as our bus wound through the canyons leading up to the high country, I couldn't believe I was headed back to the western slope. The acceptance letter we had all received stated that we had to meet the group Saturday morning at 8 a.m. sharp at the Greyhound bus terminal in Grand Junction, Colorado. This time, since I was traveling during the day, I enjoyed the magnificent scenery.

Halfway there, we reached the summit of Vail Pass, where spring was in full bloom. The aspen trees showed off their brilliant new lemon-green leaves bright against the deep greens of the ponderosa pines. Patches of white snow showed through the trees, and fluffy light gray clouds hung low in the valleys while overhead, dark clouds poured rain onto the highway. *At least it isn't snowing,* I thought to myself.

I sat next to Ellen, who had just finished her first year in our scout post. Although we had been part of the same post for the past year, we really weren't close friends as she was a couple years younger and I had hung out mostly with Mack and the boys, so we sat in awkward silence, contemplating what the next month would be like. We could hear Andy and Tate laughing and joking a few rows behind us.

Maybe they were nervous, too. Their laughter sounded a bit too loud and forced. Cinday was already in Grand Junction, having gone over a few days early to visit her grandmother.

As our bus descended from the pass, the ski lifts and gondola of Vail Mountain came into view, and I decided to break the ice with Ellen.

"Have you ever skied Vail?" I asked her.

"No, we usually ski Winter Crest," she replied. "What about you?"

"No, me neither. I really haven't skied that much except for when our class went to Loveland in seventh and eighth grades and the few times our post went to Steamboat or Geneva Basin," I answered.

Then I took a deep breath. "I'm a bit nervous about this whole Outdoor Mountain School thing," I admitted.

"Yeah, me, too," Ellen said. "Our canyon adventure last month was my first time backpacking."

"Mine, too," I said. "It was also only the second time I had ever been camping in a tent before."

"Oh. Wow. My family camps every summer," Ellen smiled at the memory. "But we normally just drive to a camping site and set up from our truck. I've never had to carry all my gear with me except when we hiked the canyons. That was tough."

"Yeah, I know. I wonder if I have the right gear, the right amount or if I brought too much stuff," I said.

"You girls worry too much," Andy shouted from behind. Obviously the boys had been listening in on our conversation.

"No, I worry just the right amount," I said, grinning back at him over the seats and feeling a bit better.

Ellen and I returned to our silent contemplation as the bus zipped past the town of Vail, whose houses and shops were crammed together in the deep, narrow gorge nestling beneath steep, snowy peaks on either side of the highway. The bus then continued down the valley as it widened out where the highway began to parallel the Eagle River. I watched scattered ranches flash past my steamy bus window as I remembered our rafting trip a year ago. The clouds started to lift and the rain began to let off.

Our route next took us through spectacular Glenwood Canyon, where 1,300-foot, red-hued walls towered above the road. To the left of the interstate the Colorado River roiled and foamed across gigantic boulders strewn through the chasm like submerged dinosaurs. As the gorge widened out again, we drove through the town of Glenwood Springs, whose hot-springs–fed pool is famous, at least to those of us in Colorado. Finally, my butt having gone numb from an entire day spent sitting on the bus, we rolled into Grand Junction, the largest city on Colorado's western slope.

Outdoor Mountain School had arranged for students coming in from Denver to stay at the local Travel Lodge Motel. Tate, Andy, Ellen and I were sharing a room so we collected our backpacks from the undercarriage of the bus, slung them over our shoulders and walked around the corner to check in. We tossed our gear into our tired little room on the second floor and headed over to the Hungry Jack restaurant for a quick bite before calling it a night. We had been given a dinner voucher, and had a hamburger with fries and a Coke as our last solid, hot meal for a month.

Back in our room, Tate and Andy gallantly let Ellen and me enjoy the dubious comfort of the extra-firm twin beds; they turned out to be hard as a rock to sleep on, with flat, bricklike, wedge pillows. The boys tested out their sleeping bags and foam mattresses on the floor, and in the end, it was a toss-up as to who slept better.

We woke up early the next morning. It was still cloudy but at least the rain had stopped. It had rained into the night; we could tell by the dripping leaks in the ceiling of our hotel room. I grabbed a Danish and gulped down hot tea while Tate and Andy both drank coffee, and we walked back to the bus station.

At least 40 people milled about waiting for the group bus to show up. I saw people there ranging from teenagers to folks in their 40s, and most people seemed to be in their 20s and early 30s.

"Wow! I had no idea there would be so many people taking this course," I exclaimed.

"Me neither," breathed Ellen, both of us feeling tense and edgy again.

After the bus pulled in, we loaded our gear into the belly of the vehicle and climbed aboard. We found seats near the rear and plopped ourselves down, ready for another long drive. Once everyone was on board, a tall, slender 25-year-old woman with blonde braids boarded and grabbed the microphone from the driver.

"Welcome to the Colorado Outdoor Mountain School," she said, smiling at us as she spoke. "You are about to embark on a journey of transformation and adventure. My name is Nicole and I will be one of the assistant instructors for this course. We have a five-hour drive to the course start, so make yourself comfortable and feel free to ask me any questions. While we drive, I'll also be passing around some paperwork for you to complete."

"Well, here we go," I said under my breath to Ellen as the bus pulled out of the station.

"Yup, it's crunch time," she replied.

"I don't think too many people die on these courses," I thought out loud. "Otherwise, the company would not still be taking folks into the wilderness."

At that moment, Nicole took to the microphone again and started telling us the history of the company.

"Outdoor Mountain School, or OMS as we call it, was founded in the early 1960s to provide young men and women with the experiences and skills necessary to survive in the Colorado wilderness," she started, looking at everyone to make sure we were paying attention. "The organization was a joint effort between businessmen and progressive educators dedicated to helping people learn through challenging experiences so they could grow individually in terms of self-esteem as well as discover some of their innate leadership abilities. Students also develop a sense of responsibility toward others. We have become one of the premier outdoor education organizations in the world," she concluded with a big smile.

"Did you hear what she said?" Ellen asked me. "The part about challenging experiences? What do you think she means by that? What challenges do you think we're going to face?"

"I don't know," I answered, feeling more nervous by the minute. "I suppose it could mean anything from being physically demanding to the idea of working and living with a group of strangers. We might be rappelling off mountains but I really have no idea. I guess we're about to find out."

Watching out my window, I saw we were driving through a beautiful, open landscape. In the distance loomed amazing, snow-clad peaks, which seemed to tower above the encompassing, high grasslands. The emerald green of the pastureland contrasted with the sparkling high peaks and the occasional dark green cottonwood tree along the Uncompahgre River.

Ellen and I tried to sleep, without much luck. I dreamed about my backpack being too heavy to carry and that I kept falling farther and farther behind the group until finally I was lost in the woods by myself. Every time I got to that point in the dream, I started awake. I'd look around, see I was still on the bus and then try to go back to sleep.

About the third time I woke with a jolt, I realized the bus was climbing. It was traveling slowly now on a narrow, two-lane highway, taking the sharp S-curves at a snail's pace.

"Where are we?" I wondered out loud.

Tate, who overheard me, replied, "We just left Ouray and are heading over Red Mountain Pass on the Million Dollar Highway. The pass is over 11,000 feet in elevation and the grade is steep. That's why we are going so slowly."

Being the brainiac of the group and enjoying a captive audience, he continued, "Did you know that Ouray was founded in 1876 by prospectors? By 1880, silver and gold had been discovered in the mountains around town, and Ouray had grown to 3,000 residents. With that, along with the spectacular location and natural hot springs, the town was a draw for families with children, which was pretty uncommon in mining communities."

"I had no idea," I said, realizing I had never even thought about this part of our beautiful state before.

Tate concluded with a grin, ignoring the sarcasm of my comment, "The town was named after the most famous chief of the Ute Native American tribe who made his home in the Uncompahgre Valley near present-day Montrose."

He added, "You two were asleep when we passed through Montrose."

"Oh, darn," I said and then added, "I really was only just trying to rest. I didn't sleep that well last night at the Travel Lodge."

"Yeah, I know. We didn't either," Andy chimed in.

Slowly the bus made its way to the top of the pass, the road characterized by steep cliffs, narrow lanes and, I noticed with a shudder as I peered out the window, a definite lack of guardrails. Much of the way was cut directly into the sides of the mountains.

To avoid looking down at the abrupt drop-off, I turned my eyes upward toward the tops of the mountains and was surprised to see that even though we were well above tree line, even higher summits of red, orange and white hues surrounded us.

"Gosh, I wonder how high we are?"

Tate jumped right in with a factoid. "The pass is just over 11,000 feet high! And did you notice the remains of the Idarado Mine?" He was obviously getting excited and about to share some more inanely boring facts with us, so I distracted him with another question.

"Why is it called the Million Dollar Highway?" I asked the boys.

Andy responded, beating Tate to the punch for once, "No one knows for sure, although there are a couple of legends. One says that it cost a million dollars per mile to construct this road in the 1920s. Another says that the fill dirt around the highway contains a million dollars worth of gold ore. Another romantic notion says that the views are worth a million dollars. You choose whichever one you feel is most appropriate," he finished.

From the top of the pass, the road wound back down with more sheer drop-offs out the window. I stared straight ahead even though we were now on the cliff side of the mountain. Soon, the quaint Victorian houses of the historic mining town of Silverton came into view straight beneath us. I gasped. If we had stopped along the road, I could have thrown a rock and hit one of the homes a thousand feet below me, but it took the bus another 20 minutes to tortuously wind its way down the narrow road.

Tate tapped me on the shoulder and I looked up. "Did you know that Silverton is one of the highest towns in the United States?"

Ellen shook her head while I tried to stifle an impatient sigh. Tate was my friend, after all.

"Yeah, it is situated at a literally breathtaking altitude of 9,305 feet above sea level!"

"Wow!" Ellen said to be polite. Then she exclaimed, "Just look at how steep those nearby mountains are!"

"I know," Tate said enthusiastically, eyeing the snow-clad peaks. "That one," he pointed out the window, "is called Storm Peak. And that one over there is Grizzly Mountain. And Kendall Mountain is just back there," he waved his hand behind us.

"Whadcha do? Memorize the topo map?" I asked him incredulously.

Tate turned bright red, and Andy ribbed him good-naturedly, "Pegged you, she did!"

"Oh, Tate," I said, smiling at my friend. "You are such a mountain geek. Oh, wait! I forgot! You're just a geek!"

He swatted at my hair as I ducked out of the way.

Passing through town, we drove by the small station for the Durango–Silverton Narrow-Gauge Railroad and continued east along the two-lane road. I felt better after the playful banter with my buddies.

Plenty of evidence of the region's mining glory days still remained. Tunnels, ramshackle buildings and colorful tailings piles littered the slopes of the nearby hills. I wondered what it was like to live here back then, trying to imagine life here so high in the mountains without easy access, running water or electricity. I shuddered. Not for me! We drove past dilapidated, abandoned buildings. An old boarding house on the hillside above us looked ready to fall over with the next strong gust of wind.

The Animas Valley was wide here, with mountains soaring on all sides. Flocks of crows circled above the river, catching thermals as they spiraled upward. Piles of round river rock lined the far side of the road, which turned to dirt just past the ghost town of Howardsville. The bus slowed to a crawl to navigate the deep ruts and potholes, which jostled and tossed us about like laundry in a clothes dryer.

We hadn't gone far when the bus slowed to a stop and Nicole came back on the microphone.

"This is it, folks!" she said chirpily, spreading her arms wide to take in the whole surrounding area.

"Oh, joy," I mumbled to myself, looking out my window and seeing nothing but mountains and wilderness. "Here we go."

"Don't worry about your gear," Nicole smiled. "We will take care of it at the campsite. Make sure you have your tennis shoes on now because we will be doing a little warm-up run." Again she smiled, trying to dispel our fears. "See you outside," and she bounced off the bus.

"Great," said Ellen's dismal voice, echoing my thoughts exactly.

Chapter Sixteen

We all piled off the bus. Some people started stretching and warming up. I just stood there wondering if I would survive the next month. Then, suddenly, without warning, folks were running. I hadn't heard a starting gun or anyone shout "go," so I was caught by surprise.

"Well, here we go," I said to Ellen as we took off toward the middle of the pack.

Although the road looked flat from the bus, it had a slight uphill grade that I noticed immediately. Plus we were at nearly 10,000 feet in elevation, so I was winded within about 500 feet of starting.

Oh, man, I thought to myself, being unable to speak at this point, *this is going to suck.* I panted and clutched the stitch in my side as we ran.

I couldn't say a word to Ellen but I saw she was sucking wind almost as hard as I was. Some of the group sprinted ahead and soon disappeared out of sight around the next bend. Several, though, ran even slower than we did. I kept thinking of images of Army boot camp commercials. You know, the kind where new recruits got up every morning at the crack of dawn for a little five-mile jaunt before heading out for a day of hiking. The Army slogan "Be all you can be" kept running through my mind.

I really had no idea if I would survive this month or not. I had gained about 25 pounds over the course of my senior year, between poor food choices, emotional eating and the binge eating that came with smoking pot. Even though I ran daily, I had not lost the weight and as a result I felt sluggish.

We only ran about a mile down the dusty road, but it was enough. By the time our camp came into view at least a quarter of the group was walking and I was pooped. I still had a side stitch and gulped for air. As we rounded a curve in the road, we saw a few tents erected in a spacious meadow by the river. The bus was there, too, but there were not nearly enough tents set up to accommodate all 40 of us. You could see the unasked question on people's faces: "Where are we going to sleep?"

A group of men and women stood near the center of the clearing, and bubbly Nicole directed us over to them.

"Alright, folks!" a burly young man in his late 20s with black, shoulder-length hair shouted over the milling crowd. "Alright! Alright! Settle in. Just have a seat anywhere on the ground around us. My name is Bruce Hawkins and I am the course director. I would like to go over a few details before we break out into groups, or what we at Outdoor Mountain School like to call teams."

Ellen and I found a large rock and sat on it near the edge of the semi-circle of people. Ten men and women ranging in age from about 20 to 30 or a bit older entered the middle of our circle. Nicole was among them. She smiled brightly at everyone, having already bonded of sorts with us during the long bus journey.

"Welcome to your Outdoor Mountain School experience," Bruce said, his voice deep and rhythmic. "Nicole has already told you the history of the school, so I won't go into that." Some of us, myself included, breathed a sigh of relief.

"Your course has been created to be an experiential learning situation, meaning that to the best of our ability we will design events and circumstances to safely allow you to go beyond your edge, beyond your comfort zone, in order for you to learn and grow from your experiences. Without challenge and stretching, there is no growth. There will be times when you will be deeply tested, mentally, physically and emotionally." Ellen and I looked at each other and I mouthed the word "Yikes!" and saw my concerns echoed in her eyes.

"You will be physically exhausted. Your emotions will be strained and at times, your mind will be taxed to its limit. As a result of surviving these challenges, you will become a better person. You will acquire leadership skills, self-esteem and confidence." He paused and glanced around at everyone, and somehow I felt strangely calmed when he caught and held my eyes for the briefest of moments before moving on.

Then he continued, "You will leave with basic mountaineering and wilderness travel skills, but more importantly, you will leave with a better understanding of yourself. You will know your own strengths and weaknesses. You will develop decision-making and problem-solving skills. You will gain an appreciation of our wilderness areas. You will come to understand the need for cooperation with others and will have the opportunity to develop your own personal values and beliefs. Finally, you will become more responsive to the needs of others. Over the course of the next three weeks there will be periods of intense involvement and physical activity followed by periods of reflection." He paused for a breath as he judged our reactions to his words. He nodded his head, seeming to like what he saw.

Then he said, "I would like to introduce you to the staff before we tell you a bit more about the course. First, I would like to ask the instructors to step forward." Four of the staff moved out from the line.

"From left to right we have Maggie Rogers, Jim McBane, Marcia Brown and Pedro Luna. These folks will each be in charge of one group or team of approximately 10 students. They will be your leader, your mentor and hopefully your friend for the next three weeks. There will also be one assistant working with each instructor. You have already met Nicole. Marcus, Carol and Ted, would you please step forward?"

The assistant staff members moved out toward the middle of the circle for us to take a look at them. Marcus was short and stocky, and looked to be of either Hispanic or Native American descent. His last name, Mitchell, didn't give any clues. Carol was a redhead with freckles covering every inch of her exposed skin and Ted's deep tan set off his blond hair in a California-surfer kind of way. They each looked around the circle, making eye contact with as many students as they could and nodding in acknowledgment to some. Marcus caught my eye and smiled. I felt myself blushing.

"Thanks, everyone," Bruce said, and the instructors walked back into the crowd. "As I mentioned, I am your course director, meaning I run everything. The buck stops here. I won't travel with any one team, but I will pop in and visit with each group to see how things are going. I may travel with a team for a day or two. If I am not available for any reason, my assistant course director, Susy Lathrup, will be. Susy, could you step forward, please?"

A tall, slender woman with dark brown braids and a quiet air of confidence and authority moved toward the center of the circle. She seemed to be about 30. With her tanned skin and muscular arms and legs, she looked like Athena, the Greek goddess, to me.

"Man," I whispered to Ellen. "She's beautiful. I want to be her when I grow up."

"Yeah, me too," she murmured back.

I heard Andy give a low whistle. Obviously, he felt the same way we did.

"Susy, would you like to continue with our briefing?" Bruce asked.

"I would love to," Susy replied in a breathy voice perfectly suited for a sultry jazz singer. "Once we have broken out into teams, the course will have three phases. The first week is what we call the training phase. During this time, you and your team, along with your instructors, will travel through these mountains. You will learn the skills necessary for safe backcountry travel as well as hopefully begin to bond together." She glanced around the group to make sure we were following her.

She continued, "The second week is considered the expedition phase. At this time, you will use the skills you've acquired to travel through the backcountry more independently from your instructor. This is when peak climbs, rock climbing and/or rappelling will typically happen." Tate and Andy looked at each other excitedly when she mentioned peak climbs.

"At the end of the expedition phase is a period of contemplation we call reflection. You will learn more about the reflection experience from your instructor. The last week of our course includes the final expedition, which you will learn more about later, along with a marathon and your course graduation. And that is a rough idea of what to expect for the next 25 days," she smiled encouragingly as she glanced around at the group's faces, which showed a range of emotions from nervous worry (me and Ellen, among others) to giddy excitement (Tate and Andy, for sure).

"Thanks, Susy," Bruce said. "Now, I would like the instructors to get their teams together. Please stay where you are until your name has been called. Then head immediately to the location your instructor has given you. I will see everyone at dinner tonight."

Pedro Luna, a six-foot-two hunk with broad shoulders, bronzed skin, cobalt eyes and wavy, shoulder-length, chocolate-colored hair, was the first instructor to step forward.

"Hey, everybody," he said nonchalantly. I could practically hear girls swooning over him and I saw a couple of friends nudging each other out of the corner of my eyes. *Oh, give me a break,* I thought.

"When I call your name, please gather your gear from beside the bus and meet Marcus over by the lone pine tree in the meadow back by the river. Do you all see the spot I mean?"

Marcus was waving at the group.

Murmurs of assent and nods followed. I looked at Ellen and asked her incredulously, "Are they ALL godlike?"

"It appears so," she sighed dreamily.

"Great," Pedro continued. "Please listen closely for your name and keep the conversation to a minimum as you get your stuff. It will get hard to hear your name called as we start moving around. Here we go." He recited names, and people began to move around as he called. "Steve Anderson, Betty Austin, Evan Byrd, Lucy Dakota, John Evans, Toma Funke, Joshua Gamble, James Lovett, Marcia Trimball, Ken Young."

Chapter Seventeen

A s soon as I heard my name, I looked at Ellen, shrugged and moved off to grab my stuff and go stand by the tree. I watched as the other teams formed. Tate and Cinday were in a group together, with instructor Jim McBane. Andy was in another team with Marcia Brown as his instructor and Ellen was in Maggie's team. I was disappointed I would not be with any of my friends, and that colored my initial reaction to my team. I didn't want to be with any of them. With the exception of the leaders, they all looked like a bunch of losers and rednecks. I wanted to go home. I hated having to meet people and make new friends. It always felt awkward and uncomfortable and I feared being rejected or ridiculed. I was particularly self-conscious about my weight, especially with all the staff looking so lean, fit and tan. *Ugh! I hate my body,* I thought, comparing myself to them. I immediately admonished myself for thinking that way because it was my own fault for eating so erratically and poorly.

Looking everyone over at the pine tree, I felt lost and hopeless already. Fortunately, our group was relatively young. None of the really old people had been placed in our team. No one looked over 35 to me, although I would later discover that two of our members were 38 and 42. A woman named Betty had a bossy attitude that immediately rubbed me the wrong way. A guy named Joshua, although handsome, seemed like a lost little boy, more out of place than I felt.

I heard a deep, throaty laugh from one of the other teams and looked over to see a woman of around 24 with jet-black hair, guffawing with her team. She seemed completely comfortable and at ease. I could hear her Boston twang as she spoke and my heart lurched as I remembered my crush on Dean Bryans last year. I wished I were her: confident and beautiful with an exotic accent.

My own team members were shuffling around nervously, trying really hard not to look at anyone else in the group.

Soon Pedro came over to join us.

"OK, gang. This is it," he said. "This will be your family for the next three, almost four, weeks. By the end of that time, you will have created deeper bonds with these people than some of you might have with your own friends or family back home. We'll see. Meanwhile, we need to get to know one another."

I could feel a collective groan go through the group. This was the hardest part, meeting new people. At least it was for me, and I sensed it was for the others as well.

"Look to the person on your left," Pedro continued. "This will be your partner. I want you to sit down with this person and then I will tell you what to do next."

I looked to my left and the girl named Toma Funke. We nodded at each other and sat down on the ground facing each other.

Looking around, Pedro asked, "Does anyone not have a partner? Great! Well done. Before we start our little get-acquainted activity, I'd like to ask you a question. Does anyone know why we refer to our groups as teams?"

"I do," Betty announced loudly.

"OK, um, Betty, is it?" Pedro replied. "Tell us what you think."

"Well, a team is a small group of people that has a particular task and that is what we are, small groups." Under her breath she added, "…with the task of surviving the next month."

"That's excellent, Betty," Pedro said. "You are absolutely right. Does anyone else have something they would like to add?"

"Well," started Joshua in a lovely southern drawl. "I think we're all a team because we're gonna try to work togetha on this here adventure and teams always have a leader or instructor, which is you, and we'll all have to follow that leader." He smiled shyly and ducked his head.

"That's an excellent thought, Joshua," agreed Pedro. "Teams definitely have to have leadership, a common purpose and a banding together. Does anyone else have something they would like to share?"

I tentatively raised my hand.

"Yes? Your name is Lucy, right?" Pedro acknowledged me. "What do you think?"

"Well, when I think of a team, I think of a sports team, like a volleyball team or something." Pedro nodded his head, urging me to continue. "And sometimes when people come together, I mean really connect and bond with each other, like on a sports team, and they have good leadership and a common goal, something magical happens: The team members support each other's strengths and help overcome each other's limitations and everyone benefits," I finished shyly as everyone in the group stared at me.

"That's beautifully said, Lucy, and you're absolutely right!" Pedro praised me enthusiastically. I felt myself turn red. "A team member is someone who is actively contributing to the achievement of the goal and has the best interest of the team at heart. Now, why do you think Outdoor Mountain School refers to its patrol groups as teams?"

"That's easy," James said. I looked more closely in his direction. I hadn't noticed before that he was very handsome, tall and dark-haired with a polished, preppy look. He said, "Outdoor Mountain School wants us to be actively involved in our own learning and our own process, and help facilitate the growth and learning of the others in our group."

"Yeah," Toma cut in excitedly. "OMS wants us to take responsibility for ourselves and for our group."

"That's right," said Pedro. "Well done. Now I want you and your partner to take the next five minutes and interview each other. Find out some interesting facts about one another because when the time is up, you will introduce each other to the rest of the group."

He added, "Any questions?"

No one raised their hand.

"Great," Pedro raised one hand in kind of a stop motion and then lowered it sharply. "Begin!"

I looked at my partner, Toma. She was young, with mousy brown hair and a long, thin body. She looked back at me and I started to feel self-conscious.

"Do you want to start?" I asked her.

"Sure," she replied. "Tell me a bit about yourself."

"OK," I said, frowning a bit because I thought I would get to ask the questions first. "I am 17. I just graduated from high school and I am an only child."

"Where did you go to high school?" Toma interrupted.

"I went to Green Peaks High," I replied.

"No way!" Toma cried out. "I go to Lakevalley!"

"Cool!" I said, realizing that we already had something in common. Lakevalley was the high school closest to mine. I would have gone there if they hadn't built Green Peaks four years earlier.

"OK. Tell me more," Toma encouraged.

"Let's see," I thought for a moment. "Hmmm. Well, I really don't feel like I am athletic, I have only been camping three times and I am really nervous about this whole thing. I am only here because my adventure post director, Carl Lewis…"

"Wait," Toma interrupted again. That girl would get on my nerves if she didn't quit butting in when I was talking. "I KNOW Carl Lewis. Does he have a son named Mack?"

"Yes, Mack is my boyfriend," I replied a bit petulantly, still steaming over the interruption.

"I race with Mack," Toma raved. "We're on the ski team together at Winter Crest!"

"Oh, that's cool," I said, still a bit annoyed at her and now a little jealous because she got to spend every weekend during the winter with Mack.

"Anyhow," I continued. "Carl applied for a scholarship for me to attend this course, and I got accepted."

"Wow, that's great!" Toma gushed. "You are so lucky!" The girl seemed to have a natural ease and enthusiasm about her. It was contagious and I was starting to like her, especially if I could get her to quit interrupting. "Now let me tell you about myself," she continued.

"OK, go on," I said.

"Well, you already know I go to Greenvalley. I am 14. I just finished my freshman year. I am the middle child of five and the only girl. My last name is pronounced Funk, although people call me Funky 'cause it has an 'e' at the end. I am a ski racer and my family has a condo at Winter Crest. We ski in the winter and camp all summer! Oh, and I'm named for my father, Thomas."

I was so envious of Toma. Not only did she spend weekends with my boyfriend; she had brothers and a seemingly loving family who spent time in the outdoors together.

"Time's up!" shouted Marcus.

When everyone had quieted down, he stated, "You should know a little something about your partner by now. Who would like to go first?" he asked.

Pair by pair we went around the circle introducing each other.

Joshua was 17 and from Georgia; no wonder he had that lovely accent. James was 25 and from Connecticut. Betty was 22, from New York, and had never been camping in her life.

Great, I thought grudgingly, *we almost have something in common.* From the get-go, I was determined not to like her.

Steve was a lanky 30-year-old from Houston. His family had come out to Colorado skiing when he was younger but he had never gone camping before either. Evan and John were both 20. They were from Denver, and neither one had much outdoor experience. Marcia was from Seattle and Ken was from Scottsdale, Arizona. So, despite the fact that I had not grown up in an outdoors-oriented family like Toma's, she and I seemed to have the most camping and outdoor experience of anyone in our group. It was another little piece in our affinity, so even though I was envious of her life and her family, I could tell we would become friends.

"Alright, gang," Pedro was back. "It's time to do some initiatives that will help us strengthen the connection between our team members. There will be times over the next three weeks when the success or failure of our expedition will depend on how well we have bonded as a group."

More groans, both audible and unheard.

"OK," Marcus prompted, taking up the reins from Pedro. "Form a tight circle with everyone facing inward." Marcus and Pedro joined us in the circle.

"Excellent," said Marcus. "Now, reach your hands into the circle and clasp hands with two different people. In other words, your right hand grabs the hand of someone while your left hand holds the hand of someone different. Make sure you are not grabbing the hand of the person next to you." Giggles and grunts ensued, as we followed directions and the circle was pulled tight into a gigantic "Gordian knot."

"The object is to untie this Gordian knot we have formed without letting go of hands," Marcus continued. "This activity will require patience and great communication. There is no time limit, so we are not in a hurry. We want everyone to feel safe. No one gets hurt."

Slowly, we started to untie ourselves. It was a challenge as some people had to kneel down so that others could climb over them in order to undo a section of the knot. We had to move at a snail's pace so no one's arm was bent too far or no one's shoulder was dislocated. Those of us with short arms sometimes found ourselves stretched to the limit.

There were a couple of times when we thought we were stuck and could go no further. Somehow, though, usually with James' help, we found a way to get through the tough spots, and after about 30 minutes of laughing, groaning and occasional tension, we were free!

What a sense of accomplishment! Miraculously, we seemed friendlier toward one another, and I started thinking it might not be such a horrible three weeks after all.

It was now time to begin dividing up the equipment. There were some individual items to be handed out also. These included ice axes, helmets, webbing, ropes and slings—safety gear, Pedro explained, that we'd use later.

There were stoves, pots, pans and other kitchen paraphernalia to share. Fuel for the stoves was poured into leak-proof aluminum bottles, and the large group tarps, three of them, were pulled aside. A couple of team members were sent over to the food table to gather up the supplies that would feed us for the next seven days. There were bags of pasta, beans and bulgur wheat; cans of sauce, tuna and soup; chunks of Parmesan cheese; ramen noodles; cartons of fresh eggs; tortillas and bread; peanut butter; and freeze-dried meat dishes such as beef stroganoff, chicken enchiladas and beef stew.

We had bags of tea, cans of instant coffee, powdered milk and drink mixes. There were granola and chocolate bars, nuts, and our fresh foods included oranges, apples, lettuce, cheddar cheese, carrots, onions, zucchini and green peppers.

I wonder what these are for? I thought as I picked up two collapsible shovels.

When we had collected all the group equipment and food and had laid it out on one of our tarps, we gathered around Pedro as he explained our next steps.

"OK, folks, we have a lot to get accomplished before the sun goes down. I am going to list what needs to be done and let you figure out how to do it. Tonight, we will eat a final freshly cooked meal and camp here by the river. We need to have two people from our patrol volunteer to help with the meal preparation and cooking. That's first. I looked around and saw James, Steve and Ken each nodding as they mentally ticked off our assignments.

"Second, we need to divvy up our group supplies including gear and food, making sure everything is accounted for and the weight of these additional items is equally distributed. Third, we have to set up our tarps for the night; we need a place to sleep and it looks like we might have rain tonight.

"Finally, I want each of you to take a few minutes before the evening meal to reflect on why you are here and what you expect out of the next three weeks. Write your thoughts down in your journal. We will share what you have written after dinner.

"Are there any questions?" Pedro concluded, searching the group's faces for any signs of concern.

"Only one," I said as I raised my hand.

"Yes, Lucy?" he asked.

"Are we supposed to make smaller teams to handle tasks or just take volunteers for the various jobs each day?"

"That's a good question," Pedro responded. "It will be up to each team to decide how they will manage the daily tasks. We will be talking more about what those tasks are tomorrow. For tonight, I would suggest that you each take a minute and think about Lucy's question.

"That's it for me for now, as I have a staff meeting with Bruce. See you in an hour or so. Oh, by the way, I assume everyone brought all the gear listed on your checklist?" he looked around for a sign from anyone that they were missing any of the required equipment. Everyone seemed to have what they needed.

"Excellent!" Pedro exclaimed. "The cooking delegation needs to meet over where Carol is standing. Good luck," he said as he turned on his heel and left us with a dazzling smile and a flash of those amazing blue eyes.

Chapter Eighteen

Steve naturally fell into a leadership role; he wasn't the oldest of us, but his quiet authority made him seem to be the most mature in our group. So, everybody listened when Steve spoke up, "I say we decide who is going to help cook tonight and then we'll figure out the rest. Does anyone want to help with making meals?"

Marcia raised her hand, saying, "I could do it. I don't know how to cook in camp, but I'm a very good cook at home and I'm sure someone will help me."

"Great! Thanks for volunteering, Marcia," Steve said.

"Anyone else?"

Betty spoke up, "I guess I will. It would be good to get it over with. I don't like cooking and tend to just eat out a lot but I'll give it a try."

"Perfect," Steve agreed. "Why don't you two head over to see Carol?"

Betty and Marcia left the circle, walking over to where Carol was starting to organize the kitchen workers. The rest of us looked around at each other and waited for someone to take charge.

James spoke up, "Well, it looks like we need to get the tarps set up and the gear distributed. How do you guys want to manage those chores?"

"I think we could use six people to set up the tarps," Toma suggested. "Two people for each of the three tarps. There would be two people left. They could take a look at the gear and food and separate it into equal piles. Once that is finished and the tarps are up, we could all look at the gear piles and if we agree that the weight seems to be reasonably distributed, we could each take one and load it into our backpacks."

"That sounds smart to me," Joshua drawled, flashing her an easy, lopsided grin.

"What about tomorrow's breakfast?" I inquired. "Shouldn't we think about what we will have to eat in the morning, and then make sure we can get to it before we pack everything away?"

"Yeah," said Evan, uttering the first words I think I had heard him say since introducing his partner, Ken. "I think the breakfast food should be counted in the weight distribution and then that pile should have more in it, 'cause we'll be eating the food first thing in the morning."

"Or," Toma cut in, as usual, "we could separate out the breakfast items for tomorrow and not even include them in the allotment of the rest of the group gear."

"That makes sense," John agreed. "What do you guys think?"

We already sounded like a team, asking questions and making suggestions that benefited everyone. No one was getting upset or needing to have their way.

Everyone agreed with the idea of having two people deal with the group gear while the rest of us set up the tarps. Steve, Evan, Joshua, Ken, Toma and I all volunteered to set up the tarps while James and John split the group materials into 10 roughly equal piles.

As we looked for a good spot to rig the tarps, we realized that none of us really knew how to set them up. We were each doing our own thing at the end of the tarp we worked on, tying at least six different types of knots. The tarps sagged in the middle and looked a lot like crumpled heaps of laundry. Marcus saw us struggling and came over to see if he could help. "What's up, guys?" he asked.

"We're setting up the tarps like Pedro asked us," I responded.

Then he asked us, "What kind of knots are you using?"

"A half hitch," replied Steve.

"A square knot," said Evan.

"No idea," Joshua admitted.

"So what will you do in the middle of the night, when the center of the tarp is sagging from collected rain? How will you tighten it back up?" Marcus inquired.

"I don't know," Ken confessed, and the rest of us nodded our heads in agreement.

"Would you like to learn a special knot that works really well for securing tents and tarps? One that you can tighten easily and doesn't slip?" he asked us.

"Oh, yeah," we all agreed enthusiastically.

"OK, gather 'round," Marcus said, and we did. "This is called a taut line hitch."

He began to demonstrate the knot by taking the rope that ran from the corner of the tarp and running it around a small tree trunk. He then took the loose end and passed it under the taut rope, leaving a small loop on the left side of the main rope that looked like a number four with the tight rope making the straight side of the four. I was trying my best to follow what he was doing but knots had never been my forte. I remember struggling with the bowline knot in Girl Scouts. I could never remember if the rabbit went in the hole or out of the hole.

Marcus then coiled the loose end over the taut rope twice, making sure to stay inside the small loop he created by making a number four, stacking the coils on top of each other toward the tree trunk. On the second twist, he took the loose end of the rope and passed it under the bottom of the "four" and created one more hitch beneath the two loops that had just been created. The finished knot looked like three fingers grasping the main line, with the rope passing between the second and third fingers.

After the knot was completed, Marcus said, "The advantage of this knot is it will bind up under a load, meaning it won't slip much once it is tied. However, you can adjust it tighter. It has a one-way pull." He showed us how it worked by slipping it a bit tighter.

"Ka-ou-ool," said Joshua admiringly, his southern accent creating a three-syllable word out of what ordinarily would be a single syllable.

Everyone got busy trying their hand at the new knot. I had to get help a couple of times as I couldn't remember if the coils went above the four or below it. Ken and Joshua both came over to lend a hand, and soon we had three lovely blue tarps set up under the trees. By that time, the boys sorting through our stuff had it sectioned off into neat mounds in the grass. They looked pretty evenly distributed and it was clear they had thought of everything: People carrying the fuel didn't have to carry any fresh food that might get contaminated if bottles leaked.

Just then a clanging pot announced it was time for dinner. All 40 of us sat around in a big circle enjoying chicken breasts, baked potatoes and salad, our last purely fresh meal for a month.

Chapter Eighteen

Bruce and Susy stepped into the center of our loosely formed circle as we were finishing our food. "Before you retire for the evening, we just wanted to wish you the best time of your lives," Susy said.

Bruce added, "Remember what the progressive educators had in mind when they created Outdoor Mountain School. This experience was created for those who would not shirk from leadership and who would, when called upon, make independent decisions, put right action before expediency and the common cause before personal ambition. The founders had all of you in mind nearly 40 years ago and their goal was to better the world, one person at a time."

"Finally," Susy concluded, "remember the Outdoor Mountain School motto as you head out tomorrow morning: 'Always be of service to others, do your best and never give up!' Go forth, conquer your fears and doubts and have fun."

Pedro stood up and said, "Pedro's team, please gather back at the pine tree where we met this afternoon." The other instructors called their groups to their meeting points and everyone stood up to make their way over to their assembly spots.

When our group had gathered, Pedro reminded us of the task he had assigned earlier in the day. "So, did everyone finish their journal entry on why you are here and what your expectations are?" A few grumbles erupted; clearly not everyone had made the time to do their writing.

"Who would like to share first?" said Pedro.

I raised my hand when it became clear that no one else was going to go first.

"Great, Lucy. Thank you for volunteering," said Pedro.

"Well, I am here because my explorer post leader, Mr. Lewis, applied for a scholarship for me and I was accepted. What do I expect from the course? I really have no idea. I guess I expect to survive, that's about it. I assume it is going to be harder than anything I've ever done and I am a little bit afraid that I might fail."

"Thanks, Lucy. We appreciate your honesty and your willingness to share first," Pedro responded warmly.

After I had broken the ice, everyone took a turn at revealing his or her worries and concerns. I was not the only one on a scholarship. Evan, the only African-American in the group, had been given a grant from the

Garber Foundation. That gave us something in common besides the fact that we both lived in Denver. At 38, Marcia was older than I had thought, and like me, she was worried about how she would do on the course.

As I listened to everyone speak in turn, I realized I had something in common with everyone in our group. Maybe that was what Pedro had in mind by asking us to share our concerns. Not only did we discover more commonality between us; we showed a little of our own humanity to each other. Both actions helped our group become a more cohesive team.

The sun went down around 8:30 p.m., just after we had finished sharing our thoughts, and it was time to sleep. We learned that five of us would share each of two of the group tarps, with the third tarp used to protect our gear. Clouds had been gathering since late afternoon and Marcus' prediction of a rain shower seemed inevitable.

When the sun set and the wind came down off the snowcapped peaks, it started to get chilly, triggering my fear of being cold. After my experience with hypothermia on the rafting trip two years ago, I was scared to death of being too cold.

I skipped brushing my teeth and jumped into my sleeping bag, making sure I was in the middle of the tarp surrounded by other people, not near the edge where the chill could seep in.

The rain started about midnight, waking me up as it thrummed against the nylon above my head. Thunder boomed across the valley, shaking the earth beneath us, and lightning bounced across the sky and peaks. Once I was awake, the noise of the storm and the snoring of one of my tent mates was all I could focus on. There was no going back to sleep for me. The temperature had dropped a good 40 degrees since the afternoon and my fear of being cold had a stranglehold on my mind. I was sure I was freezing even though I was snug inside a toasty down bag with all my wool clothes on and a wool hat on my head. Pedro had told us earlier that it was better to wear a hat to sleep than a pair of socks. It would keep us warmer. So I tried it. I wasn't yet convinced.

I finally dozed off at some point, and the next thing I remembered was hearing Marcus coming around to the tarps to wake us up. The sun had already risen and although it wasn't yet shining into the valley, everything around us was lit and clear. The summits of the peaks were just losing their rosy alpine glow.

"Rise and shine, campers," Marcus called out cheerfully.

Moans and groans greeted him as he came to our tarp.

"Do we have to get up?" Betty whined.

"Only if you want breakfast," Marcus replied with a grin.

I understood how Betty felt. It seemed like I had finally fallen into a deep sleep only a few minutes before. My body felt stiff from sleeping on the ground, my eyes were blurry, my mouth felt like a furry animal had taken up residence and my head ached.

"Not a great way to start out," I mumbled under my breath as I crawled out from the tarp, stretched and walked over to my pack. The advantage of sleeping in my clothes was that I was ready in about two minutes. All I needed to do was brush my teeth, detangle my hair and step behind a nearby tree to relieve myself.

I loaded my pack with the tarp, cooking stove and fuel, and took out my rain jacket. Although the rain had stopped sometime in the early morning hours, patches of dense fog remained in the valley and it felt like 30 degrees outside. I was so cold my teeth were chattering and I could see my breath frosting up when I exhaled. I couldn't wait for a hot cup of tea. Donning the rain jacket broke the wind and kept my body heat in, so I immediately felt warmer.

"Good morning, team!" Pedro called out enthusiastically. "The staff has gotten up early to prepare breakfast for you! If you will form a line at the end of the picnic table on the far side of the campsite, you will be served the last meal you don't have to prepare yourselves." He smiled widely as he finished his sentence. I got a sense of foreboding as he spoke but I shrugged it off and joined the others in line.

It was a delicious breakfast of pancakes, sausage, melon slices and hot beverages. After a night of restless sleep, and accompanied by the pungent scent of pine trees wafting on the glacier-tinged air, the food was nearly gourmet. I gulped it down like a ravenous dog, barely bothering to chew at times. I didn't realize how hungry I had been.

After breakfast, we gathered in a circle for a final pep talk from Bruce. "Alright, folks. This is it," he smiled in a way I am certain he thought was encouraging. Looking around the group, I knew there were several people who had experienced even rougher nights than I. It made me feel a little better.

Bruce continued, "This is the day your life will change forever, from the moment you take your first step." He stopped and looked around at everyone. "As you begin your journey, I would like to share with you one of my favorite quotes by Rob Parker."

He spoke in a clear, strong voice: "'In the mountains there is the promise of...something unexplainable. A higher place of awareness, a spirit that soars. So we climb...and in climbing there is more than a metaphor; there is a means of discovery.' I wish you all an extraordinary journey of discovery and look forward to seeing each of you on the trail sometime this week," he concluded.

Pedro immediately called our team together.

"Is everyone packed up?" he asked, and we all nodded.

"OK, before we head out I want to go over the route with you." We all gathered around one of the picnic tables and Pedro pulled out a packet of maps. "Please hand these around so everyone gets a copy," he said to Joshua, who was standing closest to him.

We each took a map and looked at it. It was titled the "Howardsville Quadrangle." I had seen topographic maps before on our trek to the Colorado River in May, but I was not yet very adept at reading or folding one.

"I can see from the way some of you are handling your maps, I need to show you how to fold them," Pedro remarked with a grin, watching us fumble with our maps. He quickly demonstrated how to fold them so the area we wanted was on top.

"OK, now that we have that out of the way, everyone find the town of Silverton," he said. We all looked, some struggled, and eventually everyone found the town in the lower left-hand section of the map. "Excellent," Pedro exclaimed. "Now follow the road through town along the Animas River. This is the road you drove in on yesterday afternoon." We all did as we were told. Poor Marcia was really having a time of it. Fortunately, Ken took her under his wing and helped her find her way.

"See the ghost town, Howardsville?" Pedro inquired. Most of us nodded that we did. "Continue along the road to Middleton. If you get to Eureka, you have gone too far. Has everyone found Middleton?" He checked again to make sure we were following his instructions. Everyone peered intently at their maps.

"Fantastic! Now, see where a secondary, jeep road veers off toward the east at Middleton? It heads up Minnie Gulch." Most of us found the intersecting road, including Marcia with some help from Ken. "That is where the bus dropped you off yesterday and you did your half-mile run."

Looking at the map, he continued, "Our first week will take us up Minnie Gulch—we'll camp just below the snowline tonight. Tomorrow, we'll continue up the gulch; there is snow above 11,000 feet, so we'll cross the pass on snow. We'll descend into the Middle Fork drainage and camp down in the valley. It will be a long day; we will cover about eight miles and gain 1,500 feet in elevation. We will rest on the third day and try some rock climbing and rappelling. The fourth day, we head up one of the drainages leading toward Sheep Mountain and cross one of the passes between Sheep Mountain and Canby Mountain, both decent thirteeners. Our fifth day takes us up to Stony Pass at 12,588 feet in elevation. We will camp near the pass, and on the sixth day, we'll descend to resupply and then return to camp. After that we begin week two.

"I'm sure there will be questions. Marcus and I will try to answer them as we walk; however, it is time for us to get going," Pedro concluded, looking at the sun cresting the nearby peaks and swinging his enormous green pack onto his back. We followed suit, hefting our own backpacks onto our shoulders as we started walking.

Chapter Nineteen

The initial part of the hike was fairly easy, following the old jeep road as it wound through a dense pine forest. A couple of times along the lower portion of the trail, we spotted deer foraging in the shade. Steller's jays and gray jays perched on the branches over our heads, hoping for a handout every time we stopped for a rest or a snack. The first was a striking bird that looked very much like the common blue jay found in the eastern and central U.S. but with a black head and crest. The latter was less distinctive with its gray, black and white coloring, but much more aggressive in its search for food, even becoming so bold as to hop down on the ground at our feet. Some people call the gray jay the "camp robber" because it is nearly fearless in begging for scraps.

Slowly our muscles loosened up and we grew accustomed to the hike. Right about that time, the trail became steeper, cutting deep switchbacks into the side of the mountain.

There wasn't a lot of talk as we walked. Participants from lower elevations, still adjusting to the higher altitudes, found it a challenge to breathe at 10,800 feet above sea level, and even those of us from Denver labored as the trail grew steeper.

As we rounded one sharp curve in the road, we came across the foundations of another turn-of-the-century mining operation, the Caledonia Mine, according to our maps. Not much of the mill remained beyond 12-by-12-foot supports and stones stacked two to three feet high, but the old boarding house was well preserved. There were even a few window panes left.

I could clearly visualize the buildings clinging to the mountainside and tried to imagine what life would have been like in those long-gone days. I found myself sympathetic to the miners. It had to have been a harsh, lonely existence.

A few hundred yards beyond the mining ruins, snow covered the road. Pedro told us to stop for a rest while he and Marcus explored ahead up the trail. After about 15 minutes, they returned and reported that we would be camping right there.

"Aww," Toma sighed. "I was just getting my pace down."

Betty threw herself on the ground and looked as though she would never move again. I swung my pack off and stretched my back, noticing how wet my shirt had gotten.

"Better change your T-shirt," Steve said, seeing how sweaty it was. "You'll get chilled quickly if you stay in wet clothes."

"Oh. Thanks. I hadn't thought of that." I went behind a tree to change shirts.

"You guys need to find an appropriate spot for us to set up our tarps," Pedro said. "The trail is covered in snow the rest of the way to the pass. There are no dry spots among the trees up higher and we aren't prepared for snow camping at this point."

Steve and Toma volunteered to scout out a campsite. As a group we decided it shouldn't be too far from the trail, and that camp needed to be close to the stream so we would have a source of water. We also determined it would be best to set up the tarps within the shelter of the trees so we could use the trunks or branches for our tie-down ropes. And we would want additional shelter in case we had another rainstorm overnight.

With our instructions in mind, they left to search out the perfect spot. Meanwhile, I suggested to the group that we discuss what tasks had to be performed regularly, and assign ourselves camp chores on a rotating basis so no one got stuck doing the same chore day after day.

"That's a great idea, Lucy," said Ken.

"I don't like it," whined Betty. "What if someone doesn't cook well? Why should we all have to suffer eating their food each time they have to prepare a meal? Some of us aren't any good at finding campsites, so why should the rest of us suffer because of them? Plus, I am not at all interested in doing latrine duty. I think we should each do what we do best; that way, each person is happy and the rest of the patrol is happy, too."

"You have a good point, Betty," Pedro chimed in, having overheard our conversation. "However, we are all here to learn and grow, and you won't do that by sticking to tasks that you are familiar with."

"Yeah, but I don't need to expand my comfort zone by eating disgusting food or digging the latrine," she shot back.

"No, you don't and no one can force you to do something you don't want," Pedro agreed. "Does anyone have a suggestion for how we could resolve this?"

"Perhaps," Joshua started and stopped as Betty stared him down with a look designed to kill. He cleared his throat and began again in his soft southern drawl, "What I mean is, maybe, those with special talents or skills in an area could assist or train others in their skill. For example, as a musician, I'd be happy to teach ya'll some fun songs to sing as we hike or around the camp at night. Maybe Marcia is a great cook, so she could help the chefs with meal preparation. And, I'll bet Ken is great at route-finding, so he might be able to teach us how to read a map better. Plus, some tasks may be more appealing than others so it wouldn't be fair to someone who got stuck doin' a distasteful task day in and day out."

"That's an excellent perspective, Joshua," Pedro said, nodding his head in approval. "What does everyone think of that as a solution?"

Everyone agreed, although Betty was reluctant to do so and showed her disapproval through a pouty face.

"OK, then," James said, "What are the tasks we need to consider?"

"Cooking is one of the obvious ones," I said.

"What about cleanup afterward?" asked Marcia.

"Yeah, should the chefs also clean up?" Evan inquired.

"I think they should," I said. "Otherwise, there is less incentive to use few utensils and pans than if someone else were cleaning up."

"What do you guys think?" James asked the rest of our patrol.

Everyone agreed that the same people would do the cooking and cleanup. We also decided that the other daily chores included the digging, maintenance and closing up of the group latrine and setting up the tarps. As we couldn't determine any other regular tasks, we checked in with Pedro.

He agreed with our list, but added that each day, a new leader would be assigned for the day. This person would be in charge of route-finding, setting the pace and maintaining morale on the trail, as well as handling, to the best of their ability, any disagreements that came up. Of course, Pedro and Marcus would be available to assist the leader with problem-solving. Since this first week was all about learning, they would be helping with the other aspects of leadership, as well. We decided that the leader for the day would still belong to a group that had to handle some of the other daily tasks.

Just then, Toma and Steve returned to tell us they found the perfect campsite about 10 minutes further up the trail.

"But Pedro said there was snow up there," Betty groused, still unhappy with the idea of latrine duty, her nasal voice pitched just loud enough for most of us to hear.

I swear, I thought to myself. *If that girl doesn't turn her attitude around, there is going to be some trouble between the two of us. Her negative attitude could affect the whole group.*

"Yes, there is," Steve responded. "But the spot we found faces south, so there is no snow where we would be camping. The site is dry and level and has about a dozen sturdy pine trees we can use to anchor our tarps. There is also a small tributary of the river running right behind the site."

"We think you will really like it," Toma added as Betty continued to pout, and her poor reaction looked likely to spread to others. We were all tired after our first full day on the trail, and susceptible to negative influences.

"Alright, guys," James spoke up. "Let's pack it up and go take a look at this site. If we don't agree that it is ideal, we can always keep looking, and you can help locate it, Betty, if this one is not satisfactory," he concluded with a significant look in Betty's direction.

Groaning, we heaved our packs back on and trudged up the road. Around the next bend, old snow covered the road. It was crusty and slushy, but fortunately it was not very deep or our feet would have been soaked as we sank straight into it. It reminded me of the slush on the lower trails of a ski hill at the end of a spring day.

Toma and Steve had been right, though. After less than 10 minutes walking, about five of it on the snow, we rounded another corner, putting us on the south side of the mountain and once again the road was free of snow. There was a beautiful open site under a dozen Colorado blue spruce trees. Off to the northwest, we had a lovely view of Dome Mountain.

"This is a wonderful site," gushed Marcia as she dropped her pack on the ground and collapsed beside it. She looked exhausted and grimy.

Her hair had come out of her ponytail and was sticking out in a dozen different directions and her face was flushed. Somehow she had smeared dirt across the front of her nice white T-shirt, giving her a distinctly grubby appearance.

Note to self: Don't wear white when camping, I thought.

James led us through a discussion about forming into task groups and dividing up camp chores. In the end, we settled on four groups, each with a mix of males and females. The groups would rotate through the chores. Betty happened to land in the group that was responsible for our bathroom facilities that night.

"Why do we have to dig the latrine first?" inquired our favorite girl.

"Because if we do it today, we won't have to do it again for another three days, dear girl," said John in a false British accent mocking James Bond.

"Oh, alright," Betty said in a huff as her group headed into the trees with a couple of shovels to find an appropriate spot for the patrol members to attend to their bathroom needs.

"I guess we'd better get busy," I said.

"Yep, it looks like it might rain later," Steve said and Joshua nodded.

We got the tarps out from our packs; by some stroke of luck, two of us were carrying tarps. The third one would be set up later and used in the kitchen area if it rained.

It took me a minute or two to recall how to tie the special, taut line hitch knot we learned yesterday but after a couple of attempts, I got it right. Steve and Joshua were faring much better with their knots. Soon, we had two lean-tos set up and our own gear set beneath them.

"This would be an ideal time to journal," Pedro commented as he came by to inspect our tarps. "You guys did a fantastic job setting up the tarps. I would, however, suggest that you look at the slope of the land. Although your sites are relatively flat, look behind the second shelter. See how the hillside slopes down toward where you have the tarp set up? Where do you think the water will run when it rains tonight?"

"Into that tent?" I answered timidly.

"That's right," Pedro said. "Would you like to be sleeping there in a big rainstorm?"

"No, I guess not," I smiled. "It seems I already knew that intuitively as I put my pack under the other one." I gestured toward the second shelter, in which I had stashed my own gear.

"OK, gang," Steve ordered us. "Let's strike this tarp and re-pitch it in a better location."

"I guess that's one of life's lessons," I said. "Do it right the first time, or redo until it is right. I learned that one at my dad's engineering firm. I worked there last summer, soldering printed circuit boards. I was paid what they called 'piece rate,' which meant for every board I finished, I got paid a certain amount. However, anytime I made a mistake, I had to redo the work on my own time, without pay. So it makes sense that the same ideal would apply to other areas of life," I sighed as we untied the knots and moved the tarp about 15 feet to the west of where it had originally been set. The new site was level, but wasn't located at the base of a hill where water would run under the tarp in a storm.

Wiping our hands off, we surveyed our handiwork.

"Good job men, uh, and woman," Steve said, smiling at me and putting his arm around my shoulder like we were buds.

"That looks like a much better placement," agreed Pedro. "Now, as I was saying before, this is a great time for some personal reflection and journaling while dinner is being prepared."

"Can we help out with other tasks?" I asked, at the moment not relishing the idea of sitting around writing and thinking about myself or what I had learned.

"That is an option," Pedro answered. "But you need to get permission from the group performing the task with which you want to help. Also, some of our writing and reflection time will be mandatory, so you will have to do it one way or another."

"Oh. Alright," I said sulkily. "As long as everyone has to write, I guess I am OK with that."

"You'll see, Lucy," he replied gently. "There is a method to my madness. Do you trust me?"

"Yeah, I guess so," I said, looking into his eyes, not at all sure why I should trust him yet since I had only met him yesterday. Yes, he was the leader and supposedly he had been trained in this position but you never really knew a person well after such a short period of time.

"OK," Pedro cleared his throat and looked to the others. "I would like you to consider the following question and be prepared to share either at dinner or afterward. Think about your identity, and what you base your sense of self on. Got it?"

We all nodded and headed toward our packs to get our journals and pencils. We had about two hours of sunlight left although the northern slopes of the hills across from us were already shaded.

Thank God our campsite faces west, I thought, *so at least we have the longest possible amount of sunlight and warmth.* I could already feel myself getting cold, so I threw on my rain jacket and my wool cap before heading over to a sunny rock to sit and contemplate.

Chapter Twenty

H mmm. On what do I base my identity?" I asked myself quietly. I thought about the fact that I was a daughter and an only child. Those were aspects of my identity. I was redheaded, well, sort of. I had reddish-brown hair that people always called auburn.

I kept my inner dialogue running: *What about my accomplishments? I'm smart and good at school, with straight A's. I graduated at the top of my class. I don't consider myself athletic and I am a native Coloradan. Thank goodness I am not from New York,* I added to my internal conversation as I overheard Betty griping from clear across the campsite.

"I guess she has just learned of our assignment," Joshua whispered in my ear, startling me as I hadn't realized he had sat down next to me on the huge outcropping.

"Yeah, she probably doesn't even know her voice carries so far," I whispered back, happy to have someone share my space.

"I sure hope she settles down and stops being so bossy," he continued in his slow, melodic voice.

"Me, too," I replied. I wondered if there was a way to help her see herself as others did, and then started wondering about myself and how others saw me. *How do I come across to others? Do I really pay attention? Nope. Maybe I should start?*

"We'd better finish our writing," I said, as my studious, straight-A student side asserted itself.

"Yes ma'am," Joshua grinned, mock saluted me and turned back to his journal.

OK, I said to myself. *What are more aspects of my identity?* I glanced around at the other members of our patrol to be sure everyone else was engaged in their writing.

My private conversation inside my head continued: *Well, I learned about my ethnic background in Girl Scouts, and I'm proud of the fact that I am one-sixteenth Cherokee Indian on my mother's side. Hmm, I guess affiliations like Girl Scouts or Boy Scouts are another side of me. Wow! There's a lot more to identity than I thought.* Feeling amused, I was starting to have fun with our assignment.

I continued thinking about how I categorized myself until we were called to dinner, when everyone gathered around the kitchen area.

"Mmm," Joshua sighed, inhaling deeply. That boy seemed to always be hungry and yet somehow, like Tate, he remained thin as a rail.

"It does smell delicious," John said and I looked at him curiously. He was truly a man of few words, having not spoken much since yesterday, except his James Bond teasing of Betty earlier. I wondered if he was just a quiet guy or if something was going on with him.

We scooped plates full of noodles with tuna marinara sauce and garlic bagels on the side.

"Wow!" I exclaimed after my first mouthful. "This is as good as it smells!"

"Yeah, it is incredible!" came comments from the others in our group.

"It turns out that Toma is a wonderful camp chef," Evan said proudly, clapping Toma on the back like an old pal. She dropped her head bashfully.

"You guys did an outstanding job," agreed Pedro. "While you finish eating, I would like for those in group one and two to share some of your ideas regarding where you derive your sense of self."

"Alright," I said—I was never one to shy away from a task, once I had accepted that I would have to do it. Plus, I was already starting to feel comfortable with my group. "I thought about how I am a daughter and an only child. I am also a good student and a rather poor athlete, though I always try hard. I look at my ethnic background and get some of my identity from being a small part Native American and a native Coloradan."

"Great, Lucy," Pedro complimented me. "What about some of you others?"

"Well," Joshua began without hurry. "I have some of the same aspects as Lucy—bein' a son, a brother, a friend and a male. I also get some of my identity from bein' a musician." As I listened to Joshua speak, I thought of guitar strings being twanged.

"Of course," he continued, grinning at the group, obviously enjoying the realization that his slow manner of speech was driving Betty crazy. She practically danced in her seat with impatience. "The fact I am a southerner plays a role in my idea of myself. We southern boys are considered true gentlemen. I also think of myself as a calm person; nuthin' much riles me up, and I am very pleased with that character trait."

"Excellent," Pedro commented as he looked around the group for someone else to contribute.

"Well," began Betty, breathless from having had to hold her thoughts in for so long. "I have the same superficial traits—a female from New York City, *not* upstate," she emphasized the latter. "Daughter, sister, aunt, niece, and so on just as Lucy and Joshua have mentioned. However, no one has yet mentioned religious affiliation. I am Jewish and that is a very huge part of my identity."

"Yeah, being Catholic is a big part of who I am," James added, cutting Betty off. "I went to a parochial school all through grade school and high school." Betty gave him a sour look and huffed her bangs with a dramatic breath.

"What about our habits and our thoughts?" asked Marcia. "Are those parts of our identity?"

"Good question," Pedro said. "What do you guys think?"

"Absolutely," Steve responded emphatically. "I've heard it said that your thoughts become your actions, your actions your habits and your habits your character. So definitely our thoughts are part of our character. Think of people you know who are always cranky or complaining. Those habits eventually become ingrained as part of their character..."

I looked sideways at Betty to see if she had taken offense at Steve's comments. I couldn't tell but I don't think she had. *Maybe she doesn't even know she's so critical and negative,* I thought.

I realized I had tuned out what Steve was saying, and heard him comment, "...just like our hobbies and interests."

"Can you elaborate, Steve?" asked Pedro.

"Sure. What I mean is, for example, I am a skier and an outdoorsman even though I have never been backpacking before. I love the fresh air and the wide-open spaces. I would rather be outside than inside any time. I am a runner. I have run the Boston Marathon twice and I cycled 10,000 miles across the United States one year with my best friend. All this, plus the hobbies and interests that led to them, make me who I am." Steve's accent was not as pronounced as Joshua's, but when he got excited you could hear the rounded vowels and drawn out words common amongst those living in the southern parts of the United States.

"Fabulous," said Pedro. "Anyone else have any thoughts they would like to share?"

"Yes," said Marcia. "I agree with Steve that our thoughts are also part of our identity. For example, Toma—you don't mind if I use you as an example, do you?" she asked Toma.

"No, of course not," said Toma.

"Toma seems to be a naturally optimistic and enthusiastic person. I think that makes up part of her identity. Whereas someone else..." she continued, glancing around the group and surreptitiously eyeing Betty.

"Who will remain nameless," I whispered to Joshua next to me.

"...might be always on the lookout for problems or issues and could be seen as a perpetually negative person. That would be part of their identity," Marcia concluded.

"I see what you mean. However, I would regard what you described as behaviors, not necessarily thoughts," Pedro agreed, nodding his head.

"Yes, but it is likely the thoughts inside a person's head lead to their behaviors," suggested John. "For example, a very spiritual person may be continually thinking about how their actions affect others and therefore will likely behave in an uplifting, positive manner. On the other hand, someone whose self-esteem is low and who doesn't think very well of themselves will likely not think well of others either, and could very well treat them poorly without even realizing it."

"OK. I can concede that is a very real possibility. Any other ideas?" Pedro inquired. "No? Well, excellent discussion, people. I really appreciate everyone sharing their views on this subject. I hope those of you who were preparing our delicious meal will take a chance before you fall asleep to jot down some of your own opinions about the sources of your personal identity. Now it is time to clean up and call it a night. Thanks again for a great meal!"

Cries of "Yeah, thanks," rang out from around the circle.

"It was a lot better than I expected camping food to be," said Ken.

"Before we head to our tents, let's talk about tomorrow's schedule and I'll answer questions," said Pedro. "As I said earlier, we'll continue up Minnie Gulch to the pass, then cross the pass and descend into the Middle Fork drainage. It will be a long day and we will be traveling on snow for a good part of it. Get some shut-eye tonight so you will be rested for tomorrow. Any questions?"

"How should we dress in the morning?" asked Marcia, concern for the snow travel evident on her face.

"Just like today—wool pants, a T-shirt with a wool shirt on top, waterproof pants handy in case it rains or if you have to post-hole in the snow and gaiters to help keep your feet dry. The earlier we start, the firmer the snow," replied Marcus after Pedro nodded to him to field the question.

"Which brings me to the question of who will be tomorrow's leader," Pedro said.

"Why don't we just go down the list, alphabetically by last name?" suggested Steve, who would get to be leader first according to his proposed system.

"I'm OK with that," said Evan.

"Fine with me," agreed James.

"Yeah, we will all have to be leader at some point, so it doesn't really matter if it's tomorrow, the next day or the day after," I said.

"Agreed, then?" asked Ken.

"Agreed," we all said.

"Excellent," Pedro concurred. "So Steve Anderson will be our first leader."

"What time do you want us to wake up tomorrow and what time would you like us to leave camp?" Marcus asked Steve.

"Well, if the best snow conditions occur early, I'd say we wake up at five o'clock and start hiking by seven," replied Steve.

"Oh, man," groaned Evan as he turned to walk to the shelters. "I never wake up that early."

"Me, neither," complained Betty. "I never get up before eight o'clock if I can help it."

"I'd like group one to get together for a minute to plan breakfast," said James.

"Goodnight, everyone," I called out as I headed toward the tarp I was sharing with Joshua, Toma, Ken and Evan. The other five team members were sharing the second shelter while Pedro and Marcus shared a backpacking tent.

Soon, I had my teeth brushed and my pack stored under the kitchen tarp and had crawled into my sleeping bag. It was freezing! The snow and the nearby river both added moisture to the air, making it seem colder than it probably was. I put on my wool cap and snuggled deep inside my bag, hoping my body heat would warm up the down quickly. I was once again wearing all my clothes plus my socks and my hat.

As I lay there, I listened to the sound of the river. I distinctly heard voices in the babbling of the little brook. Marcus had shared with me earlier on the trail that his people on his mother's side, the Huichol Indians from north-central Mexico, believed some of our ancestors' spirits went into the rivers, and if we paid close attention, we could hear them speaking to us. All that night I heard the voices in the wilderness. I couldn't understand what they were saying, but I could tell they were using words. My ears strained to capture their speech and comprehend what they were telling me, but to no avail. It made me think about the ancient people who had shaped the arrowhead I was carrying in the front pocket of my pack.

At 4:30, the cooks from group one started stirring, getting dressed and heating water. I was sleeping restlessly, so it didn't take much to awaken me. I lay in my bag, hoping to return to sleep for one final half hour before we all were supposed to wake up. No luck. Thirty minutes passed and I heard someone coming around to awaken us.

"Hey, guys," he called out quietly. "It's five o'clock. Breakfast will be ready in 15 minutes."

"OK. We're up," groaned Joshua.

"How'd you sleep?" I inquired.

"Not so hot," he replied. "How 'bout you?"

"Not well. Do you remember Marcus talking to us yesterday about the ancestors' spirits being in the rivers?" I said.

"Naw, not really," Joshua shrugged into his shirt as we were talking.

"Well, he was talking to a group of us as we walked yesterday and he told us how some Indian tribes in Mexico and the southwest

United States believed people's souls went into the rivers when they left this world. He said that we could hear them in the waters of rivers as they babble along. I guess my mind took that story to heart because all night long I heard people talking. I checked a couple of times but there wasn't anyone around except us, and everyone but me was asleep. So, I didn't sleep very well."

"Oh, that's kind of strange, don't you think?" he said as he stuffed his sleeping bag into a small sack and shoved it into his backpack. "I mean hearing the river talking. Did it tell you anything specific?"

"No, I couldn't tell words, just voices. Sometimes it was almost like they were singing," I said, feeling a bit embarrassed that I had shared my experience with Joshua and he had found it unusual. I worried that he probably thought I was odd. "Yeah, it probably does sound weird. Anyhow, the point is, I didn't sleep great."

"I know what you mean," said Evan, evidently listening in on our conversation. "I was awake all night because there was a tree root or stone or something under my back and I couldn't get comfortable. I thought I heard voices a couple of times, too, Lucy. I just figured it was Pedro and Marcus talking. I hadn't heard Marcus' story about the souls, but it makes sense. The river that runs through Silverton, the town we passed through the day before yesterday, is called the River of Lost Souls. Maybe that is where it got its name, from the native legends."

I gave Evan a grateful look. His support of my story made me feel better about myself and my credibility.

Soon enough, we had our gear packed up for the day, except the group equipment used for breakfast. We took down the tarps and folded them neatly. Even though the sun had risen, our side of the mountain was still shaded, so it was cold. I was still heavily bundled up and felt like I had when I was a kid and Mom had dressed me in three or four layers of pants and shirts to go play in the snow.

A hot cup of tea would be perfect right now, I thought to myself just as group one called us over for breakfast.

They had prepared oatmeal with nuts and dried fruit. It was hot and delicious, filling up the corners of my stomach and warming my body and soul. Topped off with a steaming mug of tea, I felt snug and cozy inside my bundles of clothing.

Chapter Twenty-One

After breaking camp, we headed out. We rounded the first bend before 7 a.m. to find the trail covered in snow. It was icy, but my new boots gave me good traction. As we climbed up out of the trees, the trail became steeper, and we began seeing drop-offs where a wrong step could mean a screaming 500-foot slide down into the valley below. Pedro stopped us to teach a few lessons about snow travel.

The first thing we did was untie our ice axes from our packs. We learned to always carry our ax in the uphill hand. He explained that when we traveled in a zigzag pattern up a steep slope, we would get into the routine of continually switching the hand that was carrying the ice ax. We also learned to put our thumb under the adze, or flat end of the ax head, and keep it facing forward. We held the remaining fingers on top of the head with the pick, or jagged, sawlike end, facing backward. Then we walked forward using the spike-ended shaft as a walking stick to help maintain our balance. This also provided a sense of stability because the spike at the end was jabbed into the snow so the hiker had a solid point to hold on to.

Pedro also told us to practice walking in each other's footprints. This would become more important, he said, as the day warmed up and we started sinking more deeply into the snow. It was challenging for the lead hiker, Steve, who was six-foot-one, to take shorter strides to accommodate everyone in the group.

Finally, near the top of the pass, on a steep slope where the snow was beginning to soften up, Pedro had us practice what mountaineers call a self-arrest. Basically, we had to mimic slipping on the snow and fling ourselves down the mountain. As we gained speed on the icy pitch, we rolled over onto our stomachs and dug our ice axes into the snow to arrest, or stop, our plummet.

On the first try, I was certain I would never halt, and that I would die smashing into the rocks at the bottom of the mountain at a tremendous rate of speed. When I did stop, it became more fun to practice the self-arrest. It reminded me and the others of when we went sledding as children on school snow days. The kid came out in each of us and soon we were laughing and giggling as we raced each other down the mountain, seeing who could stop first.

We practiced throwing ourselves down the hill feet first, face up. Then we hurled ourselves feet first, face down. Next, Pedro had us flip over to travel head first on our stomach and finally head first, upside down on our backs. Each time we sailed down the slope, we'd flip over to drive the pick into the snow along with our toes, elbows and any other body parts we could use to end our fall.

After an hour or so of practicing self-arrests, we were soaked and exhausted but everyone was jovial. We were also starving, and looking at watches, discovered it was already 11 a.m. Steve pushed us the final 500 yards to the top of the pass, where we stopped for a 12,700-foot-elevation lunch.

The view was spectacular! Off to the northwest was Middle Mountain at just below 13,000 feet. It was rounded with patches of brown soil showing through streaks of snow. To the south rose Canby, Sheep and Greenhalgh mountains, all well over 13,000 feet high and still heavily covered with snow. To the north we had a straight view of a ridge of peaks lining up in a succession of arrowhead-shaped points accented with glistening, blue glaciers, ending at the highest summit, Half Peak. To the east we could observe the rolling descent of the valley we would later hike down. The sunlight glowed warmly against our skin, and there was no wind; we heated up enough to take off our jackets and hats. It felt like heaven just to hang out on the quiet summit and luxuriate in the energy that comes from having worked your body hard. A tingling aliveness coursed throughout my body even though I was supremely relaxed. There was a sense of connection to everything around me I hadn't been aware of before. I felt at peace and could have stayed on top forever.

As we were finishing lunch, Pedro called us together.

"Hey, gang. This is the perfect spot to share with you one of my favorite quotes. It is from the French poet and novelist Rene Daumal, and it came to mind as I sat here," he said.

Pedro opened his notebook and began to read, "'You cannot stay on the summit forever; you have to come down again. So why bother in the first place?…There is an art of conducting oneself in the lower regions by the memory of what one saw higher up. When one can no longer see, one can at least still know.'

"So guys, as we descend from our summit, think about Daumal's words and what they mean to you. We'll talk about your thoughts at dinner," Pedro concluded.

"Time to pack up and head down," Steve called out after a signal from Marcus and we all got to our feet and slung on our backpacks.

I hated leaving! *Daumal was right,* I told myself grudgingly—*you can't stay on the summit forever.*

At first it was much more difficult descending on a snow-covered trail. It felt like we might slip and slide down to one of the frozen lakes below us. However, our morning practice with self-arrest had given us confidence, so after about 10 minutes of walking, we all started glissading, or sliding down the hill on our feet. Basically we lowered ourselves into a crouch, using our boots like skis with the bottom of our packs dragging the ground and the pick end of our ice axes serving as a rudder to help us steer. Before long, everyone was whooping and hollering! We soon discovered we could cover in less than 30 minutes what would have taken us an hour or longer to hike down, and we were having a blast!

Our snow-clad trail soon ended and we started hiking again. We stopped and retied our ice axes to our packs and set off downhill at a good clip. The trail was gently sloped and rolling, not nearly as steep as the other side had been. Shortly, we descended back within the tree line, but this side of the mountain had a lot fewer trees than the western slopes of the day before. Scattered patches of blue spruce and fir trees grew here and there while multi-hued grasses and brilliant purple, red and orange wildflowers covered the open areas.

It was beautiful to see early spring in the high country. Everything I saw looked vivid, fresh and new. Not a dull tone in sight.

After three more hours of hiking, the freshness of the day was lost to me as my legs burned and my back ached from the unaccustomed activity. I felt like a six-year-old, wanting to whine out to Dad, "Are we there yet?" Instead, I just kept putting one foot in front of the other.

Suddenly John Denver's "Rocky Mountain High" popped into my head to distract me from my misery. I focused on trying to remember the words to the different verses as the song repeated itself over and over again in my mind.

"Rocky Mountain high, Colorado. Hmm, mmm, mmm, mmm," I hummed to myself. "It's a Colorado Rocky Mountain high."

"Hey, Lucy, you sound good, girl," Joshua drawled behind me, startling me out of my reverie. I hadn't realized I had started singing out loud.

"Thanks," I said, blushing but feeling on top of the world once again.

"We'll have to sing together sometime," Joshua said.

"Yeah. Sure. Maybe," I replied and kept the song going in my head.

Finally, as the shadows were growing long, we arrived at the spot where Pedro said we would camp.

"OK, gang," Steve said as the leader of the day. "Betty will be tomorrow's leader; group two will prepare the meal tonight and tomorrow morning, group one will set up the tents and group three will handle latrine duty."

Group two: That was my group. Bummer. I was not looking forward to cooking for the whole crowd.

Oh, well, I guess I need to adjust my attitude and get on with it, I thought to myself, remembering my grandfather's words over the years: "You can do anything, Lucy, and with the right attitude, anything you do can be rewarding, even fun," I heard him say.

"Alrighty," Steve said, rubbing his hands together like he was excited about the prospect of cooking for a dozen people. "What are we going to make tonight?"

"What do we have?" I asked.

"Let's see," Joshua said, starting to look through the pile of food on the tarp. "We've got ramen noodles, peanut butter, some veggies and rice. Could we put together a stir fry? What do ya'll think?"

"Sounds good to me," I said.

"Yeah, me too," said Steve, "however, I am a pretty basic cook. The guys at the firehouse are not real picky about their food."

"No problem. Just so you know, I worked as an apprentice chef at Ray's, one of Atlanta's best Asian fusion restaurants, so if you don't mind,

I'd be happy to put the meal together," Joshua smiled as he started pulling out ingredients.

"Sounds wonderful to me," I said, feeling exhausted after the day on the trail yet amazed at Joshua's varied talents. "What do you want me to do?"

"Grab a couple of onions, peppers and the zucchinis and chop them up," he replied.

"Can do," I said.

"That's what I like about you, Lucy," he flashed his boyish smile my way, "your 'can do' attitude."

"What do you want me to do?" Steve inquired.

Joshua turned to face him and responded, "Take the pots to the stream and fill them with water. We'll need one for the rice, one for the noodles and at least one for hot water to clean up with."

"You got it, boss," Steve grinned and snatched up two of the four pots.

Soon the rice was done and the smell of vegetables sautéing in peanut sauce wafted over camp. The sun colored the sky gold, pink and orange as it started to sink beneath the horizon. We had been in the mountain's shadow since arriving to camp, so I was already bundled up against the cold.

I could hear Betty complaining about her legs hurting and the placement of the latrine being too far from camp. James was trying to console her. Toma was writing in her journal, no doubt penciling her reflections about this morning's quote. Ken and Evan were talking together on a rock. Pedro and Marcus were sitting, heads together, at the front of their tent, probably going over tomorrow's plans.

"That's it," Joshua drawled. "Dinna's ready." We stationed ourselves behind the pots to serve our guests and Joshua hollered, "Come 'n' get it!"

Everyone got a double scoop of rice and a scoop of stir-fry with a fig cookie for dessert. Water bottles were passed around to wash dinner down. It was one of the most exquisite meals I had ever eaten.

As we ate, Pedro started our discussion, "Who would like to share their thoughts on Monsieur Daumal's words?"

"I would," Marcia said, and we leaned in to listen to her. Marcia was one of the quietest members of our team. "This quote really touched me for some reason. I saw it as a metaphor for life because life has ups and downs, and when I am in a down spot, or lower regions, as Mr. Daumal put it, I try to remember the good times, the high points, and that helps me keep going. Plus, I know that neither the good moments nor the bad ones will last forever. There is constant flux between one and the other. That's what I thought of when I heard the quote," she finished.

"Thank you," Pedro said. "Who else would like to share their ideas?"

"I think similarly to Marcia," started Ken, watching her with gentle eyes. "However, I think of the quote in terms of the 'seeing' to which Rene referred. Being on the summit or on top to me means being able to visualize or observe the bigger picture, the vision or the grand dream. Being down below implies being caught up in the details that are necessary; however, it is more effective to work the details when one has the vision or the end clearly in mind. That way, the day-to-day activities and events are contributing to something. They have a focus, or purpose, and are not just random proceedings."

I could see the other group members nodding their heads as they listened to Ken. I guess he was making sense to people. I got what he was saying but for me it was simpler than that. I had taken the quote literally and suddenly my hand shot skyward.

"Yes, Lucy?" Pedro looked my way.

"I took the quote more literally," I said, voicing the thoughts that had been running through my head. "I was thinking of today, when we were on top of the pass. As I looked around at the pristine, snow-covered mountains stretching out as far my eye could see, I was overwhelmed by a sense of the magnificence of our planet and I felt a desire to protect and take care of the earth. So for me, the 'art of conducting myself' in the lower regions after having been at the pinnacle means I will be more conscious of my impact on the world and I will be more aware of the beauty around me."

Marcus nodded and smiled at me. His dazzling white teeth shone brightly because his dark features were obscured by the night that had fallen as we talked. Pedro said, "Thank you for sharing, Lucy. Does anyone else have something they would like to add?" He looked around the group. No one else seemed inclined to speak, so he said, "OK, before we call it a night—we had a big day today and you guys did very well. We are proud of you." We all smiled at each other despite our exhaustion.

"Marcus and I want to go over the schedule for tomorrow and give you another question to contemplate." He nodded in Marcus' direction.

"Tomorrow," he started. "Tomorrow is going to be a memorable day. How many of you, if anyone, have ever rappelled?" he asked, looking around at the group. James and Steve both raised their hands, as did Toma. Others, including Betty and Marcia, looked surreptitiously at the team to see who was or wasn't raising their hands. I felt my stomach jolt and my heart start to beat a bit faster. The idea of running backward off a cliff, tied into a rope, did not appeal to me. I wasn't necessarily afraid of heights; however, I was afraid of falling.

I'm so glad they told us before bed, I thought sarcastically to myself.

"Now I will really be able to sleep well," I mumbled to Toma, who was sitting to my right.

"Oh, it's fun, Lucy," she whispered back. "You're going to love it." Perhaps her enthusiasm could win me over. I had my doubts.

"So, as you might have guessed, we will be rock climbing and rappelling tomorrow," continued Marcus." We will use our same campsite tomorrow, so there's no need to pack up in the morning. Plus, you will get to sleep in until eight o'clock tomorrow, as we don't have far to hike to reach the climbing area."

"Yeah!" Evan said and I concurred with his excitement over the prospect of more sleep.

"What do I get to do as the leader?" Betty griped. "I wanted to be the trail leader like Steve today."

"I am sure you'll get a chance to be a trail leader, Betty," Pedro assured her. "We have 25 days in the field and only 10 group members, so there will be another opportunity. Besides, you will be one of the only group members who gets to lead on a rock climbing day!" he concluded enthusiastically.

"Well, I don't know how to rock climb and I am not looking forward to it," she responded defensively.

"I understand," Pedro said. "You'll do just fine, both as a leader and as a rock climber."

"I'm still not happy," Betty grumbled under her breath.

"And I'm glad she is not sharing our tarp," I mumbled to Toma.

"Me, too," she murmured back.

The rest of us went to turn in while Pedro and Betty continued to talk. They must have finally worked things out because I heard Betty grumbling to herself as she made her way to her tarp.

I slept soundly that night. There was no babbling brook to keep me awake and the day's energy expenditure had been great. The fact it was a clear night without wind or rain also helped.

Eight o'clock came all too soon. Actually, our group woke up at 7:15 to start preparing breakfast. We decided to cook some of the freeze-dried eggs because we had more time and didn't need to worry about hiking uphill right away on a full stomach. We attempted (and mostly succeeded) at creating a cheese omelet out of the eggs and some of the fresh cheese. We found some powdered orange juice and some beef jerky that we heated up as sausages.

It made for a tasty and filling breakfast.

As soon as we had the pots and pans scrubbed clean and dry, Betty, as the day's leader, had us grab our water bottles, helmets, webbing, prussic ropes and the main climbing ropes and we started hiking cross-country. Because there was no trail, Betty consulted her map frequently; however, she would not let us know where we were going. I was bothered by that particular idiosyncrasy but I couldn't figure out why. I just knew I started feeling agitated about not knowing where we were headed. I felt out of control.

After about half an hour, we came to a river. Apparently we had to cross to the far side, as Betty instructed us to stay where we were while she started scouting along the bank for a suitable place to cross.

As we sat, Steve began voicing the same concerns that had been running through my head. "How do ya'll feel about not knowing where we're going?" he asked.

"I don't like it," Evan said.

"Me, neither," concurred James.

"I don't think any of us do," I added. "It makes me nervous. What if we are going the wrong direction? What if we get lost?"

"Yeah," Ken agreed. "What if something happens to the leader? None of us would know where to go."

"OK. We'll tell Betty when she gets back," Steve said. Pedro and Marcus sat off to one side, listening in but letting us figure things out ourselves.

Soon Betty came back, enthusiastically telling us she had found a place where we could safely cross over without getting wet. We all looked at each other and Steve cleared his throat.

"Betty," he began. "Before we continue, we would like to share something with you. We've been talking while we were waiting and we think it's better for the group to know where we are going than to just be following the leader."

"I knew you guys would be talking behind my back," Betty exploded angrily. "That's why I didn't tell you where we were going! I can't trust any of you!" she shouted.

"Now that's not true," Ken said soothingly. "This has nothing to do with a lack of trust. We feel it is a safety issue."

Betty had crossed her arms defensively and clearly did not want to listen to this conversation. Pedro and Marcus moved in closer.

"We all expressed a sense of discomfort about not knowing," Ken continued. "And as we told our own feelings, it became clear to us why we were uncomfortable. We trust you to get us to the right place because so far you have proven to be a good map reader, but what would happen if something went wrong? What if you were seriously injured and could not communicate? None of us would know where we were going. That would be a problem, don't you agree?"

"Well, possibly," Betty agreed reluctantly. "But nothing's going to happen to me."

Pedro stepped in at that moment. "It is true we have few severe accidents with Outdoor Mountain School," he said. "We take safety very seriously. However, it does happen. Several years ago on a course near Marble, Colorado, a group was climbing Snowmass Peak when an enormous boulder accidentally dislodged. It fell on the group leader, crushing him instantly. It continued to crash down the mountain, knocking a couple other group members unconscious."

Wow! We were all stunned. I could tell as I looked at the faces around our patrol.

"I hadn't planned to tell this story until our peak climb next week, but it seems appropriate now because it illustrates the importance of everyone in the group knowing the leader's planned route and backup plans," Pedro ended solemnly.

"I guess I was being arrogant," Betty said sheepishly. "In New York and in the corporate world, it is so hard to trust others because everyone is out for themselves and if you don't think that way, you can get trampled. I am sorry, guys."

"Thanks, Betty," Steve said. "I think we understand where you were coming from better now, and we appreciate your listening to our concerns."

"Yeah, thanks, Betty," the rest of the group mumbled.

"So, gang," Pedro started. "Today will be a day to build trust with each other but we need to get to the rock face before too much sun hits it; otherwise, it will be very hot and uncomfortable for climbing. What do you say we let Betty get us across the river and to the wall now, and this afternoon before we return, she can show us the map and the route home?"

"Yeah, alright," Steve and Ken said simultaneously. Everyone else nodded their agreement.

Betty led us downstream to where a gigantic pine had fallen over the river. The branches on the upper side had been broken off and it appeared to have been used as a bridge before. A well-worn, two-foot-wide path led across the top of the log to the other side.

"Nice find, Betty," Pedro praised her. She smiled at his compliment and for a moment, she actually looked pretty.

The crossing was only about 50 feet wide, but the water underneath bubbled and churned, with white foam spitting up toward the underside of the log bridge. Marcia and Evan both looked doubtful about the prospect of crossing over while James and John seemed excited by the undertaking.

"I'll cross first," Betty said. "That way we'll know if it is stable and safe."

"I think a man should go first. No offense, ladies," said Steve as he glanced around at the females in the group, "but most of us are taller and stronger, and we're probably better swimmers if we fall in."

I expected Betty to bristle at the comment about men being better suited to go first; however, Pedro's earlier remark seemed to have softened her up a bit. She thought it over briefly and then agreed to the suggestion.

"Who would like to walk the plank first?" she asked jokingly. I had never heard her make a joke before and it caught me off guard.

"I think Steve should go first," John proposed. "He is the tallest and probably the most experienced of any of us. What do you think?"

"I would be happy to cross first," Ken said. "Steve, did you want to go first?"

"I could go first or stay on this side to help. I have swift-water rescue training through the fire department back in Houston, and could help anyone if they fall in," he replied.

"That's excellent," said Betty, reassuming her role as leader. "Why doesn't Ken go first and you go last?" she said, looking at Steve. "Everyone else can cross according to their preference in between."

Marcia had looked briefly relieved when she learned about Steve's training; however, the fear returned to her face as she watched Ken cross swiftly and easily to the other side.

"I'd like to go next," Evan said. "I want to get this over with. Standing here just makes me nervous." And with that, he stepped up onto the log and began walking slowly toward the far side.

"There's a bit of moss in the middle," Ken shouted over the raging water. "It is a little slippery."

Evan had reached the slick spot on the log and tried to step across it. His stride was not quite long enough, and we watched as his foot came down on the slimy patch of moss, and then slid sideways. The next thing we knew, Evan was down on his butt, one leg off the log and the other bent awkwardly behind him. He crashed down hard. We could all feel the jolt as his body slammed into the wood.

Everyone held their breath as he appeared to teeter on the brink of falling into the torrent below him. Steve, faster than anyone could imagine, was on the shaky span in an instant, just after Evan bounced on his backside. Right before he toppled into the river below, Steve grabbed the waistband on his shorts and lunged backward. Both men tumbled over backward, crashing off the log onto the river's bank where they started.

We gathered around them immediately.

"Good save, Steve," James said admiringly.

"Are you OK, Evan?" Pedro and Marcus asked simultaneously.

"Yeah, I think so," Evan replied. "My left knee hurts, though."

"Try to stand on it," Marcus said while James and John each put an arm under Evan's shoulders to help him up.

Chapter Twenty-One

"Oh, man, it hurts," he said, standing gingerly on his leg.

"Let's take a better look," Pedro said, gesturing for Evan to sit on a nearby rock.

Pedro poked all around Evan's knee, eliciting grimaces and groans. "I think you just strained the tendons stretching it back like you did when you fell. As far as I can tell, it is going to be OK. Did you hear any loud 'pop' when you twisted it?" he inquired.

"No, I didn't," said Evan.

"Good, then you probably didn't tear your ACL," Pedro said reassuringly.

"How are we going to get him across the river?" Marcia asked, clearly even more worried about the river crossing than before.

"Good question," Pedro acknowledged. He turned to Betty. "What would you do, leader?"

"I don't know," she replied. Then she looked at Evan. "What do you want to do?" she asked. "Do you want to return to camp and rest your leg, or do you want to cross the river and watch the group rock climb?"

"I'd like to try to get across so I can at least watch you guys," he said.

"Can you walk at all on your leg?" Betty questioned.

"Let's see," he said as he tried to walk. It was evident he couldn't get far.

"If we send him back to camp," Betty said, turning to Pedro, "who will go with him? We can't let him return alone."

"I agree," said Pedro. "Marcus would go back with him."

"I could go back with him," Marcia quickly volunteered. "I don't need to go rock climbing and rappelling."

"I understand and I appreciate your willingness to help," said Pedro. "However, I feel you would be best served if you joined us today."

Looking Evan in the eye, he said, "It is up to you whether you come with us or go back to camp to rest. After trying to walk around, do you still want to join us?"

"Yes, I do," Evan replied.

"Alright, then," Pedro smiled. "Let's get to the other side of the river."

"Could we try crossing two or three at a time?" Toma asked. "We could link arms to keep each other balanced. What do you think?" she asked the group while looking at Pedro to see if he approved of the idea.

"Let's give it a shot," James said and Pedro nodded.

Betty, James and Toma linked arms and slowly crossed to the other side. Marcia, Joshua and John followed them safely across. Marcus nimbly walked the log on his own, practically dancing to the far side. The only ones left were Evan, Steve, Pedro and me.

"I'll cross with Evan and give him a hand," Steve said. "We'll go last. That leaves you, Lucy, and Pedro."

Pedro looked at me and asked, "Do you want help or would you like to cross over on your own?"

"I'll try it on my own but I would love it if you were behind me, just in case," I replied.

"OK," he said. "Let's do it."

"That's a brave girl," Steve said admiringly.

I started across. The path was wide and I wasn't carrying my backpack. *Just watch where you're stepping,* I told myself as I gingerly placed one foot in front of the other.

"Come on, Lucy!" Toma shouted from the other bank.

"You're doing it!" came encouragement from Ken.

Behind me I heard Pedro say, "Nice and steady. You're doing a fine job, girl!"

About three feet from where I stepped onto the log, I was suddenly aware of the rushing water beneath my feet. My head started spinning and I felt dizzy. My body wanted to sway with the movement of the river.

"Look up," I heard Ken yell. "Look at me. Don't watch the water!"

I wanted to raise my head but I was afraid. My legs started shaking and I couldn't move. My breath came quick and shallow. I was panting. Sweat started to run down my cheek by my ear. Right in front of me lay the patch of slick moss where Evan had fallen. I could see the skid marks his feet had made, tracing a brown trail through the brilliant green.

I was nearly in a trance. The sparkling light and the white foam crest dancing on the waves had me mesmerized. I could feel my feet starting to slip sideways. I was losing my balance.

I couldn't look up for fear of stepping on the slick, mossy surface. Evan's fall kept replaying in my mind. Then, I heard Pedro behind me say, "You're doing good, Lucy. Stay steady and keep moving. Take one step at a time and look at Ken. I am right here behind you." He tapped me gently on the shoulder to show how near he was.

I gained courage from his presence and began to inch my way across the log to where the rest of our group was waiting. Even though my breathing was still rapid, I raised my eyes and looked at Ken. Joshua stood there beside him. Beautiful, gentle Joshua. I hadn't really thought of him like that before, but all of a sudden, he seemed like a hero to me. He was my golden-haired rescuer, even though he hadn't said a word. The next thing I knew, I was across and Marcia and Toma were hugging me.

Together, Steve and Evan limped slowly along the log with Steve helping support most of Evan's weight. They made it past the slick spot and soon joined the rest of us.

"Nice work, gang," Pedro said. "Let's get to the rock before it gets too hot."

Betty made her way out front again, consulting her map. "This way, guys," she said, pointing east toward the hills.

Chapter Twenty-Two

It was a 15-minute walk along a gentle path before we reached the lower part of the mountain. We could see rock cliffs above us but a good stretch of hill remained for us to climb before arriving at the base of the cliffs.

Finally, after another 30 minutes of steep, cross-country climbing, negotiating fallen logs and slippery, sandy soil where two steps forward included one step back as our feet slid back down, we arrived at the foot of the cliffs—sweaty, dirty and tired. Evan was still making his painful way up the hill with Marcus walking beside him. He had found a five-foot length of pine branch to use as a walking stick.

"This is it, gang," Pedro said, smiling like a kid in a candy store. His enthusiasm was contagious. "Have a snack and a drink of water while Marcus and I set up the top ropes." Marcus and Evan had just joined the rest of us at the base of the rock wall.

Pedro and Marcus took off, scrambling around the back side of the cliff with ropes on their backs. Soon we heard a whipping sound and watched the ends of the ropes come flinging through the air, bounding off the rocks to thud in a tangled pile of spaghetti at the foot of the cliff.

In a matter of moments, Marcus had rejoined the group. Pedro remained at the top of the rock face, tying off the ropes he had just tossed over the edge.

"Before we begin, we have to go over matters of safety," Marcus said. "First, everyone get your length of webbing."

We all dug into our packs and pulled out eight-foot-long pieces of red, black or blue, one-inch-wide nylon.

As soon as everyone had their webbing in hand, Marcus continued, "Take both ends of the webbing in your hands. One end in your left hand, one end in your right." And we did. He looked around the circle to be sure everyone was caught up before proceeding. "On one end, and it doesn't matter if it is the end in your left hand or the one in your right hand, tie an overhand knot."

"I'm not sure what an overhand knot is," Marcia said embarrassedly.

"No problem," Marcus assured her. "An overhand knot is the one everyone most commonly ties. Make a loop with your webbing and then bring the loose end through the middle of the loop and pull it. Don't pull this knot too tight. You'll see why in a minute." Again, he checked to make sure we were all following along.

"Hold your loosely knotted end in your dominant hand, right or left, it doesn't matter. Grab the free end in the other hand. Now, you are going to trace the knot in reverse direction with the free end. Follow it exactly and be sure you don't have any twists in either one. You should end up with the two free ends heading off in opposite directions when finished and your knot will look like this." He held up his webbing so we could all see. "This is called a water knot or a follow-through knot. You'll see that your webbing is now tied to itself in a circle."

He walked around the group, helping with the knots. Soon we all had beautiful water knots tied into our webbing. Pedro returned from up top and checked our work.

"Nicely done, everyone," he said and we all beamed with pride.

"Alright, now untie your water knots," Marcus said, amid groans and complaints.

"Aww! We'd just gotten them to look nice," Joshua drawled.

"Speak for yourself," Betty said in a teasing tone. *Wow! She's really showing us a different side of herself this morning,* I thought.

We undid our knots and then Marcus said, "Now you are going to learn how to make a Swiss seat or a seat sling, which you will use for climbing. First, fold your webbing in half so you have two even lengths about four feet long. Grab the center fold with both hands. Next, move your hands apart from the center so there is a six-inch length of webbing in the middle between your hands. Got it?" He looked around and nodded.

"OK. Now, let go with your left hand, take the webbing in your right hand and make a loop of about eight to 12 inches. Tie an overhand knot here, leaving the 12-inch loop."

He and Pedro walked around helping as we struggled to create the loops. "OK, everyone got it so far?" Marcus asked. "Now, move six inches over from the knot on your loop, along the longer side of the webbing, and make another 12-inch loop, and tie an overhand knot. You should have two loops with about six inches in between and about two and a half feet of webbing on either end. Everyone with me?"

We were all pretty quiet as we focused on tying our knots correctly. I glanced up. Toma had her tongue out between her teeth and Betty's brow was deeply furrowed as she worked. Yep, we were all concentrating hard.

Marcus continued, "Great! Next, step into your loops and pull the webbing all the way up your thighs to your crotch." He watched as everyone balanced themselves and stepped into the loops in their webbing. Marcia almost toppled over but Ken grabbed her just in time.

"Good. Take the loose ends and bring them up to your waist. Wrap them once around your waist, twice if you have a very small waist, from back to front so the loose ends are in front of you."

"Excellent," Pedro said, walking around and reviewing our work.

Marcus continued, "Now, you get to practice your water knot!" he smiled. "Take one of your loose ends and tie an overhand knot just like we did before. Then continue following through with the other loose end until your knot is done. You want to make the knot far enough back from the end of the webbing so that when the knot is complete, the circle around your waist is fairly tight. You'll probably have to adjust it a time or two until it fits comfortably."

It took me a couple of tries before I got the waist of my seat sling to fit correctly. The first time it was way too loose and the second time it was too tight. Finally, on my third try, it fit just right.

"Alright, gang." That was Pedro's favorite way to start a lecture. "Now that you have your seat slings tied, take out your locking carabiners." I looked around to see others grabbing the roughly circular metal loops we had been carrying. I pushed mine in on one side and it opened like a little gate so a rope could enter the loop. "Clip your carabiners in between the waist belt and the six-inch segment of webbing between your legs. You'll feel a little like you are wearing a diaper. Be certain to lock your carabiners."

"Find a buddy," Marcus added. "And check each other to make sure the 'biner is locked."

We all turned to a partner and checked each other's knots and carabiners. When I turned, Joshua was right there, so we partnered up.

"Wanna check my webbing?" I asked.

"Of course I do," he answered softly as he thumbed the 'biner to make sure it was locked and then pulled on the webbing. "Ya might want to tighten this knot on the end," he suggested, pointing to one of the over-hand knots I had tied in the loose ends once the water knot was finished.

There was lots of nervous chatter among our patrol members as the moment of truth was fast approaching. I heard Marcia giggling uncontrollably with Ken.

"Let me check yours now," I said to Joshua and he obliged by holding his arms away from his body so I could thumb the carabiner and pull on his knots. "Looks good," I said.

"Why, thank ya, ma'am," he grinned and exaggerated his drawl.

"Alrighty." Pedro called out, bringing us back to attention. "Now there are two important roles in climbing. Can anyone tell me what they are?" he asked.

"Obviously the climber," said Evan. "But I am not sure what the other one is."

"What about the holder-guy?" asked Marcia. "I've seen movies where people are climbing or rappelling and there is a person holding the rope. I bet he's the other important role."

"You're absolutely right, Marcia," said Pedro. "Well done!" She smiled shyly at Pedro.

He turned toward the group. "As each of you climb, there will be someone from the group who will be belaying you, or holding the rope. It is their job to stop you if you fall. Each of you will have the opportunity to climb and each of you will have the chance to belay."

"How in the world will I be able to hold Evan?" Betty asked, her anxiety showing in the whiny tone her voice took. "No offense, but you must weigh at least 200 pounds, and I only weigh 110. That would be impossible."

"Yeah, I am not sure I could hold Evan or even Marcia," said Joshua, who was also on the thin side.

I was thinking the same thing. Upper-body strength had never been one of my assets. And what about Toma? She was only fourteen. How could she be expected to handle the weight of an adult?

"I understand your concerns," Pedro said. "I can assure you that even the smallest person in this group can save the largest person. We use our ropes and techniques to break a fall, not our strength or body weight. You will see. You have to trust me in this right now but soon you will trust each other."

"Right now," Marcus took up the thread of conversation, "we are going to go over some basic rules, commands and techniques. Please pay close attention because this is a matter of life or death." He looked us each in the eye to emphasize the importance of his words.

He continued, "First rule, NEVER, EVER, EVER step on the rope. Always be aware of where the rope is underneath you. The reason it is vital not to tread on the rope is that every time someone steps on the line, small pieces of rock, sand and dirt get lodged in between the rope strands. Over time, with the tension placed on it from climbing as well as the rubbing against rock edges and corners, the rope begins to deteriorate from the inside. This means you can't see it like you would a cut or fray. Little by little the grit on the interior wears away, strand by strand until one day, someone falls and the rope snaps because it was weakened. So NEVER, EVER, EVER step on the rope. The consequence for doing so here will be 20 pushups the first time. Fifty the second offense. One hundred for the third offense and if there is a fourth time someone treads on the rope, they will not climb again. Have I made myself clear?"

"Yes," we all agreed.

I gulped, imagining someone falling and the rope breaking. *That conversation has not helped my nerves at all! What if we're using a rope someone already unintentionally stepped on? How would we ever know?*

Pedro cut in, reading my thoughts, "Don't worry about the ropes we are using. OMS changes its ropes every season and you are the first group out this year, so our ropes are brand-new."

I could see the relief on everyone's faces, especially Marcia's. She was already anxious about this whole adventure. I felt my own tension relax a bit as well, even though I was still nervous.

"Next are the commands," Marcus resumed. "Since your belayer will likely be high above you on a top rope climb, or well below you if you are doing a lead climb, you must have a way of communicating with this person. Their job is to keep you safe, so clear communication is vital. When you first tie into the rope—we'll show you how to do this in a moment," he said, looking Betty's way as she started to interrupt. "When you first tie in, you yell 'on belay.' This means that you are tied in and ready to start climbing. But you don't move yet! Your belayer responds by yelling 'belay on,' meaning they are in position and ready to catch you should you fall."

"On belay," I whispered to myself as I heard others doing the same.

"Once you have heard 'belay on' you can safely approach the wall."

"Your next command," said Pedro, taking over the instructions, "is 'climbing.' This means you are starting to work your way up the wall. Your belayer typically cannot see you, and so they have to rely on your verbal commands and the feel of the rope to know what you are doing. When the belayer hears 'climbing' he or she will shout 'climb,' and that is your cue to start climbing. Do not start climbing until you hear 'climb.' Even though your partner has said 'belay on,' something may have happened to make them unprepared for your ascent. Once you hear 'climb' you can begin scaling the rock. Got it?"

He looked around the group, each face focused intently on what he was saying. We all nodded that we understood.

Marcus interjected, "Some of you will climb more quickly than others. You may even move faster than your belayer can keep the rope coming up. You don't want to get too far ahead of the rope. All this will do is give you a longer fall before your belayer can stop you. If you experience this, stop at a safe, comfortable spot and shout 'up rope.' This tells your partner to bring the rope up more quickly and to take up any slack until they feel tension again in the rope. This is also the case for those of you feeling a bit nervous. You will want your partner to keep a good amount of tension on the rope."

"The opposite may also be true," Pedro chimed in. Listening to the two of them was like watching a well-choreographed dance; they obviously had worked together before and that helped ease some of my nervousness. "Some of you will want to have the rope looser so you can explore a bit and find the best hand- and footholds. In this case you will call out 'slack' so your partner will let out a bit of rope and give you more room."

Marcus finished, "Once you have reached the top of the pitch, your belayer will not relax until you tell him or her 'off belay.' This means that you are finished climbing and no longer need protection. Your partner will reply 'belay off' and you will untie from the rope, throw it down the face for the next climber and start the sequence all over."

"Before you throw the rope over the cliff face, however," Pedro said. "You must yell 'rope.' That way those who are below will know to duck and cover. The same goes if you dislodge a rock. Immediately shout 'rock' and those below, rather than looking up to see what is happening, will lean in against the rock and shelter their heads as the rock goes whizzing by."

I remembered the boulder flying by my head on Bierstadt, a chunk of which was in my pack back at camp.

"Is there anything we shout when we fall?" I asked.

"Yeah," John said with a grin. "You'll yell 'Oh, **@@!!' or something equivalent."

"Very funny," I replied back.

"It is possible that you might say something like that, Lucy," Marcus said smiling. "However, there is a formal command rock climbers use. Can anyone guess what it might be?"

"Falling?" speculated Toma.

"Absolutely right," Marcus responded. "Pretty easy, huh? Pretty self-explanatory."

"Yeah, it is," I muttered. "I just don't want to have to say it."

"Me, neither," Toma said and Joshua nodded.

We all looked around at each other, smiling nervously.

"So are you guys ready to get started?" Pedro inquired.

"Yeah!" James, Toma, Steve and Ken all replied eagerly.

Maybe, I thought, and could see by the grim set of her mouth, Marcia wasn't too excited about the prospect, either.

"Who will be first?" asked Pedro.

"I will," James said enthusiastically.

"Great! Who will belay James?" Pedro wanted to know.

"Oh, I will," said Marcia resignedly. "That way I won't have to climb very soon."

"Wonderful!" said Marcus and Pedro together.

"Marcus will take you to the top and show you how to belay him," Pedro said as Marcus beckoned Marcia to follow him and they disappeared around the corner.

"While Marcia is getting tied in and being briefed on the technique, I would like you to take out your prussic rope, the narrow, round rope about three feet long," said Pedro. "We are going to learn how to tie into a rope with or without a carabiner."

We each dug out the three-foot-long, slender nylon cord we had been carrying.

"OK," started Pedro. "Everyone knows how to tie an overhand knot by this time, right?"

We nodded our heads.

"Great. This next knot is called a figure of eight and it begins with a basic overhand knot. So begin your overhand knot, but don't take the loose end through the loop you have created. Normally you would poke the loose end up through the bottom of the loop and pull it tight, making an overhand knot. This time, rather than putting the end through the bottom of the loop, bring it around and poke it through the top of the loop. When you pull it tight, your knot will look like a figure eight."

We all did as he said, and were delighted to find that this was an easy knot to tie! Everyone got it the first time.

"The figure of eight is just the beginning," Pedro continued. "You can tie a figure of eight on a bight, meaning with a loop of rope coming out one end and the two loose ends leaving the other. This is used when you are connecting to a carabiner or other mechanical climbing device, like we are today. Sometimes, however, you won't have a carabiner with you and you will want to connect yourself directly to the rope for safety. In that case, we use what is called a follow-through figure of eight."

"Hey," Toma said enthusiastically. "That sounds almost like a water knot, right?"

"Yes, Toma, you're right," responded Pedro. "Do you want to demonstrate how you think the knot should be tied?"

"Sure," she said as she moved forward a bit so everyone could see her. "OK. You have your figure of eight tied in the rope," and she showed us her knot. "Then I guess you would take the loose end of the rope—pretend that the other end goes up the cliff to the belayer—run it up through your seat sling and then follow your figure of eight backward until the loose ends are both headed in the same direction." She tied her knot as she spoke.

"You would end up with something like this," she concluded, showing us her knot, which was now connected to the webbing around her waist.

"Outstanding," Pedro praised her. "Toma is exactly right. Did everyone catch what she did as she was talking?" We all nodded, tried our hands at it and showed him our knots.

"Yeah, I think I did," said James, who was impatient to get started with his climb. He shoved his knot Pedro's direction, walked up to the base of the cliff and reached for the rope.

"OK, let's see what you've got," said Pedro, looking at James' knot. "It looks good. You ready to climb?" he asked as James began twisting the climbing rope around. James nodded. Soon he had a beautiful figure of eight with a four-inch loop on the end. Pedro took a closer look at it.

"Everyone come gather around," he said. "See how James made his knot smooth, with no twisted areas? The rope runs evenly throughout the knot. Well done, James! Take the bight and secure it onto your carabiner," he said.

James did so, locking off his device as soon as the rope loop was through it. Pedro pulled on the rig to be sure it was connected correctly and gave James the nod.

He took a deep breath and then shouted, "On belay!"

"Belay on," came the clear but faint reply from above us. Marcia was ready.

"Climbing," yelled James.

"Climb on," responded Marcia, and James walked up to the rock wall. The rope moved upward, pulling slightly at James' waist when tension was obtained.

"Good luck, James," I said.

"Have fun," Toma added.

James reached above his head and found a spot to hold onto with his right hand. Then he searched with his left foot for a small ledge to place his toes. When he found one, he put his weight onto that foot and lifted himself with his arms, moving 18 inches off the ground.

"Alright, man!" Joshua said, practically jumping up and down with enthusiasm. "You're doin' it!"

Slowly James worked his way up the rock face. He shoved his hands and feet into cracks in the rock, and small protrusions became shelves he could stand on. When he was 15 feet off the ground, we were a frenzy of enthusiastic cheers. No professional athlete ever had such a supportive crowd. He slipped once about 18 feet up on the climb. Everyone held their breath but Marcia was steady. The rope caught him and he dangled there for a moment before finding a foothold once again and quickly scrambling the final eight feet up the cliff.

We heard him yell, "Off belay," and Marcia replied, "Belay off!"

Shortly, Marcia came sauntering back up to the group.

"Hey, Marcia! Way to go, girl!" Toma had a high-five ready for her.

"Yeah! You were magnificent!" I said, giving her a hug "How did you manage to hold him when he fell?"

"It was easy!" Marcia beamed. "Once Marcus showed me what to do and I visualized it in my mind, it came almost naturally when I felt James fall. This is awesome! I can't wait until it's my turn to climb!"

Wow! I thought. *What a turnaround!* I started feeling more excited about the prospect of climbing. Hey, if Marcia was excited, I could be, too!

"Rope!" came the cry from atop the cliff and we heard the whistling rush that meant the nylon lifeline was plummeting back down to earth.

Chapter Twenty-Three

W ho's next?" Pedro called out.
"I'll go," John said eagerly.

"Wonderful!" Pedro replied. "Clip in."

John clipped the rope onto his carabiner, gave the commands and began to climb. He moved much more quickly than James had. Even though he was a bit shorter, he easily discovered different hand- and footholds from those James had used. I could tell James was having a hard time keeping the slack out of the rope.

In less than 15 minutes, John had gracefully climbed the entire pitch and was readying himself to belay.

Toma went next; her athleticism showed. She moved as gracefully as John for the first 12 feet or so, and then came to a section that stymied her. "Move your right hand up about six inches," Steve shouted to her. "There is a knob poking out that looks like a good handhold."

"She can't reach that high up," James said. "Her legs are all the way extended. She needs to find a foothold higher up."

"If you can walk a bit to your left, Toma," Ken said encouragingly, "you can bring your left leg up about four inches to a crack, and then use that to push yourself up so you can grab the knob Steve is talking about."

She tiptoed an inch to her left.

"Just a bit more," Ken said.

She eased herself away from the wall and her feet slipped off the rock.

"Falling!" she screamed as she slid a foot or so along the stone. The rope jerked to a stop as John applied his brake hand. I held my breath.

"Are you OK, Toma?" asked Pedro.

"Yeah, just a bit shaky," she replied. Then she yelled, "Tension!" up to John so he would keep the rope taut.

Her feet found a comfortable hold and she straightened out her legs. Reaching above her head with her right hand, she found a place to grab hold while her left hand pushed against a ledge. She moved up another foot, then found new holds and quickly moved past the spot that had challenged her. Toma's confidence seemed to soar again after that; she traveled quickly up the rest of the face and was soon off belay.

"Next!" Pedro cried out once the rope was tossed back down to the base.

"I'll go," I said, and clipped in. I wanted to get going before I lost my nerve.

My breath quickened. I had never done anything like this before but I had just watched three people do it, so I figured I could manage it. "Climbing," I yelled. "Climb on," I heard Toma reply.

Facing the rock wall, I couldn't see any place I could put my feet, let alone a spot to hold on to. I saw tiny little pebbles sticking out of the wall but there was no way those would hold my feet! Plus, I didn't have any real upper-body strength, so finding a great handhold was not going to do me much good.

"You can do it, Luce," Joshua said, trying to inspire me. "There's nothin' to be afraid of."

I didn't feel afraid; I just couldn't find the perfect hold for either my hands or feet. Frustration was just about to get the best of me.

I suddenly realized: *That's it! I'm always waiting for the perfect something. All the protection is in place. I am not going to die or even fall very far and yet I can't make myself commit.*

I was becoming embarrassed as I stared at the wall and ran my hands over the stone.

I shouted at myself: *Come on! Do something! There is no perfect something!*

Then I heard Pedro say, "Lucy? Can you raise your right hand about four inches above your head?"

I nodded, feeling tears well up in my eyes.

"OK," he said gently. "Do that and you will feel a big, wide crack where you can place your entire forearm."

I reached up and found the spot, and shoved my arm in sideways. That felt stable, although I was now standing on my tiptoes.

"Alright," Pedro continued in a soft voice. "Take your left leg and try to put your foot on the bump about knee height."

I did that. Now I had my arm jammed into a crack above my head, my left foot on a rock bump and I was straining my right foot by standing on my toes like a ballerina.

"Now," Pedro said. "This is when you have to commit. You are going to stand up on your left leg, bring your left hand next to your right hand and place your right foot in the crack by your knee. Ready?"

I shook my head hesitantly and then decided. Suddenly I was standing on my left foot. My right arm was wedged in so tightly there was no way I could fall; my right foot found the crack and lodged itself in.

"Yeah!" I heard Marcia say.

"Nicely done," Pedro said. "Now try the same thing to move up another foot. That's all you have to do, one foot at a time. Don't think about the whole wall. Just focus on where you are at the moment and moving up another six or 12 inches."

I explored the rock surface with my hands and found a great, round, river rock protruding from the face. I grabbed that with my right hand and shoved myself upward. My feet found the ledge where my right hand had been and I was soon three feet off the ground. Then five! Then 10!

I was doing it! I was climbing! Toma kept the tension tight on the rope. I never felt like I was going to fall or even slip (except in my head). At the 15-foot mark where Toma had encountered her challenge, I found the holds easily and moved right past. Another 10 minutes and I was up and over the top.

"I did it!" I shouted, jumping up and down, starting my victory dance. "Oh, yeah," I remembered when I heard Marcus clear his throat. "Off belay," I said.

"Belay off," Toma replied and I unclipped. She ran over and gave me a big hug.

"Good job, Lucy," she smiled.

"Thanks," I said. "You, too!"

"How are your arms?" I asked, knowing she had scraped them when she slid.

"They're OK," she said, holding them up for me to see the scratches.

"How's belaying?" I asked.

"Fun!" she replied as she turned to follow the trail down to the base.

Marcus showed me how to run the rope around my back and to sit with my legs apart, braced on a boulder in front of me. Then he had me move the rope by pulling it toward my stomach with my right hand, my brake hand, and then sliding my hand forward on the rope again while the left hand pulled the slack away from my body. My right hand never left the rope.

"If your climber begins to fall," Marcus said. "Just pull your arm into your stomach, hold on with your left hand and straighten your legs to keep from being pulled forward. You can hold a several-hundred-pound person using this technique."

I smiled and nodded, all the time thinking: *Oh, man, I hope I am not tested on that.*

Soon I heard, "On belay!" shouted up from below. I didn't recognize the voice, only that it was male. *So, one of the men trusted me to bring him up safely,* I mused to myself. "Belay on!" I replied loudly.

"Climbing!" was the reply.

"Climb on!" I called out as I began to haul the rope in. It took me a couple of minutes to get a feel for the nylon cord running through my hands. I didn't want to pull the guy up, and I didn't want him to have too much slack in case he fell. Shortly, I had the hang of it. Whoever it was moved steadily, not too fast and not slow. After about 10 minutes, the movement stopped. *He must be at the tricky spot,* I said to myself.

I waited to feel the tension go out of the line and then I heard, "Slack," called up. I let out a foot of rope. "More slack," came the command.

OK, I thought. *You're asking for it.* I let out another foot of nylon.

Marcus was at my shoulder. "Keep an eye on the rope," he said. "Whoever is climbing now has about two-and-a-half feet of slack. Should they fall, they will gain a bit of momentum before the rope catches them. I just don't want you to be caught off guard, Lucy."

"Right, chief," I said. I wanted to salute him but I couldn't release my hand from the rope.

Without tension on the line, I couldn't tell if the climber was moving or was stationary, trying to find a hand- or foothold. Time moved slowly. I noticed the breeze picking up from the west. It lifted the hair off my neck, which was now sweaty with anticipation. The sun was burning intensely on my face and arms, and my mind began to wander.

I wondered what my boyfriend Mack was doing at that moment. I knew he was wrangling at a dude ranch in the northern part of the state.

About as far from me as he can get, I thought. But I had only been to the ranch once, this past spring, to help clean cabins in preparation for the season, so I didn't know where he was or what his schedule looked like.

Suddenly, the rope whipped through my hands as I heard the cry, "Falling!"

"Oh, crap!" I almost panicked. Luckily, the repetition of the first 10 or 15 minutes of belaying had worn a groove in my brain and I automatically closed my hand, shoved my arm against my waist, straightened my legs and pulled the rope in my left hand tightly against my body.

The impact of the fall jolted me to a standing position, but my belay held. No more rope moved through my grip. I could feel the weight of the person below, hanging off my body. The tension rested mostly around my hip bones, and my thighs absorbed the impact.

After a couple of minutes of straining, the rope went slack and I heard the familiar command, "Climbing!" shouted up.

"Whew!" I was relieved. "Climb on!" I called out and began my belay again.

Slowly but surely the climber made his way up the rock. Within 15 minutes of the fall, shoulder-length, golden locks came into view and I recognized Joshua. It suddenly dawned on me how cute he was. Maybe it was the sunlight glinting off his hair or his slow, gentle way of speaking, but when he said, "Off belay," and looked me straight in the eyes, I felt a jolt run through my body that took my breath away.

"Belay off," I replied, feeling shaken. "Are you OK?" I asked him. "I mean, you didn't get hurt when you fell, did you?"

I worried I had not done well with my belaying.

"Don't cha worry none, Luce," he said, his accent suddenly exaggerated. "See?" he showed me his arms where they had scraped the wall. "They're just li'l' bitty scratches. It was my own darned fault for gettin' cocky on that tough section. Good thing you weren't watchin', 'cause I could have been accused of showing off for ya."

Oh, my God! Why hadn't I noticed him before today?

"Hey, Joshua? You through flirting with Lucy and ready to learn how to belay?" Marcus inquired, giving him an elbow to the ribs.

"Well, I'm not done flirtin' with Lucy," Joshua drew the words out slowly. "But I reckon I'd better learn to belay so's someone else can come up those rocks."

I smiled and waved as I turned to head back down to the base. My heart was racing and I don't recall my feet touching the ground.

When I reached the bottom, Ken was most of the way up the climb. Of course, being the athlete he was, this seemed natural to him. He moved steadily, never hesitating, and was over the rim in less than 15 minutes, a team record, the fastest time yet.

Man, he moves well, I thought. I would have liked to have watched his entire climb. I probably could've learned something from him. But I wouldn't have missed those few moments with Joshua, either. I smiled at the memory.

Betty insisted on going next as she wanted Ken to be her belayer. She moved jerkily, making a decision quickly as to where she wanted to place her hands and feet, moving there rapidly and then stopping to determine her next move. Despite the stop-start motion of her climb she actually did very well, only getting stuck for a few minutes on the challenging section that baffled most of us. I was really surprised because she hadn't struck me as particularly sporty.

I was so absorbed in watching Betty that I hadn't noticed Joshua come down the trail to stand behind me. "She's doin' better than I thought she would," he said, voicing exactly what had gone through my own head.

"Yeah," I whispered back to him, keeping my eye on Betty. She soon crested the rim of the wall and disappeared from sight.

That left only three climbers. Evan's leg was still painful from his fall earlier in the day, so he chose not to go. Marcia was much too nervous to allow Betty to belay her, so Steve went next.

He was beautiful to watch. Young and athletic, he instinctively knew where to place his hands and his feet, moving with an ease I was envious of. He looked like a dancer on the rock.

"I'll bet he's climbed a lot of times before," Joshua said in my ear, his breath sending shivers throughout my body.

"Maybe," I said. "Even if he hasn't, he is amazing to watch. Somehow, his moves are both conservative and explosive. I would love to be able to climb like he does one day."

"I bet you could," Joshua whispered, looking at me admiringly.

I couldn't think or speak, so I kept my eyes on the rock wall as Steve crossed the top.

"Alright, Marcia," Pedro announced cheerfully. "It's your turn!"

"Yeah, I know," she responded begrudgingly as she moved toward the wall to await the rope from above. Marcia tied in with shaking hands and looked around at our little group with tears in her eyes.

"You can do it!" Toma said encouragingly.

"Yeah, we're all behind you," Joshua added.

"We'll help you find the hand- and footholds," I promised.

"Plus, you have the best belayer," said Betty, rounding the corner. I hadn't even noticed she wasn't with us, I was so caught up in witnessing Steve's climb.

"Well, here goes," Marcia said. She took a deep, calming breath, then she shouted, "On belay!"

"Belay on!" came the reply from Steve.

"C...c...climbing!" she called out, barely loud enough for us to hear her.

"You have to shout it," Betty prodded. "Otherwise, your belayer won't hear and will just keep waiting for you."

"Climbing!" Marcia called out more strongly.

"Good girl!" I cried, trying to fortify her.

Marcia tentatively placed her hands on the wall. Tears streamed down her face. "I'm so afraid," she whispered to herself. Her legs and back shook as quiet sobs ran through her body.

"You can do it!" Toma shouted again.

"Steve won't let you fall," I said.

"Look above you to the left," Ken said calmly. Marcia looked up. "See that protruding rock?" She nodded her head. "Great," Ken said. "Reach up with your left hand and grab a hold of it." She did. "Now," Ken continued calmly. "Glance down toward your feet. Do you see that line of rock running across the face about six inches above the ground?" Again she nodded. "Excellent. Now place your right foot on the ledge created by the line of rock."

Marcia did as she was instructed, one foot up on the rock, knee bent and her left hand outstretched above her head.

"Now, before you straighten your right leg, look at the rock around where your left knee is now. You'll see a crack about three inches wide."

She looked down and nodded her head.

"Fantastic," Ken coached. "That is where you will put your left foot once you straighten your leg. Always remember to have three points of contact on the rock at all times. In other words, move just one extremity at a time. One hand or one foot. Second, use your legs; they are much stronger than your arms. So look for solid footholds and use your hands and arms for balance.

"Ready?" Ken asked and Marcia nodded. "Great, then straighten your right leg and lift yourself up to the spot where you can put your left foot in the crack."

Marcia tried once but didn't really commit herself to it and she slipped back to the ground.

"Come on, Marcia!" Everyone was doing their best to encourage her now.

She tried a second time and again slipped back. I could see the frustration returning to her face. Then, a look of determination overcame her features and she boldly straightened her leg and jammed her left foot into the crack.

"Yeah! You did it!" Toma shouted.

A smile broke across Marcia's face and she began to look at the rock wall inches from her nose to see where else she might find a place to hold on.

"One more detail," Ken said, "and I think you've got it. Sometimes you have to stick your butt out toward us."

Joshua and Toma both giggled at that idea, and we could see Marcia blushing.

"Not so we can get a better view of your rear," Ken laughed, "but so you can get a better view of the rock. You can't see much when your nose is pressed up against granite."

We could see Marcia mulling the idea over and then she quickly pressed her body away from the rock. The next thing we knew, she had found half a dozen holds in a row and swiftly moved about 10 feet off the ground.

I think it abruptly dawned on her where she was, because at about the same instant we all recognized how well she was doing, she froze up and a look of sheer panic crossed her face. Her legs started shaking violently, a reaction I later learned was called sewing-machine legs.

She could neither move up nor down. Tears started streaming down her face again. Poor Steve was up top holding all of her weight on the rope as she stood there, paralyzed.

"You're doing great, Marcia," Pedro called up. "What's going on for you now?"

"I'm afraid I am going to fall," she moaned.

"I understand," he replied. "Have you fallen yet?" he asked gently.

"No, but I'm higher up now," she said.

"I see," said Pedro. "You feel you have more to risk now?"

"Yes, I guess," responded the frightened woman.

"Do you want to test the rope and see if it will hold you?" Pedro inquired.

"No," Marcia cried out, her voice rising in panic. "No, I just want to come down," she pleaded.

"How are you going to do that?" Pedro queried. "It's much harder to down-climb than it is to ascend."

"But I'm almost to the point where everybody fell!" she wailed.

"Now, Marcia," Pedro said compassionately. "Not everyone fell on their climb. Call 'tension' up to your belayer, Marcia," Pedro commanded.

"T...t...t...tension," she called out hesitantly.

"Remember at the base when you were indecisive? Do you recall how you couldn't even get on the rock until you firmly resolved you were going to climb and then it was easy?"

She inclined her head in acknowledgment.

"It is the same here. Once you become unsure of yourself and vacillate in your commitment, the same wall that was user-friendly a second ago becomes scary and too challenging. It has a lot to do with your mindset.

"Are you with me?" he asked. "Do you trust me?"

She nodded to both questions.

"OK," Pedro continued. "You are going to demand tension from your belayer. Once the rope is taut, you are going to let go of all your hand- and footholds. You are going to dangle freely so you can learn to trust your belayer as well as yourself. Can you do that?"

I could see Marcia take another big, deep breath before she gave a resigned nod of her head. Another deep breath and she called out firmly, "Tension!"

I saw the rope tighten up and she let go of the rock. She slipped about three inches, bounced against the rock face and dangled there briefly. Then a big grin split her face and she swung herself around to face the rock once again.

She jammed her toes into a crack and grabbed a protuberance near her head. Her feet found a new place to land; she straightened her legs and swung her right hand above her to thrust it into a vertical crack. Suddenly she was moving methodically up the rock and before we knew it, she pushed herself over the top.

"Yeah! She did it!" Toma exclaimed and we all breathed a sigh of relief for her. Before long, Marcia came bounding around the corner with Steve following her. Her smile was nonstop. "I've never done anything like that before," Marcia gushed.

"You did really well," I congratulated her.

"Nice work, everyone," Pedro said. "Take a break for lunch, and while you're eating, Marcus and I are going to set up the rappel line."

We grabbed our gear and sat down in the sun.

"Oh, yeah," I said. "We're going to rappel next."

"I can't wait," Joshua enthused next to me.

"I can," Betty groaned. "It was hard enough climbing up but to hurtle myself through space—I'm not sure I can do it."

"You don't hurtle yourself," Steve said. "You just walk down the wall. Like Spider-Man, only you have a rope."

"I've never done it before," James admitted. "But I've watched people do it off the rocks called the Flatirons in Boulder. Looks like fun."

"I think I might actually enjoy it," Marcia said as she nibbled on her crackers. "When Pedro asked me to just hang there, I immediately felt really safe and secure. It was weird. Once I had tested the belay and knew I could trust it, the climb became easy."

"I hope you're right," I said. "I'm pretty nervous about rappelling."

We ate in companionable silence, waiting for Pedro and Marcus to return. We were nearly finished when they did.

"Wrap it up," Pedro said. "It's a short walk to the site and we want to make sure there is plenty of time for everyone to give it a go."

It was a 15-minute hike, uphill again, to the top of a ridge. Looking east, the slope was steep but relatively gradual. That was the way we had just come. However, looking west we could see the start of a cliff and then nothing but the ground below. Marcus was down there waving up at us.

"What we have here, gang, is an 80- to 90-foot rappel. You can see we have the rope tied off to the large ponderosa pine tree to the left and another anchor set around that enormous boulder to the right. When setting up a rappel, it's vital that your anchors are secure. I don't like to use two trees, because what if one comes loose because the soil is shallow and the roots have not sunk deep enough? Would you trust a second tree just a few feet from the first?" Pedro asked us, looking around the circle as we all shook our heads. "I wouldn't, either, and I don't," he said. He continued, "We have about 30 feet of rock face and then about 50 feet of free rappel below an overhanging ledge."

I heard Ken whistle under his breath and saw Joshua dancing slightly with anticipation. I stifled my own groan.

"When it is your turn to descend," Pedro went on, "You will clip into the descending device. Your brake hand, the hand you used in the same way when you were the belayer, will grab the rope underneath you, behind your butt and upper thighs. Its job is to slow or stop your descent. Your other hand will follow along the rope above the descender. Its main purpose is to help you maintain balance. You will set your feet wider than shoulder width apart and walk backward toward the cliff. When you reach the edge, you will stop walking momentarily and lean backward. This is the scariest part for most people. You have to trust yourself."

I saw panic in nearly everyone's eyes. Only Ken, Steve and James looked calm and collected. Both Joshua and John were practically panting with excitement while the women looked slightly sick, although Toma seemed less so than the rest of us.

Little outdoor freak, I thought crossly to myself.

"Once you are almost perpendicular to the rock wall," Pedro kept on, "you will continue walking backward down the wall. At the overhang, you'll do the same as you did at the start of the cliff over there. You'll stop and lower your upper body until your hands are below the lip of the overhang so you avoid smashing them into the rock when you step off into space. Then, you'll walk off just like you did up here. Once you are free descending, just use your brake hand to slow your rate of descent until you reach the bottom where Marcus is. Marcus will help you unclip once you are stable at the bottom. Then, it's just a matter of waiting off to one side and encouraging your other team members on their rappel.

"Any questions?" Pedro asked.

"Can I go first?" Marcia inquired.

"I don't see why not," smiled our instructor, beaming with pride at her newfound courage.

Marcia walked smartly to the rope and followed Pedro's instructions precisely. Once she was clipped in, she straddled the rope, grabbed on below her butt with her right hand, and lightly held on with her left hand above the figure-of-eight descender. She began walking backward, grinning from ear to ear.

At the cliff's edge, she stopped and leaned out into space before starting to walk again. And that was it! She dropped out of sight. I wanted to run to the edge to watch her but Pedro had asked us not to approach the ledge out of safety for the climbers; we could knock rocks off the edge and hit the person on the rope, as well as for our own sake, because someone could slip and fall to their death.

I wondered if she had reached the overhang and how she had managed to get over that obstacle. Sooner than I could have imagined, I heard Marcus shout, "Off rappel. Up rope!" and the next person in line, Joshua, of course, hauled the rope up, hand over hand.

"I wonder how it went for Marcia," I said to Toma.

"I'm sure it went well," she replied. "There were no cries for help and it didn't take her long at all. I don't think it's too bad."

"I hope not. I'm getting a stomachache just thinking about it," I smiled weakly.

Joshua was bouncing up and down on his toes as he clipped in. His boyish enthusiasm made him appear even younger than he was. In less than a heartbeat he was walking backward over the edge. He caught my eye just before he went over and waved nonchalantly with his left hand. "Au revoir, cherie," he called out, and then disappeared from sight.

James went next, then Betty. I was getting anxious so I asked if I could go after her.

When it was my turn, I clipped in. My heart was beating in my ears, threatening to deafen me. My hands were sweaty and my breathing grew shallow again.

Breathe, I commanded myself. *Calm down. If Betty and Marcia can do it, you can, too.*

"Ready, Luce?" Pedro asked.

I nodded and started walking backward. The rope slid slowly through my hand.

OK, this isn't so bad, I thought, and then the cliff's edge loomed up behind me.

"Oh, God," I groaned as I stopped and started leaning backward into space. My mind said: *This is it. I'm going to die!*

Then, as if I had done it all my life, my feet started walking once I was perpendicular to the wall. My brake hand slid easily and controlled along the rope, the figure of eight putting so much tension on the rope I nearly had to jiggle it to make it move a bit more quickly.

This is fun! I could do this all day!

Then, the overhang appeared.

OK, I said to myself, stopping and planting my feet at the edge. *Just keep leaning backward until your hands are even with the lip.*

"There's nothing below me but air," I called out, nearly panicking. Fortunately, my grip on the rope below the descender was firm and steady. Just as I started to feel like I was going to be upside-down on the rope, I let my feet slip over the edge and I was immediately uprighted.

There I was, dangling 40 feet above the forest floor with Joshua, Marcia, James, Betty and Marcus all cheering me on.

"Yeah! Way to go, Lucy! Woohoo! Good job!" they called out.

I felt like a hero arriving home after a battle as I landed.

"Off rappel!" I called up happily to the top of the cliff. I untied my rope and went to join the others. I felt strong, powerful and brave.

No one had any trouble with the rappel and in no time at all, we were gathered at the foot of the cliff, ready to return to our camp.

Chapter Twenty-Four

The hike back to camp was almost boring after the climb. Everything went smoothly. Evan's leg was better, so he was limping less. Betty let go of her dictatorial style of leadership and allowed someone else to look at the map; they discovered a bridge crossing the stream about a half-mile downriver. It meant more hiking but without the risk of someone else getting hurt or Evan re-injuring himself trying to cross the log again.

We were all exhausted when we arrived at camp, so dinner was simple. I could tell Pedro wanted to talk about the day's experiences, but he deferred to the fact that we were walking zombies and let us turn in right after we ate.

I slept peacefully all night. No river talk to awaken me and no nightmares about climbing or rappelling. I had thoroughly enjoyed the day. It hadn't been a difficult climb, but for someone with no prior experience and no upper-body strength, I felt like I had done well. Rappelling had been a blast. I loved the free-hanging section when we went over the lip of the overhang. The descender made the journey smooth, and the effort didn't require any real strength. I had also enjoyed the belaying of another climber. I felt empowered having actually stopped Joshua from falling and hurting himself.

With peace of mind and tired muscles, I slept until Pedro's call, "Wake up, campers!"—which seemed to come much too early. "Ugh!" I groaned, feeling spots in my arms and shoulders I never realized actually had muscles.

Oh, good, my legs are sore, too, I thought as I crawled out of the tent into the bright Colorado morning air.

I heard groans and moans from the other team members and was sure Evan felt especially sore today.

"How's it goin'?" Joshua drawled close by my ear.

I nearly jumped out of my skin. Once again I hadn't realized he was standing so close behind me. I guess I had been caught up, gazing at the beauty of the peaks surrounding our campsite, their pristine, clear summits standing stark in the crisp, cold air. The atmosphere was so unspoiled the summits appeared to be just feet away, rather than miles distant. It took my breath away, or maybe it was Joshua? No matter, I was breathless.

"Um, good, I think," I replied, stretching tentatively. Then I added, "How are you? How are the scrapes and bruises from yesterday?"

"Well," he started slowly. "I've been better and I've been worse."

He showed me his forearms where they had scraped the wall. They were bruised and cut. It looked painful.

"Ouch," I said sympathetically.

"Yeah, but you should see the bruise on my thigh," he winked and smiled. I blushed.

"Breakfast is served!" The call came from the kitchen, saving me from my growing awkwardness.

I swore that I would not fall in love on this trip. I had Mack back home, or at the ranch, somewhere, waiting for me. We had plans to get together after my course. I was going to be a waitress at the ranch for a few weeks before I headed off to college so we could be together, and I was looking forward to that time. At least I thought I was.

Oh, man, said the little voice in my head. *This could get confusing.*

After breakfast, Pedro wanted to debrief us on yesterday's climb before we headed out.

"Although we don't have time for a long discussion this morning, there are some points I want you to consider throughout the day," he started as team members groused imperceptibly.

"I know, I know," Pedro smiled his gorgeous smile. "You all want to hit the trail knowing it's a hard day."

How could he misinterpret our grumbling, knowing the groans came from both sore muscles and the reluctance many of us still felt for self-reflection?

"We experienced a major event yesterday," he continued. "For some of you it will be a pivotal moment that you'll look back upon your whole life, so some reflection is important. Thus, I want you to think as you walk today." More groans. Sometimes it felt like Pedro was giving us homework!

"I know. I know. It's kind of like dribbling a basketball and chewing gum at the same time for some of you. No matter! I want you to think of rock climbing or rappelling as a metaphor. It could be a metaphor for your life, life in general, life and death, or anything else you want. Tonight, I want you to be ready to talk about what yesterday's activity meant for you."

Marcus took up the leadership at that point. "Alright, gang. Listen up. We're here," he said, pointing to his map, "in the West Fork drainage. We need to get to Stony Pass this evening. If you look here," he jabbed his finger at the piece of paper and continued, "we came this way. It took us three days of hiking. So we can't take that route back and expect to arrive to Stony Pass tonight, right?"

We nodded our heads although I could see Marcia was a bit lost.

"So," he went on. "We will have to cross one of these passes by Sheep Mountain. The one to the west is the most logical choice because it's less steep and brings us closer to Stony Pass than the others."

It made sense to me but I was having a hard time focusing because Joshua was pressing up against me in order to see the map. My heart thumped in my chest as my body brushed up against his.

"Get yourselves packed up and head up the trail," I heard Marcus saying as I came back to reality. "Who is the leader today?" he asked.

"Evan is," Toma answered before Evan could say anything.

"Yeah, I'm the leader," he said.

"Great," said Marcus. "Stick to the trail until you reach the valley leading up to the pass. Do you know which one we plan to cross?"

"Yes, I do," Evan said pointing to the fourth, unnamed valley upriver from where we were camped.

"Good," Marcus nodded. "Pedro and I will scout on ahead to make sure we can cross the pass we have in mind. We'll meet the group somewhere up ahead on the trail."

We watched the two leaders take off just as we finished packing up.

"Let's get going, guys," Evan called out. "There's sure to be snow on the pass and we want to get there before it is too soft."

"That's for sure," I grumbled, struggling to get my pack on.

"Let me help you with that," Joshua smiled as he lifted my 50-pound load so I could easily slip into the straps.

"Thanks," I said as I adjusted the waist belt tight and hunched my shoulders to settle the pack into place.

"Can I walk with you, Lucy?" he asked, putting on his own pack.

"That would be great," I said.

"How's your leg, Evan?" Steve asked.

"It's stiff and sore," he replied. "But I'll make it. That's another reason we've got to get started. I'll be walking slower today."

And we started out. Evan had Marcia walk in front with him right behind her since they were the two slowest hikers, he because of his bruised legs from yesterday's climb, and she because she was out of shape.

Our pace was leisurely, so Joshua and I could talk. He told me about his brothers and sisters back in Georgia, six of whom were older than he and two who were younger. I couldn't imagine living in a family of nine siblings and thought it must have been chaotic.

He seemed to have read my mind because he mentioned that it was often crazy in his house with the noise and everyone trying to get their parents' attention, especially back when most of the kids were younger. Now that nearly everyone was in their 20s and out of the house, it was better. He explained that it was the insanity that led him to become a musician. Music had been his solace during the hectic days of his youth.

I told him about my struggles with being so unpopular in junior high and my challenges with boyfriends in high school. "It sounds to me like you've been lookin' for love in all the wrong places," he said, grinning, as we stopped for a snack. We'd hiked about three miles and were resting at the juncture where we'd turn left and start up the valley toward the pass.

"Yeah, I suppose you're right," I said.

"How's everyone doing?" Evan asked as we passed around some cookies and sipped from our water bottles.

"Good," we all called out.

"I'm not good," Betty grouched. "I'm getting a blister on my left heel."

"So am I," I mumbled to Joshua. "But you don't hear me complaining."

"Take off your boot and sock, Betty," Steve instructed. "We have some moleskin in the first-aid kit. Let's get some on that hot spot before it gets worse."

We rested while Evan and Steve took care of Betty. "I think she just wanted the attention," I said to Joshua and Toma as we sat. "Probably," Joshua agreed. "Don't we all?"

"Yeah. OK. You're right," I said reluctantly. "She just gets on my nerves with all her complaining and whining."

"I know," Toma said. "You'd think she'd have learned by now that your attitude makes all the difference between a good experience and a bad one."

"I think she gets everything she wants back home," Joshua said. "So maybe she hasn't had the chance to learn that lesson."

"Maybe," Toma replied thoughtfully.

"Alright, gang," Evan called out, imitating Pedro. "Let's keep moving. I haven't seen Pedro and Marcus yet."

We started up the right-hand side of the canyon following a faint trail that wasn't marked on our maps. It was a lovely walk. The stream burbled beside us as we meandered through an old-growth forest. Strands of gray-green moss hung from the branches like party streamers.

"They call them 'old man's whiskers,'" Toma said when she saw me fingering them. "Supposedly they grow thickest on the north side of the trees."

"Hmm," I said, inhaling the musky scent of the forest.

Before long we came out of the trees, the bowl before us opening up in snow-covered glory. Marcus and Pedro's footprints stood out clearly, so we followed them.

As the trail got steeper and the sun climbed higher in the sky, the snow grew softer. We were now sinking up to our ankles and it was getting slushier by the minute. We gradually worked our way up into the higher reaches of the valley. The pass was clear ahead of us. We were almost there.

Probably another hour of slogging through this, I thought, sweat streaming down the sides of my face despite the bandana I had tied across my forehead.

Suddenly, James cried out, "Hey! Isn't that Marcus up ahead?"

We had all been so intent on watching where we placed our feet, we hadn't been looking up. Now as we all did so, we saw James was right. Marcus was about a quarter of a mile above us, shouting and waving his arms.

"What's he doing?" Marcia asked.

"I don't know," Evan said. "Maybe we should stop here and see what he wants?"

"I can go on ahead if you would like me to," Steve volunteered.

"I guess that would be OK," Evan agreed. "We can see you the whole way up and you are our fastest walker."

Steve left his pack with us on the snow and started on up the path. Marcus was still shouting and waving his hands; however, his voice and actions became hysterical once Steve left the group and continued up on his own. Marcus began to run down the trail.

"What the heck?" Ken said.

"Something's wrong," Marcia said, worry creasing her brow.

"Yeah," I agreed. "Something is definitely wrong."

"I wonder what it is?" Toma said.

"I don't know," said Joshua. "But we're about to find out."

"Where's Pedro?" I wondered.

Marcus soon caught up with Steve, who had kept on jogging up to meet him. Their exchange was animated, with Marcus doing a lot of hand-waving. We saw Steve nod and then he turned around and began running back down toward us.

"It's a slab avalanche!" he shouted as he approached.

"What?" John said. "I don't see any avalanche."

"It hasn't happened yet," Steve panted as he gasped for breath. "Pedro fell through the snow about a quarter of a mile up the trail. He was post-holing, but when his feet fell through, there was nothing underneath him but running water."

"What's that mean?" Betty demanded.

"It means," Ken said, "that there is a big slab of snow sitting on top of more snow with a layer of air and water in between. Like a big layer cake. The problem is, the cake is tilted sideways and the top layer is perched on the bottom layers. It's no longer attached to the bottom layers except along the edges."

"So," Steve interjected. "If 12 of us start walking on it, it's likely to break apart and start a massive avalanche with us in it."

"Oh, my God!" Marcia cried out. "We've got to get out of here!"

"Where's Pedro?" I asked.

"He's OK," said Steve. "He was just taking a breather after falling through and getting soaked while Marcus came down to stop us from getting on the slab."

"So what do we do?" asked Evan.

"We turn around, go back down to the trail and take another valley up to a different pass," Steve said as everyone gave a collective groan, thinking about the two hours of hiking we had just wasted. "Marcus and Pedro will join us shortly."

We turned around and started backtracking along our path. We had just entered the trees again when we heard a deafening roar. The ground shook like we were having an earthquake.

"What's that?" Betty asked.

"It's the slab!" Ken called out over the noise and gestured toward the left. Fortunately, our trail at this point was well above the stream, because as we looked where he pointed, we saw tons of snow and ice roaring to a stop like a freight train slamming on its brakes below us.

"Thank God we got out of there in time," Marcia said, breathing a sigh of relief.

"You can say that again," said James as we all imagined the worst. No one was complaining about the extra hiking now.

"Do you think Pedro and Marcus are OK?" she asked.

"I don't know," Ken said.

"I hope so," she looked worried. We all were.

"There they are!" Evan shouted with relief and we all looked where he was facing. There in the trees above us, Marcus and Pedro were descending toward us. We all gave a collective sigh of relief. "We're OK! Let's get going, gang!" Pedro called out as he approached. "We have a lot of extra miles to cover today."

We retraced our route to the main trail and backtracked downhill to the next, wide valley. This one led right to the shoulder of Sheep Mountain.

"We'll try to contour around the upper section of the mountain and get back as close as possible to where we would have crossed the first pass," Pedro said when we took a quick break.

"There's a wide, gentle pass to the west once we get above this ridge," he indicated the narrow, steep hillside running to the right of us. "And this drainage is wider so there is only a slim chance of running into another slab or any other avalanche danger," he added, seeing Marcia and Betty's looks of concern.

"Let's keep moving, guys," Evan called out encouragingly. "We have a long way to go."

It wasn't a hard climb, although the snow was getting soft near the top. We were sinking in up to our knees in places, but following in the footsteps of the person ahead of us made it much easier to walk.

Although Evan was the leader, Steve, Ken and James all took turns breaking trail, making the going more manageable for the rest of us. We finally made the pass just after midday and stopped for lunch.

The view was fabulous, with the rocky summit of Sheep Mountain looming over us. A brisk breeze blew so we took shelter among a group of boulders about the size of Porta Potties. They made great backrests and looked vaguely like a miniature Stonehenge. We were leaning against them, quietly munching our crackers, cheese and sardines, when Toma suddenly looked up and pointed behind us. She didn't say a word, but her body was electrified and we felt her excitement across the gap between us.

I turned and there, less than 20 feet away, were a female mountain goat and her kid. Their shaggy white coats were dense and ragged, and they looked solemnly in our direction. "Keep still," Pedro whispered. "They will come closer. They are very curious creatures."

So we sat silently watching the pair observe us. After several minutes, the nanny lay down among the rocks, resting yet maintaining a wary eye on us humans. Her kid, however, just like a cat, let curiosity get the best of it. Slowly it made its way toward our little group, creeping forward, halting and then bolting back a few feet only to repeat the process until he was within five feet of Betty.

Betty looked torn halfway between terror and inquisitiveness. If Pedro hadn't been nearby, providing reassurance that this creature was not about to eat her alive, I think she would have jumped up and run down the mountain.

As it was, we watched the young goat tease us for 15, maybe 20 minutes before Pedro announced, "We have to get going, gang, if we are to make it to camp before dark. As it is, we may not go as far as we had hoped."

We got up, stretched and began our trudge around the mountain, trying to keep as high as possible to avoid losing altitude only to have to hike back uphill again. It was treacherous walking. We had no trail to follow, just the contours of the land. The snow was slushy by this time, and we were walking on a steep angle. No matter what, our feet kept slipping out from under us as we plodded along.

Soon we were all soaked. It could have been fun had we been going downhill. We could have taken advantage of the slippery snow and glissaded down like the other day, but no, here we had to avoid going downhill. It sucked. I had a tension headache from concentrating on not sliding down the hill and my right leg hurt from always being the one uphill. A nasty blister was indeed forming on my heel. The only saving grace was that it was a beautiful, warm, sunny day so even though I was wet from head to toe, I wasn't cold.

After a torturous hour, we finally began our descent. We used the same sliding technique as a couple of days ago, using our boots like toboggans and our ice axes as rudders. In what felt like a matter of minutes, the snow had run out and we were back to walking on dirt.

I realized we were on a four-wheel-drive road. Because this was the south side of the mountain, the snow had melted much more quickly than it had on the north slope. There were just scattered patches of the white stuff with lots of rivulets, small streams and waterfalls showing how quickly it was melting.

Our morale dropped low as we slogged down the long, muddy road. I could see Evan and Marcia both limping at the front of the line. Betty grumbled to herself behind me when Toma began to sing in an effort to cheer everyone up.

It wasn't long before I joined her in an old Girl Scout camping song: "If I had a wagon I would go to Colorado, go to Colorado." Singing at the top of my lungs while trying to keep walking uphill was more challenging than I had anticipated, and I was out of breath before I knew it. I kept trying to sing, gasping for air every few words, "Chevy...drive to...drive to Colorado. Airplane...fly to Colorado...where a man can walk a mile high."

It worked, though. When Toma and I finished, Joshua and Evan took up with John Denver's "Rocky Mountain High." They especially liked the part about sitting 'round the campfire, getting high, so they sang it extra loudly. Everyone's spirits lifted and the walking felt easier. Soon everyone was offering up a favorite hiking song.

We finally reached the top of the pass around 7 p.m. We were all done in, every last one of us. Evan figured we had hiked about 11 miles with nearly 4,500 feet in total elevation gained, lost and regained. Our legs ached. My blister had broken open and made a bloody mess inside my coffinlike boots. Little bits of my sock, which also had a hole worn through it, stuck to the flesh. They hurt like heck to pull free from the wound. Yuck!

Dinner was a quick, cold affair. No one wanted to cook. Plus, the clouds had built up and it started to rain just as we dove into our tarps.

There weren't any trees up on the pass at 12,600 feet so we had to use our ice axes to anchor the corners of the tents. This meant our tarps were about two feet off the ground. This was a good thing as the wind had begun to howl, sending the rain pelting sideways. Lucky for me, I was in the middle of the dog pile under the flapping nylon contraption.

Somehow Joshua had ended up next to me in the tarp. As others drifted off to sleep, I could feel him nudging his bag closer to mine, spooning me from behind. My heart pounded so loudly I was certain it would wake Evan, who was snoring softly on my other side. I could also hear Steve grunting and gurgling on the other side of Joshua but I didn't know if Toma was asleep yet or not.

It was the first night, though, that Joshua and I slept snuggled together. And it was the first night I was not cold at all.

The next morning dawned gray and overcast. It had rained all night and most of our gear was soaked. Everyone was sore and miserable as we crawled out of the tents. Everyone, that is, except me. I wanted to sing and dance or at least skip down the trail.

Breakfast was another cold, hurried affair, just like dinner the night before. We were running out of supplies and needed this resupply day desperately. Pedro and Marcus had left camp before sunrise, so we were on our own. Our objective was to meet them around noon at the resupply spot. Although it was my day to lead, because I had gone to bed right after our evening meal, John had apparently taken my spot.

"Sorry, Lucy," he said. "Pedro was looking for you last night but you were already in your tent."

"I wasn't asleep," I said, feeling let down, disappointment clouding my happy feelings. "I didn't hear any call for me."

"I can let you lead if you insist," John said grudgingly. "I just need to show you where we're going to meet Pedro and Marcus."

"That's OK. I'll lead tomorrow." I instantly felt pissy, much like the weather.

"We don't have to pack up," John told the team. "We'll return to this campsite tonight. All we have to do is pack out our trash from the week and take the stoves and fuel bottles down to be refilled. Everything else can stay here."

"That sounds good," Evan said gratefully, rubbing his lower back. "I'm still sore from falling on that stupid log."

We had two large, stinking bags of trash. Ken would carry one and John had the other.

While everyone was organizing themselves, I saw John and Joshua walk over the top of the pass to the far side. Curious, I went to follow them.

When I topped the ridge, it became clear what they were up to. John had his hands cupped around a small flame and it looked like Joshua was trying to light a cigarette.

"Hey, Luce," he called out when he saw me approaching. "Come on over," he beckoned.

I shook my head. I knew what they were doing. They were trying to light a joint.

Good luck in this wind, I thought.

I didn't want any part of it. I hadn't smoked any pot since graduation night and I was feeling more healthy and clear-headed every day. Smoking weed was something I never had really enjoyed but I kept doing it because Mack did. Now that I was away from him, there was no incentive to go back to smoking. My lungs and my body felt cleaner.

I waved at the two boys, feeling disappointed in Joshua, and walked back to camp. I hadn't known Joshua smoked pot, although I guess I could have figured it out if I had thought about it. Many musicians did. My happy feelings for him evaporated like mist over the valley.

I stewed about John taking over my leadership day, and me not sticking up for myself, and then my discovery that Joshua smoked pot. Maybe he wasn't the perfect southern gentleman, shining knight I had made him out to be. Perhaps he was just a silly high-school boy.

Great. Now my mood matches this lousy weather, I thought as I angrily kicked a rock out of my way.

When Joshua and John came back to camp, we were all ready to go. I noticed John's backpack looked lighter, less full than before and so I asked Joshua about it.

"Oh, yeah," he said giggling slightly. "We decided the trash was too smelly to carry all the way down to resupply. There was a big snow bank down below where we were with a huge hole at the bottom of it. So John slid the trash down into the hole. No one will ever find it."

He sounded pleased with himself.

I got a funny feeling in the pit of my stomach. We were told to bring out all the trash. Not to leave any trace. That was part of the Outdoor Mountain School legacy. Here, our team had just left half of a week's worth of stinking garbage in the wilderness. It made me ill.

And to top it off, my "boyfriend" had been part of it. That made me even sicker. I couldn't walk beside Joshua that morning as we hiked down to our rendezvous point.

Soon enough the weather changed. By noon it was sunny and bright again with a few fluffy clouds drifting by. The temperature began to rise and by lunch we were all lazing around in the sun waiting for the truck.

Apparently, the road had gotten so muddy from the recent rains that Jonathan, the man who did odd jobs for the course such as driving the resupply truck, was having a hard time getting up the road. We wouldn't know that for a while longer, though, so for the time being we lapped up the sunshine.

Joshua came to sit with me. "Hey, Luce," he said, smiling his beautiful smile, hair all golden in the sunlight. "What's up? You've been distant all mornin'."

"Have I?" I asked, trying to appear innocent and keep the sneer out of my voice.

"Yeah, you have. Didn't you like snugglin' with me last night?"

The memory made me tingle all over again. "Yes, that was nice. I really appreciated being warm for the first time."

"Then what's up?" he insisted.

"I don't know," I said. "I'm feeling disappointed." I fiddled with a stick on the ground, trying to get up the nerve to tell him what was up. He waited patiently. Then I blurted out, "I'm bummed that you smoke pot."

"Whoa, there, girl!" Joshua said. "I don't smoke regularly. John just asked me if I wanted to try some with him today. It's really not my thing."

"Oh," I said, feeling relieved. "OK, but what about the trash? I'm worried that we'll all get in trouble for John throwing it into that snow hole. And besides, that is way beyond littering. It's…" I struggled to find the right word. One that was harsh enough. "It's…well, it's polluting!" I practically shouted the word.

"Settle down, Luce," Joshua said, trying to soothe me. "It's going to be OK. No one will find out."

I had to admit, part of my concern was being found out, even though I had not participated in the wrongdoing. The other part though was a real concern for the wilderness area. Even though my dad had been inconsistent with regard to caring for the environment, some of his well-meaning lessons must have rubbed off on me because I was genuinely worried about that big ugly plastic bag of trash.

"I don't know," I told Joshua after a moment of brooding. "I just hate to think of us hiking along some beautiful trail after all the snow has melted and coming across a big sack of stinking garbage. It would really spoil the experience for me."

"Yeah, I hadn't really thought of that," he admitted. "We were just feeling lazy after the joint and John didn't want to have to carry the bag. It was dripping and smelly and heavy."

"He should have asked someone else," I said sarcastically, not feeling a bit generous toward either of them at the moment. I also felt conflicted. What was I going to do when Pedro and Marcus joined us again? Should I tell them and betray my friend? Where did my loyalty lie—with the wilderness and telling the truth, or with my friend?

"Are you starting your period or something?" Joshua asked me. "I mean you're really cranky. You seem to be having PMS." It was the first mean comment I had heard him make toward anyone the whole week and it hurt my feelings.

Wow, I was getting to see a completely different side of him that I didn't like. Suddenly I missed Mack. He was my best friend as well as my boyfriend, and August couldn't come soon enough now. I got up and walked over to where Toma and Marcia were sitting.

Just after I sat down, we heard an engine gunning in the distance and Jonathan showed up with the new supplies. Hallelujah! Everyone jumped up in a flash to help him unload the truck. Then we had our first fresh lunch in a week—one that didn't include a single can of sardines! It was the best meal I had eaten in days. Sitting in the sunshine, I felt sleepy waiting for Pedro to finish his meeting with Bruce. I lay with my head on a rock, soaking in the warmth and hoping I was getting a tan.

I had begun to doze off when Pedro came storming into our little spot. "Everyone gather around," he ordered.

"Uh-oh," I said to Toma. "He's unhappy about something."

"Yeah, he looks a little scary," she said.

He did look furious. His eyes glinted, his hair stood out in all directions and he was breathing hard.

"There are a couple of things we have to discuss," he growled, looking around at us.

I snuck a look sideways at Joshua and John, who were sitting together, attempting to look nonchalant. "Does anyone have a clue as to what has me so upset?" Pedro demanded angrily.

Everyone looked around at each other.

Oh, man, I thought. *Here we go. Do I rat out Joshua and John or keep what I know to myself? Will they confess? If they don't, what do I do?*

I was starting to panic, so I took a deep breath and sat up straight in an effort to compose myself.

"No one has any idea?" Pedro asked again, his rising voice indicating his anger.

"OK, I will tell you," he said loudly. "What really has me upset is that I have noticed in your groups that most everyone is depending on three women to do all the work, especially the cooking, cleaning, latrine maintenance and organizing the group."

"OK, that's not what I was expecting," I whispered to Toma.

"Me, neither," she whispered back.

"Lucy, Toma and Marcia are getting the brunt end of all the chores. I don't know about you men, but I am embarrassed by your lack of chivalry and ability to take care of yourselves. These ladies are not your mothers," his voice started rising again at the end as he lost control of his feelings.

Chapter Twenty-Four

"Wow," I said quietly as the rest of the team turned to look in our direction.

"Pedro," Toma started, and then stopped to look at me for courage.

"We don't have a problem doing extra work," she said. "None of us complained about it."

"Yes, I know, but you should have," he said angrily. "Marcus and I have been observing the group even when we weren't with you. It is part of our job as we prepare you for the expedition phase of the program."

I breathed a sigh of relief. Good ol' brave Toma. She just let everyone know we hadn't told on anyone. I was eternally grateful and yet simultaneously ashamed of myself for not speaking up.

"Thanks," I muttered out of the side of my mouth.

"So," Pedro shouted. "I expect from now on that the rest of you will pull your own weight, and then some. Am I clear?"

Everyone nodded. Betty looked unhappy to have been the only female not mentioned among those handling more than their share of the workload.

It was true, though. She would do anything to get out of latrine duty and cooking.

"That brings me to the second situation that has me annoyed," Pedro said, grinding his teeth to keep from shouting, the veins standing out in his forehead and neck. "Anyone want to try and guess what this one is?"

John tentatively raised his hand and Pedro acknowledged him with a nod.

"Well, sir," he started. "You see, Joshua and me," John was practically stuttering at this point. Joshua was sitting stiffly beside him.

"Yes, I know about you guys smoking dope on this trip," Pedro interrupted him irritably. There was a gasp among a couple of the group members but most seemed unsurprised. I guess the boys had done it more than once and others had seen them.

"In general, I am not opposed to occasional recreational marijuana use among adults," Pedro started off. Then his voice began to rise. "However, there is no place for it on an Outdoor Mountain School course. You two have been inconsiderate of the other members of your team!" he yelled, spit flying and his hair getting wilder as anger overtook him. He seemed to mentally wrestle with himself, and then quietly added, "You will be in situations where you must have your wits about you. Your friends' lives could depend on you, and if you are not all there mentally…" he left the last part hanging for a bit.

"Well, let me just say, an accident like what could happen would scar you for the rest of your lives," he ended sadly, his rage leaving as quickly as it came.

"Would the two of you please come over here?" Marcus asked, and Joshua and John stood up to walk over where Bruce, Pedro and Marcus were gathered. They walked farther away from the group and began an animated discussion.

"I think something must have happened to Pedro," I said. "I mean, some sort of accident where someone he was responsible for was seriously hurt or killed as a result of his being stoned or something."

"Yeah, I was thinking the same thing," Toma agreed with me. "Maybe he was involved in that OMS accident on Snowmass Peak."

"He's seems pretty upset by it," Marcia said as she came over to sit with us. "I mean out of proportion to what happened."

"Yeah, he does," I nodded. "I can't imagine what it would be like to be belaying a friend and have them fall to their death or get paralyzed."

"I know. I can't imagine living with that," Toma said.

"I wonder, will he tell us the story sometime?" Marcia asked.

"I don't know, but here they come," I said, looking up at the men who were returning to our gathering. Joshua and John both looked uncomfortable but neither they nor Pedro said anything more.

We finished packing up our backpacks with fresh food and fuel and headed back up to camp. Clouds were moving into the high peaks again, meaning it would probably rain that night. The rest of the day passed in a blur of walking. The team pretty much fell silent following Pedro's outburst. Dinner proceeded quietly and we were off to bed before the rains hit.

I again snuggled with Joshua that night, glad for the warmth but a bit sad at what had transpired. The day's events had clouded my feelings toward him. I was mostly just disappointed. I did want desperately to know what Pedro had said to him and John, but he wasn't sharing. He just seemed to need to be close to someone.

Chapter Twenty-Five

The next week passed without incident. We hiked about six miles each day on average, some days more. We saw no other mountain goats and had no further outbursts. We were jelling as a team. Everyone did the best they could to carry their own weight regarding camp chores, and even Betty was not particularly whiny.

I was happier than I had ever been in my life. The joy of waking up in the morning, just below a high peak or in the forest, and watching the alpine glow light up the rocks and scattered, dwindling snow patches took my breath away. Despite our earlier disagreement over the trash, I had made a friend in Joshua. We were together all day and every night.

We could talk about anything, and we did. He told me about his parents' divorce and how that had devastated him. I told him about my dad's erratic, sometimes abusive nature. He recounted the turmoil he and his mom had gone through when his younger sister had become pregnant last year, and he shared the pride everyone felt when his older sister graduated from the University of Georgia with honors. I described how I had always longed for a sibling and how my cousins never did make the grade. They lived far away in Arizona and because my dad didn't get along with his family we only saw them once every few years.

Walking every day was making me stronger. I didn't realize it at the time but I was losing weight, lots of it. All I knew is that I felt strong and alive, and that I had a sense of being connected to something bigger, which only fueled my growing wonder with the world around me. I smiled a lot and burst out into song spontaneously along the trail, especially when I was the leader or when someone was struggling. I was truly on top of the world.

One night we camped inside an old mining shack at the top of a pass. The wind blew too strongly to keep our tarps down. Plus, we were above tree line, so there really wasn't anything to tie them to. Pedro and Marcus slept outside in their tent. It was pretty cool. There were a few things left in the cabin: an old bunk bed with a chewed-up mattress, a rusted wood-burning stove and a few cans of beans. There was just enough space for all 10 of us to squeeze into the cabin, side by side on the floor.

We were soaked from post-holing all day on the trail. We had climbed up to the Continental Divide and then followed a long, basically flat, snow-covered ridge for miles. As the sun rose in the sky, the snow grew mushier and mushier. By 10 that morning, we were sinking up to our knees in wet, sloppy snow and by noon, it was up to our thighs. The trail-breaker often had to roll over in the snow to get out of the hole, and we changed lead hikers frequently because it was such hard work. We were all exhausted.

We decided as a group to eat a cold dinner and just go to bed. As we lay there listening to the wind howl past the shack, I wondered if it would blow down. I figured it wouldn't because it had been standing as long as it had, but wind was always the weather phenomenon that freaked me out the most. I had been terrified of tornados ever since I was a child visiting my grandparents in Oklahoma. I had never seen a tornado but I had been down in the storm cellar on their farm a few times and that was a creepy enough experience.

It was hard for me to get to sleep that night. I could hear everyone else breathing deeply in the dark. Joshua, of course, slept curled up behind me, cradling me in his arms. Although I still loved Mack, I barely thought of him these days. It was comforting to have Joshua there with me. I doubted he could do anything to save me should a disaster strike, but he was warm and our friendship was strong.

Just as I was about to fall asleep—I had been drifting in and out of a weird dream for a few minutes—I felt Joshua cuddle in closer. I thought he had been asleep. I felt so warm and safe that I didn't move. I kept my breathing even and quiet although my heart was pounding in my ears.

A little voice in my head asked me: *What about Mack?*

Shh! I told the voice. *Who asked you? I'm happy and who knows what Mack is doing at the ranch.*

I pushed away any thoughts about the possibility that I might be betraying my best friend and scootched in closer. Soon I fell asleep, imagining how it might feel to make out and hook up with Joshua.

The next day, I really didn't feel much like being with Joshua so I hiked with Toma. We had to climb the last hundred yards or so to the pass above us, follow a jeep road around the mountain and then cross a second pass before descending back into the forest to prepare for our period of solitude and reflection. It was a long day, but we would have four days of rest following it, so everyone hung in there.

My boots were too large, and even with all the hiking, had never really broken in. I had developed a bleeding, open blister about two inches wide on the back of my left heel. I kept covering it with waterproof tape to keep it from hurting and to prevent it from continuing to tear open.

The big toe on my right foot had jammed into the front of my boot so often and so hard, it felt like walking on a knife every time I brought my foot down on the ground. I kept praying for snow because it didn't hurt when I walked or glissaded on the cold, white stuff. Unfortunately, once we descended the first pass, the snow disappeared, so by the time I limped into camp, I was the last one to arrive and tears were streaming down my face.

The spot Pedro selected as a staging area for our reflection experience was beautiful. A clear mountain stream rushed alongside the jeep trail opposite where we camped so I washed my hair and cleaned up before dinner. The warm sun dried my hair quickly. Joshua came around the bend shortly after I had finished. Maybe he had been watching from afar.

"Hey, Luce," he called out, walking slowly toward me.

"Hey," I said, keeping my head down so as not to show the mixed emotions I was feeling. On one hand, my heart still thrilled to see him, his halo of hair glinting in the warm afternoon light, his boyish face. On the other hand, I felt confused and conflicted about Mack and whether or not my feelings toward Joshua were a betrayal of our relationship.

"Hey," he said again when he drew near where I was gathering up my toiletries. "Do you wanna talk?"

My heart broke open hearing the bewilderment in his voice. He truly had no idea why I was upset or being distant!

"Yeah, you can sit down," I said, gesturing toward a large rock.

"Will you sit by me?" he asked.

"Sure," I said resolutely as I walked over to the rock and hauled myself up onto it.

"You've been ignoring me all day," Joshua said. "What did I do wrong?"

"I'm not sure you did anything wrong," I said, struggling to find a way to say what I was feeling, my fear of his rejecting me or not liking me rising sharply. I stopped speaking and searched my heart for the right words.

"It's just…" I said finally. "I really like you and I love our friendship. At times, I feel I love you and I definitely find you physically attractive. I would love to take our relationship closer but I have a boyfriend at home. His name is Mack and we've been together almost a year now. I feel that I am betraying him every time I cuddle up with you."

There, I had said it with a rush.

I watched his bright, earnest face fall.

"Oh, Lucy," he said sadly, "I understand. I don't want you to feel conflicted. I think you're one of the neatest girls I've ever known and I'd love to take our relationship further, but I don't want to hurt you."

Now my heart was breaking. I had hurt my best friend on this trip and he was so darned understanding.

"I know, Joshua," I said. "Let's try to stick to just being friends for a while. OK?"

"Yeah, that's alright," he said, a small smile lighting up his face again. "You are the best friend I've got here."

"Yeah, I know. You're mine, too," I said.

We walked back to camp and gathered with the group to hear what Pedro had to say about the upcoming days. "Alright, gang," Pedro called out. "Is everyone here?" We nodded as we looked around, making sure the entire team was present.

"The next few days will be different from what you've experienced so far. Tomorrow morning you will begin a three-day period we call reflection. It is a time of contemplation and fasting," Pedro said.

"Fasting!" I heard Evan and Toma exclaim under their breath.

"You will each be given a mini tarp for shelter and Marcus will take you to your reflection site. You must remain at your site for the entire period. Someone will come by daily to check on you and if you are not at the location where we placed you, emergency rescue procedures will be put into action and the cost will be yours to bear."

Marcus took up the instructions, "You can take your sleeping bag and whatever clothing you feel might be necessary. All food items and cooking equipment, stoves, et cetera, will be left here in the main camp. You can take your water bottle and your toiletry items."

"You will also have your journal and writing instruments," Pedro added. "Are there any questions?"

"Yeah," John said a bit belligerently. "What are you going to be doing while we're starving alone in the woods?"

"It is not really important what we will be doing," Pedro answered calmly despite the attack. "Know that we will also be fasting and reflecting. We will also be taking care of course business with Bruce or Susy."

"I still don't like the idea of doing nothing for three days," John said sullenly.

"I understand," Pedro said. "I suggest that you all pay attention to the emotions you go through during this period. Some of you will have strong emotions and you may feel intimidated by them. You will be OK. That's why we check in with you daily. No one has ever died on a reflection event, and nobody has ever been seriously injured, but that is why you must remain in your space. Anyone who does not will be immediately taken off the course, no refunds and no opportunity to participate in the expedition phase, which is most students' favorite part of the course."

"Are there any further questions?" Marcus asked.

"Can we take a book if we have one?" Marcia asked. I remembered seeing her nose in a book on the rare occasion we had extra time on our hands.

"We prefer that you leave your books with the other stuff you'll keep here in camp. The whole point of the reflection is to look inward and if you have your book along, you'll be focused elsewhere."

Marcia nodded, though I could tell she was not excited about the idea of spending three days without food and without anything to distract her. I wasn't too happy either but I trusted Pedro and Marcus and figured OMS had a lot of experience teaching people, so they probably knew best.

Our dinner that evening was tasty but light. Pedro told us that eating a heavy meal just before a fast made it that much more difficult the first day. "Your hunger pains will be sharper and your mental desire for food will be more demanding," he explained.

I slept restlessly that night. Joshua and I slept next to each other but no longer cuddled together. I was worried about the fast but more worried about being alone for three days. What would I do? What if a wild animal came to my campsite? How would I stay warm? These thoughts swirled around my head as I tossed and turned, remembering prior adventures. Even though I was an only child, I had never been completely alone in my life. I was scared.

It was a warm night at this low elevation, and my sleeping bag felt too hot. There was a rock underneath my shoulder and a lump under my hips. I wanted to cuddle by my friend again. Over and over I turned, getting twisted up inside my sleeping bag. Round and round my thoughts chased each other.

I finally fell asleep deeply just before sunrise, only to be awakened by Marcus' call of "good morning." I was dragged out of a bizarre dream involving Mack and Joshua. They were competing in a bull-riding contest, a sport that Mack participated in and Joshua did not. I was the clown who was trying to rescue them when they were bucked off the bull. In my dream, Joshua was just about to mount the biggest, wildest, most fierce bull known on the rodeo circuit, when Marcus' voice penetrated my consciousness. When I awoke, I felt strangely groggy. I shook my head to clear it as I crawled out from under the tarp.

"Rough night, Luce?" Evan asked, glancing at my hair, which stood out in all directions.

"Yeah. I couldn't get comfortable, and I was worried about the reflection period."

"I was, too," he said. "I'm worried about going without food for three days."

"Yeah, I know what you mean," I shook my head and smiled sympathetically at him.

We separated our gear and clothing into two piles, one that we could take with us on the reflection and the larger pile of stuff that would remain here in the base camp. We stuffed all of our reflection gear into large black garbage bags and then we gathered around to have a light breakfast.

"All right, gang?" Pedro asked as we tried to savor our last meal of fresh fruit and yogurt. "How's everyone doing?"

"OK" and "Fine" were the muttered replies. Some of us, including me, didn't answer. I probably would have snarled had I opened my mouth.

"I'm scared of the whole idea," Marcia said.

"That's a perfectly normal response," Pedro assured her. "Marcus and I will be nearby, out of sight, but we will be checking up on you at least once a day."

"I'm not sure I can go three whole days without eating," Evan said and several others, including Joshua and John, nodded their agreement. I wasn't worried about not eating. I had fasted a couple of times last year in an attempt to lose weight. It didn't work, but I knew I could go a few days without food.

"I would like to share with you one of my favorite quotes about being in solitude," Pedro said.

That man sure likes quotes, I thought grumpily.

"It is by a man named John Lubbock; he was an English biologist and politician. He said, 'The whole value of solitude depends upon one's self; it may be a sanctuary or a prison…as we ourselves make it.' So, that will give you something to think about as you spend time alone with yourself. How will you make your reflection experience? Will it be a sanctuary or a prison?" Pedro asked.

I was definitely worried about being alone, although thinking about it, I really shouldn't have been. Without any siblings, I had been basically alone most of my life. But the idea of not having anyone around to interact with, or in case of an emergency, had me worried. That, plus my fear of being cold. What would I do without the pack of humans I was accustomed to sleeping with? How would I stay warm at night?

Pedro had been instructing the team during my reverie because I suddenly became aware again when I heard him say, "Excellent. If we're finished with our meal, let's pack up and head out to our reflection sites. From this moment on, until you return to this camp Monday morning, you are to remain in silence. Remember, this is a time of inward contemplation."

Chapter Twenty-Six

We backtracked along yesterday's route, following the jeep road and the burbling stream that rushed by our base camp. I didn't recognize any of the trails. I guess I had been in more pain from the blisters than I had realized. Maybe that was what was causing my brain fog this morning. Fortunately, it was lifting as we walked.

After about a half mile, Pedro veered off the road and onto a well-trodden trail as he began to lead team members to their reflection sites. Marcia was the first one dropped off. She had a beautiful, grassy spot just out of view from the trail. She seemed happy with her location as she waved goodbye to the group.

John was next. He was dropped off on the opposite side of the trail in a forested area. Back and forth like that it went. One team member to the right of the path, the next settling in on the left.

Joshua was given a site on the far side, then Steve on the river side. *Please, please let me be placed on the side by the river,* I kept repeating in my mind.

Soon, only Toma, Ken and I were left. I was the next one located. I said to myself silently: *Yesss!*

I was to situate myself on the right side of the trail next to the river. My spot was beautiful! The stream meandered here, creating a peninsula with an expansive view of the valley. The tinkling sound of the water soothed my anxious mind. A large boulder jutted out into the stream where I could sit surrounded on three sides by water.

I located a spot for my tarp a little way back from the peninsula in a small valleylike depression that received lots of morning sun. I used the trunks of a small grove of aspen trees to tie off the support ropes, and soft meadow grasses cushioned the level ground nicely. It was perfect! For the first time, I felt less nervous and a little excited for this adventure.

I looked through my pack and organized all my gear, spread out my sleeping bag under the tarp and then went to sit by the water.

So far, so good. Lots of sunshine, no clouds in sight! I observed.

Everything was great for the first hour or so, and then I started to get hungry. As my stomach grumbled and growled, my anxiety level rose. I filled my water bottle and took a deep sip, hoping to stave off the hunger pangs that felt as if my stomach was trying to eat itself.

Looking at the sky, I judged it to be about noon. What the heck was I going to do with myself for the next two-and-a-half days? I was already starving and bored. I supposed I could draw a picture in my journal but artwork had never held much appeal for me.

I pulled out my journal and tried to write about what I was feeling. I really had no idea. There was a vague sense of being angry and being bored plus the ever-present hunger. All I could think of was food. So, I made a list of what I was craving. Pizza. Ice cream. French fries. More ice cream. Thinking about all that food made me even hungrier. It was a good thing no one was around—I would have bitten their head off, I was so crabby.

I stared at the river and it no longer gave me pleasure. I watched the sun cross the sky and suddenly realized it would not be long before my little valley plunged into shadow as the sun passed behind the surrounding mountains. "Crap!" I said out loud, realizing I could say anything I wanted. No one would hear me or complain or tell me to clean up my mouth! I vented, letting loose with a string of curses. I felt better for a while, and then I was bored again.

Plus, now I felt scared. I was deathly afraid of the cold, of that bone-chilling numbness I had experienced on the river only last year.

I wondered to myself: *What would I do if I got hypothermia again? I could die before Marcus or Pedro came through to check up on me.*

I put on my hat, gloves and my jacket, even though the sun was still shining on my camp. I couldn't even admire the beautiful golden afternoon light. I drank more water and as the sun dropped behind the hills, crawled into my tarp and sleeping bag.

It was probably only 4:30 in the afternoon, but I was ready for bed, desperately focused on trying to stay warm. I had already convinced myself I was freezing.

The night was horrible. I had to pee and was afraid to leave the warmth of my sleeping bag. I had all my clothes on again, even though I knew this was not the way to stay warm. I was sweating inside the bag but I was still afraid that I would get colder and not be able to survive the night.

All my childhood fears of the dark came to bear as the night wore on. I didn't have any friends to cuddle with. There was no one around to protect me should a wild creature come around to attack me. I could hear the river and the voices there but this time they were not soothing. They reminded me of aboriginal tribes preparing to attack.

Plus, my hunger had returned. It had left sometime during my afternoon rant and I hadn't even noticed it had gone until it returned with a vengeance in the middle of the night. When it did come back, it came on strong! It felt like my insides would tear themselves apart with their grumbling and roiling. My head hurt and my belly ached.

So, once again, I tossed and turned all night. I worried about not sleeping, even though I could sleep all the next day, if I chose. That thought never entered my mind. I tried counting sheep. I attempted to relax my body, one part at a time beginning with my feet and ending with my head. I tried making a movie in my mind of all the beautiful experiences I could think of, anything to keep me entertained and help me fall asleep. Nothing worked during that endless night.

Fortunately, the sun did finally rise. And as I had suspected it would, the warm rays hit my little enclave early. Despite the chill in the air, I pulled myself out of my bag and tarp and went to sit near my lovely stream.

Ice coated the rocks and the blades of grass on either side of the flow were silvery slick. It was beautiful. Tiny rainbows glinted off the ice as the sun struck it, rising even higher into the sky. At that moment, everything felt right with my world. I felt happy and light. I wanted to dance for joy. It must have been the lack of sleep but I didn't care. I burst out in song and got up to pirouette around my campsite. I was happy to be alive!

I got out my journal and began writing. I wrote of my family and my grandparents, particularly of my granddad, who had died three years earlier. I wrote of the sister I wished I had and of the life I would have in the future. I composed poems about all the feelings I was experiencing and those I had experienced before. I wrote and wrote for hours without a thought to my grumbling stomach. I noticed my belly didn't ache much anymore and that I was hardly thinking of food at all.

The day passed quickly but soon it was afternoon and the sun was sinking behind the mountains again. Damn it! My fears came screaming back to me as soon as the shade hit my little valley. I scurried back into my tarp and my sleeping bag and tried desperately to sleep. I tossed and turned and again made movies out of my life in my mind. I relived my middle-school and high-school days, reviewing the highlights again and making the low points better in my mind's eye. I thought about the crushes and boyfriends I'd had: Kenan, Matt, Stephen, Dean and Mack.

Time passed slowly, but it did pass and eventually darkness fell. I listened to coyotes howl in the distance and hoped I wouldn't die this time. I wished I were brave enough to step outside my tarp and look into the deep night. I wanted to see the millions of stars dotting the inky black sky appearing so close as to be within arm's reach, but I wasn't brave. I hid within my little tent, just waiting and waiting for the night to pass.

The third day dawned clear and beautiful. I had a little routine down by now. I'd get up when the sun hit my tarp and go to the river. I'd wash myself, brush my teeth and brush my hair. Then, I'd lie in the sun for a while, soaking up the heat and warmth after a cold night. I'd write in my journal, then spend hours watching nature around me. I hadn't seen Pedro or Marcus this whole time, although I trusted that they were checking up on us like they said. I just must have been busy when they came by.

That last morning, though, as I wrote in my notebook, I became aware of being watched. I could feel eyes upon me so I looked up from my writing. I was startled to find a black bear gazing at me from up on the hillside.

Oh, God! What am I going to do?

My heart raced and my mind switched into panic mode. I had glanced down as fear tore through me. I remembered my close call with the mountain lion in May but when I looked up again the bear was gone. Instead I saw Marcus standing there looking down at my little campsite. He gave a short nod and a wave and disappeared up the trail.

"OK, that was severely weird," I said, breaking the spell and the still-ness. Yesterday I had gotten into the habit of talking out loud to myself. It made me feel not so utterly alone. Now, however, in my fear and panic, I started jabbering like a magpie. "Where did the bear go? Should I get up and look for it? Was there ever a bear?" I wondered. "Maybe the bear was Marcus. Maybe Marcus is a shape-shifter like some of the shamans of his mother's tribe. God, I hope so. I hope it wasn't a real bear. Or maybe I wish it were. I've never seen a real bear."

Once I heard myself, I thought I sounded like a crazy woman, so I quit talking out loud and returned to writing in my journal. I kept looking up every few minutes but I never saw the bear again, nor did I see Marcus return back down the hill.

After a while, my emotions calmed down and I felt at peace again. It was then I remembered my green washcloth with its treasures. I had taken it out of my pack pocket two days ago to bring with me on my reflection experience but in my worry about the cold and being hungry and alone, I had completely forgotten about it.

Laying my artifacts out on the cloth in the sun, I thought about my life so far.

OK, parts of my childhood weren't all that great, I thought—namely being an only child and Dad's unpredictable behavior when he was drinking, and middle school totally sucked. Despite that, there had been positive moments and highlights. One was Mom starting to intro-duce me to the outdoors through Girl Scouts even though it wasn't her thing. *It certainly looks like it might be becoming mine.* I smiled at the thought. The green cloth stood for another. Although it may not look like a high point on the surface, in fact that day had been one of my real growth experiences. I discovered the kindness of others through the woman the cloth represented. I also got a nudge to start listening to my own inner voice. *Of course there are times I am still working on that one!* I admitted.

In high school everything changed, mostly for the better and mostly because of my involvement with the explorer post. I looked at the piece of granite from my first climb. As I rolled it through my fingers, I remembered not only the pride I felt at having accomplished such a big goal but also the suffering that had gone along with it—the cold and wet and my brush with altitude sickness. Then there was the smooth stone from the Colorado River, one of the west's mightiest and most important rivers. That journey taught me never to give up and, ironically, started my extreme fear of being cold. I lay the stone back down and picked up my last and greatest treasure, the perfect inky arrowhead. *This little baby,* I said to myself, *this one reminds me of my most transformative outdoor experience so far. Just think it was only a month ago!*

That trip really started me appreciating the strength and beauty of nature as well as the importance of taking care of my physical body. I thought about the strength and courage I had discovered within myself during that trip, remembering the cougar outside my tent and the flash flood and the challenge of hiking with a torn-up hip and ill-fitting equipment. It also made me value my history both in terms of my short life so far but also regarding my ancestors and the ancient ones who are ancestors to us all.

I shook my head and looked at my journal. I had written nearly 10 pages as I contemplated my precious reminders of my growth. *I should find one to represent this adventure,* I thought, and looked around. Right there in front of me, unobserved until now, lay a flawless chunk of milky quartz! It was beautiful and at a little less than two inches long, was just the right size for my collection. I picked it up and placed it in the washcloth with the others and put them back with my gear.

The rest of the day passed uneventfully and my last night alone under my tarp, I slept deeply, without dreams. It was the first good night's rest I'd had since being placed on reflection. I wasn't thinking about food, and even my fear of the cold had dissipated.

I woke up feeling refreshed and enthusiastic. I packed up my little camp after my morning ritual and sat by the stream to await Pedro and Marcus. With a wave of sadness, I realized I was going to miss this beautiful spot. I also felt a sense of calmness and clarity I had never felt before. I felt a tingling aliveness and a connection to everything around me, similar to what I had felt on top of our first pass but at least twice as strong. It was exhilarating as well as strange. I had no idea I would feel this way and no one would have been able to convince me of this three days earlier. I was glad I found the small piece of quartz yesterday to remind me of this moment and the feelings I experienced.

Around mid-morning, Marcus came over the rise into my camp. He quietly told me to join him and to remain in silence. We walked over to the trail and I fell into line with Toma and Ken. Toma looked the same to me but Ken appeared different. I couldn't quite place it but something had changed about him.

As we made our way slowly down the trail, I observed each new member as they rejoined our team. Marcia and John were practically unrecognizable. John's green eyes were piercingly sharp and clear and his face had lost all traces of fat (there hadn't been much to begin with). He looked like a hawk.

Marcia was beautiful. Her eyes were also clear, but the loss of fat from her face made her features stand out that much more distinctly. Her sculpted cheekbones set off her full lips and her dark brows highlighted her blue eyes perfectly.

Wow! I wonder what I look like.

When we arrived to camp, Bruce and Susy were there ready to serve us a bowl of fruit and yogurt. We remained in silence as we slowly reintroduced food to our bodies. Finally, Pedro broke the silence, "Does anyone want to share about their reflection experience?"

No one spoke for a while. It felt really strange to be with others again and to be talking.

"I found it very hard to not eat," Toma finally said. "I had to eat my toothpaste the first and part of the second day. It started to make me feel sick around noon on the second day, so I quit but it was really hard."

"Yeah," John agreed. "I didn't eat my toothpaste but I thought seriously about trying to eat some pinecones or plant leaves. I didn't because I didn't want to poison myself or get sick."

"I found being alone the hardest at first," I said softly. "That surprised me because as an only child I am alone a lot but I always have music, books or the television to keep me entertained. Plus, I know that someone is always around, nearby. I never have had to just sit with myself. That was hard."

I saw most of the others nodding their heads in agreement.

"I thought I was gonna go crazy," Joshua said. "I always have someone with me, either my brothers or sisters, coworkers or my folks. There is always another person around even if we don't talk to each other."

He took a breath and then added, "I thought I saw a mountain lion the last day. It was weird. He was just looking at me for a moment and then he was gone. I didn't see him again after that but I got a little worried." He looked down sheepishly as if he were embarrassed to admit this.

"Wow! You're lucky in a way," John said. "Most people go their entire lives without seeing a cougar."

"Yeah, I know," Joshua said. "But I've read too many stories about people being attacked by them to have really savored the opportunity. It was a little too frightening."

I nodded my head, remembering the mountain lion that had visited my tent just a few weeks earlier and how frightened I had been listening to it skulk through camp.

"I saw a big elk," Betty said. "It looked like it took up the whole side of the mountain. It was pretty freaky. We don't see wild animals in the city, except the occasional rat or raccoon. It was so huge! I was afraid it might trample me."

I glanced over at Marcus and saw he was grinning and looking at me. *Hmm,* I wondered. *Did he have anything to do with the others' animal sightings?* I wasn't going to tell anyone about the bear. I didn't think it was a real bear. I thought it was a vision, or Marcus doing some hocus-pocus shape-shifting, and there was no way I was going to share those thoughts with the others. I worried way too much about what they might think of me.

We continued talking quietly around the circle for a while, then Pedro told us to gather up our gear and repack our packs. We were going to head back down to the main base camp where it all began a little more than two weeks before.

Chapter Twenty-Seven

The hike out of the mountains and back down to the river valley was easy. The days off had helped my feet heal, as had soaking them in the icy cold water of my little stream. Even though I was dizzy from the lack of food, I felt light and energized. I was happy to be alive!

I love my life! I wanted to shout to the mountains, to God, to anyone who would listen.

It was great to see Joshua again. He looked as cute as ever following his fast, his smiling brown eyes glowing subtly with an inner fire, and the few days of separation helped us both look at what we enjoyed about each other. It was good to have a friend again.

When we arrived back at the base camp at the entrance to Minnie Gulch, Jim McBane's team was already there setting up their tarps. We were the second group in, followed shortly by Maggie's team. Only Marcia's group was not in yet.

You could tell everyone had just finished with their fast. We all looked lean, tan and ready for anything. In fact, we were beginning to look like the gods I had thought the OMS staff appeared to be the first day I saw them.

I had lost a lot of weight. I didn't have a mirror but I could tell by the way my pants fit. I felt strong and alive, connected to the universe and sure of the existence of a benevolent energy or force running through nature and myself. It was an incredible sensation and it was the first time in my life I had ever felt this way. I wanted it to continue forever.

We hung out, connecting with friends from other teams for a couple of hours while waiting for Marcia's group. I guess they had been pretty far out in the field. Tate, Cinday, Ellen and I found each other right away and started swapping stories. Tate told of one of their team members having to leave the course. He had broken his leg on a zip-line crossing when his belayer had accidentally allowed him to ram into a tree on the far side of the ravine they were traversing. Ouch!

I recounted the incident about Pedro coming unglued and screaming at us and told about Evan's mishap on the river crossing. Ellen's team had no mishaps to report. Everything had gone perfectly for them. They had bagged a couple of peaks and had seen mountain goats just like our group did.

It was great to be with my Denver friends again.

Once Marcia's group arrived that afternoon, Bruce called us all together again. "Gather 'round, folks," he shouted. Everyone started to quiet down. It was tough because we all had exciting news to share.

He waited patiently for us to stop talking. "I hope everyone has had a productive couple of weeks," and a roar went up as we expressed our enthusiasm for what we had already been through.

"You look fantastic," he said once we had quieted down again. "I love seeing students right after their reflection experience. You are all so clear and bright. I hope you'll hang on to whatever you have gotten from your three days alone in the wilderness for the rest of your lives."

I looked around at everyone. We did look great. There wasn't a sullen face among the group.

"The last phase of your Outdoor Mountain School experience begins tomorrow. This is what we call the final expedition phase."

A thrill of excited energy ran through the gathering as he spoke.

"Shortly, you will be given assignments for a new team."

"Ugh!" a collective moan replaced the previous enthusiasm.

"Each team will have a special characteristic as well as an objective for the next four days. You will travel completely on your own without an instructor."

More moans met this last announcement.

"We will be keeping an eye on you just like we did during the three days you were on reflection. You will be given specific instructions as to how, where and when you will check in once you are separated into the new groups. The instructor who reviews your itinerary with you will provide details for checking in.

"Are there any questions or comments?" Bruce asked.

No one said anything.

"Excellent! Susy, would you announce the new teams?" he asked his assistant and she stepped forward with a smile. "The final expedition is usually everyone's favorite phase of the Outdoor Mountain School experience. It is your chance to use both the hard skills and the soft skills you've learned over the past 19 days, and most everyone shines during this phase. Your natural leadership abilities will be honed. I am certain it will be an unforgettable adventure for each of you," she smiled reassuringly as she looked around the group.

Then she continued, "Your instructors have been working to determine the exact makeup of the final expedition teams while you've caught up with your friends. Looking over the plans, I think they've done an outstanding job," she glanced down at the papers in her hands.

"When I call your name, please remember the instructor or assistant with whom you are to meet and remain here until all the finals teams have been called. That way, I won't have to shout over a lot of noise. Does everyone understand?" She looked around the circle to make sure we were in agreement with her.

"Fabulous! Let's begin."

Susy began to name off teams. I could guess the "nature" or plan for a couple of teams. Tate and Andy were together in a group that I assumed would be the kick-ass boys group. It was a small team of only five guys, including some of the best, most experienced outdoorsmen of the course. Steve from our team was in that group as well. The rest of the teams had anywhere from six to 10 members.

There were a couple of groups that seemed to have taken all of the men and women who were mediocre and placed them together. I assumed the purpose of those teams was to help people who typically held back to step up and become leaders.

Then I heard my name. I was to meet with Maggie Rogers when all the names had been called. Toma was in my group, as was Ellen. The woman with the deep, throaty laugh was also in our new team, as were two other gals I hadn't noticed before. In all, we were six women, and it turned out we were the only all-female team. That in itself was both exciting and terrifying.

Although Fluffy had been my friend my last year in high school, I hadn't really socialized much with girls since Keri. My experience with her and with the bully girls had left me jaded with regard to females. Toma had been a fine hiking companion and I liked Ellen a lot, but a group of six women? I was not sure how this adventure would work out. I imagined a lot of backstabbing and catfights, as that was my prior experience with women.

Once all the new teams had been formed, we gathered at the meeting spot. The girl with the throaty laugh was Sarah Simons. She was a law student at Brown University in Providence, Rhode Island. Not only was she beautiful and socially adept; apparently she was brilliant, too. *Great. She's everything I am not,* I thought. I felt extremely jealous of her at that moment.

The other two girls were Karn Walker from northern California and Hope Bradley, a native of Telluride, Colorado. *I've never even heard of Telluride,* I thought when she introduced herself.

Maggie came over to brief us on our final expedition.

"Hello, ladies," she greeted us cheerfully. "I have great expectations for you all. We don't often put together an all-female final expedition team; however, you women seemed talented and ambitious enough for us to give it a go." She smiled at us as she looked around our small group.

We glanced at each other and I am sure the doubt I felt was echoed in the others' minds. Maggie pulled out a map and continued, "The next four days will take you from where we stand now, up Cuba Gulch, down to the Cottonwood River, up Boulder Gulch, across the shoulder of Handies Peak—one of Colorado's fourteeners—through American Basin and down Grouse Gulch to this rendezvous point," she jabbed a long, slender finger at a spot on the map near the Animas River, several miles upstream from where we were now standing.

She then said, "I would like this team to take some time now to discuss your proposed camping sites, where you feel appropriate checkpoints would be located each day for the staff to check in with you and how you will handle leadership responsibilities over the next four days. I will return to see how you are doing in 30 minutes or so." She looked at each of us to make certain we had understood her request of us. We all nodded and she left to work with another group.

"So," Sarah began, naturally taking the leadership role as the oldest woman in our group. "How do we want to handle leadership of our group?"

"Our team switched leaders daily," I suggested. "It worked well for us."

"Yeah, we did the same," said Ellen.

"Do you guys want to use that same system?" Sarah asked in her sexy, sultry, nightclub voice reminiscent of Susy's. "There are six of us and only four days on the final expedition."

"True," I replied, already feeling more comfortable with Sarah because her leadership style did not seem dictatorial at all. "Although we could count this evening as a day."

"Yes, but one person would not get to lead," said Karn with a pout.

"We could elect a leader for the whole trip," Toma suggested.

"Or we could just not have a leader," I countered.

"The problem with not having a leader," Sarah said, "is who would be responsible in the case of an emergency?"

"I have found that usually someone with the right skills and knowledge steps in when a leader is needed," I said, hoping I was not going to offend Sarah. I knew she wanted to be the leader but I was secretly hoping the group would pick me to be the leader. My grandfather had always told me to be a leader, not a follower, and I felt like this was my chance even though it seemed so natural to have Sarah lead. She just had a way about her.

"Why don't we try it without a leader and if it doesn't work, we can always change methods?" Hope suggested.

"What if Maggie wants to know who our leader is?" Ellen asked.

"We'll tell her that we are all leaders," I said. "If she doesn't like it, she'll tell us and then we will choose someone to be our leader."

"OK, I agree since what you just said seems right. We are all leaders. But what about pace-setting?" Sarah asked.

"In our team, we always had the slowest person set the pace. That way they never had to play catch-up. A group can never hike faster than their slowest member anyway," I said. "Besides, we don't know, maybe we were selected to be together because we all have a similar pace."

"That may be true," Sarah conceded, sizing each of us up.

"OK, then," she continued. "We'll play the pacing by ear and see if we do hike at a similar speed. Let's look at the map and figure out where we think we will be camping each night." We pulled out our topo maps and began reviewing the route Maggie said we would follow.

I took a piece of string and ran it along the basic route to determine, more or less, how many miles we would be covering. "It looks like we have about 18 miles to cover in four days of hiking," I said, checking the key. "Plus, we have an elevation gain of about 2,600 feet followed by a loss of about 2,000 feet. Then another gain of almost 3,000 feet and a final loss of 3,300 feet." I glanced around and saw Karn's eyebrows raised. I don't know if she was surprised or impressed. It didn't matter. Reading maps was something I had gotten very good at.

"Pedro always told us to plan on a mile per hour, plus an hour for each 1,000 feet of elevation gain or loss. So, we'd have to cover approximately four and a half miles each day, plus add time for elevation gain or loss," I finished.

"Alright, then," said Sarah, looking at the map. "How many feet total do we have in elevation gains or losses?" she asked me. I loved hearing her voice. *Man, I wish I had a sexy voice like that,* I mused.

"It looks like, um," I said, adding up numbers in my head. "I think it's about 10,800 feet total or approximately 2,700 feet each day."

"OK, then. If we plan on hiking about six hours each day, that would put us near the top of Cuba Gulch tomorrow night," Sarah said, looking around at the group for confirmation.

"That looks about right," Toma agreed. Karn, Ellen and Hope all nodded.

"So, where would you have us camp for the second night?" Sarah asked Karn. She looked at the map and took the string from me. She laid the string along the Cuba Gulch trail and calculated about four miles.

"It looks like somewhere down here near Cottonwood Creek," she said and pointed to a spot on the map.

"I agree," I said, nodding my approval of her calculation.

"Me, too," smiled Sarah.

"OK, Hope," she continued. "You tell us where our last campsite could be."

Hope smiled happily to be included in the decision-making and took the map from Karn. Using the string to determine mileage, she followed Boulder Gulch up toward Handies Peak.

"I think somewhere here in the American Basin," she said, pointing to an area on the map below the fourteener. "There is Sloan Lake, which might be a good campsite as we can probably get water there. It is above tree line but I don't think we can make it across the second pass that day since it is mostly bushwhacking without a trail."

"I think you're right," said Toma as she looked closely at the map. "That will be our hardest day with the most elevation gain, and like you said, there is no trail. If you look at the route, it is pretty steep most of the way." She pointed out the trail we planned to take and the contour lines did run pretty close together. The closer they were to each other, the steeper the terrain. When the lines were spaced out, it meant a flatter trail.

"We might even be better off planning to camp before the first pass and then hit both passes early on the last day before the big downhill push," Ellen said. "I don't know, what do you guys think?" she asked at last.

"You may be right," Sarah said, looking at the map and apparently calculating time in her mind. "Do you see what they're thinking?" she asked Hope.

"Yeah, I do," she said. "And I agree with them. I was so focused on measuring the distance, I didn't pay attention to the steepness of the trail. Let's plan on camping near that small lake at the top of Boulder Gulch," Hope said.

"Great! We have our campsites," Sarah said with enthusiasm. "How many miles does that leave us for the last day?" she asked Ellen.

"Hmm. It looks like about six miles and about 3,300 feet total in elevation, about 800 feet up to the pass, a couple of hundred feet up and down as we contour around the basin and the rest downhill to our meeting point," Ellen said, proud to show off her map-reading skills.

"Excellent! Now where do you think we should plan to have checkpoints?" Sarah asked the group.

"Maggie may already have some checkpoints in mind," I said. "I think it will depend on where other teams are headed as well, since there are more finals teams than staff members."

"Actually, there are exactly the same number of finals teams as staff members if you count Bruce and Susy," said Karn.

"You're right," I said. I had completely forgotten about them. It made sense that there would not be more groups than staff.

"So, maybe the best place for checkpoints would be a place where we might get lost," I suggested.

"Yeah," said Toma. "Like where a trail meets another trail. See here, where the Cuba Gulch trail meets trail number 836?"

"Exactly," I said, smiling. I looked to Sarah for confirmation.

She nodded, "That makes sense to me."

"So checkpoint one will be there," Toma said.

"Yep," Sarah and I said together and we smiled at each other.

"So maybe checkpoint two should be where Boulder Gulch leaves Cottonwood Creek?" Hope suggested.

"I think so," Sarah said and I nodded. We already felt like a team working together. This was going to be so much better than I had anticipated. Maybe being with a group of women was going to be fun rather than drama.

"Where do you think our last checkpoint should be?" I asked Karn.

"I dunno," she said and I got the sense that she was feeling left out.

"Here, take the map and let us know what you think," I said, handing the map over to her.

She smiled a little at that and peered at the route we'd be following.

"I have a hard time understanding the difference between our campsites and our checkpoints," she said. "Why do they have to be different?"

"I don't know that they do," I said. "What do you think, Sarah?"

"So far they really aren't much different. There's maybe half a mile between where we might camp and the checkpoint. I don't see any reason why they can't be the same, except that we may try to make a few more miles one day if we're feeling good or if the campsite we had in mind turns out to be a lousy spot once we are there in person."

"The one thing we might want to keep in mind when determining a checkpoint versus a campsite," said Toma, "is that the checkpoint should be easily locatable. So it should be near a distinguishing spot like where two trails cross each other or by a lake or where a stream flows into a river. Places like that so the staff doesn't have to search all over a large area to find us or the cairn we leave."

"OK, then," said Karn. "That makes sense. What if our third checkpoint is near the western end of Sloan Lake?"

"That makes sense if we are camping there; however, we just decided to back the camp up and set it near the lake at the top of Boulder Gulch," I said to her.

"OK, then, what about at the southeast end of that lake?" Karn asked.

"Perfect," Sarah and I said in unison. We looked up and saw Maggie heading back our way.

"I think we're ready," Sarah said with a smile.

Maggie walked up to our group and we shared with her our plan. I could tell she approved and was excited to see how well we were already working together. I had a feeling we were her "pet" team and she had probably been instrumental in seeing to it that an all-female team was created. She thought our checkpoints made sense and that our campsites were well chosen.

"What if there is an emergency along the route?" she asked us. "What will you do?"

We looked at the map again. I spoke up, "It depends on the emergency. If it requires evacuation, and it occurs on the first day, a pair of runners can return the way we came along trail 836. On the second day, we would send runners toward the Mill Creek Campground on County Road 30. There are bound to be some vehicles there and someone can drive us to a public phone if their cell phone doesn't work," I paused to take a breath and see if anyone else wanted to jump in.

No one did, so I continued, "On the third day, I would say that would be the same plan and head toward the campground. The last day, we'd send runners down to the rendezvous point. On any of those days, the rest of the team can work on bringing the injured person down."

"That sounds reasonable, Lucy," Maggie said approvingly.

"I think you ladies are right on track," she continued. "Carol and Ted have redistributed the group gear into piles along with food for the four days. Have someone from your team go to them and bring everything back here so you can figure out who will carry what. I'd also like you to come up with a name for your group." She smiled again as she left us. I could tell she was happy with our progress.

"I'll go get the group gear and food," Toma volunteered.

"I'd like to come, too," said Ellen and the two of them headed over to where Carol and Ted were standing.

"Let's think of some names while they are away so we can give them suggestions when they return and we can vote," Hope said.

"Do you have a name in mind?" asked Sarah.

"I have a couple," she replied. "What do you think about the Amazons? Or maybe the Six Chicks?"

"Those are good possibilities," Sarah said. "What about you, Lucy? Do you have any ideas?" I hated it when people asked me to be creative. That was definitely not my strong suit as I saw it. Clever sayings and cute words didn't easily pop into my mind.

"Hmm," I said, trying to stall. "I don't really know."

"We'll come back to you," Sarah said kindly. "What about you, Karn?"

"Well, I was thinking Strong Gals or Heavenly Hikers," she said.

"I like those," I said. "Especially Heavenly Hikers. It's got a ring to it." I was still struggling to figure out something clever. Then I remembered I had recently read the book *Even Cowgirls Get the Blues* so I blurted out, "What about the Cowgirls or Blue Cowgirls?" I felt my face growing red with embarrassment. I hated having to do this.

"Hmm," Sarah said. "Those are cute ideas. Very Coloradan."

"We could make a play on the Hikers idea," Toma said, coming up to our gathering spot again. "What about Hearty Hikers, or...?" she stopped as she tried to think of another idea.

"What about Hairy Hikers?" asked Hope with a grin. "I definitely could use a shave." She showed us her legs.

Yep, we could all definitely use a shave. My legs were covered with black fur. I hadn't really paid it any attention since all of the Outdoor Mountain School staff had hairy legs and underarms. It seemed like a chic mountain girl kind of thing.

"What about Mountain Chicks?" I asked, having a momentary brainstorm.

"I like that," said Karn graciously.

"I'd like a name that stands for strong women," Sarah said. "What about the Femme Fatales?"

"It's OK," Toma said. "But I like something that makes me think of mountains and hiking."

"What about the Mountain Amazons?" I asked.

"Hey, that sounds good," Ellen said.

"What about Hiking Amazons?" asked Toma. She really did want hiking in the name.

"OK," said Sarah. "Let's take a vote. The best we have so far are the Mountain Chicks and the Hiking Amazons. Do you all agree to vote on one of these two names?" We all nodded our agreement. The vote was taken and the Hiking Amazons won out four to one.

I didn't particularly like the word Amazon because it made me feel like we were man-haters and I didn't think we were. It did imply female strength without the need for men, so I guessed it would be OK.

We shared our name with Maggie, who seemed to like it, and then we divided up the food and group gear. It seemed that each of us would be carrying about 50 pounds on our backs.

Just before sunset, Bruce called us back together as one group. The staff had prepared a special meal for us as a celebration to end the first phase of our journey, to mark the conclusion of our reflection experiences and to commemorate the start of the final leg of our adventure.

It was a glorious dinner of roast chicken, fresh green salad, baked potatoes and ice cream. We were warned not to eat too much as our stomachs were still shrunken from three days of fasting. Most took that advice seriously and quit when they felt full, but a few foolhardy boys couldn't help but gorge themselves on the ice cream following a huge meal and I could hear them later that night, puking out in the trees. *They had been warned,* I thought.

We all slept with our original team that night, our final night together as a team. Bruce wanted the instructors to do a last briefing with us before we started out on finals.

Pedro took each of us aside for a few moments during dinner. He asked me what the highlights of the expedition had been so far for me. I told him reflection had been way more rewarding than I had ever anticipated. That it had been scary for me at first, particularly at night, but that by the end, I felt good—elated and connected to the nature around me.

He also asked me about the group and how we worked together. I told him I thought we worked well together, especially after he had blown up at us about not sharing the chores load evenly. I liked everyone in the team and had really grown close to Joshua over the weeks.

After he had spoken to everyone individually, he called us together before we headed to our tents. "You guys know me," he said sheepishly, pulling out his journal. "I have a quote I would like to share with you before you begin your final expeditions. For nearly everyone I have ever instructed in Outdoor Mountain School, these next four days are the most memorable. I wish you the very best experience and the most growth possible." His fingers searched through his journal to find an appropriate quote.

"Ah," he said as he silently read the words he was about to impart to us. "This will do very well," he smiled.

"It is a quote from Sir Francis Younghusband, a British officer, explorer and spiritual writer who in the 19th century explored remote parts of the Karakoram range, on the border between Pakistan, India and China. He said, 'To those who have struggled with them, the mountains reveal beauties that they will not disclose to those who make no effort.'" He looked around at all of us for a moment.

"I don't know why that quote jumped out at me," he continued, "except that for the past two-plus weeks, each of you has struggled with the mountains. You have also struggled with yourselves in one way or another. And I believe you have reaped rewards, far greater than you anticipated, as a result of those struggles. You still have some struggles ahead of you during the next four days. Keep this quote in mind so that you keep your head held high, despite the struggles, on the watch for the beauty and rewards that will surely be yours."

Although it was almost dark, I noticed a tear run down his rough, unshaven cheek as he finished, "It has been a tremendous pleasure being your instructor these past weeks. I am immensely proud of each of you and I look forward to learning of your adventures during finals.

"Marcus, is there anything you would like to say?" Pedro turned toward his assistant instructor.

"Yes, thanks, Pete," Marcus said as he stepped forward.

"Pete's been rubbing off on me," he grinned sheepishly. "I, too, have a quote I would like to share with you guys. First, let me say that you've been an amazing group. I loved the opportunities I had to share some of my culture with you and it was a joy watching you grow in strength and ability these past weeks. I leave you with words from Goethe: 'Whatever you can do or dream you can, begin it. Boldness has genius, power and magic in it.' So, go forth tomorrow, and every tomorrow from now on, and follow your dreams."

We turned in for our last night as a team. I felt a strange mixture of feelings. I was tremendously sad to think this was our last night together. I didn't know if we would spend time with each other at the end of the course following finals or not. I felt exhilarated and excited to be starting a new adventure in the morning with the Hiking Amazons.

Of course, I found myself nestled against Joshua but this time we were near the outer edge of the tarp, not in the center. My heart felt happy again to be near my friend and I snuggled readily into his arms. I fell asleep there, peacefully dreaming and warm.

Chapter Twenty-Eight

The next morning, the Amazons were anxious to get going. I could sense Sarah chomping at the bit at breakfast. We ate together in our new teams even though everyone in the course ate together. It was kind of like the first day, 19 days ago, when we set out as a brand-new team headed up Minnie Gulch.

I was happy to be part of the all-women's team, even though butterflies of anticipation and excitement fluttered around my stomach. I felt like we were making history. I could tell from Maggie's comments yesterday that it wasn't common to have an all-female team.

I was so fired up I really couldn't eat much for breakfast, just a quick bite of yogurt. I also felt a rumbling in my intestines that didn't bode well. *Hopefully nothing will come of it,* I thought to myself and I was glad I wasn't able to eat a lot.

Once the meal was finished, Susy and Bruce wished us Godspeed and we took off. We soon discovered that, as we had thought, we were well matched in terms of pace. We kept up a steady rhythm and no one felt rushed or fell behind. As we walked, we talked about a variety of topics. I was curious about going to college in the fall, so I fell in with Sarah to find out what it was like her first year.

"It was great," she said, remembering her freshman year. "There were lots and lots of parties and I made dozens of new friends. The homework was challenging at first, but if you create a routine and stick with it, you'll do fine. Where are you going to go to school?" she asked me.

"I've been accepted at Colorado Liberal Arts College, CLAC, in Durango," I replied.

"Oh, I've heard that's a good school," she said generously. Obviously it was not an Ivy League school like Brown.

We talked a few minutes more, and then fell in with the rest of our team. The day was glorious, with not a cloud to mar the brilliant blue mountain sky. The temperature was perfect and the views as we made our way past the Kitti Mack Mine grew more and more spectacular.

It was a long uphill trudge that day but our jovial spirits kept us pumping along. We reached our checkpoint at about 2 p.m. and found Maggie waiting there. We reported no problems, that everything was going great, and kept on walking toward our first campsite. We arrived at the site and set up our camp just below the highest point of the pass to avoid the strong winds that often rush over the tops of the peaks and passes in summer.

We were above tree line, so there was nothing to which we could tie our tarp lines. Hope got creative and figured out we could use our ice axes along one side of the tarp and rocks on the other to create a very low, triangular shelter. It would be warm, snug and nearly windproof.

Toma and I made dinner; accustomed to working together from our previous team, we easily fell back into a routine. We had spaghetti with tuna marinara sauce put together in no time.

We watched the sun set over the surrounding peaks before retiring that evening. Inside our shelter it was like a slumber party. Everyone had something to say. Sarah took charge and asked us to share one thing about the day that had been special for us.

I started, "I really liked today and the fact that I am part of an all-women's team. I enjoyed learning about each of you and look forward to the next few days. I have had some distrust of women ever since my best friend turned on me in junior high and high school."

Toma went next, saying that she, too, liked being part of an all-women's group and had had fun talking with each of us.

Ellen said that the highlight of the day had been watching the sunset with all of us. She felt like she had found the group of sisters she never had (she had three brothers).

Hope's best part of the day was figuring out how to set up our tarp in such a successful, creative way. Karn's highlight was not getting any blisters on her feet and Sarah's favorite part of the day was how well we had all worked together and that there were no fights among us. She ended the day with a favorite quote from Oliver Wendell Holmes, "A mind that is stretched by a new experience can never go back to its old dimensions."

Sarah concluded, "I feel all of us had a new experience today and so tomorrow we will be different and better people. And for myself, I hope that is always true—that each day I am a better person. Good night, ladies. I had a great time on the trail with you today."

The night started off uneventfully. Everyone was sleeping soundly when the wind suddenly came up. It howled through our camp like a freight train, ripping up the side of our tarp tied down with rocks. Obviously, we had not selected stones that were heavy enough because one minute I was sound asleep and the next, the tarp was flapping wildly in my face.

Karn screamed as she was awakened and panic set in. I did not want to leave my warm sleeping bag. It was cold outside and the wind felt like a crazed beast trying to tear us apart. All I wanted to do was crawl back inside my bag, tuck my head in like a turtle and go back to sleep.

Sarah and Toma were already up and out of their bags.

"Lucy!" Sarah shouted above the wind. "Get up! We need your help!" They were attempting to wrestle the tarp back into place.

"We need to find another spot to tie down our tarp or else another way to do it here!" Toma cried out.

Reluctantly, I got up and threw on my rain jacket. I already slept with my hat on so I was ready in seconds. My boots had been at the end of my sleeping bag and were easy to tie on quickly.

I grabbed a flapping corner just as Hope took the fourth.

"Let's use ice axes for all four corners," I shouted above the roar. "It's too dark to look for a new spot tonight!"

"Good idea!" Sarah called back. "Ellen, take out two of the axes and tie the loose corners to them!"

Ellen pulled two axes out from the center of our stable side of the tarp and tried to tie them to the out-of-control fabric while the four of us held onto it to keep it from flying away. Karn just sat there huddled among the sleeping bags, rocking back and forth.

"Karn!" Ellen shouted. "I need help! I need someone to hold onto the tarp or the ice ax while I tie it down!" Karn looked up. Tears were streaming down her face. She looked terrified, but we all were scared.

"Come on, Karn! We need your help!" I yelled at her. I was closest to where she was hunched over. "Here, come hold this corner and I'll help Ellen!" She looked at me gratefully and scooted over to take hold of the blue nylon.

I stood up and tried to walk to where Ellen was battling the beast. The wind nearly knocked me over. It must have been gusting about 80 miles per hour!

Stumbling over sleeping bags, backpacks and other gear, I reached Ellen just before the tarp was torn from her hands. I snatched it out of the air and held on tightly as she tied it to the ax head. Then, Ellen took one of our original tie-down rocks and pounded the ax into the ground.

We staggered over to the fourth corner and repeated the process. The tarp was no longer flapping wildly but it still made a horrible crackling noise as the wind rippled under the edges, lifted the center and then dropped it back down as the gust died, only to do it all again a few seconds later. No one would be able to sleep with that horrendous noise. Sarah and Hope used large stones to pound the first two corner axes deeper into the soil. Now our shelter was flat and only about eight inches above the ground at the highest point.

"What if we took the other two axes and put them together, one on top of the other, and then used them to lift the center a bit higher so we'd have some headroom?" Hope suggested.

I looked up at the sky at the moment, and shouted back to her, "No time! Look! It's going to dump on us!"

Sure enough, within moments, rain started pattering on us. We dove into the makeshift shelter just as the deluge began. At least we were warm. There wasn't any dead air that needed to be heated up and so our body heat warmed our space quickly. The rain slammed against our tarp and the wind tried to pull the axes back out of the ground as we lay huddled in the center, far away from the edges of the tarp so we would stay dry. No one slept well as the rain continued for the rest of the night.

Chapter Twenty-Nine

There was no way we could speak over the noise of the water and air. At some point I must have fallen asleep because the next thing I knew, it was morning and the storm had passed. My head was resting on Ellen's feet when I awoke. It looked like a bomb had gone off in our shelter. Gear was tossed about willy-nilly and my companions were lying every which way. I stretched and tried to disentangle myself. The other women stirred and we crawled out from under our tent. The only evidence of the night's torment was a few puddles of water where the rain had not yet soaked into the ground.

"Well, that was quite a night," Sarah said as she stretched in the crisp air.

"You can say that again," I smiled at her disheveled hair knowing I looked just as frightful.

We checked our gear and we still had everything—a miracle in itself. Our sleeping bags were all wet, though some like mine and Karn's were wet just at the foot where rain had gotten under the tarp. We had been in the center of the huddle, so rain had not gotten us on the sides. Toma's bag was soaked. She had been sleeping on the outside edge of the group and had gotten the brunt of the storm. In typical Toma fashion, she didn't complain but just laid her bag out in the sun to start drying. Hope's was the other very wet bag. She had been on the other outside edge. Thankfully, the weather was now beautiful.

"I think this calls for a nice hot breakfast," Ellen said cheerfully. "I'll whip us up some mountain oatmeal." That was our name for oatmeal cooked in powdered milk with fruit and nuts. It was delicious and after eating that, along with a cup of hot tea sipped under the rising sun, I started feeling a little less like a war survivor and a little more like a human.

The day's hike started out well. We were tired from the night's adventures, but everyone was in good spirits. Karn set the pace as she seemed to be the most affected from the evening. She hadn't really spoken all morning and seemed to have shrunk into herself. The rest of us were either tired or introspective as well, so we mostly walked in silence.

It was another glorious day. The wind and rain had served to wash the atmosphere and the peaks clean, and everything stood out in crisp relief. Our trail took us across a high tundra plateau with views of majestic mountains all around us. We saw evidence of mountain goats or bighorn sheep but didn't spot the animals themselves.

A ptarmigan that had been nesting on the ground flew up as I approached and startled me out of my trance. She had blended in so well with the surrounding rocks and grasses that I hadn't seen her before she sprang up from the earth and started limping away with a pitiful cry like she was injured. She was obviously trying to lure us away from her nest. It didn't work. We stopped to have a quick peek at the eggs she had been sitting on.

At the head of Cuba Gulch, the trail took a downhill turn. It was a steep, rocky path, apparently well used. We had no problem following the deeply rutted, dirt and stone route as it took us high above Cuba Creek.

Right after lunch, my stomach started acting up. It had felt rumbly all morning but I was beset by a sudden case of diarrhea, causing me to run off the trail, unbuttoning my pants as I went. After having to stop four or five times, I felt my energy draining out of my body. I was walking slower and felt listless. The rest of the team was feeling excited and happy, even Karn, as we lost altitude and got back down among the trees. She was smiling again and seemed to be more like herself, not optimistic but at least not completely down.

Toma came back to hike with me as I was lagging a bit behind the group. "How's it going, Lucy?"

"Not well. I've had diarrhea five times now. My butt is sore and chafed and I feel weak."

"Man, that sucks."

"Yeah, tell me about it."

"Have you told Sarah? She has the first-aid kit. Maybe there is some anti-diarrheal medicine in it. I can go check for you," she said as she sped back up to catch the head of the group. When Sarah found out, she called a halt to the hike immediately and came back to where I had sprawled myself on a big rock in the sun.

"Luce," she said. "You should have said something to me or someone else before now. You are probably dehydrated and that's why you are feeling so lethargic." I nodded, not really wanting to move at all.

"I checked the first-aid kit," she continued. "We do have some Imodium A-D and some electrolyte solution." She handed me a small pill and searched in my pack for my bottle of water. It was full. I hadn't had anything to drink since lunch. No wonder I felt so terrible!

I took the pill and then Sarah poured the powdered contents of the foil pouch into my water and shook it well. "Here," she said. "Drink half of this now and then I'll refill your bottle and put more solution in it." I did as she said and immediately started to feel better. It was crazy how being dehydrated had made such a huge difference in how I felt. My butt still hurt because we weren't allowed to use toilet paper on the trail. Marcus and the other staff had taught us how to find soft leaves to use, and which grasses to use as native toilet paper. It usually worked really well, except when one had to wipe every 20 minutes or so.

Karn came back while Sarah was tending to me and offered a possible solution to the butt issue. "Hey, Lucy," she said. "I know most everyone was taught to use native materials as a toilet paper substitute." I nodded, not sure I wanted to discuss my issues with her, or anyone else, for that matter.

She smiled. She really was beautiful when she let her guard down and relaxed a bit. "Our instructor, you know, the one everyone calls Gentleman Jim because he carries an umbrella? Anyhow, he taught us another technique that worked really well, once we got over our initial shock."

I was curious now. What could be more repulsive than wiping your butt with a freshly picked leaf?

"Jim always made us take our water bottle and soap with us when we used the toilet; in fact, our group latrine had a soap on a rope thingy that was set up with it every time."

I made a face as I was starting to get an idea of what she might say next.

"Anyhow, Jim had learned in Nepal to use his hand with water on it to wipe himself."

Yep, it was exactly what I thought she was going to say!
Yuck!

"Then, of course, you wash your hands thoroughly with soap once you're finished," she concluded.

"Wow! Thanks for sharing that, Karn," I said while thinking to myself there was no way on earth I was going to use my hand to wipe my butt after I have pooped!

"I know it sounds gross and it took me a while to get used to it but it does work really well and you don't get a rash from using an unknown plant. Plus, when I tried the leaf thing, my hand got dirty anyway," she said with a shrug. "I thought I would just share it with you in case you were tired of having dirt and grass parts in your crack." She turned around to walk back to her pack.

I will certainly view touching Karn's hands differently in the future, I thought.

Sarah smiled at me as if she read my thoughts, "I know how you feel, Lucy. I grew up in Manhattan, upper west side." I hadn't known that about her. "And I come from a very conservative family. We didn't even discuss personal stuff, let alone body parts, and we certainly didn't talk about how to tend to ourselves in the toilet."

I smiled at her. It sounded like my family in terms of our inability to discuss stuff.

"Maggie had the same idea as Jim of using water and soap. She was super concerned about the environment and us making as minimal an impact as possible. I refused to even give it a chance a first. I was enraged that people I didn't even know were talking to me about my personal hygiene matters, let alone telling me how to keep clean!" She sounded indignant and I realized I could easily visualize her in a courtroom. She would make a great attorney.

I nodded in understanding.

"By about the third day of our first week, though, my butt was sore from choosing the wrong plants. I even tried sticks and pine cones. Rocks. You name it. I tried everything but the water and soap technique. There was no way I was going to touch my dirty butt with my bare hand! To make matters worse, we hadn't come across a stream so I could stop and wash thoroughly during all that time and I was starting to smell myself," she said disgustedly. I could imagine her discomfort. She seemed like a pretty classy gal.

"The fourth day, we did finally come to a river and we had time to wash our hair and clean up. As I was scrubbing, I realized I was touching my butt and that I did so every morning in the shower. With soap and water. Furthermore, I figured out my rear was probably dirtier at that point than it had ever been in my life and I had just cleaned it. So I said to myself, 'Sarah, why are you being such a priss? Why not give Maggie's technique a try?' So, I did and I have been very pleased ever since. No more sore butt or stinking crotch. You really should consider it, Luce." She smiled again and then went to her pack to stuff the first-aid kit back in.

Great, I thought. *Now I know way more about both Sarah and Karn's hands and toilet habits than I ever wanted to know.*

When I had finished a full liter of Gatorade, we started back along the trail. I was definitely feeling more energetic and I only had to stop once. It seemed that things were getting back on track in my system. I sucked it up and tried the water technique and discovered that the cool water was soothing. I scrubbed my hands well and checked to make sure there were no lingering smells.

It wasn't so bad. *Maybe I could do it again,* I thought.

The trail grew more gradual as we came closer to Cottonwood Creek. At the creek, we had to hike along a jeep road and to our dismay, we encountered non–Outdoor Mountain School people for the first time in three weeks. Our first contact with the outside world came in the form of an overweight middle-aged man who must have thought he was cool beyond belief. He wore a faded muscle shirt and skull doo-rag over his long, straggly, gray hair. He gunned his motorcycle, trying to impress us. I think the vision of six lithe, young mountain girls walking down the road was too much for him.

He shouted out, "Hey, hey, hey, girls! Where have you been all my life?" with a leering grin. I'm sure he thought he was hot and sexy and that one of us would jump on his bike with him to go riding off into the sunset.

"Oh, man, is he totally disgusting," whispered Toma, who was hiking beside me.

"Yeah," I replied. "Even worse considering we haven't seen anyone but fit mountain gods and goddesses in weeks and now he is our first vision. Yuck!"

"This is worse than a truck full of rednecks!" muttered Ellen.

"No doubt," murmured Hope.

We did our best to ignore Mr. Potbelly motorcycle guy even though he rode up and down the jeep trail twice, backtracking each time to taunt us with his prowess. Finally, no doubt tired of being ignored, he rode on and we all breathed a sigh of relief. The hike down the road was an easy, gentle slope and happily, we didn't encounter any more backcountry four-wheelers or biker dudes.

The river here was wide and fast-flowing, and the road was filled with rocks. Ponderosa pines grew thickly along the way and a sign marked the location of a national forest campground five miles down the road where our jeep trail intersected County Road 30 on the Colorado Scenic Byway.

I hoped there would be a bridge leading across to Boulder Gulch. Checking the map, Sarah stopped us after about a half an hour of hiking.

"This looks like it should be our turnoff," she said, placing the map on the ground so we all could take a look. "See this steep wall?" she asked as she indicated a spot on the map along Cottonwood Creek.

We all nodded.

"I believe that is what we see over there," she said, pointing across the river.

"Yeah, I think you're right. We came into Cottonwood Creek here," Toma added. She showed us a spot on the topo. "That's about two miles up from where Boulder Creek comes into the main river. Two miles should take us about 30 minutes to hike downhill on a good, easy trail."

Karn looked at her watch. "That would be about right. I think you're right on, Sarah."

We looked across the river. No bridge existed here and we could find none on the map unless we hiked five miles downriver to the campground. Then, there was no trail on the far side of the river to follow, so not only would that add 10 miles to our route (an entire day's worth of hiking on a good trail) but we would easily double that time because of the route-finding and backtracking necessary when bushwhacking cross-country.

"This is our next checkpoint," Hope said. "Maybe we should wait here for the staff person who is going to check up on us. They could help us get across."

"Yeah, we could do that," Sarah agreed. "But, we're on a roll now and I don't want us to lose momentum."

"I agree with Sarah. Besides, we're the Six Chicks Hiking Amazons," I said, spontaneously making up a new name for our group out of two of the previous favorites. "We don't give up that easily!"

"But how are we going to get across this river?" Hope asked. "It looks pretty fast and deep. We might even get in trouble for crossing without a staff person."

"Yeah, we could," agreed Karn.

"Let's put our heads together and try to think of solutions rather than problems," Sarah said. I really liked and admired that woman. She made a great leader.

"We could scout up and down the stream to see if the river gets any narrower or safer looking," Toma ventured.

"There might even be a fallen tree or other natural bridge," I added, remembering the tree trunk we used to cross the Rio Grande the day Evan fell and hurt his leg.

"That's a good suggestion," Sarah smiled.

"If we don't find a place, we could use our rope to cross," suggested Ellen.

"How would we do that?" asked Karn.

"Well, the strongest and most surefooted of us all could cross, holding onto the rope. We'd belay her to help with her footing. Then she could tie the end she carried to a tree. The rest of us could cross, holding onto the rope for security. The last person would have to cross just like the first, bringing the far end of the rope across."

"That might work," Sarah said thoughtfully.

"We could also form a human chain," I said. "We could link arms and cross together in two sets of three. We could help hold each other up and maintain our balance."

"I like that idea, Luce," Sarah said. "It might be the most practical of all of them. What do you guys think?"

"The only problem with Lucy's idea," Karn began. "No offense,

Lucy, but we don't have any idea how deep the water is. I would hate for three of us to get stuck midstream in water too deep to forge."

"That's a really good point, Karn," I agreed. "So, what are we going to do?" I asked no one in particular.

"Let's scout first and then decide, if we don't find a good place to cross," Sarah said.

Toma, Ellen and I headed back upstream, this time walking along the river's bank. Sarah, Hope and Karn headed downstream. We agreed to meet back up within an hour. We were looking for stones that could be used as stepping blocks, fallen trees that would make a bridge, or a narrow or shallow area that was easier to cross than the spot directly in front of Boulder Gulch.

When we met up again, no one had found a place any likelier for crossing than where we currently stood.

"So, what are we going to do?" Karn asked Sarah again.

Sarah looked at Ellen and me and said, "Do you two want to give it a go and set up a line for the rest of us to cross? You two seem to be the most athletic and mountain experienced in our group. You could buddy cross with a line. We'll belay you. Then, you set up the static line and Karn and Hope will cross using prussic lines for security. I'll bring up the rear, buddy crossing with Toma while you belay us. What do you think?" she added.

"I like the idea," I said. "You've combined the best of both suggestions and I think it is the safest bet we have, considering the makeup of our group. Let's do it!"

I wondered to myself: *Who was that speaking? She's sure not the same girl who once cowered in her English teacher's office, afraid of being seen and beaten up at lunchtime.*

I guess these mountains have changed me. I like who I am discovering, I thought with a smile.

Ellen and I put on our webbing seat slings and I tied in directly to the main rope as I would be crossing in front. Ellen tied in using her prussic rope. Then we linked arms and started edging out into the water.

It was colder than anything I had ever experienced—cold enough to take our breath away. Within seconds my feet and calves went numb. Within 10 feet of the bank the water came up to our knees and it was moving swiftly, trying to yank our feet out from under us. An added challenge came from the boulders we couldn't see until our shins barked on them. Thankfully our legs were so numb we really couldn't feel the full extent of the pain.

"Make sure you guys have a good grip on us!" I shouted over the water's roar. "This water is really hauling through here."

Slowly, we inched our way across. When we reached midstream, about 20 feet from either bank, the water was up to our butts, threatening to pull us down with every step. We were soaked and freezing but we kept going, holding each other up while the rest of the team kept the rope taut.

Gradually the water crept back down to our knees and then our calves. We were almost across! Suddenly Ellen slipped and fell into the water, pulling me with her. The shallow water made it easy to regain our footing without being dragged back into the deeper waters of the center, especially with the other girls hauling on the rope.

"Stop pulling on the rope!" I yelled. "You'll pull us back in!"

I struggled to my knees and stood up, drenched. Then I got a hold of Ellen's arm and helped her stand.

"I'm sorry, Lucy," she stammered.

"It's alright," I said, trying not to shiver.

"No, I mean, not only am I sorry you're cold and wet but I am sorry because I am not sure I can walk," she explained.

"What do you mean?"

"The reason I fell was that my foot got caught under that boulder there and I think I might have broken my ankle," she said.

"Oh, God," I said, freezing now that I was soaked through. "Well, let's see if we can get you to the bank and then we'll figure out what to do."

Ellen leaned on me and hopped, one-legged, the remaining eight feet to the riverbank. There, we stripped off our soggy backpacks and stood dripping in a patch of sunlight.

"Sit down here," I told Ellen. "I need to tie off the rope and then I will take a look at your leg."

"OK," she said, shivering and clutching her arms around her chest.

I ran the perlon rope around a huge ponderosa, then tied a bowline knot to secure the static line. I waved to the others across the river to indicate they could begin crossing and walked back to Ellen.

"Let's get out of these wet clothes," I said as I watched her shake with cold.

"Ggggood ideeeaaa," she said, her teeth chattering together.

We stripped off our wet pants and T-shirts and stood there in the sunlight in our bras and panties. I put on my hat for added warmth.

If only Mr. Potbelly could see us now, I thought contemptuously. *He'd probably have a freaking heart attack.*

I looked over to where the others were preparing to cross. Karn and Hope were tying on their prussic knots. I noticed they had taken off their pants and were getting ready to step into the water. I gave them a thumbs-up and a big smile for encouragement. They linked arms and began creeping across the river, feeling for rocks with their feet. I could tell by the shocked looks on their faces that the water was much colder than they had expected. I was glad I had worn my pants even though they were now sopping wet. They had given me some protection from the frigid water.

I turned back to Ellen and her ankle. It was starting to swell and was already turning purple.

"Oh, man," I murmured. "Does it hurt a lot?" I asked.

"Nnnnot yyyyet," she stammered. "I thththink I I I'mmm tttoo ccccold," she said.

"Yeah, probably," I agreed. Sarah had the first-aid kit, so I could only do simple things for her at the moment. I had her sit on her backpack and put her foot up on a rock, then covered her with my rain jacket to keep her warm; everything else inside both my pack and hers was wet. I glanced back at the river to see that Karn and Hope were nearly across. It looked like they hadn't had any mishaps.

Good for them, I thought. Then I took my bandana and tied it tightly around Ellen's ankle. She grimaced, so I knew the pain was starting to break through the cold.

"Sorry," I said. "I remember my volleyball coach a couple years ago taught me the acronym RICE, which stands for rest, ice, compression and elevation. We're doing all of those right now for your ankle," I said with a smile.

Just then, Karn and Hope joined us, having successfully crossed the river without incident. They were cold, too, and stripped off their wet shirts. They traded them out for dry ones and put on dry pants.

"I'll belay Sarah and Toma," Karn said. "You guys still need to warm up and start drying out your gear."

"Great!" I said. "Thanks. Do you have an extra sweater or something for Ellen? She's freezing."

Karn got out a dry fleece and handed it to Ellen. She smiled as she put it on over her head.

I pulled out the stuff from my backpack, opened my sleeping bag and spread everything out under the sun. Then I did the same with Ellen's gear.

She was no longer shivering.

That's good, I thought as I glanced up to see the last pair crossing the river.

Soon Sarah and Toma were across, again without problem.

"Sorry it took us so long," Toma apologized. "We had forgotten to leave our checkpoint list for the staff member, so I quickly wrote that while Karn and Hope were crossing."

"How's Ellen's leg?" Sarah asked.

"It's her ankle and it could be broken or badly sprained," I said. "She caught it under a rock and twisted it when she fell."

"Bummer," both Toma and Sarah said at the same time.

"Let's have a look at it," Sarah said as she knelt down to untie the bandana.

"Does it hurt much?" she asked Ellen.

"Yeah, now that I am not freezing, it is really starting to ache," she said, attempting a smile.

Sarah looked at the injured limb and prodded here and there.

"I think it is just sprained," she said. "I've done this several times playing field hockey. Let's get you back over to the water's edge so you can soak it for a few minutes. Then, we'll tape it and see if you can hike with the use of a stick."

"OK," Ellen agreed and we helped her hobble over to the water. She gritted her teeth as she put her foot back into the icy water.

"Toma," Sarah called out. "Would you and Hope look for a sturdy stick about four feet long, and thick enough to bear Ellen's weight? She can use it as a crutch. Lucy, would you and Karn redistribute Ellen's gear so she doesn't have to carry any weight?"

We started to work while Sarah massaged around Ellen's ankle. Toma and Hope returned with a nice, tapered stick that would be ideal for a crutch, while Karn and I had put all of Ellen's gear into everyone else's packs and Sarah had quickly and expertly taped Ellen's ankle.

Ellen tentatively stood up to test both the tape job and the stick.

"I think it's going to work," she said with a smile.

"The good news is," Sarah grinned, "we don't have far to go. Remember we had decided to camp somewhere near where Cottonwood Creek and Boulder Gulch intersected? All we have to do is find a good campsite, away from the road. Tomorrow we'll head up Boulder Gulch. That will give Ellen's ankle some time to heal."

"Awesome!" I said enthusiastically.

Karn said she would like to find the campsite, so she and Hope took off without their packs to locate where we'd set up for the night.

"Do you think we should leave a message about Ellen's ankle for the staff at our checkpoint?" I asked.

"That's a good idea," Sarah nodded. "Unfortunately, it means crossing the river twice more."

"I would be happy to do it," I said.

"I'll go with Lucy," Toma said.

"OK," agreed Sarah.

"Let's do it now," I suggested.

"I think that is a good idea. That way, we can dry out before nightfall," said Toma.

She and I tied into the rope again and Sarah belayed us back across the river. It wasn't nearly as hard to cross the second time. I remembered where most of the rocks and deep holes were and the water didn't feel as cold as it had earlier.

We walked the quarter of a mile back up the road to our checkpoint cairn and added a note that Ellen had sprained her ankle and that we were camping near where our third day's hike would begin. We left the last a bit cryptic in case someone else disturbed our marker and read our note.

In less than 40 minutes we were back at the river, ready to cross for the third time. Sarah saw us and motioned that she would belay us again. We tied in and stepped back into the icy water.

I must have been getting tired because halfway across, my foot slipped and before I knew it, I was falling face first into the frigid snowmelt. I jumped up gasping almost before I had completely submersed. Fortunately, I had not pulled Toma under and she was still relatively dry. We made it across without further incident but my teeth were chattering when I reached the far side.

"Mmmmaaannnn, iiitt'sss ccccolldd," I stuttered.

"Change your clothing, Lucy," Sarah instructed.

"Aaaaalll mmmmyyyy ssssttttuffff iiiissss wwwweeetttt," I said, trying to speak normally.

"Oh, yeah, I forgot you had fallen in when Ellen hurt her ankle," Sarah said. "Hmmm. You're about my size. Why don't you borrow a T-shirt and pants for now and we'll lay your stuff out to dry at camp. The others are there now, setting up our tarp and getting ready to fix dinner."

I looked at the sky. We probably had two hours of sunlight left. Our stuff might dry out.

"'Kkkkkkkk," I stammered and stripped off my wet clothes for the second time that afternoon. Sarah handed me a faded blue T-shirt and a pair of jeans. They felt like heaven when I put them on, warm and cozy despite the shivers that continued to run through my body. I couldn't believe they fit me! Sarah was so beautiful and sexy. I knew I had lost weight but never in my imagination would I have thought she and I were the same size. It was amazing!

"Better?" she asked me.

"Yeah," I said, still shaking but at least my teeth weren't clacking together anymore.

"Let's get to camp, then," Sarah said and she, Toma and I set out.

It was less than a quarter of a mile to the campsite the gals had selected. It was a beautiful site, thick with trees and meadow grasses just where the canyon leading up Boulder Gulch opened up to intersect with Cottonwood Creek.

Ellen was resting with her foot propped up on a log. Hope and Karn were busy getting dinner prepared. Somehow they had managed to get the tarp set up and water boiling for dinner in the time it had taken us to add to the message under the rocks and get me dried off after my fall.

With a hot cup of tea in my belly and wearing Sarah's warm clothing, I stopped shivering. I enjoyed our pasta dinner and took on the cleanup duties since I hadn't been available to help set up the camp. The night was thankfully uneventful. Everyone slept well and there weren't any storms to awaken us. Even Ellen slept despite her pain.

Chapter Thirty

When we woke, Ellen's ankle was purple but the swelling had gone down. Sarah re-taped it and Ellen was able to bear some weight on it. The five of us carried her portion of the group gear as well as her personal belongings so she didn't have to carry extra weight. It was going to be a challenging day, for her especially, but probably for all of us as we had no marked trail to follow.

Our route was smooth and easy at the start. We followed Boulder Creek for about half a mile, enjoying the sunshine and gentle breezes before our route took us up a steep, grassy slope. We left the trees down below following the creek bed as we turned to head uphill.

With a 60-pound pack on our backs, we had to zigzag across the slope, walking 20 or 30 feet on an angle uphill, then reversing and heading back across the slope in the direction we'd just come from, only 15 to 20 feet higher up. This slow process required a lot of energy from the upper muscles in our legs but saved our calves a ton of pain in the long run.

Ellen hobbled along with her walking stick, doing her best to keep her spirits up. Gradually we reached the top of the hill only to discover a steep, rocky slope before us. The stream ran through the bottom of a deep gorge a thousand feet below.

For the first time we could see Handies Peak, one of Colorado's magnificent fourteeners at 14,048 feet above sea level. It towered above the hilltop where we stood, stark and rocky against the clear blue sky. A few patches of snow remained on the southern face of the peak, and deep within, I felt a longing to reach the summit. Unfortunately, our schedule would not allow us the opportunity this time.

We took a short break on the hillock before setting out again. This time the angle of the slope was such that I felt I would tumble to my death if I lost my footing. Fortunately, there were plenty of rocks, small shrubs and patches of tuft grass that we could use for footing. I wondered how Ellen was faring, knowing it had to be twice as hard for her. As we gained elevation, we spread out along the slope so as not to damage the fragile vegetation. We enjoyed a simple lunch around noon.

After nearly six hours of slow, uphill slogging, sweat was streaming off each of us. Somehow, the higher I climbed, the more invigorated I felt. Energized, I again had that sense of being intensely alive. Everything I observed stood out in clear, sharp relief. It was almost as if I were seeing the glow of life in everything that my eyes set upon as I glanced around at the miraculous setting.

We had reached the basin underneath the peak. A lovely, emerald green glacial tarn, or little lake, rested at the apex of the hollow, dug thousands of years before by an enormous sheet of ice. Its smooth surface perfectly reflected Handies' summit as well as the ridgelines leading up to the top. Deep chocolate- and coffee-colored mountains, all leading up to the main peak, surrounded us. Patches of pink-tinged snow ringed the upper reaches, with old cornices hanging precariously over the edges. I had never seen a lovelier sight.

We didn't want to descend all the way to the lake to set up camp because it meant having to gain that altitude all over again tomorrow morning, but there was no level spot near where we were standing.

"Well, ladies," Sarah started. "We have a decision to make. We can stick with our original plan and descend 500 feet to camp by the lake, or else contour around this upper basin, cross the pass and look for a campsite on the far side." Ellen limped up with Hope by her side as we were speaking. "How's your ankle feeling, Ellen?" Sarah asked.

"It's hurting," she said. "But I can keep going. I know you guys are discussing whether to go on or set up camp. I'd rather quit earlier today," she grimaced as she leaned on her walking stick.

"I know what you mean," Hope smiled as she wiped sweat off her face. Toma stretched the backs of her calves while we talked.

Sarah pulled out the map and we all gathered around. I pointed out where we were on the map. "We are approximately here. We have about 400 or 500 feet to lose to get to the flatter ground around the lake. We still have about 600 feet to gain before we reach the pass and then another 400 feet to lose before we're in the flatter terrain of American Basin. It's probably a mile and a half total in distance."

"So, we're looking at about three more hours of hiking at our current pace, right?" Toma said.

"Yeah, about that," I agreed.

Sarah looked at her watch, "It's two o'clock now. I think it's a bit early to call it a day if everyone is feeling good. Crossing the pass means we wouldn't be getting into camp until five or six o'clock this evening. We'd still have enough daylight left for dinner and camp chores. I just don't want to overdo it on Ellen's ankle."

"One advantage of going on today is that we can take it easy tomorrow morning," Karn added.

"Yeah, and if we needed help for Ellen, there is a well-established trail," I said. "We could send runners down and bring back a rescue team."

"Let's take a look at your ankle," Sarah said to Ellen as she sank down onto a rock to rest.

They unwrapped the tape. It looked terrible, purple streaked with red and some yellow. It wasn't swollen, though, and I guess that was a good thing.

Sarah prodded it with her finger. "How does that feel?" she asked.

"It's painful," Ellen said, "but not horrible."

"Can you make it another three hours?" Toma asked her gently.

"I think so," she said. "It has really helped not having to carry a heavy pack."

"OK, then, Six Chicks Hiking Amazons," Sarah declared with a twinkle in her eye. "Let's bag this pass and get it over with!"

"Hoo-ha!" Toma cried.

"Hoo-ha!" we all replied, feeling strong and empowered.

"What about the checkpoint?" Karn asked. "Didn't we say we would have it set at the outlet of that lake down there?"

"Oh, man," Sarah groaned. "We sure did."

"Well," I said. "We have a couple of options. We could build a big cairn over there," I pointed several hundred feet behind us to an open area, where a pile of rocks might be visible from down by the lake. "And make it easier to spot by tying a bandana or something brightly colored to it. Or," I continued, "two of us could hike down there, set up the checkpoint and then catch up with the group. We're definitely hiking slower than two of us could go on our own."

"You're right about that," Sarah agreed with my assessment of our speed.

"Hmmm," she said, thinking over the options. "What do you ladies think? Make a checkpoint here and risk having it missed or send someone down to set it up below?"

"One thing to consider," said Toma, "is that the staff knows our route and our proposed campsites. If they don't find a cairn there below, they might just keep on hiking toward Sloan Lake to see if we are there. In that case, putting a rock pile, made visible with a bandana or something, there," she pointed toward the pass, "might make more sense. They are bound to see it no matter what."

"That's a great idea!" said Sarah enthusiastically.

"I think so, too!" said Karn and Hope almost simultaneously.

"Great, then," Sarah said. "Let's keep going and we'll stop to rest up ahead where we will set up the checkpoint."

We continued trudging uphill. I wasn't trudging; I still felt exhilarated and alive but I could tell the rest of my group was getting tired. It only took another 45 minutes to reach a wide-open spot on the hill above the pond and just below the pass. There were plenty of stones around for creating a cairn and Ellen rested with her foot propped up on a large boulder.

We built a large pile of rocks, hoping the staff person checking on us would be able to see it from down by the lake. Hope wrote the day's note advising the staff that we were still on track but that we had elected to cross the pass and have a shorter day tomorrow rather than camp by the lake as originally planned. She commented on Ellen's ankle and noted that it was doing better. The pain was less despite the discoloration. Everyone was in good spirits, she wrote.

Then, we put the note under the top stone and wedged a large, bright red bandana, tied to a stick like a flag, between the upper rocks.

"That should be visible from down below," Toma said as she wiped dirt from her hands.

"Yeah, it looks good," I commented, proud of our work.

"I'll say," said Sarah. "Nice work, Six Chicks Hiking Amazons!"

We rested and ate our snack on the side of the hill, overlooking the water, which now looked tiny nearly 500 feet below us, like an emerald in a solitaire ring setting. Above us, Handies Peak towered another thousand feet, silently witnessing everything that happened in its vicinity.

Sarah, being Sarah, pulled out her notebook while we sat quietly munching our trail mix. She wrote for a while. I preferred just sitting, enjoying the view and the contrasting feeling of the sun and the air on my skin. When Sarah put down her pen, she said, "I have some thoughts I'd like to share."

We all smiled in her direction. I really liked and admired her and hoped I would be like her when I was older. Her patience and wisdom, beauty and athleticism, and her high spirits and ability to lead others were all traits I aspired to.

"I came across a quote from T.S. Eliot, one of my favorite poets, and it was totally appropriate for us and our situation right now. I can't remember the exact words, but it basically spoke to the idea of taking risks and challenging ourselves further than we think is possible.

"I know from my own experience that when push comes to shove I can do much more than I think I can. There was a time in field hockey when our team was in the championship tournament. We were the wild card team because we hadn't had a great season but it had been good enough to get us to the tournament," she smiled at us as we listened intently to her story.

"Anyway, because we were the wild card, we had to work to earn our way to the finals. I mean, we had to play and beat almost every team in the tournament. It was incredibly tiring but we wanted the championship badly. Finally, we got the chance to play the best team in the final round. By that time we had played three or four games a day for four days straight! We were dog tired and wanted to give up but our coach shared with us an idea he had learned."

Sarah continued, "He told us that win or lose we had played amazingly and there was no disgrace in losing. The loss would be temporary and because we had come together as a team he could see us winning next season. However, if we decided we were too tired and gave up now, rather than playing at 100%, we would not only lose the tournament, we would also lose our self respect and the respect of the other teams. In our minds we would become losers and therefore make the loss permanent. You can guess what we did," she looked at us for a response.

"You went out and kicked butt!" Toma said enthusiastically.

"You're right, we did! We found our second wind, and we won that tournament and went on to win it for several years in a row.

"So my point is..." she concluded.

"Your point is not to give up," Toma finished for her.

"Yeah," Ellen said with a smile. "You want to inspire us to keep going the remaining two hours we have to hike."

"That's right! We're the Six Chicks Hiking Amazons!" Hope cried.

"Hoo-ha!" I shouted to the peaks around us.

"Hoo-ha!" echoed Karn.

Sarah nodded, grinning ear to ear. "We're lucky to have such great weather, and you guys have done fabulously! It's been a hard day and I am so proud to be part of this team."

At that moment a song popped into my head, and the next thing I knew I was belting out, "I've been working like a dog. Hmm, hmm, hmmm, I should be sleeping like a log."

Everyone joined in at once. We were off key, but it was fun. After that we went straight into John Denver's "Rocky Mountain High" and kept singing it as we continued the last 30 minutes to the saddle.

I've got to learn some new songs, I thought wryly to myself when I realized I had sung "Rocky Mountain High" at least a dozen times in the past three weeks.

"From here on out, it's downhill today, ladies!" Hope cried out at the top.

We could see Sloan Lake below us, shining Caribbean turquoise color beneath the peaks and looking cool and refreshing. A lot more snow hung on the pass across from us, bringing with it a chill on the breeze. *We'll cross that in the morning,* I thought, but for now it was great to see our destination so near.

"Woohoo!" Ellen whooped as she crossed the summit. She seemed to be limping less. The sight of our proposed campsite raised everyone's spirits.

Toma did an impromptu victory dance on top and then we started downhill. About a hundred feet below where we crossed, we ran into a well-marked trail, making our descent much quicker and easier than it had been when we were traveling cross-country.

"I guess that is the trail to the summit of Handies," I said to Karn, who was hiking beside me.

"Uh-huh," she grunted. "I guess it is." She seemed to be getting tired. We all were, and we still had about an hour to go.

I started singing again in an effort to help us both forget about our burning legs and aching backs. I sang every song in my repertoire, which was filled with show tunes like "Whistle a Happy Tune" from the musical *The King and I* and the title song from *Oklahoma*, all learned during my piano-lesson days. Unfortunately my selection was fairly limited in terms of modern songs people my age actually listened to. At least Karn didn't seem to mind—she didn't tell me to shut up—and it helped pass the time.

We reached the lake around 5 p.m., but couldn't find a decent camping spot nearby; it was rocky and unevenly sloped. So we kept hiking around Sloan Lake searching for an ideal place to spend the night. Thirty minutes later, at the outlet end, the ground was too swampy.

"Bummer," Sarah said sadly. "It looks like we have to hike on."

"Why don't Lucy and I look for a campsite while you guys hang out here?" Toma asked.

"That's a good idea. I know most of us are getting really tired," Sarah said.

"Yeah. I'm all done in," said Karn, wearily sinking to a rock.

"No problem," I said brightly, somehow still feeling energized. "We'll be right back." And Toma and I took off. I felt light and free, having left my heavy pack behind.

We hiked down the trail a distance but didn't find a good spot, plus we didn't want to get too far from the lake.

"Let's try the other side of Sloan Lake," Toma suggested. "People climbing Handies from this side have to have a place where they camp."

"You're right," I said. "That was one reason I recommended this area to begin with. I just assumed there would be campsites galore."

We hiked back up to the outlet, jumped across the small stream that left the lake and rock-hopped as we navigated the muddy sections. Rather than having a well-defined river for the lake's runoff, the water just seemed to seep out all along the west end of the lake.

Once past the swampy stretches, we came across a leaf-green plain.

It was flat and cushy underfoot and covered with mosses, short grasses, marsh marigolds and other high-tundra plants.

"This is perfect!" Toma called out.

"Yeah! We just have to get Ellen across the swamp."

"She'll do fine. She has her walking stick. In fact, she might do better than the rest of us."

"Yeah, you could be right. Let's go tell the others," I said and we hiked back to where we had left the SCHAs. Everyone was lounging around as best they could, given the limitations of the terrain.

"We found the perfect spot!" Toma called out as we approached.

"Let's go, then," said Sarah.

"How much farther is it?" groaned Karn. "You guys were gone a long time."

"Yeah, I know," I said. "We hiked down the trail quite a ways and decided we were getting too far from the lake. So we came back and went around to the other side, thinking climbers going up Handies from this side must camp somewhere. And I think we found the somewhere. You guys are going to LOVE this campsite! I promise."

"We'd better love it," Karn grumbled as she shrugged back into her backpack.

"How are you doing, Ellen?" I asked her as we started out again.

"I'm hanging in there. My other leg is hurting now."

"Yeah, probably from having to do most of the work. It's been a long, hard day."

"You can say that again."

"Have you enjoyed it?" I asked her.

"I have. Even these past couple of days with the ankle thing. What about you?" she asked.

"Yeah, I have, too. It surprises me because I didn't really expect to like it so much."

"I know what you mean," she said and then we walked in silence.

Everyone made it across the rock stepping stones without mishap and despite being dead tired, they let loose with oohs and aahs upon seeing the site we had selected for our camp.

"This is amazing!" breathed Hope. "I've never seen anything such a brilliant, vibrant green before in my life."

"Yeah, and it's cushy!" exclaimed Karn, who had dropped her pack right where she stopped. She sat down and sprawled her tired limbs across the grass. "It's heaven," she sighed.

"Nice job, ladies," Sarah said and I smiled. I loved it when she told me I had done well. If I had been a dog, I would have wagged my tail.

"Let's get cracking with the tarp and dinner. We're all tired and hungry," said Toma, rubbing her stomach. After dinner that night, we sat bundled up outside our tarp, talking and watching the sky.

"I've never seen stars like this before," whispered Karn in awe.

"It's amazing," Hope agreed.

The Milky Way streched directly above us, filled with so many stars that in some places it was difficult to distinguish individual stars. We could identify the Big Dipper and Orion. I saw Cassiopeia, a collection of stars I recognized from my visits to the planetarium during elementary school. Sarah showed me the constellation Scorpio, which was my sun sign. It was a huge pattern with the red-hot star Antares forming the heart. We made up constellations based on what we could see, like creating animals and figures out of clusters of clouds.

It felt safe being here, high in the mountains with this group of women. I never wanted to go home. I never wanted this night to end. I felt really at peace in the mountains.

"Hey, guys," I said. "I was just thinking about how I felt so at home here in the mountains, almost like it was my destiny to be here."

"Yeah," said Toma encouragingly.

"I don't know. I'm just sort of getting an idea or a sense that I might want to find a way to keep doing this. I know, it's probably crazy, what with me going off to college in a few months. It's probably dumb," I finished, feeling a bit embarrassed.

"No, it isn't, Lucy," Hope said. "It sounds like you have a dream, and that's important."

"I know it is, Hope. Thanks," I said gratefully. "I'm not sure yet if it is a dream or not, or just the start of something, but I agree with you about having a dream. I think it's vital. Maybe that's why I got so lost my last few years in school. I didn't have a dream. I didn't have vision for my future. I was just sort of hanging out, if you know what I mean."

"I know what you mean," Karn said. "I've felt that way in my life."

"It's funny, too, because the only poem I ever memorized was by the African-American poet Langston Hughes. It had to do with dreams and how important it was to have a dream for your life. I guess I had forgotten that for a while but it's coming back to me now."

"So what do you think your dream could be, Luce?" Ellen asked.

"I don't know right now," I said. "I'm going to college in the fall and I'll see my boyfriend, Mack, after the course. I've always wanted to have a family. You know, get married and have kids. I want to have three children—all boys."

The girls smiled and laughed knowingly.

"What about a career?" Sarah asked. "I'm going to be a lawyer."

"Yeah, I know," I said. "You'll be a good one. But as for me, I don't really have any career plans in mind. My parents own their own business. My grandfather is a doctor and my other grandpa owned a business. I guess I just wanted to be like my mom was when I was little, you know, staying at home and taking care of the kids, but now that might be changing. What about you guys?" I asked, looking around the circle.

"I want to be an Olympic racer," Toma said. "I've been skiing all my life and that's what I want more than anything else."

"That's fantastic!" Karn said with genuine admiration. "I didn't finish high school so I've just been working. I'm a receptionist at a nice hotel but I always wanted to be a dancer."

"Are you dancing now?" asked Toma.

"No, I haven't danced since my parents divorced when I was a kid. There wasn't enough money for me to continue with it," she said with a sad grimace.

"That's too bad," Toma agreed sympathetically.

"What about now that you are on your own?" I asked. "Can you afford to dance now?"

"I don't think so," she replied, and then I understood better why she was always so pessimistic and down.

"What about teaching dance? Do you know enough to teach younger girls?" I persisted. "Maybe there is a way that you can be involved with dance and not have to pay a lot. I don't know, but I think there has to be a way."

That was one of the things I knew about myself—if I wanted to do something badly enough, I would find a way to make it work out, like climbing Mt. Bierstadt or paddling past a gigantic whirlpool.

"You might be right, Lucy," she said. "I can look into it when I get home." She smiled, and I again saw how pretty she was when her face was not furrowed with concern or darkened by a frown.

"What about you, Hope?" Sarah asked. "What is your dream?"

"I've always wanted to join the Peace Corps," she said. "But I moved in with my boyfriend, David, a couple of years ago and that was the end of that dream."

"Why did your dream die when you moved in with David?" I asked.

"I'm not really sure," she said. "I think I just got distracted. You know, caught up in the day-to-day living. I don't even think I ever told David of my dreams. I know he's never told me about his."

"Oh," Toma said sadly.

"What's your dream, Ellen?" Hope asked.

"Well, I still have to finish high school," she replied. "Then, I am going to college like Lucy. I do know that I want to be an architect. I love designing buildings and producing the drawings. I would like to create some earth-friendly, aesthetically pleasing structures. I guess that is my dream, isn't it?" she said, wondering. "Hmmm."

"That sounds awesome, Ellen," I said with admiration. "I'm sure you will do it."

"You might be right, Lucy," she said with a smile.

"You just made me think of another quote I have in my journal," said Sarah. "I think it is a good one to end the day with."

She thumbed through the pages while holding her flashlight in one hand, then put the light in her mouth to free up both hands. "Mphr ess et?" she mumbled unintelligibly.

"Oh, well," she said sadly, taking the light out of her mouth. "Darn! I can't find it but I'll tell you about it because I just love it. It was from the Pulitzer Prize–winning American journalist Walter Lippmann and it spoke about those of us who do things we feel are worthwhile, whether or not anyone else thinks they are valuable, such as climbing mountains or creating beautiful art or whatever. Those are the ones that make the world a place worth living in."

"I don't know if we dreamers, climbers and artists make the world a place worth living in," I said, "but I do know something I am learning is that no one can live your life for you. You have to do it yourself and so you might as well do the things that make you deeply, truly happy. I guess that means following your dreams."

"Well, we certainly are dreamers and doers of brave, useless and possibly foolish things," Karn laughed.

"You can say that again!" Toma laughed. "I mean, what good is being a ski racer, except that it makes me happy?"

"I think that's the point," Karn replied, looking happier than I had ever seen her. "Just like Lucy said, we need to do what makes us happy and then it is worthwhile."

"Hmm, that's something to think about," said Ellen.

"You bet it is," Sarah replied. "Now I think it's time to hit the sack. Even though we don't have to leave as early tomorrow, I always feel better once we've made our destination, so I don't want to lollygag around here too long."

"You slave driver," I said, poking fun at her.

"You bet I am," she said, grinning back at me.

We all slept well that night. The tranquility of real friendship and the bond of shared work gave us all peace of mind.

Chapter Thirty-One

Everyone woke up refreshed. After a leisurely breakfast, we looked at Ellen's ankle; the purple discoloration was fading and the swelling was minimal. Even better, she was able to put more weight on it than the day before.

"I think you'll make it," Sarah said.

"It looks like," she replied with a grin.

"I know it's beautiful here," Sarah called out wistfully, "but we should probably hit the trail."

"You're right, of course," I said, shouldering my pack one more time even though I longed to stay in this stunning location. I felt like nothing in life could stop me.

"Let's head out!" called Toma. Apparently, she was feeling great, too.

I looked around and everyone seemed happy and alert. No one harbored any negative feelings or discontent.

The second pass was a breeze to cross. Yes, we faced a 400-foot elevation gain immediately after breaking camp but I'd discovered that nothing in the world makes me feel better than good, hard exercise first thing in the morning.

We lingered for a while at the top, enjoying our final vast view of the Colorado Rockies.

Ellen surprised us all by some of her thoughts.

"The whole OMS staff habit of reading and thinking about quotes is beginning to wear off on all of us," she said mischievously. "I was looking in my journal this morning while we ate breakfast and I came across a quote that Maggie shared with us our first or second week. I really liked it so I copied it down. When I read it this morning, I got an even deeper insight. Do you mind if I share what I'm thinking?" she beamed at us.

"Yeah, go ahead, Ell," I said.

"Right on! Sounds great," said Karn.

"OK. The quote was from Lionel Terray. I didn't know anything about him but Maggie told us who he was. Have any of you heard of him?"

"No, I haven't," I said.

"Nope," said Karn.

"Me, neither," Sarah said.

"I have," Hope said. "David is a big climber and the author's name sounds familiar."

Ellen continued, "He was a French climber known for several first ascents. I believe he was on the first climb of Makalu, the fifth-highest peak in the world, located in Nepal."

"Wow, Ellen, that is an impressive memory you have there!" I said with admiration.

"Yeah, I can remember a lot of useless facts," she smiled, tapping her head. "Anyhow, the quote Maggie shared dealt with the idea of freedom and taking one's destiny into your own hands despite potential dangers. At least that is what we discussed when we talked about it with my former team."

Ellen read the passage aloud and went on, "Obviously since Terray was a climber, he was referring to the physical and mental peril faced when attempting a major peak, like Makalu or Everest, and I feel we have done that—taken our destiny into our own hands at least for a while, both in this team as well as my first team. The quote also speaks to a sadness at leaving the summit as well as departing from the deep bonds of friendship and connection that are created when a group of people goes through a challenging experience together. It was that sense of sadness that struck me this morning because that's how I am feeling. Even though it is a lovely day and my ankle is mostly healed, I feel a bit down to be leaving this magnificent place and our incredible team," Ellen smiled as she looked around the group.

"Wow!" I said. "That really captures what I'm feeling right now. Even though I am elated, I feel this strange sense of melancholy. I don't want this to end. I don't want to leave the Six Chicks Hiking Amazons. I feel more despondency about this ending than I did about graduating from high school a few weeks ago."

Others were nodding their heads in agreement and several mumbled, "Yeah. I know what you mean."

"We need to do something to make sure we stay in touch," Toma said. "That way, we will never lose the connection."

"Yeah, let's make sure we exchange phone numbers and addresses," said Sarah. "We can do it down at the rendezvous point tonight, but now I think we need to keep going." She glanced at the sky, and I was surprised when I looked up for the first time in a while to see that clouds had begun to gather to the west and were starting to stream in toward us.

"Yeah, it looks like we might get some weather this afternoon," Hope agreed.

We began our descent; the trail along Grouse Gulch was clear and obviously well used. Although the mood had grown more somber as each of us thought about our futures after Outdoor Mountain School, we were all still in good spirits and the day's trek passed quickly. Just after our lunch break under a cloud-laden sky, we came out of the gorge leading down from American Basin, enjoying the expansive vistas of the upper Animas River Valley. The mountains surrounding the valley were steep and rocky, and the river ran deep and turbulent on the far side from where we were hiking. We could smell the approaching dampness and knew rain would come soon.

"Do you see any tents or any signs of the others?" Sarah asked above the rising wind.

I shook my head and turned to look downriver.

Hope and Karn had their hands above their eyes, holding their flying hair out of their faces. I always wore a bandana tied around my forehead and that kept my straggling locks out of my eyes. I hated having hair in my eyes. I strained my vision to see if I spotted any bright blue tarps among the granite and gunmetal rocks. Nothing.

"I see them!" Toma suddenly shouted, pointing almost directly across from where we were standing. Although the terrain looked flat in the dull light of the upcoming storm, there seemed to be a dip between the road and the river and the base camp was set up in that depression. I was relieved we didn't have to hike too far in order to set up our tarp. It looked like we were going to have a downpour.

We hustled across the road and the boulder field to the depression. I thought we would be the first to arrive but I noticed immediately that the all-male group was there along with one other team.

"Third group in, not bad," Sarah said, echoing my thoughts.

"Yeah, I thought we would be first," I said.

"I did, too, but we did well. It's not even three o'clock yet. Too bad it's going to pour!"

"Yeah. We'd better get our tarp up *tout de suite*!" I said as I pulled the familiar blue nylon out of my pack.

"Hey, Toma and Hope!" Sarah called out. "Come help Lucy and me get this up!"

The wind was starting to howl down the valley and lightning crackled through the clouds. With four of us holding down the corners, we were able to set the shelter up quickly. It reminded me of trying to reset the tent our first night when the vicious storm attacked us. We used our standard alpine technique of tying the corners to large rocks and interlocking two ice axes to use as a tent pole in the center. It gave us a roughly A-frame shaped tent with low sides to keep the rain from blowing under the edges. We quickly shoved our packs into the dark interior and dove in behind them just as the rain hit.

Thunder shook the ground as lightning struck the nearby peaks. It sounded like an off-key garage band. Man, was I glad to be under something warm and waterproof. I was thrilled that we were not one of the several groups still out there hiking. Rain struck the tarp in violent waves. Rivers formed among the rocks around the shelter and began searching for the shortest way to join with the main river. I could hear people shouting outside our shelter but there was no way I was going out unless I had to.

"Another group is arriving," Hope said while peeking out from under the tarp.

"Do they need help setting up their tarp?" Toma asked.

Why couldn't I be so helpful? All I care about is my own safety and comfort, I thought, admiring Toma for her willingness to always help others.

Hope continued to peer out from under the edge of our shelter, watching as the newly arrived team struggled to set up their tent. The all-boys group, responding as Toma had wanted us to respond, rushed over to their assistance.

"No, the guys have it handled," Hope said.

So we waited out the storm. Like most Colorado weather events, it was short-lived and after about 45 minutes of pounding rain, thunder and wind, it was over. The sky began to clear and we crawled out from under our tarp.

Within 15 minutes of the storm's end, two more teams came into camp, wet but relieved.

"Two more to go and everyone will be here," I mused as I looked around the area. I saw Tate, Andy and Steve hanging out by the river and went over to talk with them.

"Hey, guys! How'd it go?" I asked as I approached the men.

"Hey, Luce!" Steve waved me over.

"It was AWESOME!" Tate and Andy exclaimed in unison.

"We bagged three fourteeners!" Tate said with pride.

"Wow! That's amazing! Which ones?"

"We did Handies first, then Sunshine and Redcloud," Steve said excitedly.

"Yeah, it kicked our butts," Andy added. "We must have hiked 15 miles a day, plus the elevation of gaining the peaks, but it was worth it!" he smiled. They were all grubby with straggly beards but their contentment shone through.

"Pedro told us we were the only group to do this in all the years he has been teaching with OMS," Tate said.

"Yeah, we're beat, but stoked!" Steve grinned. "How about the kick-ass girls' group? How did you like your finals?"

"It was amazing," I said, realizing the truth of that statement. "We covered a ton of miles and handled some situations very well, and we bonded as a group. For me that was the incredible part—to be close and trusting with a group of women."

"It was f'in unbelievable," said a sexy, throaty voice I would recognize anywhere. Sarah had come to join us.

"You should have seen Lucy! She was amazing," she continued. "We wouldn't have been nearly as successful without her."

"That's our gal," Tate said proudly as he clapped me on the back.

"What route did you guys take?" Steve asked.

"We were in American Basin and at the base of Handies, just like you guys. We didn't have time to climb the peak, and it wasn't on our agenda," Sarah said.

"We had a gnarly river crossing to deal with," I said.

"Yeah, and Ellen sprained her ankle pretty badly," said Sarah.

"Oh, man! That's a bummer," said Andy, looking in the direction of our tarp.

"Yeah, she's doing better now. She is a real trouper," I said as Andy got up to go see Ellen. I think he had a sweet spot for her.

"I guess there are a couple of teams still out, right?" I asked.

"It looks like it," Steve said. "Your friend Joshua is not back yet."

"Oh," my voice and face fell. "I hadn't noticed." That was accurate and now that he'd mentioned Joshua, I wasn't sure I wanted to see him again.

Odd, I would have expected to be excited to see him again. After all, he had been my friend for the past two-and-a-half weeks.

"I wonder what's next?" I said out loud.

"Haven't you heard?" Sarah asked incredulously.

"Nope. Haven't heard a thing," I said.

"Tomorrow we are going to run a half-marathon and then do some kind of community service," Steve said.

"Really?" I asked. "Thirteen miles! I've never run that far in my life!" I was starting to panic.

"Relax, Lucy," Sarah said. "You've just spent more than three weeks hiking nearly a hundred miles. I am sure you can handle 13. Besides, the route is mostly downhill." She smiled reassuringly at me.

"How do you know the route?" I inquired.

"Marcus told me," she said. "After the rain, I went over to the staff to see if everyone had gotten back and I asked what happened next. He sort of let the cat of the bag. Maggie gave him a look that said he wasn't supposed to say anything yet," she shrugged.

"So? Tell us more," begged Tate.

"Nope. I promised Marcus I wouldn't. Besides," she said, looking behind us, "it looks like the staff is gathering up team members now."

We all turned to look in the direction she was pointing, and sure enough, people were already circling up in a large clearing.

"Let's go join them," Steve said, and we walked over.

"Welcome back, everyone," Bruce said as we finished milling about. "You all certainly look different!" He looked around the circle, beaming at all his troupers. "Did you enjoy finals?"

Chapter Thirty-One

"Yes!" a big shout went up from everyone gathered around.

I was looking anxiously about because I didn't see Joshua or Marcia and a few others.

Bruce saw me looking and said to the group, "There is one team still out. They're doing fine, just coming along a bit slowly. They should be here in 30 minutes or so. Susy is hiking in with them."

I breathed a sigh of relief.

"In the meanwhile, I want to share with you what the next two days, your last two days with OMS, will look like."

I felt my stomach drop. This was the time I had anticipated so eagerly at the beginning, the end of the course, and now I didn't want it to end. Strange, huh?

"I don't know what you all know about OMS besides what you have learned these past few weeks, but one of the vital components of our philosophy is the concept of service. Therefore, each course incorporates some type of community service."

Several of us were looking at each other in confusion. I wondered what could we possibly do out here that would be a community service.

Bruce continued, "I am sure some of you are wondering what we could possibly do of service here." He smiled in my direction. *Had I just said that out loud?* I panicked. *No, I am sure I didn't,* I reassured myself and then realized I had totally zoned out on what Bruce was saying.

"…painting the community center in Silverton. You may be asking yourselves, 'How are we going to get to Silverton?' Looking around, you don't see a bus. That, my friends, will be the other fun part of the day tomorrow! We are going to run to Silverton!" he ended enthusiastically.

"There's the last team!" someone shouted and we all turned to look up the road. Sure enough, a ragtag band of folks were jauntily hiking down toward us.

Yep! There were Marcia and Joshua, both walking at the front of the group. Good for them! They seemed happy.

It also appeared that they were leading the group in song. Of course! Joshua was a musician, after all. I strained to hear what they were singing.

After about five minutes, they were among us, having marched in singing—what else?—"Rocky Mountain High" at the top of their lungs.

It was good to see Marcia and Joshua. They looked fantastic and the group really seemed to get along well. I waved at Joshua. It felt good to see him. My ambivalence disappeared and I wanted to go over to see how his past four days had gone.

"Hey, gang!" Bruce called out, interrupting my mind ramblings, signaling the newcomers. "I know some of you just got here but we were having a course meeting to discuss tomorrow. Come join us in the circle," he beckoned toward the rest of us standing around as a couple of folks from Joshua's group were starting to put up the team's tarp. "You'll have time to do that shortly and the weather is fine right now," he glanced up at the sky, which was clear and blue following the storm.

"As I was saying, we will run to Silverton tomorrow morning. Your staff will wake you at 5:30. You will drink some water, coffee or tea and then run 13 miles to the community center. The route is easy. Just follow this road," he pointed toward his right and the dirt road down which the last team had just been walking. "It leads directly to the community center. You'll pass our main base camp at Howardsville and run halfway through Silverton. Any questions?"

A woman raised her hand. "I have never run that far in my life. Will there be some sort of aid or something in case any of us have trouble with the run?"

"That's a good question, Christy, is it?" Bruce acknowledged her, remembering her name. She nodded.

"Yes, we have a couple of trucks we will use to transport all the personal and group camping gear back down the mountain. These trucks will also serve as sag wagons or rescue vehicles." Bruce looked around the circle again.

Marcia raised her hand. "How should we dress for the run?"

"Good question but hard to answer," Bruce said. "We are in the mountains at 11,000 feet. The weather is changeable. It is cold early in the morning when the valley is in shadow but once the sun comes over the mountains, it could get intensely hot. We are supposed to have a clear day tomorrow, so I would suggest shorts, a T-shirt and a sweater or jacket you can tie around your waist. You could wear a hat and gloves early in the day. Your call.

"Any other questions?" No one raised their hand.

"Excellent! Tonight you will eat and sleep with your finals team. Two teams can eat together if they wish. A staff member will be coming 'round during dinner to debrief each group. Have a great meal and rest well, as 5:30 comes early," he smiled. Bruce then added, "I just want you all to know how proud I am of you! You did some amazing work out there on finals. We'll share more either later this evening or tomorrow night but know that you have all done something fairly remarkable." And with that, he turned and walked off to talk with his staff.

The circle broke up and I went to see how Joshua and Marcia were doing.

"Hey," I called out as I approached their team. They were busy setting up their tarp. "How'd it go?" I asked, looking at Joshua.

"Oh, hey, Luce," he said. "It was fabulous! Right, guys?" he asked his team of six.

"Yes. It was so much better than I could have imagined," Marcia gushed in a very un-Marcia-like way.

"That's awesome!" I said. "What made it so great?"

"Our group, mainly," Joshua said. "I don't know how the OMS staff did it, but we were a perfect team! Everyone's personality complemented the others; we're all artists of some sort. Marcia not only cooks amazingly well but she has an incredible voice. She's been singin' in a local group for years. She also paints. Douglas over there is an accomplished graphic designer and photographer. Carol is a poet and author, and it just goes on! We got along fabulously!"

"And our route was beautiful!" exclaimed Marcia. "It wasn't too difficult and we were told to take in the area from a variety of artistic angles. It was incredible. We wrote poetry and made sketches of each other and the landscape. I've never had so much fun!"

Now I was jealous. Their group seemed so connected and their "theme" seemed very hip.

What a cool idea, I thought, not really thinking about how deeply connected my own group was. *Why couldn't our group have had a theme besides just hiking our butts off?*

"Wow, you guys are lucky," I said instead of what I was really thinking. "I'm glad you had such a wonderful experience. I've gotta go find my group now. We'll talk more later," I promised and I walked off to locate the rest of the Six Chicks Hiking Amazons. You would think we'd have started with a big, cumbersome name and gone shorter, simpler over time—but no, not us. Our name started small and got more complex over the days we were together.

Chapter Thirty-Two

I found everyone over by our tarp. It felt good to be with the girls again. I didn't feel so left out once I was back with the SCHAs.

"What's up, Lucy?" Sarah asked. "You seem down."

"Yeah, I guess I am," I said. "I just visited the newcomers group to see Joshua and Marcia, who were in my old team."

"And...?"

"Nothing happened, really. They had such an amazing time and a cool theme and they were so tightly bonded with each other. I got jealous, that's all," I replied.

"Oh," she said. "I see."

"Don't you feel we are a close-knit team?" asked Toma.

"Yes, I do," I said earnestly. "I feel much better now that I am back with you guys. It's just I can't figure out what our theme was besides kicking butt."

"What was the other team's theme?" asked Hope, who was listening in.

"Theirs was art. They had an assignment to absorb, soak up and take in their journey through various artistic means and perspectives."

"That is a very cool assignment," said Hope.

"Sure it is," Sarah interrupted.

"Don't you know what our theme was, Lucy?" she asked me.

"I guess not," I said. "I thought it was being burly hikers because we covered so many miles and we really did rule the mountains."

"Of course we did!" said Toma triumphantly.

"Absolutely," agreed Sarah. "However, that was not our theme. Do any of you other SCHAs know what our theme was?" she asked the other group members, who were all gathered around now.

"I thought it was female power," Ellen said.

"Me, too," said Toma.

"That was certainly a part of it," agreed Sarah. "What did you think it was, Karn?"

"I have to agree with Lucy and the others," she said. "I thought it was either female power or serious hiking."

Sarah said, "Well, I could be wrong, but I think the core of our group was leadership. Particularly female leadership. We are all great leaders. We discussed this our first day together and it was proven again and again over the past four days. Not only can we lead but we also know how to follow a good leader. In other words, we know when to allow others to lead."

"Hmm. You may be right," said Ellen. "I believe leadership goes along with power."

"That definitely makes me feel better," I said. "And it explains why I was not in the artistic group," I joked as I thought of myself being in a group of painters, musicians and other artists. Art was about as challenging for me as physical education had been a few years before. And I remembered my grandfather always admonishing me to be a leader, not a follower.

"Plus," Toma cut in enthusiastically. "Leadership is its own art. There has been lots of study on effective leadership over the centuries."

"You're right, Toma," said Sarah. "One of the first thinkers on leadership was the Chinese philosopher Lao Tzu, who said, 'A leader is best when people barely know he exists.'"

"Well," I said. "I have always wanted to be a leader."

"You already are," Hope said. "We look to you daily for inspiration and strength."

"Thanks," I said, blushing yet feeling very satisfied. "Well, we should probably start cooking dinner."

That evening, while we were eating bean and rice burritos created from the last of our team supplies, Maggie stopped by to debrief us.

"First, I want to congratulate you all! You ladies were amazing. Not only did you tackle a very challenging route with aplomb, you also handled a demanding situation—one of your group being injured—with style and grace. I applaud you!" she smiled as she looked around our little circle.

"Do you want a burrito?" Toma asked. "We have more than enough."

"No, thanks," Maggie replied politely. "I already ate with the staff. I do have a couple of questions to ask you as individuals as well as a group, if I may?"

"Of course," we all answered eagerly. We liked Maggie and wanted her to stay with us as long as possible.

"Alrighty," she said.

Obviously she's been hanging out with Bruce too long, I thought, listening to the way she got people's attention.

"First, what did you learn about yourselves?" she asked, looking around the group.

"I'll go first," Sarah volunteered. "I learned that I am an excellent leader and that people follow me pretty easily."

"I think we all learned that we are leaders," I said, jumping in next. "I mean, we were just discussing this earlier and we determined that we are all leaders."

"You are right, Lucy," agreed Maggie. "But what did you learn specifically about yourself?"

"Well," I hesitated, thinking. "What I learned is not that positive. I learned that I need a lot of attention. That I get jealous when someone else is getting more attention than I am."

I wondered: *Where the heck did that revelation come from?* I added, "I also learned that I enjoy being a leader."

"Excellent, Lucy. Thank you," Maggie said.

"I learned that I love hiking and camping," said Karn.

"Can you share more about that?" asked Maggie.

"Sure," Karn said. "I've never really considered myself to be outdoorsy. I resisted the whole experience here in the mountains until the past couple of days. I don't know if I got tired of resisting or if it just went away, but once I stopped fighting myself and the surroundings, I started having a lot of fun."

"Thank you," Maggie said.

"I learned that I am stronger than I thought," Ellen said. "I wasn't sure I would be able to go on with my ankle hurt the way it was, but I did. Granted, I had a lot of help. That's something else I learned, that it's important to receive help when it is genuinely offered. If I don't, then I am depriving the person who offers it a tremendous gift."

"Wonderful, Ellen," Maggie said.

"I learned how powerful a group of women can be when they work together to do something," Toma said.

"Fantastic," said Maggie.

"I'm not sure what I learned that is different from what everyone else has already said," Hope admitted as she chewed her lower lip.

"Take your time," Maggie said.

"Well, I was surprised," she said.

"About what?" asked Maggie.

"That we all got along so well. My typical experience with girls is that they can be catty and backstabbing and none of that occurred in our group."

"Why do you think that might be?" encouraged Maggie.

"I don't know, but everyone was honest and helpful with each other and we were all working toward the same goal. I guess then what I learned is that we, as women, don't have to be mean or catty to each other," Hope ended in a rush as if she were afraid she would forget what she was going to say before she finished.

"I agree," Toma jumped in. "I was just thinking about how I tend to distrust women in general and I think that comes from being in a competitive state of mind all the time. Here, in our team, we had a cooperative mindset and it made all the difference."

"Excellent. Thank you, Hope and Toma," said Maggie. "How can you take what you've learned through your finals, or at any other time during the course, home with you? How can you use what you've learned in the outside world?" she asked with a smile.

"I know how I can," Hope answered with a grin. "I can be more open and honest with other women because I know now that deeper friendships can be formed."

"I feel like I can tackle anything," Ellen said. "I have a strength I never knew and that can help me during any future difficult times."

"Yeah, I agree with what Ellen said," I added. "Plus, I would like to find more ways in my life to be a leader."

"Ditto to what Ellen and Lucy said," Sarah chimed in. "I am already a leader, but I feel I learned how to be a more effective leader and how to give back some of the power I have as a leader to those I am leading."

Chapter Thirty-Two

"I will take time to be outdoors more often," Karn said.

"I will take on more of a leadership role on the women's ski team and work to develop camaraderie like what we experienced these past four days," Toma said.

"Great work, ladies," Maggie said. "I am proud of you. As you know, very few courses have all-female finals teams. I went out on a limb for you guys and you exceeded all of our expectations. Bruce is very pleased, as well."

"Thanks, Maggie," Sarah said.

"Yeah, thanks," I added. "You were a great leader."

"Thank you. Alrighty, girls. Time for bed," Maggie said, standing up and stretching her long legs. "We'll see you bright and early."

"Good night," we called out as she left our site.

I slept well that night despite my anxiety about the next day. The farthest I had ever run was five miles. How would I be able to finish almost three times that distance? I had no idea but for once it didn't bother my head.

It was still dark out when I heard the staff making their rounds.

"Good morning, people. It's 5:30. Time to begin the first day of the *best* of your lives!"

I heard mumbled "we're up" and "good morning" from the other tarps and heard the rustling noises folks made as they crawled out of their sleeping bags and donned jackets, hats and gloves for the chill mountain morning.

I did the same. Shorts, followed by my wool trousers. T-shirt, wool sweater and rain jacket. Balaclava hat and wool gloves. "Ready!" I crawled out of the tarp.

"Brrrr! It is frickin' brisk at this time of the day!" I exclaimed.

I started rummaging through our gear for the stove to heat up water for tea.

"You'll want to eat very lightly, if at all," Marcus said right behind me. I jumped nearly 10 feet in the air, he startled me so.

"Sorry to scare you, Lucy," he said. "Bruce asked me to make sure everyone knew to not eat much but to drink a couple cups of tea or water. You need to be hydrated before the run starts. There won't be any aid stations along the route like in a race."

"It'so'k," I mumbled, still fumbling with the stove. "I'll let the others know."

"Thanks. How was your finals expedition?" he asked.

"It was great. We did really well, covered a lot of miles and bonded as a group."

"Fantastic," he said as he started off toward another group. "I'll see you on the run."

"'K."

Soon I had water boiling. Everyone was anxious for something warm. The sun was lighting the horizon and we could see now without headlamps. After a couple of cups of tea, we got our gear packed and stacked by the trucks and went to join the others in a big circle.

I waved at Pedro and got a wink back, and waved to Ken and Evan on the far side of the circle.

Maggie stepped into the middle of the group and everyone quieted down. She didn't have to say a word; there was just something about her that caught your attention.

"Good morning, everyone!" she called out joyfully, smiling as she looked around the circle. "It looks like you slept well."

Most people nodded. A few shook their heads.

"In a few minutes, you will begin a 13-mile run down to the town of Silverton. It is a long enough distance that you will go through some mental and physical changes and experiences along the way.

"This run is symbolic in many ways," Maggie continued. "It is a perfect metaphor for your life up to this point and it is an excellent time for reflection. How you run this route will show you how you live your life because how you do anything is how you do everything. Do you want to quit? Do you stop or do you persevere? Do you start off fast and burn out, or do you have a steady pace? Observe yourself and your mind chatter. What do you say to yourself as you go along? Are you supportive of yourself or do you cut yourself down? Do you go it alone or do you have support? These are all questions you can ponder as you run," she paused and looked around to see if we were all still with her, "and I'm sure your minds will come up with some of their own." She smiled and I sighed. *I really would like to be like her when I grow up,* I thought.

"For some students, the marathon, which is what we call it even though it isn't 26 miles in length, represents a break with their past and a new start. Whatever it is for you is perfect."

Bruce stepped up and added, "As we said last night, the route is straightforward. You will follow this road all the way into the town of Silverton. You will pass a couple of old mining camps along the way, and then you will see the site of our original base camp at Howardsville. The road is downhill most of the way, but there's a small hill just as you come into town. You'll run up this and descend along Main Street. About midway through town, you will see a staff member directing you to turn left. This will be the last three blocks of the run to the finish. Anyone who has arrived before you will be there to cheer you across the finish line."

"Once you've crossed the finish line," Maggie picked up the instructions, "grab some electrolyte solution and water and then come back to the finish to cheer others across."

Pedro came forward then. "After everyone has completed the run, we'll have a light lunch and then begin our service project. I will speak to you about this after the marathon. The service project will take all afternoon. We'll have a celebration dinner this evening and one last night camping out under the stars. Then, tomorrow morning, we'll check in our group gear and you'll board the bus back to Grand Junction. Any questions about the run at this time?"

A young man raised his hand. "What if we can't run that far?"

Pedro smiled at him. "I think you will surprise yourself, Axle. You are stronger than you realize. Let's see how it goes. There will always be the trucks available to serve as sag wagons to support tired or injured runners."

Axle nodded but still looked worried.

"Although this is not a race per se," Maggie said. "We encourage all you runners to challenge yourselves. Most of the staff will be running. Some of you may want to run at the front of the pack with the leaders while others will be content to pace themselves in the middle or toward the end of the line. Marcus has been designated as the 'sweeper,' meaning he will be the last person to cross the finish line. If you have any problems and don't see a truck, look for Marcus." He waved his hands so people who didn't know him would recognize him.

He was wearing his mom's old, handmade serape poncho. It was brightly colored wool, woven in shades of red, orange and green. Even though the poncho had faded with years of use, no one would be able to miss Marcus.

"I want to remind you this is not a competitive event," said Bruce. "To help emphasize this, the start will be somewhat different from what you might expect. Each of you will remove your right shoe and throw it into a pile here in the center of the circle." He gestured toward the middle of the group.

"Marcus, Pedro and Susy will then mix up the pile so those of you strategizing to throw your shoes in last so they will be on top can stop worrying yourselves," he looked poignantly at some of the boys, including Tate and Andy, who had been whispering among themselves from the moment Bruce started speaking. "Once the shoes have been redistributed, Maggie will blow her whistle and you'll find your shoe, put it on and start running."

He looked around the circle. "Any questions? No? Alrighty, then. Go use the latrines. Take off any extra clothing and put it in your backpacks. Drink some water and come back here in 10 minutes."

Everyone scrambled to do as we were instructed. I ran to the latrine as my stomach was suddenly rumbling with nerves. Even though I was quick there was already a line.

Maggie came by and sighed, "This line will take forever to get through. Gentlemen, unless you have serious business to do, go ahead and find a tree. Ladies, you can do the same. That should shorten up this line quite a bit."

More than half the people in line headed toward the forest. I stayed in line.

After using the latrine, I put my wool pants and rain jacket in my pack and took one last, long drink of water. Then I returned to the circle, which was starting to form again.

"Hey, Lucy!" Tate called out and he and Andy came over to where I was standing.

"Isn't this great?" Andy asked excitedly. I remember the two of them getting up in the morning to run at the Colorado National Monument in May.

"Oh, yeah!" I said sarcastically, feeling extremely nervous about the whole thing. "I can't wait."

"Oh, come on," Tate said. "You're a runner. Besides, you're really fit now. Mack will hardly recognize you."

Maybe, I thought. I couldn't wait to the get to the hotel tomorrow afternoon so I could see myself in the mirror.

"Just remember to relax and go at your own pace," Andy advised. "It will be just like your morning runs. Don't think about the distance; just watch the scenery as you move along. You'll see."

"OK," I said. "I'll try to do as you suggest."

Just then Bruce was back in the middle of the circle. "Alright, guys," he said.

"Take off your right shoe and throw it into the middle of the circle in a pile." The shoes landed in a series of thuds.

Chapter Thirty-Three

It was a gigantic pile of shoes by the time all the footwear was accounted for. Pedro, Marcus and Susy stepped forward and began digging through the shoe pile. They mixed and stirred, dug and re-piled shoes for about two minutes. I saw my shoe a couple of times before it got dredged back down into the pile.

I heard Pedro tell the others it was enough and they all backed away from the pile.

"I see my shoe!" exclaimed a youngish girl near me.

"Yeah, I saw mine but it is gone now," her friend commented.

I had no idea where my shoe was at this point.

Everyone was anxiously watching the pile when Maggie called out, "Everyone ready?"

Everyone kept staring at the shoes. The shrill *tweeeeeee* of the whistle was shocking in the still mountain morning, and then we were off. People were grabbing shoes not their own and tossing them back onto the pile willy-nilly. I noticed Tate had found his shoe and was off like a jackrabbit, Andy close behind.

Finally, I saw my shoe and shoved it onto my foot. I started off with a slow jog. I felt good and strong, exhilarated by the crisp air. The descent was gently sloped and the road was graveled and relatively smooth.

Soon I found myself running faster. Passing people, even! *Wow! I wasn't expecting to be able to run faster than other people,* I marveled.

The valley widened as we lost elevation. Some people passed me, and I passed others. We were like an undulating snake making its way down the gorge. It was very cool to imagine what we looked like.

I had no idea how much time had passed, but the sun was well over the mountains before I reached Howardsville. *How strange to think that just three short weeks before, I jogged along that road over there and nearly died,* I thought as I ran past the entrance to Minnie Gulch. I was still feeling good and strong even though I could tell I had run longer than my normal 30 or 40 minutes.

I believed Howardsville was about the halfway point of the run. I was starting to feel the fatigue in my legs, so I decided I had to do something to distract my mind. *Sing,* was the answer that came to me. I didn't want to waste my breath singing out loud, so I started singing in my head.

The song that popped in and stayed with me was Helen Reddy's "I Am Woman." It had a good rhythm that matched my stride and its lyrics made me feel strong. I lost myself in the music in my mind for a while before I noticed someone was keeping pace with me. It was Sarah.

I nodded at her, not sure I could actually speak. She smiled back at me and for a while we matched each other stride for stride. It really helped having a partner to run with those last few miles even though we weren't speaking. I felt an unspoken commitment not to quit with her there to witness it, and I sensed she felt the same. I kept singing in my mind and running alongside the woman I had wanted to be the first day of the course.

Funny how it all worked out. Here we were on the same finals team and we were running together during the marathon. It was all very cool.

At the edge of town, just as Bruce had advised us, the route took an uphill turn. The rise was probably only a quarter of a mile in length and not terribly steep, but it was a challenge, coming in at approximately mile 11. Sarah and I matched each other step for step up that hill.

Suddenly I had to pee! *Aargh,* I thought, feeling a bit competitive. *I don't want to have to stop and have Sarah beat me!*

"Sarah, I have to pee," I shouted over at her.

"Thank God!" she said with a laugh. "I do, too, and I didn't want to stop and have you beat me!"

We ran off the road into the trees and took care of our business and were back on the run in less than three minutes.

I felt so good that all of a sudden, I started singing the song out loud, "I am woman!

Sarah joined in and we sang together as best we could, being a bit breathless.

"I am strong!" I practically shouted.

"Strong," echoed Sarah. "I am invincible!"

"Invincible," I echoed.

"I am WOMAN!" we sang together, laughing.

We were almost halfway through town when we saw Gentleman Jim flagging people to take a left turn. I could see the finish line about five blocks ahead. I glanced at Sarah and she glanced at me and I knew it. We were going to sprint to the finish to see who would cross the line first.

It was as if an unspoken signal passed between us because we both started sprinting at the same time. We were about the same height, and our strides matched almost exactly. My legs were churning as fast as they could and I felt powerful, unlike I had years before when my legs were churning just as fast on the 50-yard dash at school. The song was gone because it no longer suited my quicker pace but it had left its legacy in my mind. I knew I was invincible.

Sarah pulled slightly ahead of me. "Crap!" I said under my breath and sped up, catching her within a couple of yards. We were nearly at the finish line and I could hear those who had arrived before us, egging us on. Nothing like a photo finish to get people excited.

"Come on, Lucy!" I heard Andy's distinct voice above the crowd. "You can beat her!" I tried to make my legs go faster but it was almost like my brain and my legs were no longer communicating.

Come on! Don't fail me now, legs! You've only got 20 yards to go! You can do it!

Everything slowed down. It felt like I was crawling even though I knew I was running faster than I had ever run in my life. It was weird. I could see the details of the buildings I passed. Victorian-era houses with gingerbread trim painted pink and purple. I saw Steve and Ken on the side, yelling my name. I heard Sarah's old team shouting her name. I felt the warm sun on my head and the sweat trickling down my face.

Suddenly, everything sped up again and we were speeding toward the finish. A burst of lightning spread from my crotch to the top of my head, sending ripples of pleasure throughout my body. It nearly made me stop running and then, before I knew it, we had made it across the finish line. We had tied crossing the line despite the best effort from each of us, and fell breathlessly into each other's arms, laughing and coughing.

to go, Lucy," Sarah grinned, giving me a big, sweaty hug.

"Yeah, you, too! That was fun," I said, returning the embrace and then turning to my friends who were coming to congratulate me.

Remembering the strange sensation that had swept through my body a few moments earlier, I wondered: *What the heck just happened to me?*

Tate thumped me on the back, "Great job, Luce! You did really well!"

"One hour and 42 minutes! That's fantastic!" Andy was beside him congratulating me.

"What a finish!" Steve shook my hand. "No one has come in that strong since the leaders at the front of the pack. Nicely done, Lucy!"

"Thanks," I stammered, having finally caught my breath.

"Go get rehydrated," Tate instructed. "You've probably just sweated out a couple of pounds of liquid."

I looked where he was pointing and found the tables set up with cups of electrolyte drink. I downed a couple immediately and grabbed one more to sip on. Then I found Sarah again.

"Hey, Sarah!" I called out. She turned around and gave me a big grin, and then embraced me a second time.

"Thanks for running with me," I said. "It made it so much easier that last half even though we weren't talking."

"It made it easier for me, too," she said. "You're a good runner."

I felt embarrassed. No one had ever told me I was good at any sport.

"Thanks," I said. "It was fun racing you at the end."

"Yes, that was a lot of fun!" she agreed.

"Let's go cheer on the rest of the group," I suggested and we walked back to the finish line.

Joshua came across in the next wave of finishers. He raced the young man who had raised the question before. Axle was his name, I thought. Joshua beat Axle soundly but they had a good race to the end. Toma was in the same wave of folks. She looked strong and was running with a couple of other women I didn't recognize. They were all chatting as if it were a Sunday outing and they weren't expending any more effort than a picnic. They didn't bother to race each other even though the crowd was encouraging them to do so.

Karn and Hope came running in together about 10 minutes later. They looked exhausted but gave it a good last effort by racing to the finish. It was fun cheering them on. Marcia and Evan came in with the last wave. They were jogging together, with Marcus looking tired but pleased. I was glad to see that Evan's knee had healed up.

What an amazing feeling having run 13 miles and having cheered on others. I was elated and not thinking at all about the fact that in less than 12 hours, I would be leaving all of this. I would say goodbye to my new friends and I would head back to life in the city. None of that entered my mind. I focused on the moment, enjoying the sandwiches we had for lunch and concentrating on my paint job that afternoon.

It turned out that our service project involved painting a community building the town was going to use for a proposed ski area. We had some barn-red paint and dozens of paintbrushes. Not everyone could paint, though, so I was fortunate to serve as a painter. Some people were collecting garbage from what appeared to have been an unofficial landfill in front of the building. Old tire rims, a refrigerator door, paint cans, a bike frame and more "treasures" lay buried under several inches of dirt and required quite an effort to dig out. I was delighted to be painting. The junkyard brought back unsettling memories of my ill-advised knee-sledding episode a few years back.

Others were assigned KP duty to help the staff with our celebration dinner. I still felt glad to be painting. The sun was warm and very few fluffy clouds floated overhead. The hills looked green and alive as fields of yellow, orange, blue and magenta wildflowers came into their peak. My body was tired and my mind was relaxed and alert— an incredible sensation.

My muscles would probably ache tomorrow but for now I was happy with myself and with life.

Once we'd finished with the building, or our section of it, we were free to hang out and enjoy the day. I walked to the river and washed up for the last time outdoors. I dunked my head into the glacial waters of the river and got an instant headache, which went away shortly after taking my head out of the water. Goosebumps jumped out on my arms and legs as the cold trickled down from my hair and damped my shirt.

The sun dried me almost instantly and a gentle breeze lifted my hair as I sat there on an enormous boulder, soaking up the sun's warmth and ʻ ⁻ᵗⁱⁿᵍ my hair dry. I could see the others finishing up their community ᵈ heading, one by one or in pairs, to the river.

I looked for Joshua but knew he had volunteered to help with the dinner since he loved cooking so much. As Sarah helped with the trash removal, I could hear her laughter on the wind.

At once I realized I would probably never see any of them again, nor Ken, Steve, Marcia or Karn. I probably would never see Toma or Evan again, either, even though both lived in the same city as I did. I was overcome with sadness and a pain in my heart I thought would tear it apart. Before I knew it, tears were running down my cheeks.

Darn it! I don't want to cry.

"You just don't want to leave," someone said behind me and I turned around to see Pedro coming up.

"No, I don't want to leave," I said, wiping at the tears on my face, feeling like an idiot for crying.

"I understand. I feel the same way each and every course," he said. "I guess that is why I am still teaching for Outdoor Mountain School after nearly 10 years," he smiled.

"I came to chat with you about your experience, if you have a few moments," he said.

"Sure," I shrugged.

"I just wanted to find out how you liked your Outdoor Mountain School experience," he asked.

"It was good," I said nonchalantly while thinking to myself it was the best experience I had ever had in my life.

"What were some of the highlights?"

"Well, today was a high point for me. I have never done anything like that and it left me feeling, um, well, like actually high if you know what I mean." I fumbled a bit at the last, not wanting to let Pedro know I had been a pot smoker.

"Maybe," he said. "Can you tell me more?"

"What I mean is that it affected me both physically and mentally. There was this sense of strength and power I felt that left me almost giddy after the run. And I felt almost intoxicated mentally."

"Oh, I get it," he said. "They call that a runner's high. It comes from the endorphins your body produces to help you ignore the pain your body is going through."

"Well that explains it," I smiled at him, not wanting to tell him about the full-body explosion that had happened just before I crossed the finish line. It had felt so good; I didn't want to spoil the memory by talking about it.

"Another highlight for me was the finals expedition," I said to cover up the thoughts racing through my head. "It was amazing being with a group of strong, independent women who, along with their courage and tenacity, were helpful, connected and kind to each other. I had never experienced that in my life, either."

Pedro nodded and showed his lovely teeth, starkly white against his tan skin.

"I am happy to think of myself as athletic for the first time in my life," I added. "I mean, I was always a fat kid and my parents were not very supportive in terms of anything sportslike unless it was being a spectator. I believe I have finally found a place where I not only feel at home; I feel I could be really good. I am going to learn more about mountaineering, and maybe climb high peaks one day, like you," I blushed, thinking I was being too forward.

"I think you are right, Lucy. You could be a very good high-altitude climber," Pedro replied. "You have a strength about you that is not only physical but also mental, and that is vital for a climber. Plus you have a grace that will serve you well in the mountains. I wish you luck in your pursuit." With that he smiled, shook my hand and got up to go speak to another student.

"Pedro?" I blushed with embarrassment.

"Yes?" He turned my way again.

"Um," God this was hard, "I just wanted to tell you thanks and that I thought you were the best leader on the whole course." My face felt like it was on fire.

"Thanks, Lucy. I appreciate that," Pedro said and then he was off. I was tempted to ask him what really set him off the day he got so angry but decided not to ruin the moment.

I walked back to camp. Tonight we had the option of using our reflection tarps or setting up a group shelter with either our finals team or our original team. It was a bit confusing. I didn't know which group to hang out with so I decided to set up my own camp using the small tarp. Fortunately, it looked like it would be a clear night.

Dinner was an elaborate affair for a campout. We had roast chicken breasts, fresh tossed salad, and penne pasta in garlic sauce. For dessert, I don't know how they managed it, but we had cheesecake with strawberries. It was incredible. Everyone ate their fill and chatted amongst themselves. Despite the celebration, a sense of melancholy hung in the air. The talking was subdued, not boisterous like before we headed off on our finals. People shared contact info with plans to stay in touch.

"Hey, Luce," a soft voice drawled near my left ear.

"Hey, Joshua," I answered without looking. I would know that sound anywhere, even with my eyes closed.

"I've been lookin' all over for you," my golden friend said.

"I've been here most of the evening," I said, sorrow once again rolling over me as I thought of the good times we had had and that we probably would never see each other again.

"I wanted to get your cell so I could text you sometime," he said.

"That would be great," I said. "I'd love to hear from you and know what's going on in your life."

We exchanged information and then sat together, eating in silence, each of us lost in our own thoughts.

"Have you set up a tarp?" I asked when we had finished our meal.

"Yeah," he replied. "I was gonna sleep with my finals team. What about you?"

"I set mine up over there," I said, pointing to some trees about 20 feet from where we sat. "I couldn't decide if I wanted to be with the original group or with my finals team, so I decided to be alone."

"Do you want some company?" he asked.

"It would be nice to have someone to snuggle with," I admitted. Maybe that was why I had set up my tent away from the others. "But don't you already have a commitment to sleep with your group?"

"Yeah, but that can be changed," he said.

"I would like to sleep with you," I said. "I am feeling sad, thinking of leaving everyone tomorrow."

"Let me go tell my group," he said. "I'll be back soon."

Just then, Bruce whistled for our attention. "Alright, guys. Give me your attention for just a few more minutes and then you can call it a night.

"Susy will go over logistics with you in a couple of minutes, but for right now, I wanted to share with you one last quote."

Some laughter and a few groans erupted at that announcement.

"Don't worry," Bruce laughed. "Some of you will miss my quotes. Others will be delighted never to hear another inspirational quote the rest of their lives."

A couple of guys I didn't know said, "You can say that again!"

"It's alright," Bruce continued. "You can't dissuade me from sharing these last few words with you. It's from a poem written by a pilot named John Gillespie Magee Jr. Even though the poem is about flying, it inspires in me some of the same feelings I have when I climb. It is one of my favorite poems and I hope you enjoy the few words I share with you. Maybe you will be inspired to locate the full poem and read it in its entirety yourselves." He smiled at us before quoting, "'I've topped the wind-swept heights with easy grace…put out my hand, and touched the face of God.'"

When he finished those two lines, he stood there in silence, letting the poignant words soak in. Suddenly there was a burst of applause and everyone stood up, clapping for the sentiment, for the whole experience.

I knew what the author had felt. I had a similar sense of connecting to my soul during the course. I, too, felt the presence of God here in the mountains, especially at the tops of the passes and the highest points we crossed.

"Beautiful," I heard someone exclaim.

"That was fabulous," my throaty-voiced Amazon, Sarah, announced to Bruce. "Thank you for sharing it with us. It definitely expressed what I have sensed these past three weeks."

"Alrighty. Alright, gang," Bruce called out to get us to settle down.

"Thanks for indulging me one last time," he smiled at the group, winking at the boys who earlier had commented on having one last quote. "You have all done exceptionally well. This has been one of my most memorable courses. I feel hope for the future letting all of you leaders loose back in the world. Just remember what you have learned here in the mountains and take it home with you. Keep the Outdoor Mountain ʼl creed with you: 'Always be of service to others, do your best and ʼe up!' Be well and stick around to hear what Susy has to say.

I will see you all in the morning," he waved as he walked back through the circle and went over to the trucks.

That man's work is never finished, I thought.

"Hey, everyone," Susy called out as she stepped into the center of the circle.

People started quieting down and looking her direction.

"Thanks," she smiled gratefully. "It has been a wonderful course for all the staff. You have been amazing to work with."

Applause started up again, and Susy raised her hands to get us to quiet down.

"I am charged with going over tomorrow's logistics with you. We'll have breakfast together at 6 a.m. Then, you'll rejoin your finals team and we'll turn in all the group camping equipment. Once that is finished, you'll gather your personal belongings. The bus should be here about 8 a.m. for the drive back to Grand Junction. If you have arranged your own transportation and will not be taking the bus, see me after this meeting." She nodded to a couple of people.

"The bus will depart at 8:30 sharp and you will be back in Grand Junction around 1:30 tomorrow afternoon. Does anyone have any questions?"

It was getting dark already and I could see folks were tired. I hoped no one would raise their hand. Thankfully, no one did.

"OK, then," Susy smiled her golden smile at all of us. "We'll see you all bright and early tomorrow morning. Sleep well and if you are doing your own thing with transportation, come find me now."

I walked to my tarp and crawled into my sleeping bag. I hadn't seen Joshua and I was getting tired. Before long, though, I felt the edge lift up and heard, "Scootch over, Luce," as Joshua shoved his sleeping bag and pad into the tiny space.

I moved over a couple of inches and unzipped my bag. Joshua lay down beside me and opened his bag. Soon I was cuddled in his arms, snug, warm and drowsy. "Thanks for coming over tonight," I whispered. "Even though I am tired, I would have been really lonely."

"No problem, Luce," he said. "You were my best friend these past three weeks. I'm really glad I got to know you. I like you a lot."

"Thanks. I like you, too, Joshua," I yawned. I slept soundly that night, resting in Joshua's arms, not thinking about the future.

The next morning dawned clear and bright. I was surprised. I expected the weather to reflect my own mood—gray and melancholy. I didn't want to leave what had been one of the best experiences of my life. I wanted to stay in the mountains forever, breathing in pure, clean air, exercising my body and connecting with nature and amazing human beings. I was crabby and sullen.

"Good morning, Lucy," Toma called out brightly.

"Hey," I grumbled.

"Hey, Luce!" Tate called out and waved me over to join him and Andy. "Guess what?" he asked excitedly.

"I have no idea," I said morosely.

"Oh, come on! Give it a try!" he encouraged.

"Fine," I snapped. "You've been accepted to Stanford."

"I haven't even applied to Stanford, silly," he said.

"I know that. I just have no way of guessing something so random."

"OK. We'll tell you," he looked over at Andy.

"Outdoor Mountain School is hiring us!" Andy said enthusiastically.

"What? You're kidding!" I was astonished. "When did this happen?"

"Last night," Tate broke in.

"Yeah, neither one of us has applied to a university yet. We were talking with Bruce after everyone had gone to bed..." Andy continued.

"And we told him what a great experience it had been for us and how we wanted to find out how to become OMS leaders..." Tate interrupted.

"And so we started talking more and found out that they need leaders now," said Andy, punching Tate in the arm.

"So they're shipping us off to Leadville tomorrow for training and then we will be assistant instructors for a course in the Collegiate Range in two weeks!" Tate finished hurriedly, punching Andy back.

"Wow!" I said, my head spinning. "I didn't even know that was possible."

"Neither did we," they said in unison.

"But isn't it great?" Andy gushed.

"Yeah, I guess so," I said, feeling extremely jealous. Here I had been thinking I never wanted to leave. I wanted to figure out some way to always be part of OMS and Tate and Andy had gone and done it.

"I mean, congratulations! You guys will make great instructors," I said. "As long as you don't talk their ears off, Tate," I grinned at him.

Chapter Thirty-Three

He smiled and gave me a big hug.

"Too bad you're headed off to college in September," he said.

"Yeah, but it's a summer thing mostly, isn't it?" I asked.

"You're right, but Bruce said some courses go all the way through November," Andy said.

"Plus," Tate added, "they have winter courses in the deserts of the southwest."

"You guys are so lucky," I said wistfully.

"I know," said Andy and he gave me a squeeze.

"Well, we'd better get busy turning in our group gear," Tate said. "We just wanted you to know we won't be coming back on the bus with you today."

"Yeah, thanks. I'm gonna miss you guys," I said, turning my head because I was already starting to tear up.

I walked back to my tarp and noticed Joshua had already taken it down and folded it. He had put my gear in my pack and had everything neatly organized.

"Hey, Luce," he said as I came up. "You look bummed. What's up?"

"Oh, everything," I said, starting to cry. "I don't want to leave. I'm going to miss you and the mountains and everyone!" I was in anguish now that I was letting my feelings out.

"Aww, darlin', hush," Joshua said and held his arms out for me to get a hug.

"And Tate and Andy are going to work for Outdoor Mountain School and I want to do that. I don't want to go to college and I don't know what I am going to do with my life, and...and..." I stuttered to a stop and took a deep breath and then plunged on. "I probably won't see you or anyone else ever again and...and...I am just so bummed," I wailed.

Joshua put his arm around me, "Whoa, girl. It'll be alright, Luce. You'll see. It always is."

"I dunno," I sniffled. My nose was running onto his shirt.

Great! Just what I need, to be getting snot all over my cute friend.

We held each other for a few more minutes as my sobbing quieted down. Then I dried my eyes.

"Better?" he asked and I nodded. "Let's turn in our group gear and see if anyone needs help."

"OK."

And so we handed in the tarp and the stove I was carrying. We both had ice axes to turn in and Joshua had fuel bottles. We saw Sarah and Toma and exchanged e-mail addresses and cell numbers. Hope came by and we got her information, too.

Joshua went off to find some of the members of his finals team and I looked for Steve, Marcia and Ken.

Before long, the bus arrived and we all climbed on board for the journey back to Grand Junction.

As I watched out the window, I thought about who I had been just weeks before and who I was now. Then, I had been frightened and worried about the new adventure coming up. Now, I was sad because I was leaving behind new friends and a sport that had quickly become a passion. I was sorrowful because I was going away from the mountains and back to the city. I was again frightened because it was all so unknown at that moment. I didn't know what to expect. What would the next steps in my life look like? What would it be like to go off to college in September? How were Mack and I going to relate to each other after this time away? How would I get back to the mountains I had grown to love?

As my thoughts ran wild with worry, my hand touched a lump in my pocket. *What the...?* I wondered and then remembered I had put my washcloth with its treasures there this morning, thinking I would take a look at what it contained during the ride home. I opened it up with a gentle clink of the stones. Next to the piece of granite from my first climb, the shining arrowhead, and the smooth, swirled stone from my river adventure lay the sparkling chunk of quartz I had picked up on this course during the reflection period. *Wow! That one represents a lot,* I thought. *Not only all the great memories of these incredible past 25 days, but my own acknowledgment of my growth into an athlete and a leader.* It also was a clear symbol of my love of the mountains.

Looking at my little reminders of my life journey so far, I felt a sense of calm. *Man, I've come a long way,* I thought with a smile, harking back to one of those silly notes Kenan had passed me in middle school: "You've come a long way, baby!"

Sure, there were lots of things I didn't know, and I'd certainly continue to make mistakes—but I did know that I was brave and strong and athletic. I also knew that no matter what I came up against, I would be able to handle it. I was invincible!

I knew that somehow, someway, I would be in the mountains again, climbing and hiking. Who knew, maybe I could start an explorer scout post at college in the fall. Maybe I would even climb some of the world's highest mountains. Maybe I would travel to Nepal and see Everest and Makalu and the great peaks Bruce and Pedro and Maggie spoke about with such fervor. Maybe?

As I gathered these small tokens of my first adventures together and tucked them back into my pocket, all of life's possibilities—all the ways to set my new dreams into motion—spread out before me like a Rocky Mountain sky.

Lucy Dakota: Adventures of a Modern Explorer
Book 2—Journey to Nepal

The glacier moved and creaked beneath my feet like a living thing. A snake, slowly undulating down the valley. An eight-mile-long beast that could kill you in an instant. With crevasses opening up today where none had existed yesterday, and boulders and stones constantly falling, the route up to our high base camp at 18,000 feet changed daily. At times, the moaning of ice crushing the earth or grinding upon itself echoed eerily throughout the valley as we walked. The keening cry of anguish as the land shuddered, or a crack of thunder from deep within the earth, unnerved me to the core.

We had just heard the news that someone from the team had died. Porters and teammates were attempting to carry him down through this living hell.

Who was it? I wondered as we climbed to the high camp to meet the remaining team members. I delicately picked my way through the maze of rubble left behind as the ice of the Barun Glacier chewed its way through the mountains.

Step, climb, breathe.

Step, climb, breathe.

My usual hiking chant gave way to endless questions, doubt and fear. *What had happened? How could it be? Who was with him at the time?* Questions ran through my head as my legs automatically made their winding way through the rock field.

Who was it? They were all my friends now.

We had only heard rumors until this morning. They had started two days earlier when we ran into some Italian climbers hiking around Jark Kharka. They had said, "Someone on your team has problems," and that was all. We tried to question them, but between their limited English and our nonexistent Italian, we got nowhere. The Sherpas spoke with their guide but said nothing to us except, "Not to worry, didi. Not to worry."

"Not to worry, my butt!" I practically shouted at Ang Phurba Sherpa. "Those are my friends up there!"

"Calm down, didi," he said in his quiet manner. "It will be what it is. There is nothing to do about it from here at this time. We are in the mountains. They make the decisions here."

We spent the entire hike up to Makalu base camp—another day-and-a-half worth of walking—worrying and speculating amongst ourselves as to what might have happened or what might be happening. We had no idea how high up the mountain the team was, who had taken the lead up to the higher camps, or even what the problem was or where it had occurred.

"What do you think is happening?" I wondered out loud.

"Who do you think it is? Do you think it's Glen?" Rachel asked.

"I don't know. Gary is the oldest," Michael added. "He could've had a problem."

"God, I hope it's not Ken," Eileen moaned, worry about her husband creasing her brow.

Everything we had heard up to that point from descending hikers and climbers indicated that the climb was going well. We had met a British foursome in Mumbuk just after the last pass who'd found the team in high spirits and doing fine. Edwin had led some games with the local children and, in typical Edwin style, had passed out balloons—the colorful yet popped and deflated evidence of which now littered the trail.

Oh, God! What was happening up there?

Discover what Lucy finds at high camp and more in
Journey to Nepal, *the next book in the Lucy Dakota series,*
which promises adventures as dramatic
as the Himalaya Mountains.

ABOUT THE AUTHOR

C.S. Shride grew up in the western suburbs of Denver at the foot of the mountains. Like Lucy, she was a chubby, rejected girl during her middle-school years and surprisingly enough, she rarely, if ever, ventured forth into the nearby hills. Her pleasures were derived from armchair and bed-top adventures achieved while reading her favorite novels.

Like Lucy, Shride's life took a turn for the better when a group she was involved with in high school started introducing her to the mountains, rivers and wilderness areas of Colorado. At that time she discovered one of her lifelong passions, high-altitude trekking and mountaineering, which led to her first career as the owner of a successful, multi-million-dollar adventure travel company. For the next 20 years, she would orchestrate, conduct and lead thousands of clients through the mountains of Nepal and the wildernesses of South America. She spoke to dozens of audiences each year on the joys and beauty of traveling to remote areas of the world. Although she is no longer an international climber and mountain guide, she continues to hike and explore mountains around the world.

Shride's love of learning and her sincere desire to share with and help youth led to her second career as a classroom teacher. Even though she had taught hundreds of people the art of backcountry travel and wilderness trekking through her business and volunteer activities with the Colorado Mountain Club, at age 43 Shride returned to school for a master's degree in education and began teaching in both public and private schools. She experienced tremendous satisfaction and joy in teaching children in the classroom setting. It was at that point, during a creative writing class, that she decided to write about Lucy's adventures.

As a mother of a daughter who is about to reach those crucial tween and teen years, the author aims for Lucy to serve as a role model that anything is possible and to inspire young people to believe in themselves.

Hungry for More Adventure?

Lucy Dakota: Adventures of a Modern Explorer, an exciting
new series for young adults, follows Lucy Dakota—formerly an
overweight bookworm misfit—as she travels across the continents.
In Book 2, our teenage heroine heads to Nepal to climb among the
world's highest mountains, where she battles the elements
and loses a friend in the Himalayas.

In future books, join Lucy as she tries paragliding in Alaska,
snorkels with sharks in the Galapagos Islands, endures natural
disaster in Australia's Great Barrier Reef, lives with headhunters
in the rainforests of South America, and faces
savage beasts on the plains of Africa.
Who knows where Lucy will show up next?